MERITAGE: AN UNEXPECTED BLEND

A GELBERT FAMILY WINERY STANDALONE

KELLY KAY

ALSO BY KELLY KAY

FIVE FAMILIES VINEYARD SERIES

LaChappelle/Whittier Vineyard Trilogy

Crushing, Rootstock & Uncorked

Stafýlia Cellars Duet

Over A Barrel & Under The Bus

Gelbert Family Winery

Meritage: An Unexpected Blend

STANDALONES

SIDE PIECE

CHI TOWN BOOKS

A Lyrical Romance Duet

Shock Mount & Crossfade

Spinoff Standalone

Present Tense

www.kellykayromance.com

Meritage: An Unexpected Blend
Copyright @2021 by Kelly Kay/Kelly Kreglow
All rights reserved
Visit my website www.kellykayromance.com

Cover Design: Tim Hogan www.timhogancreative.com
Editor: Aimee Walker : Aimee Walker Editorial Services
www.aimeewalkerproofreader.com

Published by Decorated Cast Publishing, LLC

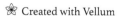 Created with Vellum

For Kristin, Kris, Krissy

Thanks for showing me how to apply eyeliner in a moving vehicle, non stop enthusiastic support and other invaluable lifeskills I use every day.
Let me grab my Dad's boots. I'll be over in a minute.

DEFINITION

Meritage:

1. People tend to Frenchify the word "Meritage" by pronouncing its last syllable with a "zh" sound, as in the U.S. pronunciation of "garage," the Meritage Alliance specifically states that the word should be pronounced to rhyme with "heritage͐ /ˈmɛrɪtɪdʒ/.

2. A Red Meritage is a blend of two or more of the five red "noble" Bordeaux varieties - Cabernet Sauvignon, Cabernet Franc, Malbec, Merlot, Petit Verdot. If the blend includes any other grape variety, it is, by definition, **NOT** a Meritage.

3. No single grape variety can make up more than 90% of the blend to qualify as a Meritage. Must be a partnership between varietals.

Family Trees for the 5 Families

Gelbert Family Winery

Jana
Gelbert ----------- Arthur >------< Tina
Gelbert   Gelbert

David   Becca   Poppy
Gelbert   Gelbert   Gelbert

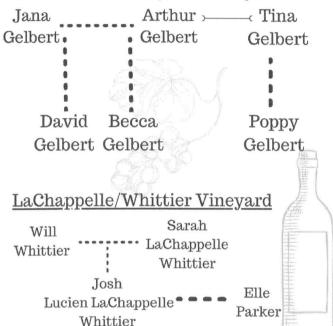

LaChappelle/Whittier Vineyard

Will
Whittier ---------- Sarah
                    LaChappelle
                    Whittier

Josh
Lucien LaChappelle •• •• •• Elle
Whittier   Parker

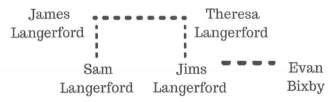

Langerford Cellars

James   •• •• •• •• Theresa
Langerford   Langerford

Sam   Jims •• •• •• Evan
Langerford Langerford   Bixby

Stafýlia Cellars

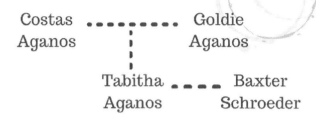

Costas Aganos ---------- Goldie Aganos

Tabitha Aganos ---- Baxter Schroeder

Schroeder Estate Winery & Vineyards

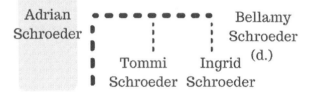

Adrian Schroeder ----------- Bellamy Schroeder (d.)

Tommi Schroeder   Ingrid Schroeder

Baxter Schroeder ---- Tabitha Aganos

PART 1

CABERNET

CHAPTER 1

NATALIE

THE PHONE RINGS, and my heart jumps. It's my first official phone call working here.

"Prohibition Winery, how can I help you?" I say with all the wherewithal of a girl who's insanely nervous about being in a new space. I don't know how to belong here yet. Baxter Schroeder hired me to be here to handle the fall out of him walking away from his senate bid. I only slept an hour and a half. I'm the only one in the office—technically, I'm the only employee—and I was here on flim-flamming time, unlike the owners. They're all scattered to the wind. This is not where I saw myself six months ago. Working with Baxter Schroeder has been the greatest job of my life—it's why when Tabi called and asked me to join the campaign, I jumped at the chance. I never take chances like that, but I believe in Bax. I knew, no matter what, he'd provide work for me. But I never anticipated he'd drop out and drop me off in Sonoma. Now I'm sitting in Tabi Aganos' chair at their winery, pretending I know what I'm doing. I've researched everything I possibly could. I do know that most of what I should say is 'no comment' if it's about Tabi and Bax.

"Yes, hello. I'm looking to start a dialogue with the Prohibition Winery folks for a feature story I'm writing. I'm Ryan Lely with Wine Spectator, and who may I ask am I speaking to? Would you mind if I recorded this conversation?"

"Nice to meet you, Mr. Lely. Yes. I'm Natalie Lloyd, the catchall employee. As far as I can tell, I'm the only permanent employee. The rest are owners, and they hire people here and there for project and harvest work. Oh. You asked a question. Um. Yes. You may record me."

"Excellent. Well, the angle I'm going for is the next-gen of it all. I'm particularly interested in the rumblings that they're looking for property to develop a brick-and-mortar. It's rare for a strong virtual winery presence to mess with their sales and build a large-scale facility and winery."

I squirm in my seat. Bax and Josh Whittier told me that was the case, but I'm not to tell anyone. I also know that many people want to do stories on them since they're the children of five substantial wineries in Sonoma Valley. "That's a trendy angle."

"I'm aware. I want to run these facts by you."

"Shoot." I open a notebook and begin to make an outline to be sure to report this call accurately.

He says, "Here's the facts everyone knows: Prohibition Winery started as a secret collaborative effort between five family-owned wineries in Sonoma. And no one knew they were working together for the better part of a year."

"That's correct."

"And now, the children, who all grew up together at those wineries, are the principal owners of Prohibition Winery. Joshua Whittier has a controlling interest."

"That's not correct. He doesn't have controlling interest. They each own an equal share. Josh Whittier, Sam Langerford, Tabitha Aganos, Baxter Schroeder, and David Gelbert. Mr. Whittier simply bankrolled the buyout from their parents. But you can get into the details with him. He can be reached at his family winery, LaChappelle/Whittier. That's his primary occupation and location these days."

He speaks, "I didn't realize he'd taken over operations."

"It's a family affair they can discuss with you."

"Now that Baxter Schroeder is back in town, is he working at Pro/Ho or his family winery?"

"That remains to be seen, but he is still a partner at Prohibition."

"And how did they find you?"

"I was Mr. Schroeder's assistant in both DC and Sacramento when he was an environmental lobbyist. I was on the senate campaign with him before, well, before that ended." I reach my arm in the air and roll my wrist around after transferring the phone to the other hand.

I say, "The best people to speak to about Prohibition and all the expansion would be Mr. Schroeder or Mr. Whittier. The day-to-day operations are currently being handled by Mr. Langerford or Mr. Gelbert. Ms. Aganos is indisposed at this time."

He asks, "I'm aware that she left the campaign, and after the scandal has gone into hiding of some sort. But I promise I don't have any wish to discuss that, simply the winery."

"That's refreshing to hear. The gentlemen currently run the day-to-day and the viticulture and agricultural elements of the business."

"Is there anything you can tell me about the expansion into a brick-and-mortar facility? I'm curious since they've had so much success as an online brand and created an air of exclusivity. Building out seems to be a great expense of time, energy, and money, all to achieve what they're already achieving."

"Here's what I know: If they do find a property and proceed, they're targeting Sonoma Valley and looking to be operational within a year. But nothing is definite. As for the reason, you'll have to ask them."

"Thanks, you've been so helpful."

"Thanks." I like being helpful. I'm really good at it.

"Can you help me set up an interviews with the 5 and send some samples?"

I say while arranging the pens on this desk, "I'll need your assignment letter before I can release any product or set up chats."

"Well, you're rather efficient, Ms. Lloyd."

"I know. Take care, Mr. Lely."

I hang up and exhale loudly. It's nine a.m. Still no sign of anyone who works here. I've dusted the office and checked the address several times to ensure I'm in the right place. Even though Bax gave me the code to get in, no one has shown up. Now it's 10:45 a.m., and I'm still on my own.

The door jangles as I'm arranging the newly washed mugs in the kitchen. They were disgusting. I've also dusted and vacuumed. I can see the hallway from here, and I don't know which of the 5 to expect. I met Sam Langerford briefly at Tabi's surprise party on my first day at the campaign. David Gelbert was too busy hitting on the other staffers to notice me. I paid him no mind as I was so incredibly busy that day and took off well before the party got going. I didn't know anyone then so I just slipped away from the party.

I say, "Hello. Hi. I'm in here."

He fills the doorway, and my chest catches. He's quite the honeybun with glaze dripping off it. I did not remember him being this yummy. His hair color, that russet red, is so much more than I remember. The tattoos are a bit of a surprise as the vines snake down his arm, peeking out of his royal blue t-shirt. He stares at me, then his upper lip in a particularly delightful way. I put my hand on the counter to steady myself. His look, his smolder, if you will, is putting me a touch off-balance. He lifts his arms up and holds onto the doorframe. It looks like he could actually expand the door if I asked. His t-shirt is pulling on the bottom of his biceps and popping up just a touch, revealing the band to his briefs and the top of his jeans. Mother, may I look at that again? He shifts his weight, and his bright green eyes sweep over every part of me, and I feel it. Then he licks his lips. We don't say anything.

I've never had a moment like this before. Where the world seems to pause and we're suspended in a lust bubble. Neither of us wants to break the spell with words and details of life. We exist in a time loop where we can just stare at each other under the weight of all we haven't said. It's languid, sensual, and wrapping around the two of us like something out of a movie I have no place being cast in.

I rock back on my heels just a bit, and it's enough to snap some sense into me. This is the most attractive man I've ever seen up close, and it's rather unnerving. He should only exist on Tik Tok and in catalogs. No. Not catalogs, in the pages of high-end fashion. Even though he's wearing a ratty t-shirt and jeans. Suddenly, I feel underdressed in my green sundress and sandals. I feel like I should have stepped up my game to be worthy of the way his eyes are worshiping me.

"What have we here?" His voice curls around the room and nudges low in my belly. I know his name, and I know I should answer, but I turn away to take in a cleansing breath and clear my eye palate from this man. He has to be a figment of my over-worked imagination. I turn back, and nope, he's still mother-trucking gorgeous.

"I was putting these away." He steps into the room, and all the molecules, ions, and electrons scatter and swirl around him. Then they recompose perfection as he walks. He gets too close for me to come up with something clever to say. Suddenly I'm

Jennifer Grey in *Dirty Dancing,* and I don't even have a watermelon.

"Natalie. I'm a Natalie Lloyd."

He extends his hand, and I can't believe he wants me to touch him. Does he not see how red my face is and how I'm staring at him? I can't touch him. I can't see a time where I can even transfer a phone call to him.

"David." He takes my hand in his, and I look up into his eyes. His way too green eyes, framed by the longest lashes, stare at me and all my nerves evaporate. The sweat forming under my breasts slows, and my breathing regulates. He shakes my hand slowly and sweeps his thumb over the back of my hand. "Gelbert. I'm one of the owners and winemakers here. And, Natalie, I'm a Natalie Lloyd, why are you in my offices? You work for Bax, right? I'll have to thank him for such a beautiful gift.

He's flirting. And it's cheesy. Bax warned me about him. He doesn't date but tends to sleep his way through a bar or a club. That's not who I am. But to each their own. Remembering this gives me power back. I smile as wide as I can and pull my hand back from him. I know exactly how to deal with a scoundrel like this one. I grew up around Washington, DC, and have worked around politics for the past eight years. I've got this man's number.

"Fate. You can thank fate." I shrug.

He crooks an eyebrow.

"You can also thank Tabi, she got me mixed up in the campaign, and Bax did put me here."

He crosses his arms over his broad chest, and the light dusting of red hair that's scattered over his freckled muscled arms thwart my resolve. Never been a girl for ginger, but he's a lot spicier than I would have guessed. I'm pretty sure I know how each and every woman ended up under him. He nods his chin at me and says nothing. I continue to prattle on. It's what I do.

"Is that an indication you approve of me, what I'm wearing, or the job I'm doing?" I ask.

He spreads his legs into a superman stance. "And what job is that? I'll bet I can think of a couple of jobs we could do for each other."

His words coil through the air like sin. Like that serpent twining around that apple tempting me. I'm no stranger to sin, but this particular brand seems extraordinarily dangerous to me.

I giggle. He looks confused.

"What's with the laugh?"

"Women really do fall at your knees, huh? I'm here to answer phones, not unzip your too-tight jeans. Where's your head at, player?" He laughs at me, but I'm faking it. If I weren't here in an office, working for my mentor and favorite boss ever, it's possible I'd already have my top down. He's that hot. There's a flush of heat rushing towards my luscious carpet below. I push past him. He turns as I get to the doorway with my clothes intact.

"Fair enough. So, if we're not going to spend the afternoon on our backs. What are we going to do today?"

"I'm going to go to lunch since it's almost noon. You will answer the fourteen emails waiting, call back the six messages I took, and sign the stack of equipment orders on your desk. Then you can open the packages in the refrigerator, which I assume are bottles of juice for you to sample."

He smiles and says, "I'm pretty sure spending the afternoon playing on my tongue would be more fun."

My entire body lights up at the thought. I exhale slowly while my back is to him. Then I turn.

"Get your work done, and maybe we can see about putting that tongue of yours to work."

He rubs his hands together like he's trying to start a fire. Too late, blood already boiling over. But I do need to douse it.

He says, "Now we're talking, Natalie. Natalie Lloyd."

"Did you say my name to prove you remembered it?"

"Perhaps. Now, about my tongue. I just want to know how much time I'm going to need to set aside." He licks those rosy lips. They're just pink enough, like the inside of a sea shell. He smells like clover. He's literally roses and clover. I will not be charmed by him. I'm too smart for that.

I wink at him. "Probably about an hour or so."

"Is that right? How much do you think we can get accomplished?"

I walk towards the conference room and can feel him follow me. I can actually feel and smell this man, and it's scary how quickly my body recognizes his pheromones. I open the door and show him the conference table filled with boxes.

I flash him a grin. "The mailing should only take us a couple of hours to stuff, seal, and stamp. But you might want to get some water to wet your whistle while you're licking envelopes." I nudge him with my hip, and he moves out of the way with a groan.

"Don't we have people for that?" He throws his hands in the air. I'm guessing he doesn't adult much.

I saunter away. I may be swaying my hips a bit too much, and I hear his breath hitch. I have power too.

I turn back to him and say, "According to Bax, Sam, Tabi, and Josh, you've slept with all the people you have ever hired and never called them after. So now there's just you and your magical tongue to get the job done. You've got this. I have faith in you." I keep walking towards the front desk.

He leaps in front of me. "Do you?"

He startles me a bit with his vulnerability. "Sure. Until you prove me wrong."

I grab my purse, knowing full well the man is watching every move I make. I wait until I get around the corner and out of sight to lean against the wall and see if I can regulate my breathing. My work ethic and personal ethics are stronger than that ginger. That's definitely not happening.

CHAPTER 2

DAVID

DAVID: Tab, there's a hot chick at your desk. The tiny hot blonde piece from your birthday party who sat in her office the whole time.

TABI: DO NOT BANG HER.

DAVID: You know that's not how I operate.

TABI: That's Natalie, in case you've already forgotten her name. I'm sure Baxter gave her a job. She's an excellent admin and picks things up quickly. I'm out for a while. Give her all the POs and boring stuff you hate. She eats it up. Have Josh teach her the warehouse software. And don't fucking tell Bax you talked to me, or I'll pay someone to cut your balls off.

DAVID: Why can't I teach her about the warehouse? I know it. I AM a partner in this winery.

TABI: Because I don't want you to touch her. I repeat. Do not sleep with her. She doesn't need a touch of Gelbert-and-run. And we are in no position to find yet another admin. Stop sleeping with our only employee.

DAVID: I will not make any promises. Where are you?

DAVID: Seriously, Bax is flipping out. Talk to me, Tab.

DAVID: U ok? I won't tell Bax a thing, but if you need me, I'm here.

TABI: *Thanks, G. I'll call if I need you. But I'll be gone a while. Take care.*

DAVID: *That was way too nice to me. Where the fuck are you, Tab? Come home. I can't take mopey Bax for much longer. And I'm worried because the only thing worse than a mopey Bax is a defeated Tabi.*

TABI: *Stop being nice to me.*

DAVID: *Takes a black sheep to know a black sheep. Talk to me.*

TABI: *Fuck off. Fuck all the way off. Fuck you hard with a razor dildo up your pristine ass. Without lube. Fuck off in a million ways. Better?*

DAVID: *Fair enough. Gotta jet. I think it's time for a staff meeting.*

TABI: *DO NOT LET HER MEET YOUR STAFF.*

DAVID: *Come home, and I won't. Your call.*

FUCK TABI. I CAN'T RESIST THIS ONE. SHE'S DIFFERENT. THAT'S how all nights begin for me, I guess. I keep hoping they're different, then they turn out to be the same. But this one appears to like me without a blood alcohol level of 1.2. She's smart, like whip crazy witty, and genuinely laughs at my jokes. Her baby doll-blue eyes, golden hair, and little bow lips haunt me. She's all I can think about. In addition to wanting to taste every piece of her, I also want to talk to her. She listens when I talk instead of just waiting for the flirting to be over with so we can get down to business. She's so much smarter than I am, but she never makes me feel stupid. I've had seven meals with this woman. I haven't had my hand anywhere but on her back to guide her into a restaurant. But my hand has been extremely busy since she showed up in my life.

I light up a little, knowing she's going to be in the office soon. She's been here three weeks, and I've made every excuse I can think of to talk to her or not make a move too quickly. First, I broke our copier so we'd have a project together. Second, I have to run home like three times a day to relieve myself of the pressure in my crotch. Third, and most significantly, I have not slept with anyone since she rearranged our office supply closet on day one when she kept bending over. Who knew that face would sweep me away as much as that tight little body?

Yeah. Not listening to Tab.

I look at the delicate little thing that seems all vulnerable and ready for big bad David to pounce. It's time. Yesterday morning over coffee, she rubbed her leg up against mine and left it there. Then licked her lips while staring at mine. I've slow-played something for the first time in my life, and I can't wait another second. I pray I'm not making any big moves and scaring away the little chipmunk.

"How much are we going to dance around this?" I'm sitting at the reception desk with my legs outstretched and my hands behind my head. I've been waiting for her to show up. I'm not usually in this early, but I'm tired of waiting. The steam from my coffee curls up like the ends of her blonde bobbed hair.

Natalie Lloyd breezed into the Prohibition Winery offices on the wings of Bax's failed senate run, now she's picking up all the Prohibition pieces. I don't care why she's here. I only care that we haven't slept together yet.

I've wooed, joked, and flirted my ass off, and she's been receptive. I don't remember working this hard to get a woman before. I'm dying to kiss her.

She just walked by me and smirked. Natalie approaches the desk, places a bakery bag down from the Basque and walks away. I call that progress. I'm going to need to taste her lips pretty fucking soon.

As everyone is focused on freaking finding Tabi, who took off without notice, I've been focused on keeping our own fucking label up and running. Sam's off building a new contraption to fuck his girlfriend. Literally calling his supplies the Erection Set instead of an Erector Set. Josh has a tiny baby and his own winery to run, and his wife is freaking pregnant again. It's just me here. I'm not the one who should be running things. I was pissed off coming to the office every day until her.

She smells like vanilla foam on top of a cappuccino with the slight smokey smell of espresso and a hint of nutmeg coming through. To look at her, she's tiny. She can't be more than five feet, maybe 5'2", but her personality and smile fill the room. Any room she's in. I've never seen anything like it. Her blue eyes are big and round and insanely gorgeous. I'm 6'2". I thought I'd intimidate her with my height. It's happened before with women of her stature. But I'm pretty sure Natalie Lloyd is afraid of nothing. Least of all me. She's called me out on every move I've tried to make on her. She's seen everything about me instantly.

Bax dropped off this tasty little treat and told me to keep my hands off her. Of course, that's never going to happen.

I haven't been out in the vineyards for two weeks. Sam's been handling the fieldwork, and it's killing me to be inside. But she's made it all kinds of exhilarating. I don't want to find a rando to bed. I want to bend Natalie Lloyd over my desk. She keeps flirting. I know she does. I don't care if she knows I don't date. I wonder if she'll be cool with that. Every woman I'm with is aware I don't date. It makes it much easier to justify when I don't call or text back.

I follow her into the tiny kitchen area, sit down at the table, and pull out the croissant she bought me. She asked what I do when I'm not winemaking. No one questions that and actually listens. And no one is this fucking sexy without trying.

She's futzing with her tea behind me in the kitchen and still hasn't answered my question. I hid all of the honey. It's on my desk. She'll have to ask for it. Beg for it. Not very nice of me, but it's not very nice of her to invade my every waking thought since we met.

"Where?" She puts her hands on her hips, and I turn around at her question. Once again, I'm drawn to her. It's as if I'm on a leash or a choke chain, and her voice is a little tug pulling me back to her. She makes me behave. But I'm aching to misbehave. I get up into her space. Her scent makes me feral. I want to rip her clothes off right here.

"Where's what?" Her face flushes and her eyes somehow open even more expansive. Her bright blue eyes take on a darker tone with a lusty feel, which I wasn't expecting. Much like I was not expecting my voice to come out like a growl. But I'm pent up and laser-focused on getting this woman on top of me. I need her to ride my cock.

I step forward, and she backs herself against the kitchenette counter. I grin and ask again.

"Where's what, Sunshine?"

Unlike her pixieish normal voice, her voice is low and gravely, and I feel it in my balls. "Where's my honey?" Her skin is the perfect hue of peaches and cream. I always thought that was a bullshit phrase grandmothers say to describe the young. But here it is, the creamiest skin with a hint of blush like the back of a luscious peach, and all I want to do is lick and bite and taste it.

"Answer my question first, and then I'll answer yours? How much more are we going to dance around this? Give me a ball-park, so I know how much longer I have to want you."

She takes her sweet watermelon-colored bottom lip between her teeth and sucks in. She's a fucking fruit salad on a hot day. Then she licks where she slightly bit them, and I throw my head back, groaning. She giggles, and I place my hands closer to her. I cage her there and lean down. We're face to face now, and she's not shying away from me. There's no way she doesn't feel this connection, this heat. I don't know if it's hot because she kept blowing me off, or if the thing I felt the moment I saw her is more. If there's even a crack of an opening in the next minute. I'm taking it.

Her tongue darts out again, and I can smell her breath. Her fresh and minty breath. She seems the type who remembers to floss and brush after every meal. Her chest rises and falls; her bosom is literally heaving. She's proportionate, but her tits are full and perfect. All of her is petite except for those full rosy lips and her eyes that seem to go on forever.

Her voice is gruff, and I feel the lust coming off her in waves. Fuck yes. This is happening. "Where's my honey?"

I grin as if I've just won the lottery. "Right here."

And I don't hold myself back any longer as I slant my mouth over hers. Her lips are smooth, robust and so fucking sweet. She throws her arms around my neck and moans. Christ, it's like a B12 shot to my dick. I deepen the kiss, and our lips react to each other. They instinctively know what to do. And then the most glorious game-on muthafucking thing happens. She jumps, and I catch her as she wraps her legs around my waist and bites my bottom lip. I'll always catch her. I open to and for her, and my tongue touches the sweetest nectar I'm ever going to taste. There is something about this woman that's not just chemistry but biology.

She gasps as I start to nibble along her jaw. "David. Oh. Crackle. Crackle bomb." I pull back. Then I unwrap her legs and place her on the counter. She's staring at me. I cock my head. "What did you say?"

"I said 'Crackle bomb.' It felt good, and I don't swear." She nods her head in a definite sharp jerk as if to say the case is closed on getting her to swear.

"Ever?" I cross my arms over my chest. She stares down at my erection. I grab it through my jeans. "What would you call this?"

Her face turns blushy pink. "That's your penis, and it has an erection. I know you swear, and it doesn't bother me. I just, well, don't tooting do it."

I pause and stare at her. "You talk like a 50's housewife on TV. Are you a virgin?"

"Far from it."

I move between her legs, caging her with my arms again. I peck her lips and pull back. I say, "That might be the only information I need, but—" She puts her hands on my forearms. She's not pushing me away, simply announcing herself. I let her speak.

"I know you're not used to it, but if we do this, please don't sleep with anyone else until we're done."

"You mean at the same time?" I curl my lip to the left.

She smacks me playfully. "No. I don't want to date you, but I'm done pretending I don't want this to happen." I growl and lean in to suck on her neck. She shifts towards me, moaning. Then tries to speak, "I...." She gasps. "I don't want you to...." She's unable to finish her sentence as my hands crawl up her back and pull her towards me.

She shifts as I kiss and suck on her neck. She arches backward to give me better access. "What?" So sexy. Such the perfect little snack-size cake.

"What happens when I say my cock is hard for you? Does that make your pussy wet for me?" A gasp that's music to my ears as her hands roam my body. "Does that crackle your bomb?"

"Yes."

She wraps her legs around me, and I pull her closer. She grinds down on my already raging hard-on. I pull back but keep my hands on her ass. I look her in the eyes. My voice is like deep molasses and commanding as I tell her what's going to happen. I'm done waiting. This flirting we've been doing eight hours a day for three weeks, that's like dates 1–4 to someone like her. Today I get inside this woman.

"You won't say fuck, but you like it when I talk to you like that, don't you?"

She bites my bottom lip, and I slide my tongue into her waiting mouth. She's open, and her tongue is waiting to dance with mine. We vie for dominance, and I let her win as her tongue sweeps into my mouth.

"I'm going to close the office for today. We're going to my house. We're not checking voicemails or emails. We're not catching up on paperwork or worrying about Bax or where the fuck Tabi disappeared to. We're not charging phones or computers. We're not checking in or buttoning up anything. The only thing on our agenda for the foreseeable future is fucking. Filthy, hard fucking. Your cunt open, and you bouncing on my cock until I come so hard, we change time zones. I need my dreams to come true."

She smiles. "What dreams?"

"The dream of you bouncing on my dick, your tits in my hands and your face in a permanent O as you come quivering around my cock."

"Oh, my mother-truck, that's dirty talk." She loves it, I can tell. This is going to be so much fucking fun.

"You're mother-trucking right it is. After that, I'm going to make you come hard on my face. I want to be buried deep inside of you, so you feel me for a fucking week. I want to take you from behind, so I can see that perfect ass up close while I drive you to another orgasm. And that honey you're missing, I'm going to pour it all over your body and lick it off until every last sweet drop of you has been relished. I want to get lost in you. Just us. Nobody else, while it's just us. Now, You in?"

Her eyes are wider than before, her smile larger, then her sweet, breathy voice gives me the green light.

"In." She gasps.

There's a heat washing over me in a wave, like I'm already post-coital. It's the most relaxed I think I've ever been as I head into sex. I pump one fist in the air and turn to carry her out of the office.

I put my forehead on hers. "You're fucking perfect."

CHAPTER 3

NATALIE

I DON'T KNOW what we're doing, but I can't stop myself. He's so hot. He's currently sitting in his office, legs spread, watching me. I'm trying to concentrate, but he keeps fiddling with a pen in his large hands. Flipping it around, clicking it, then he'll put one end in his mouth, and as he does, that tongue, the one possessed by all the saints and all the demons, flicks out on the end of it. It wasn't one night. It was all supposed to be casual, on my terms, but I'm a terrible overlord to my emotions. They run willy silly all over the place.

He's just as taken. If he's still trying to pick up one-night stands, I'd be shocked since we've been together every night for almost a month now. He would have to be some kind of sexual spy, sneaking out while I'm sleeping off the multiple orgasms he bestows on me. There's something, but I don't want to get too invested or jinx it, so I keep quiet about it to him.

We've also kept it from his friends and co-workers. But they've all been wrapped up in the property they bought out on Arnold Drive to become the winery of their dreams. They all want to own a piece that's their own, not their family's. I'm not supposed to talk about it to anyone. I'm good at keeping that secret, but terrible at the other one. The one where I might not use dirty language, but I love it when he does.

We overslept, and I bolted out of his place and back up to my little guest cottage up on the hill at LaChappelle/Whittier Winery. Will Whittier, Josh's dad, makes sure to keep it stocked with wine, and Sarah, his mom, keeps me in terrible vegan baked goods and clean sheets. Most nights that I stay at his house, I remember to pack clean clothes and some dry shampoo, but today I forgot.

David usually gets me all slippery and wanton in the morning, but I left, and now he's torturing me with that pen and his smile. His green eyes are searing into me like those electric green hills of Ireland from stock photos about travel. His red hair is pushed back on his head and flopping a touch to the right. I shift in my seat, smile at him, and refocus my attention on proofreading marketing emails and stickers. We won a couple of medals in some California wine competition, and we're going to sticker the bottles. I was trying to tell Tabi we'll be sold out by the time the stickers get here, but she insisted. She also didn't put the year on the stickers, and we were instructed to write it on with Sharpie when people bought the bottles.

Between harvest with Stafýlia, Bax's upcoming election to City Council, and them both being a little love-drunk and engaged these days, I ignored all of her demands. No one needs Sharpie on a bottle. I also forgot. She's my closest friend here but I'm also penis-drunk, and I can't tell her about it.

I do think it bothers David a little to keep the secret. These four people, his partners, are like his brothers and sister. They were everything to each other growing up, and to be honest, they're insanely co-dependent. There's not a decision or a moment in the day they don't consult each other. Whether it's a quick trip to Sonoma Market or the purchasing of major winery equipment, there are always at least two of them discussing the situation's outcome. They are each other's large and small moments of life.

I'm their only salaried employee. For the moment, David and I are minding the store. Sam's out in our assorted patches of vineyards. Since they started as an online winery, they sourced juice from their parents' wineries. Now they have blocks of grapes all over Sonoma Valley. Their dream is to have their own vines someday, and that's what the brick-and-mortar of it all comes down to.

I push send on a decent number of emails. However, I'm still thinking about the absence of my new normal morning entertainment. I shift again and sigh. I don't realize he's behind me. He leans down and puts his hands on my shoulders, and I melt. His tongue is warm and tickling the tiny hairs on the nape of my neck as he kisses me from behind. "You didn't tell me you were missing our regular morning meeting."

I know what he's saying, but we're at work. Maybe I can convince him to take an extra-long lunch. He spins my chair around, and he's on his knees. He slides his hand to the back of my neck in one motion and tugs me towards him. His aggressive and sexy tongue is against my lips, and I grant him access to my mouth. I always do. I have no self-control against his tongue. Oh, how I want his tongue in places I can't even mention in mixed company. He keeps begging me to call his member the "c" word or use the "f" word. Not even as hot as he gets me am I breaking those little internal rules. I haven't told him about my secret name for his manhood. I call it the Parade. It's big and beautiful and should be celebrated. Because I'm always happy when it comes to town. He calls it Poundtown, but I just call it town. Or when the Parade comes down Main Street, it's always a good time.

He licks into my mouth, and I moan into his. It still feels new. My chair is manipulated, and now my legs are wrapped around him. I have on a maxi dress, and his hands are slowly making their way up my calves. He's torturing me with how slow and delicately he's touching me. Finally, he pulls back from the kiss and looks at me.

"Natalie. If you aren't a vision. Just a vision of lust and want. I don't know what to do with you, woman. You're a constant drain on my libido."

I laugh at him. He puts his head under my skirt, and I feel his tongue skim the edges of my thong. I smack the back of his head. "We're in reception. Stop it. Stop."

He pokes out of my skirt. "Stop all together or stop at reception?" He waggles his eyebrows and quickly leaps to his feet, plucking me out of the chair.

He says, "Please put a do not disturb on the phones. I think there's a snack break in the conference room."

I look confused. "You, my delicious girl, I'm eating you." I giggle, flip the phones off and run after him to the conference room.

CHAPTER 4

DAVID

"OH, sweet mother of silky milk, that feels so good," she moans.

I lift my head from between her legs—my new favorite place to be—and ask, "What the hell did you just say?"

She sits up on her elbows to try and see me. Her sandy blonde bobbed hair falling out of its neatly done ponytail. I adore the crazy that spills out of her mouth every time we're together.

"I don't know, David. You have me out of my head. I say all sorts of things because, to be very honest, I don't know if I've ever felt this the way you do it. It's beyond comprehension or explanation. It's fantastical."

While talking to her, I slip a finger inside. She gasps and arches her back but moves into me. I slowly pull it in and out of her. "It is, Sunshine, it's us. It's our beyond comprehension. You are my secret slutty Sunshine who loves to come almost as much as I love watching."

"Oh. When you talk like that." She moans as I push another finger inside her and let my other hand drift to her clit. I'm holding her open and letting the air get to it, and I see her lust ratchet up even higher. I tap on her clit while exploring that one spot inside of her that makes her scream.

"You fucking love how I can almost make you come by talking about fucking your cunt with my fingers." She moans loudly as I curl my fingers into her. She gasps and thrashes her head back and forth. I swirl my thumb around her clit and am gifted with another gasp.

"It's my favorite fucking show. Then Nat comes undone, a shattering orgasm, flushed face show. I mean, silky milk, it's fucking perfect and makes my cock throb and weep." I bury my face and begin working in earnest.

I grin at her. Every time I go down on her, it gets sweeter. She's so wet and perfect. Her legs are on my shoulders, and I have little Natalie all laid out on the conference table in our offices.

I cannot get enough of her. She's so different. She's innocent and not—sweet and salty. She's screwing up my head, but I can't stop screwing her. We've not made a big deal of it all, and we're trying to be low-key in the office, so basically, they don't yell at me for screwing our only employee. Again. If Nat and I go out with my friends, we take separate cars and hang out. But always end up together at night. Mostly we stay at my house or up at the LaChappelle/Whittier guest cottage, where she's currently living. We screw and talk. And although I'm her pussy's number one fan, the talking is just as good.

She bucks her hips and moans to indicate she wants more, and I dive back in and pump my fingers in and out of her. Pretty proud, she usually tries to be quiet, but not today. So it's a personal victory when she cries out for more. My fingers find her cozy spot, and I double my speed around her needy clit. She moans loudly as I hear a creak from the front door. I ignore it and hope it will go away. Like it's the wind rushing down First Street West, rattling the cages of the random buildings that house Sonoma businesses on the south side of the Plaza.

She cries out, trying to squirm away. But I hold her in place. "David. Puck the fairy. David. I'm so close." Her crazy sex talk keeps me motivated.

And then I find out it wasn't the wind. Dick shrinks instantly at the sound of his voice. "Gelbert. Really? Who the hell are you fucking in our offices?" I still have Natalie pinned, and her giant globe baby blue eyes shoot daggers at me. I pull my finger out, and I shrug. Then I flat tongue her entire slit up to her clit, and it's fucking delicious. She smacks my head, and I raise it up.

"Go away, Sam," I yell and turn back to Natalie. I can hear him coming closer to the conference room, and I put my finger to my lips. I begin to close the door. I should have locked it when we came in here.

"Where the hell is Natalie? I need those rec orders for the new racking system." And before I can answer for her, keeping her anonymity, her efficient side pops out.

"They're in a folder on your desk along with a couple of messages from distributors that couldn't get in touch with Tabi." Then her face drops, her mouth goes to a perfect O, and she slaps her hand on top of her luscious lips, realizing what she's just done. I swipe her clit one last stroke, sit down in the office chair and pull her skirt down over her exposed perfection.

There's no stopping him from coming in here now, and I decided about a week ago nobody gets to see this pussy again until I'm entirely done with it. And I don't see that happening anytime soon. If it was anyone else, I might have kept going.

His giant body fills the doorframe as he takes in the scene. Natalie scrambles off the table and pulls her dress straight. It's such a happy sundress. It's got those tie straps and a full skirt that make you dream of running through a lush meadow, then lifting it over her head to have full access and railing her quickly.

She shouldn't be able to carry off a long summer dress. But she does. Her confidence makes her appear much taller than her actual height.

Sam cuffs me on the back of my head. "Tabi's going to kill you. Slaughter you and Bax will let her. He's going to be just as pissed off that your wanker, player ass, has her ass in the air."

I say, "I kind of told Tab, but I think she thought it was a joke."

Natalie straightens to her tiny height and again fills the room. She's a bright tulip, always reaching for the sun. "I am an adult, and I did not make this decision lightly. I am well versed in Mr. Gelbert's history and antics."

Sam rolls his eyes and scrubs his face. Then he lifts his beard, running his fingers through the end of it, and groans. Then he smacks the back of my head again.

"Stop fucking hitting me. I know what I'm doing." I shove him a little away from me. One of my brothers from another mother is pissing me off.

"Do you? Wipe your chin, Gelbert. You're frosted with our admin." He tosses me a stack of napkins from the credenza in the conference room. And I wipe with an insane grin on my face. He turns to Nat.

"You just called him Mr. Gelbert. We pay your salary. He's never been out with the same woman more than..." He turns to me, looking for the number. Natalie already knows all of this. But Sam doesn't know Nat, and I have set an all-new record. Josh suspected I fucked her once. Tabi's not totally sure we've hooked up. Bax is dick-drunk on Tabi and in the last minutes of his City Council campaign, so he hasn't really been paying attention to me.

Natalie moves closer to Sam. "Two. Two times. That was the standing record."

"Was? Have I really not been paying that much attention? So, you've only hooked up with the same woman twice in how long?"

"Like a decade or so. I was busy working." I shrug.

Sam puts his hands behind his head and leans back, staring at me. Natalie shuffles papers, and I place a hand on her back. I can't keep my hands off her. I'm insatiable.

She puts the folder up to her chest and turns to Sam. I don't know if she's trying to hide how hard her nipples are or if she's trying to look professional. Either way, it's sexy as hell. Sam needs to go so I can finish my snack. My dick is aching to be inside her. I adjust my jeans, but they're too tight. Not even mountain Winnie the Pooh, Sam, can keep my dick down. That's how powerful Nat's pussy pull is on me.

Sam glances down and gets an eyeful. "Jesus, Gelbert."

Natalie speaks, "Was the record, Sam. David and I are about to have our seventeenth date this evening. And I refuse to disclose how many times we've been intimate because I don't see any of this being your business."

"Christ! More secret fucking. How are you assholes my brothers in arms? Full disclosure from now fucking on. Get me?" He's still pissed that Bax and Tabi did all kinds of secret fucking for years.

I nod at Sam, but he's off on a rant. He continues, "Natalie, take this down and send out an emergency memo to the esteemed winery owners of Prohibition. To Josh, Bax, Tabi and David, for the case of public record. Sammy and I do it at least three times a day. And sometimes, when we get lost in a scene, I'm not calling in sick; I'm calling in bondage. We ALL good now? NO more secret fucking. Especially when it's going to affect our bottom line. Prohibition Winery can't survive unless we're all on board and acting like an actual business instead of kids in a fucking clubhouse. Which means you can't secretly fuck the staff, Gelbert."

Natalie, unfazed, puts up one finger. Sam looks at her and back to me.

He says, "Don't we have to like cover our asses or something? I mean, we are a business?"

"Please hold." Natalie rushes out of the room, and I know exactly where she's going. She leaves a cloud of cinnamon sugar in her wake. She always smells like a bakery to me. I grin and step out of Sam's reach. I don't want to get hit again.

She comes back in and hands a folder to Sam. He opens it. "What's this shit?"

"It's a letter filed with HR revealing the nature of our relationship. We've both waived any liability the company or Prohibition Winery might be responsible for. It's been notarized." My girl rocks back on her heels, proud of herself.

"I can see that. But we don't have an HR," Sam says flatly.

My girl is undeterred. "I'm HR. When Tabi went MIA, you were in the cave with Sammy or at the crush pad. Josh disappeared into baby Emma and LC/W's harvest. Bax was sporadically working, campaigning, and looking for Tabi. I stepped up."

"You're HR?" Sam looks at her skeptically.

"With the complete lack of corporate structure upheld by your Articles of Incorporation, someone has to be legally on file. You had seven unopened notices about it. And I am the ranking administrator in this office. It can be undone, but you were about to lose your corporate license. I also refiled your sales tax information, put you on auto payment with vendors and the state for tax purposes. They were getting a touch cranky at what you owed and what you all seemed to be ignoring. And all permits have been pulled for you to proceed. You have all been named officers of your departments, and HR cannot legally be one of you. Bax said to take care of it, and I did. That's what I do. I take care of things."

"You did all of that and fucked Gelbert seventeen times."

She's so hot. I answer with my mouth full of blueberry muffin, "Oh, shit, it's way more than seventeen times. A shit-ton more than seventeen times. It's seventeen dates." I swallow and smile.

Sam's jaw drops. I wink at Natalie. She can be cheeky if she wants to, and I see the glint in her eye as she turns to Sam definitively. She looks at me and says for Sam's benefit, "Approximately one hundred and thirty-four."

Sam turns to her. "One hundred and thirty-four what?"

I answer as I usher him away from her with my arm around him, "Times we boned." Blueberry muffin crumbs spray out of my mouth.

Sam whispers, "Fuck me."

I nod. We've been doing it like five or six times a day. Our record is eight and ¾. She got there that last time, but my dick raised a white flag and couldn't figure out how to stick the landing.

Nat picks up the piece of paper Sam has placed down. "And that document you have is perfectly legal."

Sam says to me, "This document says it's ok to participate in a muff carwash in our conference room?"

I stand up and face Sam. I've enjoyed this exchange, but Natalie shouldn't have to take the brunt of this. "Back it down now. That's on me." I turn to Natalie and waggle my eyebrows. "And I'm looking forward to my disciplinary review by the HR department."

She turns scarlet. I turn back to Sam. "Sorry. I thought I locked the door. It won't happen again."

"You won't forget to lock the door, or you won't eat out our apparently entire staffs' clamshell?" Sam's fingers are back in his beard.

"As the HR rep, I can say, we're verging on some pretty serious sexual harassment issues."

Sam pulls his hair out like a mad dog. "What?"

"As Natalie, I'm terribly sorry for my behavior and that I let that happen on company property. But as your HR rep, you have to stop referring to my parts in the manner in which you're speaking."

Sam turns without saying anything and stomps to the door. He yells back at us, "How about this? Don't fuck in the office. Don't fuck anywhere near me. And certainly, don't fuck anywhere I eat my lunch. Oh, and how about you don't fuck anywhere Tabi will find you. Because I'm not cleaning up that mess. You're on your own with Tab."

Natalie is standing behind me, and I see what Sam does not. I cringe.

Standing with her hands on her curvy hips, her ebony hair wild, and pulling out of her messy bun is my oldest and closest female friend and winery co-owner. Her voice is deep and raspy and full-on hurricane category 5 strength. "Don't tell Tabi what?"

She glares at Natalie, who is hiding nothing with her blush face. I wipe my chin instinctively, and her eyes dart between us. "Holy muthafucking player piece of shit. You ruined her. You broke Natalie, didn't you? Fuck you, Gelbert." She tries to push past Sam, and he physically restrains her, which is a good thing because I'd pretty much just have to take her fists of fury.

Nat's voice breaks the tension. "I'm not broken. Just bathing in orgasms in a consensual, healthy, and completely transparent relationship. I have the paperwork."

Sam slings Tabi over his shoulder. She's screeching expletives. I fucked up. But it's what I do, so I'm used to it. I'll bring her a candy cane later. It's like her secret crack. I'll apologize to her for getting caught, but not for Natalie. I turn to Nat and take the folder out of her hand. She looks worried.

"Do you think Tabi thinks less of me? I can't have that. I want to be her someday, or at least her with a better sense of decorum. The way that she—" I pull Natalie into my arms and slant my mouth down over hers. I'm almost bent in half to lower my head to hers, but it's so worth it. At first, she tries to keep talking. Something she does quite a bit, but then her lips soften and yield to mine. Kissing her is unlike anything I've ever known. There's no judgment or angling. She doesn't want my family's money, the high school athlete, or to be with the former basketball star or even a revenge fuck against a boyfriend. She's the first person I can think of that's simply kissing me for me. I feel total acceptance for all my fuck-ups in her arms, her gaze, and in her kiss.

"I adore you." Her eyes light up.

"I adore you too. From a Natalie perspective, but as HR, I am going to have to write you up for an infraction."

"Let me plead my case." I pull her closer and slide my tongue back where it belongs.

CHAPTER 5

NAT

I CAN'T HELP but fall back into him. His hands slide up my thighs and pull up my dress as he places his hands on my butt. I break the kiss and murmur against his lips as he tries to reattach us. Instead, he drops to his knees and lifts my skirt up, and buries his head under my dress. I nudge his head, trying to warn him.

"Your father is stopping by any minute to pick up the new Pro/Ho brochures for Gelbert's tasting room. And Will Whittier just warned me he was on his way over."

"Why is my Dad picking them up?"

"Becca told him he had to see me. He doesn't believe we're actually dating. Will Whittier told him where to find me."

"My sister's a monster. But Will's a mensch. He's met you like fifty times. He's seen us together, and today he finally wants to get on with the inquisition."

"You're just going to have to fold that piece of you away for a minute."

Then there's someone clearing their throat. "Natalie?" My face turns bright red instantly. David pops up like it's nothing. He's way too athletic.

"Da! What brings you in?"

"A sense of decency and lack of pride." He says drolly.

David rolls his eyes and slaps him on the back. He turns towards me, and I get off of the floor.

I stumble over my words, "This might look like something it's not, and I'm not an improper girl. I had a loose WiFi connection, and there's a new router being installed later this afternoon, and we have to disconnect the old one and box it up for the guy to take with him. If I don't, there's so much hassle and money and time and effort that no one even needs to understand. I have it all handled. Well, except for the thing David was doing under my desk. That was the one thing not handled, and now it's all figured out." David lets me babble.

Arthur Gelbert is a balding man holding onto the scraps of red tufts around his head like a crown that's too big. His coloring and stature mirror his son's, but that's about it. Where David is trim and athletic, Arthur is the opposite. Like the reverse images of each other. Arthur's stomach protrudes over his khakis but has a large barrel chest. David's body is delicious and looks like a reverse triangle. Broad on top and tapering slightly at the waist. He stares at me as I try to settle my thoughts.

"Breath, lassie, and your dress is tucked up into your underwear in the back." My eyes get wide, and David shrugs behind his father's back.

I'm going to die. David takes up a place next to me. I feel his giant, and a warm hand slid down my back and untuck my dress. He smooths it down and then gives my ass a pat. I continue to stare directly at his father as if eye contact alone will fix this situation. Then he pulls me into his side, leaving his large hand splayed across my lower back.

"Dad, you remember Natalie Lloyd, my girlfriend." My breath hitches, and David's hand grips my back. His Dad's eyebrows raise, and I'm convinced David said it to get a rise out of his father. We don't say those words. I nod, trying not to lose eye contact. Arthur clears his throat and gestures to us, then passes by headed for the conference room where I was just splayed out in pleasure. I can see through the door he's making himself a cup of coffee. Then he grabs the stack of brochures I laid out for him and skips the pastries I left. Probably a good call. They're scent is probably sex-tainted now. I didn't know if he was staying or what I should do. I like to be prepared for everything, so nothing throws me. Well, my dress in my panties, I didn't prepare for that. And for David in general, but I'm rolling with it. His father moves to exit the building and turns back.

"David, your mother expects you for dinner. No T-shirts." Then his gaze falls on me again. "And Ms. Lloyd. It's a pleasure to see you. I'm sure Jana would appreciate it if you were there as well. David, I'll leave you to do whatever it is you do at this club-house." He turns and leaves, and I'm stunned. I'm invited to family dinner. And he's gone but not without a barb directed towards David. I exhale a breath I didn't realize I was holding in.

"He's not a warm man, but he is an asshole," David says in a semi-sarcastic tone as he clutches me closer to his side and slides his hand to my hip. Then he kisses the top of my head again.

I murmur into his chest, "Girlfriend?"

"Duh. What the hell else would you call spending every second together, and when we're apart, you're all I think about?" And my now my breath is gone.

CHAPTER 6

DAVID

I WANTED to take her out. I want to take her somewhere that's not Sonoma. SF is a whole thing, but I used to come to this one club in Napa a lot. I want to dance with her. I want to woo her. She pulls her sage green dress under her and smooths it down as she hops up on the barstool. I'm there in case she needs me. She's so short I worry about her making it up there. But she figured it out. I lean sideways on the barstool, and she places her porcelain hand on my tight black shirt right over my heart. I'm about to be touched when she pushes me back just slightly.

"Do you always crowd your dates like this?"

I tug on her low short ponytail. Her hair is a long bob, so I find it adorable when she pulls it into a low pony. It's not the typical long sleek sex handle other women can sport. Instead, it's a bit stubby and altogether charming. Doesn't make me want her any less, but it's not as polished as she thinks it is. I rub my thumb along the back of her hand, and she smiles.

I say, "I'm pretty sure you're going to be my karma."

"How so?"

She's this little thing I can't hold back from. All my hidden shit behind well-crafted protective walls spills over when I'm with her. "You'll be the one to leave me because I'm already in too deep. You have all the power, Nat. I'm just hoping to stay on this ride with you a little longer. But sooner or later, you'll figure out this isn't what you want. And on that day, you'll be the first one to break my heart. But I can't stop. I can't help but be with you every second I can. Until you decide to go, I'm going to take advantage of my time."

Her mouth makes that little O. The same as when she comes.

I move to her ear so only she can hear me, "When we get home, I'm going to suck on that dripping pussy of yours. I'm parched, and my thirst is only quenched between your legs."

She smiles. "Gracious gravy. That is a lot to take in. Give me a moment."

"Is there something you'd like to say to me?" I grin, hoping I didn't just dangle my balls into a shark tank.

Her face flushes red, and just as she's about to speak, a woman places her long cabernet-painted fingernails around my bicep. The color of her nails matches the wine color in my tattoo.

"Gelbert. Look, we match." The beautiful blush I just put on Nat's face retreats. Nope, can't have that. Can't have her think this is anything. I'm using the g-word. Fuck it.

"Hey. How are you? This is my girlfriend, Natalie." This woman, who I know I've slept with but forget the circumstances —I believe she has a name like a customer service rep, Roberta or Lisa—needs to stop touching me. She's laughing as if this is a little game we play. I only sleep with people once, so not sure what this one is angling for.

Natalie puts out her hand, the woman dips her claws, and Nat ends up shaking her nails awkwardly. Then, finally, she sips her drink and tries to slink off the barstool. I move closer to Nat and face our intruder.

She throws her hair over her shoulder. "The girls and I won't believe your little ruse for long. If you don't want to have fun tonight, Gelbert, you don't have to make up a lame excuse."

I say sharply, "Not an excuse. Actual truth." She laughs harder, and I put my hand on Nat's knee. I know she's uncomfortable and squirming. I need her to see how I handle this. And I'm positive I'm handling it spectacularly wrong.

"Tell me another one." She pouts. "I was worried about your fun level this evening."

I say, "Well, that's sweet of you to worry about my fun evening, but trust me, it's taken care of." I kiss the top of Nat's head. What am I, her Uncle? I kissed her on the top of my head while telling this she-wolf I'm satisfied. Christ, I'm doing this wrong.

I look over her shoulder. The lights are swirling, the music is pumping, and I see the ghosts of hook-ups past gyrating, sipping, and sliding into VIP booths. Shit, this was a terrible idea. This person, Adrienne, maybe? I don't know her fucking name. She was clearly someone I filled time with instead of enjoyed. I recognize some of the other women, and I know some of their names. I'm twitchy. My whole body is tight as a strap. We have to get out of here before she breaks up with me because I've been a whore for a couple of decades. Shit.

Natalie scrolls her phone while the customer service rep keeps chatting with me about what an excellent time could be had with the three of us. I can't get Natalie to say the word cock, and this one wants a three-way. Oh, shit. Now I remember her. She's the three-way girl. She and her gorgeous friend. Her, I remember, her friend was the one I wanted to hook up with, Liza. She was freaking stunning. Damn. She needs to get away from the only woman I've ever wanted as a part of my life.

I remove her hands from me again. "I'm sorry, we're having

an evening together. It was great catching up, but you need to go now."

"David, that was rude," Natalie snaps at me.

The customer service rep runs her hands back up my arm again, and I cringe at her touch. "Yeah, Davie, that was rude. Your little cupcake wants to share."

I grin at the insane situation Nat doesn't even realize. I raise my eyebrow and purse my lips at Natalie. I cross my arms over my chest and step back, so Nat realizes what she's encouraging. Also, that I want no part of the offer. Nat gasps.

She says, "Oh. Oh. My. Wow. That's a bucket of paint. No shipping way, I'm sharing. No. I don't want to be rude, but I get it now, and I'd like to be alone." But, shit, does she mean without me?

The woman shrugs. "Your loss. I make him better. I'm like a value add." I roll my eyes and turn away from this woman. She walks away. And Nat is left with a whole lot of information.

I put my hands on her face and kiss her lightly. She smiles, but it's a strange smile. I back up a bit, and she slides off the barstool. It's my own damn fault. Bringing her to a fucking pick-up club was an idiot thing to do.

I look at her. "Please. Nat. Let me explain." She puts her hand up, then leans on the bar. She sips her drink slowly and seductively running her pinched fingers up and down her straw. She crooks an eyebrow at me and I steel myself for what's to come. She glances at her phone, then places it face down on the bar.

Then says, "Well, here I am. What are your other two wishes?" I shake my head slightly, trying to process what's she's doing.

She grins at me and says, "There is something wrong with my cell phone. It doesn't have your number in it." Then slides her phone to me. I start to laugh. She pulls her dress down just a little to expose some cleavage, and I couldn't adore her more as she says, "Aside from being sexy, what do you do for a living?" I laugh heartily as she tries to pick me up.

I lean down to her ear and say, "I must be a snowflake because I've fallen for you."

She doesn't hesitate and takes the sleeve of my tight black t-shirt between her fingers and rubs it. "Let me feel your shirt. You know, I think I know what that's made of, boyfriend material." She licks her lips. This fucking woman.

I rapid-fire these at her while taking her hand in mine and massaging it lightly. Suddenly all the shit around us and my sketchy sexual history disappear in her pure, unassuming laugh.

I say, "Baby if you were words on a page, you'd be fine print. Did you just come out of the oven? Because you're hot. It's a good thing I have my library card because I am totally checking you out. I was blinded by your beauty; I'm going to need your name and phone number for insurance purposes."

She tosses her head back, and her gorgeous neck is exposed, and I kiss it. She reacts by pulling away a bit. I guess my past didn't wholly disappear. I pick her up and place her back on the stool and cage her legs with mine.

"No, Nat. This is happening. Don't move away from me. Don't retreat. We go forward, and I've never wanted that before. All of this is background noise, and we never need to come back here. But I want you. And no one else."

My hands roam to the top of her ass. We were supposed to be a casual hook-up. But it's like she was always there as a Russian sleeper agent. Some code word awakened all my senses, and the assault of those blue eyes tells me everything I want in life can be found in her face. I pull her to the dance floor and hold her close, even though there's some thumping club beat in the background. She smiles and moves her arms around my neck. We dance to our own beat and rhythm. All women pale in comparison to her.

I didn't realize the moment I kissed her, all of this became my past. It's a little jarring. This is who I was for a long time. Drunken hookups, greasy breakfasts, and a quick goodbye. If I was too fucked-up to leave before they woke up my MO was to take them to breakfast as soon as possible. No round two. No sober light-of-day sex. Quick breakfast, then drop them back home. Clean and simple. No follow up.

Natalie challenges everything about me and accepts all the things I hate about myself. She actually likes the dumbass and dick parts of me. And I can't get enough of her honesty and positivity.

"David. You're looking at me differently." I keep dancing with her. We're close, and our bodies know what to do with each other. We've already done it, but I feel like we've unlocked a different level of this game. I anticipate her every gasp and hip sway as she does mine. She's such a powerful little thing. She tries to look down and dismiss my intensity. I catch her chin between my thumb and forefinger and tilt her back to me. I always want her to tilt back to me.

"I'm looking at everything differently." Shit just pours out of my mind without a filter around her.

"Stop. This isn't this." She shakes her head.

We keep swaying, and now my dick is getting involved, but it's not about lust. It's about things I've never felt before. Things I've been saving for her, apparently.

I say, "This is different. You light me up, Sunshine." I lean down and brush my lips softly over hers. Her bottom lip trembles a little, and I rub my thumb over it. She pushes into it, then I'm on her lips, gently at first. I don't want to scare her away. I sweep my lips over her jaw and up her neck to her delicate ears, intending to say what I'm feeling, but it's her who whispers in my ear.

"David. Ok. It is different. Please be different."

"I promise. I'm already different. But I promise to be different from any other man who's been lucky enough to be with you."

I back up and stare at her. She smiles. I pick her up, and she straddles my hips. She weighs nothing, but everything around us is weightless as I carry her out of this place. It may be her first time here, but it's my last. I get to be someone else now if she'll let me.

CHAPTER 7

NAT

WE BARELY MAKE it in the door when my dress is ripped off me. All the gooey emotions of the club fall away, giving rise to lust. I feel the Parade through his jeans, and he groans when I cup it. His eyes are dark and mossy green with lust. He pulls me to him and kisses me as if he's being judged. Our tongues smush and mush together in a sophisticated dance. His lips only leave mine to pull down his jeans and boxers. Then he lifts me and places me on the bed. He cages me to the bed, and I wrap my legs around his waist. He slides his hand down between my legs and is met with all the desire in the world.

"Beautiful. You're so fucking wet for me. It's perfect." He watches my face as I gasp when his finger slides into me. I arch into him. I always do. It's involuntary.

"My cock can't wait. I need to feel the end of you. I need for it to feel every fucking bit of you." He leans down and traps my nipple in his mouth. He tugs, and I gasp at the pain with how much pleasure follows. He rolls the other between his thumb and forefinger and pinches that one instead. After giving each nipple equal attention, he reaches over and rolls on a condom.

We're always careful. He slides into me, and my entire body explodes. He sits up and pulls me to him.

"I'm going to drill my cock into you by pulling you down on it. I want your tits to bounce. Play with your clit while I do this. Let me see how hot we can get you by working together."

"Mother-truck, that's so good. Geranium busterflies, don't stop. Jesus." He's got me wild. He smiles at what I just said then his look gets so intense. He pulls me to him and pushes me away. Driving deep inside me and possessing each part. I can't stop myself from screaming his name over and over. We're cresting, and the entire bed is slamming into the wall. He'll need to spackle the cracks we make. I refocus on the pleasure instead of home improvement. The banging of the bed is rhythmic and in beat with each time he slams himself into me. I stretch and take him, and I feel him everywhere. I'm so full of this man, and yet it could never be enough. My fingers creep towards my lady button, and he groans. "Yes. Yes. Fuck Yes. Touch yourself. Let me see." I swirl two fingers with a bit of pressure over my clit, and I'm not sure I can take anymore. I'm all Pop Rocks and Brulee sugar sweetly exploding and cracking all over.

"Fuck. Nat. You're so fucking hot. Feels so good. Come for me." He pulls me to the edge of the bed and stands up. He places one of my legs over the crook of his arm and begins to slam his Parade home.

I whisper, "Harder." I want it so badly.

"Did you just say harder? That's filthy coming from you. Fuck. How is it I'm harder when you say harder?" His hips piston in and out of me and I'm unable to do anything but go along for the ride. My hands are pulling at my nipples. He reaches down and swirls my 'O' button, and I'm gone.

I scream and shudder and shake. My legs are quaking with quick jerks, but he doesn't stop. He drives through my orgasm.

Then I feel him shudder inside me. He groans and loses his rhythm and I pick up a bit by thrusting so he can finish.

"Nat. Natalie. God." He groans.

Then my leg is down, and he's on top of me. He kisses me deeply without saying a word while still inside me.

He pulls back and stares at me. I see it all. And I hope I'm showing him enough.

I WAKE WITH A START. I DON'T MOVE ONCE I POP OPEN MY EYES. His arm is draped over my middle. This sexy, rakish tattooed bad boy's arm is draped over me. I regulate my breathing, so he doesn't wake up. I've never been so comfortable in all my life. The windows are open, and I hear life all around us, and no one is waiting on me to leave or make myself useful. I do have to finish my to-do list from yesterday. I let it slide so this man could slide on top of me. We had sex five times. I think every man I've been with was lying to me about stamina. He's living proof a man can, in fact, get it up again very quickly. I seem to be enough for him. For now.

He snuffles and pulls me closer to him. The closer I get to him, the more it's going to hurt when it's time to pack up and leave. What was supposed to be fun took a distinct turn last night into unmapped territory for me. I've had boyfriends and lovers. I've had some friends, but I've never had anyone that was all three.

My life is bursting with firsts lately. I don't know how to define what I'm feeling, but it tickles the bottom of my belly and heart whenever he's near. It's like an itch that can never get scratched except when he's inside me. In those moments, it's like we're in our own space pod or something—just us floating in the nothingness. We're the only ones who matter. I've never really mattered to anyone like this. I'm aware of how dangerous the situation is because I'm the only one who feels this floaty.

I do need to get to work. If I don't my job done efficiently will all end sooner than later. No one is going to keep me around if I'm not earning my keep. I want to float with David a little longer, so I need to get all the Prohibition stuff under control and running impressively perfect

I grab a pillow from the floor and pull an Indiana Jones, switching my body for the pillow, and he doesn't wake up. I collect yesterday's clothes and tiptoe into the living room. As I'm crossing the threshold away from the bedroom, I don't see his jeans and tumble. I catch myself as I'm falling. I can't stop the expletive from slipping out as I stub my toe. "Snake in my boot!"

I freeze. I hold up my clothes in front of my naked body and wait to see if he woke up. I think I'm in the clear. I turn back towards the living room.

In the sexiest gravel voice, I hear him say without moving, "Did you just say 'snake in my boot?'"

"Shh. Go to sleep."

"Did you just quote Woody from *Toy Story*?"

I whisper, "I stubbed my toe. Sorry."

He leans up, and the sheet falls like a waterfall, revealing that chest full of goodness. And now the rich auburn parade route of hair points south to his Parade. "You swear weird. Come back here."

"I have to pee. I'll be right back. And I have to write some-thing down, so I don't forget." I rush to him, kiss him quickly, and try to back away. He captures my lips and the back of my head. He holds me in place while he kisses me slowly, then furi-ously, then slowly again. As if he wants to use every ounce of energy he has left to let me know I matter. Like I take up volume, mass, and space in his world.

"Come back to bed." Then he falls to the pillow and immediately falls back asleep. He does that. I've never met anyone who falls asleep as quickly as he does. It's like he has a secret to turning his brain off to go to bed. He doesn't take stress or worries to bed. They fall away in an instant.

I don't know how to do that. I dress quickly and write a quick note. I plan to be back before he gets up to head out to the vineyards. He wants to check the sprayers and hose, they keep getting clogged, and it's going to be warm today. He wants to cool the grapes down early and douse them so they don't get too hot too quickly. I don't know what that has to do with the taste of wine, but he does. He knows it all like a grandmother remembers her Christmas cookie recipes. It's all in his memory chip of essential things.

I'M THE ONLY ONE HERE AT THE OFFICE. I FIND GREAT PEACE IN being at an office insanely early. It's 3:30 in the morning. Not usually here this early, but the quiet settles my brain. It's not about the distractions. It's about the secret of the early morning that holds possibilities and gives me the feeling I can accomplish anything I want. I love a 5 a.m. morning. Especially when I have work to get finished. I put in four hours of work, then when people show up and start to interrupt my day or veer it off course, it's ok because I'm ahead. I love being ahead.

I get all of yesterday's work done and text David. It's close to six. I can't stop yawning.

NAT: *I'm still at the office. But I'm thinking of you.*

I'm always thinking of him.

DAVID: *Duh. Who isn't always thinking of me? Catch you after I spray down the Chard.*

DAVID: *I miss you.*

NAT: *Really?*

DAVID: I did not get morning sex, and that's on you. I'll be by in an hour or so.

He misses me. I guess it's ok that I miss him too. We're kind of pathetic. We've only been apart like three hours. I grin to myself. Another first. No one's ever missed me.

CHAPTER 8

NAT

DAVID LOOKS at me with those eyes. "Tell me something." His fingers are tracing a slow seductive pattern up and down my leg, leaving a trail of goosebumps.

"What?" I curl into him a little deeper. I'm so cozy. His fingers, which gave me such hot pleasure an hour ago, are now comforting and addictive.

"Anything. I want to hear your voice while I fall asleep."

"I'm pretty sure I've never had sex before."

David leaps up. He quickly hops to my side of the bed. I'm staring at his beautiful member. It's eye level. He's gesturing, and it keeps flopping. It should be completely deflated, but it seems as if he's perking up to say hello again. It's like the Parade route is circular.

"What? No. There's is no way someone with hot ass moves like you was a virgin. Did you lie to me? Are you a sexual savant? Like it's intuitive. I've never come that hard. I'm far from new at this, but you are a goddess at sex. You are the hottest of fucks." I sit up and turn in a tight circle. "I was thinking of googling new tricks, so you don't get bored of my subpar mastery of your perfect vageeene."

I'm laughing so hard I can't correct him. "Goddess?"

He falls to his knees. "If I could sculpt marble, I'd shape your pussy into the prettiest centerpiece the Plaza has ever seen. Then everyone could worship it like I do. Goddess." He kisses my nose, and I scoot up. He whips the sheet off, exposing me completely, then dramatically gestures to my body. "GODDESS."

I grin and plump a pillow behind me as I scoot up the bed. "No. Not a virgin. It just feels as if every other time was practice for a game I might never get to play in."

He falls on top of me and kisses the hell out of me. His tongue scooping in and claiming mine. I melt into the mattress as his hands begin to roam. He pulls back and moves a piece of hair out of my face.

His voice is soft and quiet. And sexy as hell. "Suit up. You're in the big leagues now. No more riding the bench for you. Now you get to ride me. Hmm." His eyes drift to the ceiling as if he's contemplating things. As if he's controlling it with a pump, I feel him begin to get ready again, inflating like a Parade balloon. His dick is always happy and waving. Constantly rising above all expectations, and when I orgasm, I feel as if a marching band is playing. I smile at him as he rolls me on top of him. I sit up, straddling him.

He commands, "Giddy up." I giggle. "What? What's that smile about? You should be busy bouncing on my dick, but you have a secret. Spill it, and then I will."

I roll my eyes. "I named your penis."

"Tell me the nickname is cock. Or dick. Fuckstick? Say it. Come on. The thought of you talking dirty drives me insane."

I shake my head. "The Parade."

"Like, before the Parade passes by? So, you'll be on Parade pretty soon?" He grins. "Not as manly as I would have liked. I could have used a consult, but where you going with this?"

"I can ask things in public like, 'What time's the Parade coming through?'" He grabs my hips and wiggles me a little, and my breasts sway back and forth. He reaches out, pinches my nipple and rolls it through his thumb and forefinger, and I sigh.

Then I compose myself a little and say, "Or I can say, the Parade was very good this time. I like to wave to the Parade."

He asks, "How many floats are in the Parade?"

"Usually two nice and round ones." I squeal.

He sits up, and now I'm on his lap as he kisses me. "You'll be going down to the Parade later?"

"If you want me to Parade around like a hussy?"

"Fuck, yes I do." He readjusts me, and I move just a little, putting a little pressure on my lady button, and I moan as he kisses my neck while speaking. "The Parade route seems a little wet."

"Oh, it's soaked, but I think it's a safe route." He pulls back and looks at me, and I give him a soft smile.

He moves hair out of my face. "Are you sure?" I nod. I want to feel all of him. "I've only ever done this when I was stupid in high school or college. The Parade Committee is a loyal and fervent believer in making sure all avenues have been safe."

I kiss him, then he smirks. His hands move down to my ass and scoot me forward. Then he dips his head to my stiff, tight nipple waiting for the warmth of his tongue. I lean back just a touch to give him better access. He pulls and nips while his thumb and forefinger pinch the other. I gasp and rock forward on a very ready Parade. He sucks my nipple hard, drawing it deep into his mouth and releasing it with a tiny pop.

"Look, the bands, floats, and balloons are all lined up at the entrance to the Parade route. The confetti is locked and loaded. Tell me when you want it to start."

I reach down and move him slightly as I lift up and let him find me. The tip of him goes in slightly. He's not a local college homecoming Parade, he's the whole flim-flamming Macy's Day Parade, and it takes me a second to acclimate. He doesn't move and lets me set the pace. Then as I take him deeper, he groans loudly.

"Fuck, Nat. Fuck. So hot and tight. Feels so fucking good. My cock bare inside of you. Let me make you come. I know I won't last. Ride me, Sunshine. Ride me hard and fast. And if you can't get it done, I'm going to flip your sweet dripping ass over and get it done for you. Fuck, I feel all of you. I feel the end of you. Take all of me. You can do it."

I gasp for a second, then slam down on top of him. I feel the pinch of his size quickly replaced by a flood of unbelievable pleasure, and I clench.

"FUCK. Jesus, Nat. This is another muthafucking level." He picks up my hips, and I move up as he slams me back down on his Parade. My entire body clenches around him. "I can't, David. I can't monkey-leafing stop."

"Then come on my cock. Monkey-leafing come. Let me feel you. I want to feel every monkey-leafing pulse and twitch. Oh. God. Nat. Yes. Come on my dick." I let the orgasm of all orgasms toss its way from my toes up to the top of my head, then slam me back down to earth. I scream his name and lots of other animals as I climax so hard I might never stop. I feel the Parade jerk and shudder so deep inside me. I clutch onto him as he rides it out, still pumping himself up and into me. I quake around him again as a more petite, more polite second orgasm rips a gasp from me and a growl from him.

He whispers in my ear, and I shake and shudder from the slight tickle his stubble gives me. "Natalie, you're holding me so tight. Like your cunt never wants to let me go." It's not just my parts that don't want to let him go. It's all of me.

I'M ALONE IN HIS BED. I DON'T LIKE IT. I PANIC JUST A TINY BIT AND figure he's getting a snack. I pad out to the kitchen, looking for a note. I grab one of his many Golden State Warriors t-shirts and find nothing. I don't hear him shooting baskets. He does that when he can't sleep. I peek outside to see if his car is here. So odd. There's a grinding noise and sparks of light coming from his garage. His car is in the driveway. Why doesn't he ever park in the garage?

CHAPTER 9

DAVID

I DON'T HEAR her until I lift the shield and turn off the blow-torch. She knocks over a stack of license plates. The construction crew pulled them out of the old equipment barn at the new Pro/Ho property we're about to close on.

I don't know what to say. I turn towards her and help her pick up the fallen metal. All the edges have been ground smooth, so she's in no danger of cutting herself. She looks angelic in my Warriors shirt with her nipples reacting to the slight chill in the garage. I had the place airconditioned, so I could always work. I toss my gloves on the bench and put my hands in my pockets. Her eyes take in the space slowly. I converted a three-car garage into a place to fuck around. Other than going out, it's not like I ever really spent any of the money I've earned. My skill sets include wine, basketball, and I'm oddly good at saving money. About a year ago, I spent a chunk on this place. And I bought one other giant thing a couple of years ago, but I don't deal with it. It's just there. But this workshop is all selfish. I get fidgety. Sex, basketball, and this help me focus and stay on a path that doesn't end with my fists.

"This is an amazing studio," she says, looking around.

I shrug. "It's just a workshop."

"But isn't this art?"

"No. It's just stress release."

I have a big blue lounge chair in the corner, and I pull it out for her. Josh sometimes stops by and hangs out to escape the women in his life. I don't tell anyone. He often comes here when I'm not here too. He bought the chair. I can always tell he's been here because he likes to stock my mini-fridge with his winery's wine just to bust my balls. Once, it was filled with Elle's breast milk, and another time, it was filled with frozen octopus. Ages ago, we were all out to dinner to celebrate Josh's first big deal. And I puked up octopus. After that, they called me "8" for like a year. I told everyone it was after Kobe's LA rookie number, but my friends knew and love to bust my balls about it.

She sits and pulls her legs under her. I kneel down in front of her and move her hair out of her face.

She asks, "What?"

"You're everything beautiful in the world. Do you know this?" I grab the fuzzy bathrobe I keep in here and drape it over her.

She shakes her head.

"Seriously, name something more beautiful than you. I defy you. Hell, I'll even talk about all the shit in here if you can name something. And you know I do NOT want to talk about this place or what all of this is about." She thinks for a moment and then places her delicate hand on my heart. I look down and cover her hand with my bulky, awkward callused one. "What?"

"That," she states simply.

"Explain, woman. You're oddly and sweetly cryptic."

"Your heart is more beautiful than I am." I fall backward onto my ass. I overexaggerate my fall to make her laugh, but my legs went out from under me. She's not right, but her words are breaking me wide open. I cross my legs and face her. We stare at each other.

I say, "I have ADHD with a side order of some anxiety, if you couldn't tell."

"You don't say, Mr. Non-sequitur no attention span." She crosses her arms.

"Very funny little perfect Natalie who has no troubles." She scoffs. "We'll get to those. You don't think I'm opening an artery, and you're remaining unscathed." She smiles.

I hop up, pop open the fridge, and pull out a bottle of Langerford Viognier. Dammit. Since when does Sam hang out here? I pour some into two red solo cups while telling my story without telling her perfect face. "They didn't know for a long time, and Arthur's not a huge fan of patience or understanding, so when I fucked up in school, which happened a lot, there wasn't a whole lot of warm talks over cookies and milk. He still doesn't believe it's a real thing—just thought exercise would fix me."

"Is that when you started to play?" I turn around and hand her the wine and sip as I nod. Her golden hair is all over the place, but her blues are fixated on me. I pull out another chair and sit backward to face her. Almost like I've put a barrier between us. I don't share this shit. I mean, my friends lived it with me, but they don't know all of this crap. But I want to tell her. I don't think she'll judge. I know she won't. I nod.

"Basketball and the hoop at the house were a place to put it all. I started when I was like seven. I was good from the beginning. And it was a place to get out aggression. Bax played, and the other guys would do pick-up games with me. Josh and Bax were more football and baseball, respectively. But we all ran track and tore it up."

"This is delicious," she says after a sip.

"Fuck off. It's Langerford." I smile at her, and she giggles

"Continue. I'm sorry. It's good, but not nearly as good as Gelbert or your Pro/Ho blends."

I lean the chair forward on two legs and steal a kiss. Then I snap it back to four legs. "I couldn't always throw hoops in school, so my mom introduced me to her art studio. She and Sarah Whittier are both really amazing artists. I just fucked around. But it got so if I could draw during class, I could refocus on the lesson.

"You doodle on every napkin, piece of paper, or receipt."

"Habit. Drawing did it. Painting never did it for me. Auntie Sarah tried her best to get me to paint, but it never took. My mom used to make stained glass, so she had all the soldering stuff. One day I started messing around, and it stuck with me."

She shifts on the chair and leans a little more on the arm. I say, "Do you want to go to sleep?"

"Absolutely not! Are you flim-flamming kidding me? Tell me more. What happened when you started to sculpt?"

"Mess around," I correct her. "I liked it as much as hoops, maybe a little more, but that's not what happens in Arthur's world, so I ended up at UNLV with a basketball scholarship."

"Wow. Did you ever think about art school?" I stand up and head back to the bottle. I glance over my shoulder.

"I got a full ride to Pratt, but there was only one path in my household." She gasps. I don't look.

"And now you do it in secret?"

"Somewhat. I'm kind of working on this for Josh and Elle. Well, for Emma, then one for the next one." I hold up a mobile. It's different clusters of grapes with intricately woven vines connecting them created out of metal.

She comes over and puts her arms around my waist. "It's breathtaking, David. They will love it." I shrug. "You already finished this and never gave it to them. David, you must."

"We'll see."

She says, "Did you blow off the NBA draft because of your dad?"

I suck air through my teeth. I didn't know she knew that little nugget. She either googled me or asked around. I would have told her.

"So we're just going to cut deep? Yes. I got drunk and blew off signing with anyone," I say and turn back to pouring us more wine.

She slaps me on my back as she releases my waist. She's just a little pixie standing there like the Golden State Warrior fairy. I want her to go back to sitting in the blue chair. She was flashing me without knowing it. And her perfect blonde and particularly coiffed pussy was on display just for me. I love me a landing strip.

Her hands are on her hips. "Surely, you could have sobered up if you wanted to."

"I was drunk for a month."

"Oh." She takes a sip.

"In Ireland. At my great-aunt's house." She squeezes me tighter again. "But I wouldn't change anything in my life because it would mean I'm not here right now with you. Not one second of it."

CHAPTER 10

NAT

"SIT your ass down and start spilling your secrets, little pixie. I know you grew up out east. Your parents' names are? What did they do? How did they raise someone as perfect as you?"

I bristle at his words. I don't know how to do this. "You'll treat me differently."

He scoops me up, flops down on the cozy aqua chair, and pulls me on his lap. I spill wine, and he doesn't notice. "Impossible. Are you still going to have the same magical cunt and sunshiny personality?"

I roll my eyes. "Yes. And stop using that word."

"Why?" He kisses me suddenly and intensely—his tongue claiming every part of me. There must be an electrode attached to my lady button that buzzes when he kisses me. "Not only am I not going to stop saying cunt, but I'm going to get you to say it."

I hit him. "No, sir. Never."

He laughs, then the jokey atmosphere evaporates as his eyes tell me I can trust him. The world and my worries disappear as I fall deeper into his bright green eyes.

"Nat. You don't have to tell me anything. Truly, Sunshine, you don't have to tell me a damn thing. But if you do, I might throw you a Parade." I giggle at this man who seems to know exactly when I need a laugh, a cuddle, or a moment to myself.

I inhale deeply. It's not a story for everyone, so I'm going to say it quickly. I don't want pity, and I don't want him to think differently of me. "My mother overdosed in jail when I was nine. My father is still serving six consecutive sentences for voluntary manslaughter and drug trafficking with intent to distribute and sell. They went to jail when I was two. I have only one memory of them. I visited the prison just once, when I was six. They asked if I brought them anything they could trade."

He says nothing, but to his credit, his expression hasn't changed. He's providing space for us to sit in the moment. No one has ever done that. No one ever gives me room to sit with the truth. I put my head on his shoulder, and he slams his wine, tosses his cup, and wraps me inside the safety of David Gelbert. We sit like that for a while. After what seems like forever, I exhale loudly.

He says, "You know you're a true crime story ripe for Netflix." Then he pulls me closer.

"Oh, there's more. It's more Dickens than 20/20."

"Hit me."

"I don't know what you know about the adoption world. But sixty-two percent of adoptions happen within a month of babies being born. And the odds of an orphan of junkies getting adopted at almost three years old is pretty low. Or in my experience, zero."

"How does that happen? How are you this amazing, accomplished, and together?"

"First of all, I'm not that together. But mostly, anyone can do anything. I would imagine you've run across that concept." He squeezes me closer. He needs the contact as much as I need it.

"Once or twice."

"Everyone comes from their own stew of stuff. Some get lucky and—"

"And only have white people, privileged problems. Oh no, my daddy doesn't love me, and I didn't get to go to the art school where I had a full scholarship, so I had to go to the other school to play a game I love on a full ride. I'm still such a douche nozzle."

I laugh and turn to face him. I put my hand on his jaw. "No. Being born into privilege isn't a crime. It's what you do with it. I know you provide work for many people who can't get a visa for one reason or another. You're kind and aware of how lucky you've been in life. I also know about all the sports equipment that magically shows up at area rec centers of Sonoma County."

He looks away. "I can neither confirm nor deny that allegation."

I put my hand on his heart again. "I can't hold a grudge against everyone who had a better childhood. I'd never move forward."

He shifts me a little on his lap. "Did you live at an orphanage or with a family?"

"Fourteen families, actually. I'm a career foster kid, always the bridesmaid but never the adopted. I emancipated from the state orphanage at seventeen, copped my GED, and went to college on student loans."

He shifts me again so I can look more into his face. "Can I pay them off?"

"Already done. Stop with your useless guilt."

"Year to year, nothing ever looked the same for you?"

"No, not really. But I was an adventurer, a traveler, or an explorer in my mind. Some years I would get to go back-to-school shopping, and others, I might go on a vacation. One year I even got to decorate a Christmas tree."

His face falls. I was trying to be light and breezy with it all. Fail. "So that joke didn't land." His eyes are so sincere.

"Tell me you at least had an owl and a cupboard under the stairs." He feathers his thumb over my lips. Then kisses me lightly. "You know all I want to do is protect you from ever feeling hurt again?"

I whisper on his lips, "I'm ok. I've had lots of therapy, and I'm fine." Then he pulls back and gets his patented David smirk on.

"Yeah, you are." I smack his chest lightly. He says, "Thank you for telling me."

My voice is small. "Please don't tell anyone. No one needs to know."

"Same with my annoying and slightly more tragic story. I once lost my luggage in Barcelona, and it was like two weeks before I had my favorite shirt back. That was a tragedy. You moving and shucking and jiving. That's nothing."

"You know who Tiffany Haddish is?" I want him to understand, and if he really wants to help, I don't need it, but I'm sure there's someone like me that could.

"I do. She's very funny." He nods.

"She was a foster kid too. And she has this charity that gives suitcases to foster kids so they can own something."

"Get out. You owned nothing?"

"Still don't really. I had clothes and a couple of things, but they gave me a fresh, new garbage bag each time I moved. I saved the old ones, and eventually, I'd use them as an organization system. Each bag would contain a different piece of my belongings."

"That is the saddest thing I've ever heard. That's urchin sad. Are you sure you're fine?"

I smile at him. "Ok, then what are you going to do with that guilt? I don't want it, and I don't need to be saved."

He thinks for a moment. I'll pretend it's his idea even though

I led him to it. "How many suitcases are just sitting around in people's storage empty?"

"And..."

He smiles widely. "And I think Pro/Ho just found a new cause." I kiss him lightly.

"That's a start. Someday, I'd like to do more. I'd like to create somewhere or something to help kids like me. But for now, I'll be happy I convinced one person to do more." I do want that someday. I've never thought about anything past being an assistant, but someday I want to do more for people like me.

He scoops my hair up in his hands and pulls it into a ponytail behind my head. "I do look at you differently."

"You do?" My heart plummets. I knew he would. I shake my head to get him to let go. We just busted all kinds of honeymoon, Mooney-eyed bubbles. But I'm used to endings. My status quo is flex, and I guess it's time to go.

"I adore you more. As your picture rounds out with shade and form, the picture gets even more breathtaking. Don't leave me." He's so open and vulnerable. And another damn first. No one has ever said that to me before. Tears fill my eyes. He takes my breath away. Perhaps I get to stay here in his arms a little longer.

"I don't think I'm able." I've never felt there was anywhere I wanted to stay, but his lap is a pretty good place to start. I snuggle back into him, and we stay there wrapped in the security of his art studio.

CHAPTER 11

DAVID

I HAVE it all set up, and I'm dressed like a fucking baby with pink cheeks. Josh's fiancée and baby mama, Elle, my cousin Poppy, and Josh's mom, who I call, Auntie Sarah, went nuts with my idea. We call all the moms of the 5 aunties. Sam and Sammy helped string up the lights and rearranged the back of my house. My village doesn't do anything half-assed—we whole-ass everything. There's a crane with a giant disco ball waiting at Poppy's Café for later.

Nat makes me feel everything all at once and sees every piece of me without explanation. I don't have to grow on her or justify any behavior. My father is the very model of conditional love. The rest of the families do love me, but Natalie knows me. She sees things in me I never knew could be seen. Nat answers all the questions in my soul. She's the only one to ever ask what I was trying to do with the sculptures. What they were and why I felt compelled to create them. When she entered my secret studio, she entered a piece of me that's never been exposed since I shut it down publicly.

Sculpting has been on the DL since I chose basketball and my father over my art or myself. I don't regret the decision. I loved playing basketball on that level. Regret is a waste of time. You can only be here right now. What's next is a thing, but mostly I like being present. But when I look in her soulful and bright sunshiny blue eyes, I see what's next. Go big or go home. The player in me doesn't die.

I don't want her to live in her past. I don't want to gloss over whatever pain she still has to tell me about. But I also want her to make new memories. I want to give her a moment to sit in the present with me. She works and speaks so quickly, I think she's trying to outrun her memories by moving as fast as possible into the future. If she has good memories, maybe she'll sit still with me. I've been a jackass for a good portion of my life, and I'm cool with it, but I want to be her jackass. I'm falling in a real way for the first time in my life. I didn't think there were a whole lot of firsts left for me, but I can't wait to give her a lifetime of them. Fuck. I'm in deep. I rearrange my wings and pick up my bow. She'll be here any moment—she's never late. Always rushing to be on time for some imaginary deadline or perceived expectation. I'm going to break her of that. I'm going to force her to binge a show and not move off the couch for an entire day.

She knocks tentatively. I told her to dress up. I open the door, and both of us gasp just a little. She's in a cobalt blue short dress that gathers at her tiny waist and makes her perfect mouthwatering chest look even more perfect. Her dress mirrors her eyes, her honey blonde hair is tousled, and her bangs are swept to the side. She's breathtaking.

"Hiya, gorgeous." She looks down at her feet. I lift her chin to meet my gaze. "What?'

"Aside from you being dressed as what I assume is Cupid, you make my insides squirm when you say things like that."

"Good. I hope it's a good squirm. And yes. I'm Cupid. It's time to make some romantic memories. So please follow me to your first Valentine's Day celebration."

"I've had Valentine's Day celebrations before."

"Yes, but did you make traditions? Do you have memories you revisit? Because that's what I'm doing. I'm creating a legendary moment to live in your heart and soul forever. I'm shattering all other days. I'm crushing it."

"Ok."

I cock my bow and hit her with my Nerf arrow. She giggles. I take her hand and rub my thumb across the back of her warm and peachy skin. She's so soft—all the time. Every piece of her is soft to me despite what she tries to portray to the world. Her underlying sweetness is my favorite thing. Like I'm the one who coaxed it to the surface.

I pull her to the kitchen, set up like an ice cream parlor Elle loves in New York. There's one giant pink milkshake with two straws that wind up into a heart. I sit her down and pull off my wings and diaper. I grab a blue dress shirt. I'm still in my red basketball shorts, but now I'm date-ready from the waist up. I open the fridge and pull out chocolates, roses, and a card I made out of construction paper.

She opens the red kindergarten heart and smiles as she sits down. Nat reads the card. "Eat Your Heart Out I'm Taken – Taken by your beauty. Will you be my Valentine?"

"You do know it's the end of October?"

"No. It's February 14, and I need you to accept this rose." I hand her a single red rose.

"I'm a bachelorette now?"

"No. You're my girlfriend." I haven't meant those words since high school. Jane Gallagher. Everyone else has been a hook-up, a fuck buddy, friends with benefits, a hang, a stranger, a Netflix and Chill, a recreational stress release, or a giant mistake. Everyone else wasn't her.

I remind her, "You didn't answer the question."

She looks down at the rose petals all over my kitchen and

the cheesy pink decor everywhere. Then she looks at me, and her eyes sparkle just a touch with a bit of wetness. "Yes. I'll be your Valentine."

"No, Sunshine. Tonight is not about tears. It's about celebration."

"Valentine's Day." She smiles. We both sip it together. She picks up a rose and smells it.

I whisper, "No. All celebrations."

She looks confused. "What are you talking about?"

I stand up and take the dress shirt off over my head, and her eyes look at me hungrily. I grab her hand and kiss it as she raises her eyebrows at me. Then I kiss her. My lips can't help but press her to me. I crave the connection. "Happy Valentine's Day." She licks her lips and then bites down on the bottom one. I kiss her again quickly. "Definitely later. But we have a thing to do, so tuck naughty sexy thoughts away, you secret Sunshiny slut." She smacks me on the back.

We walk towards my dining room, and I grab a top hat with an attached beard and throw a green t-shirt on. She starts laughing as we enter the green and sparkly rainbow explosion of my dining room. There are seven different strings of lights that end in a pot of gold on the far side of the room. There's a pitcher of green beer, two glass beer mugs, and some corned beef and cabbage sitting at a high-top table. We stole the table from Gelbert's tasting room. I pull out her barstool.

"Look, if you're going to date an Irishman, this is a national holiday. And you are dressed inappropriately. I pull out a headband with bouncing glitter shamrocks on it. Before I put it on her head, I pinch her butt.

"Ow!"

"Should have worn green." Her lips press together in a smile that overtakes her face as she exhales loudly. Then she hops up on the stool and beckons me to her. She kisses me, and I nudge her pink and perfect lips open with my tongue. We make out, which I usually do on St. Patrick's Day, for a bit. Then I pour our beer and take my place across from her.

"Sláinte!" She touches her mug to mine, and we drink. I slam the entire warmish beer, and she laughs. Then I motion to no one. "We'll take two shots of Jameson." Nothing happens. "Hate how crowded it is in here. No one can even hear me order over the crowd. Wanna get out of here?"

She laughs and leans over. Her voice is loud like she's trying to be heard, "I hate crowds! Is there a less rowdy holiday?" I nod at her.

Then I grab her and head to the den where I usually keep my weights. I replace my hat and beard with a pair of ears. Next, I don a pink and yellow vest and bowtie and hand her a basket. She giggles as she looks around.

I say, "Better start looking."

She looks at me curiously, and I pull a colored egg from behind my weight bench. She squeals and then tears through the room. "I've never done this! Well, once at a Sunday school thing with the family I was staying with. Oh my!"

"The orphanage never did this?"

"I was never there during Easter, and if I was, I was too old and felt it was lame. Oh my God. You dyed eggs!"

"Sammy did. But I did think of it." She zooms around the room and collects three eggs. They all say her name in crayon. She turns and throws herself at me. I catch her and kiss her again.

"This is the best date I've ever been on." She squeals when I pull her towards me. I can't help but slide my hand into her hair and angle her face up towards mine. I slide my tongue into her mouth, and she accepts it greedily.

"Come on, there's more." I drag her out the sliding glass doors to my screened-in porch. I stop and pull open the drawer of the table. I exchange my green for a royal blue t-shirt and an Uncle Sam hat. I hand her a sparkler, and I take one as well. I kiss the top of her nose and pull out a lighter.

"I've done 4th of July before."

"I know, but we didn't have it together, and it's just a small memory to tuck away." We swing the sparklers around, drawing our names, and she draws a heart with hers. Red, white, and blue bunting falls from my roof, draping down to the patio.

Over the last remnants of smoke, she says, "Is that what you're doing? Making holiday memories for me?"

"Just getting started, but, yes."

The sparklers gasp their last sizzle as they hit the galvanized bucket of water, and she moves to me. She wraps her arms around my waist and squeezes. I hold her for a moment removing my hat and tossing it down. We step out back and around the side of my house. There's a corridor of bushes leading to my side door. Hanging on my hedge are two masks and two plastic pumpkins. I hand her the Wonder Woman mask as I slap a red and gold S on my shirt. She takes my hand and the pumpkin, and we enter the spiderweb-laden corridor. Prerecorded creepy sounds play while ghosts hang from the trees. I walk up to the side doorway and motion for her to knock.

She does but shakes her head. Then she jumps a bit as my mom opens the door.

I shout, "Trick or treat."

She says a little too loudly, "Trick or treat." My mom puts a ton of mini snickers, Reese's, and fun-sized KitKats in our pumpkins. I lift my mask, balance it on the top of my head, and kiss my mom on the cheek. She squeezes Natalie's arm. Nat says, "I guess turkey is next!"

Mom shakes her head. "No, dear, for the last thirty-seven years, before David was even a thought, we've hosted Thanksgiving. All are welcome. We call it Orphan Thanksgiving, and it's often employees or friends who have nowhere to go. I told David I refused to let him set up a fake Thanksgiving because I wanted to invite you to our real one."

She lifts her mask and stares at my mom. "Because I'm a real orphan." She growls at me, knowing I told my mom.

"No. Not at all. Because you're David's girl."

I say, "And, Nat, we make sure to watch the Parade every year." Her face instantly goes scarlet.

My mom squeals a bit. "Oh, do you like the parade, Natalie?"

She chokes out an answer, "I'm a big fan of the Parade."

I add to the conversation to embarrass her further, "I just love watching the Parade disappear down the parade route. In and out of the streets and snaking around the back of the blocks." I pull her into my side and kiss the top of her head. I love making her blush. Unfortunately, I'm still wearing basketball shorts. I have to conjure a disgusting image to make sure the Parade doesn't come to town right now.

Tabi's nutty mom pulls the door open more to reveal herself. She's in an orange and black caftan that shimmers and has black cats on it. She has a caftan for every occasion. She also speaks in her own way—a hybrid of Greek and English she's developed over the years—I'm used to it.

Auntie Goldie yells, "Look at that, little one, we all believe in that this is the real thing that has David so upside down and right side up finally. So you can go nowhere. You sit next to me on the turkey day. Also, this is for you. It did not get here until now because it is not part of the Easter that David is forcing on your person." She hands her a red egg, and my mom and I laugh. I look at Natalie. "It's for Greek Orthodox Easter. Ask Tabi." Goldie's laugh is big and broad and fills my house. I hand the pumpkins and masks to my mother.

"Hey. I want that candy!" She stamps her foot. Then Goldie hands me a white dress shirt, red brocade dinner jacket, and a

Santa hat. Nat's jaw goes slack as she removes her Halloween costume.

"Ho Ho Ho. We have places to go!" I pull her towards my car, and she's struggling to keep up with my long legs. If my mom weren't watching us, I'd pick her up and have her wrap her legs around me. I've never done anything like this for anyone who wasn't part of the 5. And I'm not even sure I've done anything this nice for any of them. We're all coming off the high of the last stunt we all pulled together at Stafýlia Cellars when Bax surprised Tabi with an engagement ring a couple of months ago. So this was a piece of cake for them to pull off.

CHAPTER 12

NATALIE

HE HOLDS my hand in his. I disappear into his large hand. I'm disappearing into his entire life. It's kind of exhilarating not to be me. A surge of happiness overtakes me as I look at this ginger Adonis. I giggle and squeeze his hand.

"What's up, Sunshine?"

"I'm just so flim-flamming happy right now."

He laughs. "There's no greater honor than getting you to say flim-flamming. I'd say it's actually more of a floopy belly moment myself." I shove him a little, but my smile is too big for him to think I'm actually mad he's mocking me. So instead, he kisses the back of my hand. Then as we ease to a stop sign, he leans over and pulls me into a kiss. The kiss ruptures then repairs the space-time continuum. I lose all narrative when his tongue is in me, on me, or around certain parts of me.

He pulls back, and his eyes are hooded and dark. "If Santa didn't have elaborate wooing plans, I'd have you unwrap this gift right now." He thrusts with his pelvis, and the outline of the incredibly hard and big Parade is showing. I grin at him and lick my lips. "That fucking beautifully wicked cherry-kissed tongue will be the fucking end of me." I sit back as he lurches the car towards the Plaza while adjusting his red basketball shorts. The sun is setting, but there are bright lights up ahead.

"Oh, my frosted Bundt cake! What did you do?"

He rolls down the windows, and I hear "White Christmas" blaring.

He looks at me, grinning like he does after I have multiple orgasms. "Merry Christmas, baby."

All the trees in the front half of the Plaza have lights on them, and kids are running around everywhere. I focus more clearly on them.

"HOLY SHINY SHENANIGANS. David, David. OH My GOD! There's snow!"

He eases the car into a spot. He adjusts his Santa hat. "Will you be my Ho Ho Ho?"

I scream, "YES!" I kiss him quickly and leap out of the car and run towards the snow. I love snow. I haven't seen snow in years. It was only occasional in DC. I once went on a ski trip to Vermont, and all I wanted to do was be outside. I wanted to play first, then just sit and look at it. It was a magical trip, but not because of the boyfriend. Everything is a fresh start in the snow.

It's hard to look at him and believe he's not my fresh start. I'm staring at the sky that snowing on me. I don't even notice that Elle and Sammy are standing off to the side at first. Sammy spins opening her mouth to catch the flakes. She seems so free and open. I want to be like that.

"Hi!" David saunters over and takes me in his arms.

Sammy says, "Seeing him under your spell is freaking awesome." She kisses me on the cheek.

Elle pops her hip and crosses her arms, then a grin overtakes her face. She says, "I quite like that the man who once called me a bitch is now someone's bitch." I giggle and look down at my feet. "No, Nat! Own it. Look up and be proud. You have power."

David tosses a middle finger at her, and she sticks her tongue out. Then she moves over to the bench where a man hands her what appears to be hot chocolate. They're all in harvest right now—it's kind of amazing they took a little time off to help out with his insane date.

White lights are twinkling in the prism of the snow shooting out of multiple cannons. He must have gotten permits for all of this. There's a sleigh over by the duck pond on the west side of the Plaza. David nods to the women and some very industrial-looking fellows.

He pulls me closer and whispers in my ear, "I owe Larry Ginesi and Illusions lighting design a small fortune." He draws me even closer, "But that smile, that light in your eyes, might be the most perfect, exquisite thing I've ever seen in my life."

He sways his hips as we slow down to dance to Dave Matthews, "A Christmas Song." I snuggle into his chest. Elle puts her hand on her heart and wipes a tear. Sweat drips down David's face from under the hat and heavy red brocade jacket. He must be dying, but his smile says something entirely different. I stretch my body and get to the tip-top of my toes, and he meets me halfway. He glides his tongue between my lips briefly, then nips at my neck. I whisper, "Thank you."

"Merry Christmas." His lips are full and lush. He brushes by my bottom lip.

"I'm gushing with happy right now."

"Me too, beautiful." He smiles.

He breaks our embrace and takes my hand.

I say, "David. This is too much. You don't have to do Christmas. I've been to Christmases." He hands me something from his pocket. It's an engraved cheesy brass ornament that says, "Baby's First Christmas," with our initials and the date. N & D. 10/23.

"Go hang it up." I twirl around, and Elle and Sammy throw

their arms up as a giant fake tree I didn't notice before blazes to life. He guides me over, and I hang it on the tree.

I turn around in his arms.

He says, "I know you have. I also know you've had good times. You can't have lived a miserable Dickensian life all the time."

"I was an orphan," I say with some sass. My head is reeling from his effort to give me something that's just ours. To fill my mind with happy holidays. And his mother just invited me to Thanksgiving, and Tabi's mother hugged me. I don't know what to make of all of this. I do know I should enjoy it. I'll need these memories to last so I can pull them out and wrap them around me like a comforter in the lonely winter to come. But, good lord, I'm pessimistic. Maybe, just maybe, this doesn't end. If I fit in enough. If I'm helpful enough. If I care about him enough.

I look at his face. His verdant eyes sparkling and a hint of red sideburns peeking out from his Santa hat. He licks his lips, and I watch his tongue.

"Now, now, Sunshine. Stop thinking about what this tongue can do to you."

"It's too hard not to think of." I reach for him, and he steps into my arms.

I look up at him. "Can you kiss me now, so I know all of this is real?" His arms wrap around me. His hands take up residence on the top of my butt.

"I thought you'd never ask." He leans down close enough for me to see his very light freckles. They're private and intimate. If you look at him, you don't notice them, but if he's this close, it's like looking at the stars. The more you focus, the more pop out—my own personal constellations of pleasure and delight. I drift my nails over his sharp jaw to his chin dimple. He smirks and it sends a surge of sexy pulse to my down below. As his lips make contact with mine, I dissolve entirely into his. I gasp, and he smiles on my lips. Then I whisper, "I can't help but give myself over to you. It's like I've lost all Natalie control."

We're rocking slowly in a circle while kissing and dancing. I look up at him. "Be kind to me because I can't resist falling anymore."

"About fucking time. Do you know how long all this shit took to plan and set up?" I laugh. Then he smashes his lips to mine, and I open to him immediately. My hands drift to the back of his neck, and I hold on. He picks me up for a brief moment, and I escape my brain into the float.

I pull back because there are children around in the fake snow. "This is some jacket, Santa."

"Wait until you see what's in my new bag?" He grabs his rising Parade, and I slap his hand away.

There's a tap on his shoulder. "Can I cut in?"

"If you must." He twirls me and hands me off to Elle and Sammy. They take my hand, and Sammy hitches a giant bag upon her shoulder.

He kisses me quickly. "I'll see you on the other side." I'm confused, but then he's jogging to his car, and I can't help but stare at his muscular behind move under those flimsy shorts. Those shorts will be the death of me. It's all I ever need to get me going. Basketball shorts.

Elle waddles just a bit now, her belly starting to really pop. She's in front of us, heading towards the little brick building on the east side of the Plaza that faces the beautiful old Sebastiani Theatre. We enter the Visitor's Bureau conference room, and Elle flourishes as I see three dresses hanging up. Sammy lays out make-up on a conference table.

I ask, "What's happening?"

Sammy, the pretty girl Sam dates, says, "Wardrobe and make-up for your finale holiday."

I breathe out and say quietly as I cross my hands in front of me, "New Year's Eve."

"You got it, sister. Now we have half an hour until we meet up with everyone."

"We?" I cock my head to the side.

Sammy scoffs. "You don't think I'm letting Gelbert throw a super swank party, and I don't get to dance with my mountain of a man and kiss at midnight."

"It's a party?"

"Damn, I did not think your eyes could get wider, but they just did." Sammy squeezes my arm and turns me towards Elle. Sammy takes off her long trench coat and is wearing an orangish-column dress with delicate spaghetti straps. It's so simple and stunning. That's who I think she is. She has these cool severe fringe bangs that frame her face with her wheat-colored hair. She's just so cool. I could never be as unaffected as she is. She and Sam are perfect together. They adore each other, and it's hard not to watch them when they're together. They have their own language, and they're always glowy and happy. I turn toward the other stunning woman in the room, Elle Parker. Icy blonde hair in a sharp bob. She's always so fashionable and put together. She's settling into the most stunning cream beaded dress. People say my eyes are bright, but the green from hers shines like an emerald surrounded by diamonds. Her dress is tiered lace and a tight bodice off the shoulder. It's like a cloud floating around her.

She sees me looking and smiles. "I'll only be able to wear this tonight without busting it. My tits are getting insane. But I wanted to feel buoyant and light. It's Marquesa. But you, little girl, you have quite the choice ahead of you. I think you should go with this—" She holds up a lilac dress that flairs at the bottom but looks like it's liquid. It's sleek satin that only gathers at the halter neckline.

My mouth drops open. "I'm a wreck. You can't possibly make me Cinderella?" Sammy laughs.

Elle cracks her neck to the right. "You don't know me very well. If I can pull off a spur-of-the-moment wedding in the middle of a weekday, this is a piece of cake."

I gasp.

Sammy's mouth drops open. Elle slaps her hand over her mouth. "Fuck. Fuck. God damned miserable pregnancy. The fucking girls made me do it." Wait, what did she just say? Elle's daughter, Emma, was born in the spring, and she's already pregnant again.

Sammy puts her hand on Elle's shoulder. She's calm. "Shut the fuck up."

I nod and say, "Yes, shut the front door. You're married?"

Sammy roars, "AND you're having twins?"

"GIRLS!" I squeal. I'm not a good baby person, but this woman is like a factory. In fact, I don't actually like to be around children, but I'm excited for them.

She dives for her large pink Birkin bag, which has to cost a flim-flamming fortune, and shoves a giant piece of rainbow sprinkle cookie into her mouth. She talks through chewing. "Oh My God. And now this heinous woman's rite of passage takes one more fucking thing from me. I have no filter. Zero filter. Zero chill. I hate pregnancy brain. I hate being pregnant. The babies are perfect, but this process is fucking horrible."

As an unadoptable orphan, I try not to wince. You don't have to get pregnant to have children. Not that I'm ever having children. I've seen too much. She doesn't know what she's saying plucks at a chord deep inside me. I recently learned she created a haven for women, victims of domestic abuse, in Manhattan. Her heart is good, but I can't help but feel a little triggered. Glad I'm doing none of that. Children usurp your life. Just look at Elle. She's miserable. I turn my brain towards David and all he's done for me today, and my belly gets floopy again while my smile gets dopey.

She continues to rant, "I'm so freaking foggy, and now with two of these little demons inside of me constantly begging for food or bringing on acid reflux two months early. This is supposed to be the good part of pregnancy. Instead, these little snuggly bitches have robbed me of the only tolerable months."

Sammy yells, "ANSWER US."

Elle reacts like she has no idea what we're talking about. Then Sammy shakes her head sarcastically at her for emphasis. Elle exclaims, "Oh. No. I'm not married. I'm not doing that until I'm not this large. I want the best shoes in the world, and we have no evidence my feet will return to human size, so unless Chanel starts making hobbit-sized shoes, I'm never getting married. These boats are too big for fashion. And yes. Twins. Yes, girls. Josh doesn't know yet, so please, even though I'm the babbler—" She's so confident and beautiful. She knows exactly who she is and makes no excuses for it. All these women are like that in their own way. I should be more like that.

Sammy cuts her off. "WHO the hell got married?"

Elle rolls her eyes and points to both of us. "Tell no one. Tabi and Bax."

I scream loudly. "I'm so thrilled for them." My eyes well up. I can't believe they finally found their way to each other, and I love that they secretly got married. After all, they've endured publicly, it's nice that they had a private forever moment. I adore them so much. I only wish I could have been there.

My eyes well up, and I try to blink away the tears. Elle points at me. "Do NOT cry. We don't have time to depuff you. Strip." I stand there. How are these women so close that naked in front of each other is no big deal?

"Look, we're both outsiders to the 5 as well, don't worry. We got you. There's a bathroom around the corner if you want to change without us judging your body," Sammy says, and I laugh at her. I turn around so they can unzip my dress. I didn't want them to see my lingerie, but mine is a little tamer than what Elle has spread out on the table.

Elle sits and shoves another piece of chocolate in her mouth. "Nat. Can I ask you something?"

"Sure."

"Do you honestly like Gelbert? He's a tough pill for some people to swallow, but I've grown fond of him."

Sammy sits next to her. "Same," she says and takes the piece of chocolate from Elle's hand and pops it into her mouth. I'd like a close friend like that someday. David keeps opening up different parts of me. I've never really had a friend for the long haul. I got moved around, and I learned to have what I call gym class friends. Those that are ok in gym class because no one else is around, but you aren't really close. You're just *mocking the boys in volleyball* close. Situational or work friends, that's all I've ever had, except Bax and Tabi.

Elle pulls a long candy cane from her bag and sucks on the end of it. "Are you in this? Because we've never seen him like this before." She must have taken that off the Christmas tree. Josh won't let her eat sugar while pregnant, so she sneaks it all the time.

I blush and pick up this fabulous dress. I slip it over my head and slide my other dress out from underneath. "I want to know what he wants for breakfast."

Sammy looks puzzled and asks, "Come again?"

"I want the big and the small with him. I want to continue having epic nights as well as buy the right kind of jam."

The two answer in unison, "Raspberry." Elle laughs. "He's kind of obsessed with raspberry jam." I begin to blush, thinking about the first time I learned that.

Sammy says, "Oh shit! He ate it off your nipples, didn't he?" I look up and don't answer. They're all so open, it's strange. I turn around, and Elle zips me up. I do not acknowledge that Sammy guessed what he did with the jam.

After light glitter make-up and learning to walk in shoes, I can't afford but are apparently on loan to me from Elle's legendary closet, we make our way across and up the street half a block to Poppy's Café. There's music and laughter. There are more white lights and a contraption suspending a giant disco ball. I grin as my fairy godmothers disappear into the café to find their men. I fix my hair one last time. Then I look up, and my breath stops.

When he steps into view, dashing and perfect, time stops. His hair is tamed by product, and his perfect body is wearing a fire-trucking tuxedo. He has a corsage in his hand, and when he looks at me, his hand goes to his chest as his eyes darken just a touch. I feel more beautiful than I could ever have imagined. He touches me, and my whole body trembles for a quick second.

"I *am* good. You shiver like that when I make you come, Sunshine." I smile. He pulls me into his arms. "There's nothing else in the world tonight but you. This dress is fucking apeshit insane, and you look so incredibly gorgeous. "

"Thank you. So do you."

"Nah. In comparison to you, the world is pale. You're all the color and all light." My eyes fill with tears as he kisses me gently. "Happy New Year, beautiful."

"It certainly is a new year."

CHAPTER 13

DAVID

WE'RE JUST DONE with the insane feast Pop put on our tables. Damn. I paid to have her close the restaurant tonight, which I know was hard during harvest. The place is tourist crazy right now. But my cousin wanted to do it. She's a huge freaking sap. And I think she might like Nat more than me.

Sam looks over at Nat. "Sunny, I'm not going to be in for the next couple of days."

Sammy smacks him. "No fucking work talk. We're not in harvest. It's December 31st. Remember." He leans over and rubs his hand on her jaw, then pulls her face to his, kissing him. Then she scratches his beard lovingly.

Nat turns to me, her ankles crossed and her hands in her lap. I want to pull her onto mine. I have to keep thinking about Mrs. Dotson, Josh's makeshift Gramma, to keep the Parade from lining up.

"Do you call me Sunshine when I'm not around?"

I answer, "That or crack pussy."

"How are you an adult?" Tabi hisses.

Nat's face blows up red, and I love it. I stand and pull her up to me. "Wait. You don't mean like my the..." she whispers, and it's so cute. "Crack in my butt. You mean like you're addicted to my lady bits like crack cocaine."

I put my hands on her shoulders and capture her blue eyes. "Yes. Your cunt is my junk."

Everyone laughs but Nat. Her face, if possible, goes a deeper shade of red. I continue even though I know I shouldn't. "Your slit is my spliff."

She buries her head in my chest, and everyone is howling around me. "Your way in is my heroin. Your vagine is my line."

Elle smacks me on the back, and I wrap my arms around Nat. She looks up at me with tears of laughter spilling down her face. I kiss her forehead and pull her back to me.

Sam says, "Cool it. I'm the funny one."

"Getting it on the reg has me a changed man."

Tabi throws a piece of ice at my head. "You've had it on the reg since fucking 11th grade. You whore piece of shit. That's not it."

I pull Natalie from my chest and put her in front of me to face everyone. I wrap my arms around her. "You're right." I kiss her temple. "I might not be a changed man, but I am a more complete one."

This time Poppy throws a piece of bread at my head, and I bat it away. "Stop throwing shit at me."

Poppy wipes tears from her eyes, the softie, and says, "Ten minutes to New Years', everyone load up your sparkling."

Elle groans and rubs her belly. Then her entire demeanor changes as she looks at Josh. "Please, baby. The belly just wants one glass." She pushes her lower lips out.

Tabi yells, "Oh, shit. Here come the big guns. Joshie, look at your woman. She's all cuddly and wanton."

Josh laughs and sips his own drink. He addresses the crowd, "The baby can have a glass when she can ask for it."

Sam leaps up. "Holy muthafucking shit. Josh, our alpha-hole, is going to be surrounded by pink bows again!"

Tabi throws her arms in the air. "Yes! Girls rule."

Elle moves to his lap and starts running her fingers through his thick hair. "But, Josh, what if I tell you a secret right now? One that will blow your mind."

"Hellcat, you and I have no secrets."

Sammy leans forward. "Not true." Elle's head whips around, and she puts her finger over her lips, then points at Nat and glares at her. I pull Nat to me and whisper in her ear.

"You holding out on me, Sunshine?"

"Maybe. Shh. Watch." I kiss her neck and pull her closer as I wrap my arms around her as she stands in front of me.

Then she says, "And you should know the Parade isn't starting until after midnight." She pops her butt backward into my thickening cock. Nat pulls my head down and whispers, "Twins."

My eyes shoot to Sammy. She does the same, and Sam yells, "Get the fuck out of here with that heresy."

Sam says, "Elle, I'll give you $20 cash money right now if you tell him so we can watch. Hell, I'll sneak you a glass of bubbles." Elle winks at me and then curls up.

Josh doesn't do well in the dark. He bellows, "Tell me, Hellcat. Tell me now, and you can have a sip."

Poppy squeals, "Hurry, we have four minutes."

Elle kisses Josh then makes her way up to his ear. This alpha asshole best friend of mine lets his eyes fill with joy. He kisses her deeply, and we all hear him say, "And. They're healthy?" Elle nods. I throw up two fingers towards Bax, Tabi, and Poppy, so they're in the know as well. Tabi jumps in and hugs them.

"So Josh finally got his harem," Bax yells from the back of the room. Tabi returns to him and tosses over her shoulder, "Just like all his high school fantasies."

I yell, "Careful what you wish for, I guess."

Sammy yells, "We have more to toast than two babies, trust me, Elle deserves a sip for holding on to this secret."

Bax's eyes shoot to Tabi.

I whisper in her ear, "Do you know this one too?"

Natalie blurts loudly, "They're married!"

Sam throws his hands in the air. "No more secret fucking!"

Bax pulls Tabi to him and raises his glass. "We're aware most people will want to kill us, but I'd like to toast my wife. And then have our first public dance as man and wife."

"Holy Shit Balls!" I yell.

Tabi glares at me. "Let me have a classy moment, Gelbert. I'm a fucking bride." Bax dips her and kisses her deeply. We all cheer.

Nat says, "I'm pretty sure no one had Irish triplets or planning a secret wedding on their Elle pregnancy bingo board." She shoots me a look. She helped me create the bingo boards.

"Tell me that's not a thing?!" Elle yells.

Bax says, "No. Not a thing, but do you have any salted caramels in your purse? Just asking for a friend." Sammy routes through the bag, and Elle snatches it back.

"Don't you dare violate Daphne?"

I look at Natalie. "That's the name of her purse." Nat nods.

Sammy reports, "She has four salted caramels, two candy canes, and a churro." She shrugs.

Tabi yells, "Churro! Yes!"

Josh yells, "HELLCAT! No sugar. Especially for two, I mean, all three of you! Not during pregnancy."

"I'm never not pregnant! Sugar is fine. It's not the devil, you sexy beast." She huffs. Tabi is scratching off a piece of paper.

"Keep the pouting temper tantrum coming. Look, it's not a thing you get to play, Elle. Sorry. But you should know I am cleaning up tonight. Happy New Year, everyone! Muthafucking BINGO!"

Elle yells at Tabi, "Consider it my wedding present."

Poppy screams, "10, 9, 8—"

Sam says loudly, "Hey, Gelbert, should we sing? You know Old Acquaintances be forgot..." Everyone laughs, and I flip off my friend.

Josh yells, "Hellcat, surely someone needs you to bitch about your acid reflux?"

Poppy keeps counting, "6, 5, 4."

Sammy pulls a piece of paper out. "Me! I get a bottle of my choice from all your wineries if I get bingo. Bitch about the acid reflux at a formal event, please, Elle. Do it for your best friend. Come on, do it."

Bax yells, "No! Tell me about how you hate the ultrasound wand again."

Elle throws her head back and yells, "Fuck you all."

"2, 1!"

We all yell, "Happy Fake New Year, Natalie!" just as I planned, and her mouth goes into that perfect 'O'.

I pull her close, and she says, "How are you seemingly a douche nozzle on paper but this magical person who makes the world a better place to exist?"

"Shh. Don't tell anyone."

"HAPPY NEW YEAR."

My lips take hers, and the world falls away. My friends, the moment, the make-believe of tonight, all of it falls away. All that's left are these lips, her heart, and this moment.

CHAPTER 14

DAVID

IT'S EARLY in the morning, and we all keep celebrating. Her hair has come down from the complicated updo Elle created. Her lipstick is gone. Her natural flush and lush skin shines through. I'm rubbing my thumb over her hand that's sitting in her lap again. I lean over to her.

"You're the sexiest thing. Just sitting there waiting for the world to pounce on you." She looks up from her chair. It's the first time she's sat down and been left alone all night. She's been dancing with almost everyone. Bax and Tabi are beaming at her, and she keeps giggling with Poppy in the corner. I'm sure my cuz is telling her all kinds of shit about me. But it doesn't matter because right now, I can't help but be flooded with light from my little Sunshine. I put out my hand and pull her up to me. She wraps her arms around my waist, and I hold her back and stare into that perfect face. Her delicate cheekbones are more pronounced when she smiles. Those little bow lips are fucking perfect. She's nothing I ever saw coming and everything I've always needed and wanted.

"Sunshine?"

She whispers, "Yes."

"Time to go home." She nods, and I wave to everyone as we turn towards the door. No one says anything to me. They just nod. I think they know I don't want to talk to them. I have tunnel vision right now. I only see her. It's fighting to get out of me, and I don't know if she's ready to hear this, but fuck. I don't know. I don't know how to stop it. We're getting close to my car, and I stop her. The streets are quiet except for the muffle of the crowd we just left. I'm staring down a very familiar Spain Street, one that I have been on thousands of times, but tonight seems wholly changed and new.

I turn, and her blue eyes are bright and open. Her confident vulnerability eeks out of every pore in her body. And I feel something else as well. Something more profound. There's this thing I couldn't place and kept trying to push down. It's something I know without a shadow of a doubt. I've never felt it before, and I never will again. Not like this. I know this in my bones.

"I love you, Natalie." Her breath catches, her knees buckle a bit, and she simply stares at me. She seems in shock. I'm a bit in shock, so it's cool if she doesn't know what to do.

"I. Um. I. David." Her words are stunted and breathy. I take her in my arms and bend down to her lips. I brush mine slightly over hers, and she responds with a sigh. Then I kiss her a little harder, and she finally opens her mouth to me. I didn't scare her with the words that terrify me. Thank God.

Our kiss moves into a different space, and I'm clutching at her light purple, liquid shiny dress and pulling it up. I need to feel her ass in my hands. She's clutching at me as our tongues attack each other's mouths. There's not enough of each other.

I pull her closer, and now she can feel how aroused I genuinely am by kissing the love of my life. She gasps, and I brush my lips along her jawline. I kiss my way up to her ears, and each time I pause, I whisper the words like prayers, hoping she'll answer them. "I love you. I love you. I love you. I love you, Natalie Lloyd."

When I go back to her mouth, there's a tear staining her cheek. I put my hand on her face. My large hand holding her cheek as she leans into it. "No. Beautiful. Don't cry, my love."

She finally speaks, "I don't know what to say."

I back away and spread my legs. I cross my arms over my chest and cock my head. "And?" She can't possibly fake how she feels. I know it. I see it in the way she looks at me. In the way, she touches me. No. This is not the brush-off. This is something else. I give her the space she needs to breathe after I made myself breathless.

"This is all too much. You're too much. My brain." Her voice drifts off, and the tears start running down her face. I scoop her up into my arms. I walk us to the car, and she holds onto me— my precious girl.

Her head falls to my chest, and she whispers, "Over-whelmed." I kiss the top of her exhausted head, and she whispers again, "Thank you."

I open the car and place her in the passenger seat. She seems wrung out emotionally and physically. I broke her as I tried to romance her. I'm that good at romance. I break the inner circuits of women. I'm the king of romance. Who knew? I never really tried it before.

She snuggles into the passenger seat, and I close the door quietly. I take a moment to breathe in the humid fragrant air and survey my little town. I try to comprehend the gravity of what I just said, and I can't. I'm too happy. I'm totally not worried about her reaction or the words slipping my lips again tonight.

I slide into the passenger seat. Her eyes drift closed but flutter open at my touch. I pull out and drive home. I'm trying to talk my dick down. She's tired.

It's not happening tonight. You can lie next to her and not be inside of this woman. You know the woman you just told you loved. Sure, she's tight and warm and cozy and fucking perfect for the Parade, but there will be no Parade tonight. Just empty streets and scattered confetti. My dick isn't listening, and the more I think these thoughts trying to convince him we're not getting laid tonight, the harder he gets. He's not listening. But he never really has. We don't have that kind of relationship. My dick has no healthy boundaries.

CHAPTER 15

NATALIE

I'M DRIFTING and floating on my day. I'm like one of those fainting goats. I passed out after too much excitement. He loves me. I can't wrap my head around this. No one has ever said those words to me in my life. I mean, a friend kind of said it once but not even my long-term boyfriends.

I got a lot of 'love yas' in my life, and once when I said I love you, I got a 'back atcha.' And I clung to it. But never someone, anyone, in my life telling me I love you. My parents didn't write it in the note before they took off, but I was told it was signed with love. The note was entered into evidence, so I've never actually seen it. Then when they ended up in prison, they never said it when I visited. But I only went that once. I thought if I saw them more, they'd rub off on me, and I'd never be loved. And until twenty minutes ago, I thought I was cursed with genetics.

Men have said, 'I adore you or 'I cherish you,' but not one of them stepped up to change my life and tell me they love me. And here is the least likely candidate telling me without reservation. No hesitation or explanation. Not even a lead-up, just blurts it out like we say it all the time. He's such an all-in man. He doesn't do anything in half measures.

My reaction was to pass out. I'm keeping my eyes closed as we head back to his house. He called it home, and I'm terrified I'm starting to think that. My body relaxes when I'm there as if it knows something my brain doesn't. My brain rationally knows there's no such thing as a home. Simply a house I rent or an apartment I keep. My money is the only thing that will pay for something more permanent, someday. My brain exists in the temporary because that's what I know how to do. I have a system to survive the impermanent. And then this most perfect man says the most permanent thing in the world. My body is a rush of adrenaline and dopamine, and confusion.

We arrive at his driveway. I'm a ball of nerves and energy. I know he can feel it—I can't hide things like that. I'm just that nervous.

I've never had sex with someone I knew loved me. I've never even shared a car ride with someone who I knew loved me. They told me at the orphanage that Jesus loves me. I guess that counts. Now David loves me. That's two.

I'm so nervous. He comes to my door, and I pretend to sleep again. I go limp to sell the sleeping. I don't know what to say. He scoops me up and carries me into the house like a ragdoll. He lays me on the bed, and I realize I have a side of his bed. It makes me feel rooted. I feel like I belong somewhere, and that somewhere is next to this man. I can't tell him that yet. But hopefully, he can feel it.

He takes off his tux jacket, and I crack my eyes to watch.

I'm screaming in my head, but it won't come out of my mouth. I can't let myself say that. I softly sniffle and turn away from him.

The mattress dips beside me. My eyes still shut. His hand rests on my cheek.

His voice is a light summer breeze gently kissing my soul. "Sunshine, what is it?" Tears are streaming down my face again.

I'm so annoyed with my emotions right now. They should mind their own business and stop telling the world how I feel. I'm sure I have make-up running down my cheeks. Elle would be horrified. I'm trying to center myself, and he kisses my wet cheek. I open my eyes, and his are concerned and loving.

He disarms me by kissing me. My lips respond to his in an instant. It's a chaste kiss full of all the things I can't say.

"I'm fine. I'm overwhelmed and so grateful for you." His sexy smile calms me.

He rolls onto his back, clutching me in the process. I put my hands on his chest, his tux shirt half undone. His hair still looks movie-star perfect. His hand slides to the back of my neck, but he doesn't pull me towards him.

He says, "I hope you liked it all. I'm sorry we can be a bit extra."

"It was lovely. All of this. You're so incredibly sweet. Thank you."

"I need to put that guy away right now. I need to fucking tear this dress off of your sexy perfect body, toss you back on this bed, and slide inside the love of my life. Not sure that I can be gentle. All those moments tonight when you'd glance at me, showing me how much you trust and care for me. Well, let's just say, the Parade is way overdue." He pulls me to him roughly, and the only thing I can say before his lips are possessing mine is, "Yes."

His other hand yanks my skirt up and rips my thong from my body. "Hey, that was new."

"Don't fucking care." He picks me up and tosses me on the bed, and the liquid material of this dress slides up. He's out of his pants in a moment, and the Parade is all ready for launch, but his shirt hangs open, and it's so lip-smacking jellyroll sexy. He stands at the end of the bed, stroking his long and thick beautiful member. He bites his lip as he continues but stares at me. "So fucking gorgeous." I don't squirm away or retreat into myself. I open my legs a little wider.

"God, yes." The dress is pushed up higher as he grabs my ankles.

He grabs my ankles and yanks me to the end of the bed, leaving one leg over his shoulder. He bends down and sucks my button deep into his mouth, and I arch into him. He explores me with his fingers and groans. "All this beautiful wetness needs to be coating my cock. All this Sunshiny slutty goodness."

I reach down and gather it up and grab the Parade. I smear myself onto him. "Fuck, yes. Jesus, that's the most perfectly filthy thing." Then, without ceremony, he leans forward and slams himself into me all at once. I gasp at the pinch of pain. He holds himself there, staring at me, my leg in the air. He can feel me relax around the Parade, making room for him in all parts of myself. Then he pulls out and thrusts back in. I close my eyes.

"No. You watch us. Listen to me." On his next thrust, he says, "I fucking love you. And love fucking you." He lifts my leg to his shoulder and stands on the end of the bed. He yanks me to the edge and plunges back into me. I'm at his mercy and loving every hot hard second of it. With each thrust after that, his words drill into me that there's no escape from him. I surrender to my climax as well as the idea that I deserve all this love.

CHAPTER 16

NATALIE

I STOP and pull my dress closed again over my breasts. This dress keeps popping the buttons open a little in the front. I should have ironed it flat. David says he didn't notice, but I think he's full of bullpoop. He always notices my breasts. I can't help it when my lips tug into a small smile, thinking about his adoration for my breasts. They've never been celebrated quite as much before. He calls them the Parade floats. We're all about the celebrations lately.

David's wearing dark pressed pants and his royal blue button-down. It makes the color of his russet hair pop. I won't tell him that, though. His tie is a subtle green and amber stripe. He said this outfit reminds him of game day. I might have snuck a peek at game footage on YouTube. He always arrived and left dressed up. I'm sure that's why he got laid all the time. I have limited knowledge of basketball—I own a Washington Wizards t-shirt and have watched The Last Dance on ESPN, but he was very good by all accounts. It's a bit like watching pornography when I see him play. One time I had to actually go over to his house and attack him after I watched. He was pleasantly surprised, but I didn't want to say I was turned on by his younger self.

He won't talk about basketball, only that he blew off the draft. Or assorted stories here and there. He plays every day in some capacity. He says it's for the ADHD, but I feel as if his connection to the game is deeper. It's almost like if he admits the joy he gets from it, his father wins.

He squints his eyes at me and cocks his head. He says, "What?"

"Do I look ok?" He strides back two long steps and scoops me into his arms. His lips touch mine and I can't help but bite his bottom lip. He sweeps into my mouth. I sigh, and he looks me right in my eyes. His green marbles make my knees weak. He knows I'm nervous. I have a thing about people liking me enough to keep me around. I know everyone inside, but still, I'm nervous about them altogether. All five families and their children and the one grandchild, Emma Whittier, will be inside those doors sitting down to a family meal.

He says, "No. You look like shit. Now get your lumpy, disfigured ass inside. I don't want to be seen with you." He smacks my butt, then grabs my hand and pulls me towards the door.

I scamper behind him. "What did your other girlfriends wear to Thanksgiving dinner?"

"Never brought one here. You're the first."

"I seem to be your first at a lot of things. Why is that?"

"I've been waiting for you."

Swoon.

He opens the door, and there's a bit of bedlam. Tabi is up on a chair with a Sonos speaker in her hand. Bax is bent over laughing. Jims Langerford, Sam's little brother, is dancing with Elle and Tabi's mom, Goldie. Everyone else seems to be forming a circle around Will Whittier, Josh's dad, taking center stage doing the worm. And then Tabi sees us and motions for us to come to her.

David's father and Adrien Schroeder are sipping scotch in the corner with his sister Becca. His Aunt Tina and cousin Poppy are moving furniture out of place with the help of Poppy's non-boyfriend and our resident Mafia Don, Sal. He's a little intimidating but seems very nice underneath that gruff exterior. David told me he actually does run a crime family that's moving away from crime. It's all fascinating but I'm too nervous to talk to him.

Tabi screams down at us. "This is a warm-up act. I've been waiting until you got here. Gelbert, I'm gonna make you lose your mind."

Bax yells, "Up in here. Up in here."

He whispers in my ear, "One of my favorite songs from the past. But whatever Tab has planned you know it's batshit crazy so hold on."

And then Tabi changes the music on her phone, and "Yeah!" by Usher blares from the speaker. Out of the corner of my eye, I see Tabi's ancient grandmother. She's dressed in a dark jumpsuit and a baseball hat cocked to the side. Lately she's been forgoing clothes so it's great she's wearing something. Each time Usher sings, "Yeah Yeah." Everyone in the room yells it, and grandma throws her hands up in the air.

David moves to Tabi's grandmother and mildly dances with her to the middle of the circle. The way that man's hips move has my full attention. And then I realize they're chanting, "Yia, Yia" instead of "Yeah, Yeah."

Tabi looks down at me from her perch and says, "It's her walk-out song."

And then the most amazing thing happens. Bax hands Yia Yia a microphone, and she beings rapping the Ludacris part. Every word. We all scream with her, "Lady in the street but a freak in the bed!" With Will Whittier doing the robot on the beat.

David yells, "Shit! This is the greatest fucking thing I've ever seen." Everyone is roaring with laughter, and as she finishes with a minor hip flourish, David catches both Yia Yia and the microphone.

Tabi fades the song out, and Yia Yia is still humming, "Yia, Yia." Goldie puts her arm around her mother and guides her towards the great room where dinner is set up for everyone. David walks over and throws his arm around Tabi.

"How the hell did that happen? She was just all in on *Men in Black* and thinking it was documentary."

"I know. She found out that Will Smith was a singer and thought his songs were code. She listened to the theme song from *Fresh Prince* about a thousand times."

Costas, Tabi's father, finishes the explanation. "The Spotify machine kept playing after *The Prince that is Fresh* songs were done. And eventually, "Yeah, Yeah!" came on all the time."

Tabi says through a laugh, "They couldn't shut it off. They called me to come over and explain how to shut up the Google speaker. Fucking classic. I walk in the house, and Jay-Z's – 'Blank In Paris' is blaring, and my father is red-faced and screaming at the Alexia to shut up."

I smile. Tabi says, "He forgot they have a Google and not an Alexa. But Yia Yia thought the aliens were reaching out to her. I set her up on YouTube to watch the video. It's all she does. Bax started to dance with her one day, then we set up this. She loves Luda."

David pecks Tabi on the lips and Bax slams his hand on his shoulder. David turns around, and the two embrace, while Tabi hugs me.

Bax says, "You have your own girl now, hands off my wife."

Goldie yells from the table, "You are not married under the

eyes of God, so you are not the husband. You are not the thing now Baxter, do not say that. You will curse my grandbabies." She spits on the floor then rubs her medallion necklace and looks to the sky.

Josh hits Bax on the back of the head. "Jealousy over Tabi isn't going to play well here. Take her out in the city and let someone hit on her if you want to get possessive."

"I'll just go kiss Elle on the cheek and hug her a little too long."

"Feel free. I'm done comforting that woman for today. She's extra. Mrs. Dotson is showing up here after she has dinner with her gentleman friend, and I'm passing off Emma to her for the night. Then I'm going to shove some Popsicles down my girl's throat, wait for the twins to knock her out, and then it's booze, cigars, hot tub, and no women for me tonight. Checking my ass into Sonoma Mission Inn for the night." David nods at him.

Sam startles us and says, "So, except for location, just like your old life in Santa Barbara then." We all cheer. It's the first joke he's cracked since Sammy disappeared a couple of weeks ago. It was so abrupt and strange. David and I retreated back into our sex bubble, but Sam's a mess. Elle walks over to our collective, and holds Sam. They feel her absence more than the rest of us. He pushes away from Elle. And turns towards me.

"Hi, Sam. How are you feeling?" He scowls at me. I don't like grumbly Sam.

"Just fucking comfortably numb." Then he looks around the room and asks no one, "Why the hell am I talking about any of this with our employee?" My breath catches and my body floods with worry. I made someone upset. Shit. I don't do that. Fuck.

David intercepts before he can say anything. "Go be an asshole to someone who deserves it. My dad's over there. Go be a dickwad to him."

Sam steps to David. They're similar in height, but David is a lot more fit and built up, where Sam is a big guy, but not so muscular. "No."

David says, "Get the fuck out of my house then." Sam bumps him with his chest and David shoves him. Sam stumbles backward into Evan, and the two go down. Jims runs over to his husband. "Are you ok, Bae? What the fuck, Gelbert?"

Evan says, "Yes, but keep your mountain of a brother off of me."

Jims says, "With pleasure." He doesn't look strong, but his slight build is deceiving. He whips Sam off the floor and pushes him out the front door slamming it behind the two of them.

Becca joins us and greets me with a hug. "What was that about?"

Elle puts a hand on Becca's forearm. "Sammy. I can't know what he's feeling. I miss her every day. I'm depressed, angry and confused as to where she went, but I can't tell you what I'd do if Joshua left like that."

Josh waggles his eyebrows at Elle. "Bitch about your cankles one more time, and you may find out."

She shoves him and says, "They're your fault. It's all your fault."

"You keep thinking that." He kisses her on the forehead and walks away from his annoyed and pregnant wife.

We all sit down, and Bax says across the table, "Nat. You're way too quiet to be here. Speak up, or we're going to have to ask you to leave." I'm not saying anything after pissing off Sam.

David whispers in my ear, "Sam picked the easiest target. It doesn't mean anything. Relax, my love." My shoulders lower a touch.

Mel, Bax's sister's girlfriend, yells from the end of the table, "I fucking agree with Bax. You're like a little mouse. Enough with that shit. If you're boning Gelbert, surely you have some stories. I've seen his string of women. You're not them. Start yapping." I grin and nod. But Bax's words about me leaving have me in a panic to come up with something entertaining. My stomach rolls, and my palms sweat. How can I possibly be as entertaining as they are?

David bumps me with his shoulder, then steals a quick kiss. The whole table, all thirty of them, say "awe" in unison. I thought I would crumble from the attention, but somehow, I take it all in and muster to speak. "Are we going to eat or just bust my balls?" David leaps up and throws his hands in the air. He kisses me roughly and as sexy as ever.

"That's the first time I've ever heard her say balls. Woo-Hoo! Can cock be far behind?"

David's father's voice cuts through the revelry. "That's quite enough, son. We have guests. This is Thanksgiving." David stares at his father, and they both nod and sit down.

Bax whispers, "The Gelbert détente. It's a classic."

Everyone laughs. There's an ease to the room I'm unfamiliar with. I don't think I've ever known someone well enough to tease them. Or be teased. Add another first to our ever-growing pile. His arms slide to the back of his chair as Yia Yia stands and begins singing the Greek national anthem. To credit of everyone in this extended and odd family, they either join in or stand up. All of them put their hands over their hearts instantly.

Mr. Aganos says in his deep baritone voice, "That is as good as grace. Let us eat the food now!"

I sip my wine and let the warmth wash over me.

PART 2

PETIT VERDOT

CHAPTER 17

DAVID

I'M HUSTLING from Gelbert Family Winery's large tank and barrel room over to the blending lab. It's behind the old house that serves as our tasting room, kitchen, and merchandise area. My parents' home is up on the hill overlooking the family vineyards. I haven't been out here lately. But with the holiday rush, I thought I'd lend a hand in the tasting room so my mom can decorate all the millions of themed trees on the property and in the tasting room lounge area. There's actually a walking path around the property to view all the trees. She's insane with Christmas.

Locals come here just to sip a glass and are surrounded by her winter wonderland. She's never met a Michael's sale she didn't like. We used a lot of her stuff for the Plaza when I surprised Natalie. My mom decorates for every season, but Christmas is her Superbowl. These holiday weekends are madhouses. Pro/Ho is out of wine and waiting on more product, so we all have a little time on our hands. The five of us picked up shifts at our respective family wineries to help out. Nat's pouring wine over at Bax's winery, Schroeder Estate.

I left Nat naked in my bed, and it about killed me, but the

woman does probably need a rest. You know how they say show don't tell, well I showed her just how much I loved her last night. Jesus. It's nearly Christmas, and the Parade has been a well-loved and honored tradition in my house lately. She still hasn't said she loves me, but she shows me every day. I was supposed to see her tonight, but it's the first time I need to cancel on her after five months. It's Nutcracker night in the city with Mom. Becca argued her way out of going to the ballet when she was seven, but I always go with my mom. I don't love ballet, but I love the ritual of it. We go to dinner, the show, drinks after. It was special enough to get hot chocolate way after my bedtime when I was little, but now we make a night of it. Even though my parents have a place in San Francisco, we get hotel rooms and sip champagne late into the night at the Top of the Marq.

Today, I'm grabbing some juice that my dad offered Pro/Ho. I'll blend for the next couple of days with Gelbert Estate Merlot juice and the Cab samples Sam pulled off the new property. It probably won't amount to much. Still, I want to explore the idea of creating a series of limited-release Meritages using our family winery grapes and our own. I'm starting with Gelbert's, but Josh, Will, and I will sit and sample next week and see if we can develop something for the partnership with LaChappelle/Whittier. Tabi wants to work with the Grenache from Stafýlia Cellars, and a some sort of Syrah we pressed last week from .

I answer the phone in my dad's office as I'm about to bug out of here. He hates it, and I like to fuck up his schedule, so I answer it.

"Shit. Thank God. David. You need to come to the tasting room, now." This is strange. I don't have time for whatever shit this is.

"Chris? Handle it. I'm done for the day." The tasting room manager. I've just put in a full shift, and I need to shower and dress for the Nutcracker.

"Only you, man. Get your ass down here." Chris has been with our family for a long time. He was a finance guy in a former life, retired early, and wanted to pour wine. He's fantastic at managing anything, so I can't fucking imagine what this is. I start the trek back towards the big white and gray house with the wraparound porch. There's Victorian gingerbread trim framing the archways around the entire porch. They were preserved from the original owner's home. Very turn of the century California. Very cool. My great grandparents used to live in the house. It was the original farmhouse on the property, and rumor has it the owner's wife had a Green Acres thing going on. She wanted no part of farm life, so she built this decadent Victorian house in the middle of the farm and demanded her husband plant vines to have wine on demand.

I have no desire to run a winery this big. It's a beast, and my dad runs it "the right" way. My asshole of a father will never step down. They'll need to pry his pruning shears and cluster hook from his cold dead hands. He loves it so much, and he's good at it. Most of the time. He got cocky a couple of years ago and bought land that didn't pay off, but we don't talk about that. We don't talk about the fact he's the one who almost lost our family winery because I'm the one who's always been the fuck up. Not that any of that shit got blamed on me. But not a day goes by he doesn't talk about how he and the families of my four best friends created Prohibition Winery and handed it to us. Like we couldn't do it on our fucking own. Like we didn't build that business. It was just their juice and their idea.

It was awesome to grow up here, but it's not mine. I do love winemaking, though. It truly is in my blood and on my palate.

I always had a corner in the lab to experiment with blending. At first, my father and mother thought it was cute I'd blend unfermented juice as a kid. Now I know what each grape will taste like before it hits my tongue.

Gelbert mass-produces many grocery store wines so our high-end stuff can be sold exclusively here at the winery. We also put on a lot of weddings and events in the warehouse barrel space. But our name is heavily distributed, and when tourists come to town, they make this a destination.

My mother grew that tourist business. She created a brand for us, and now coming here is a bit like winery Disney World. You can taste wine, but you can also meet the woolly weeders. The sheep who roam and eat our property and weed under the vines. There's a riding tour all over our vineyard with tour guides and signage to walk you through the winemaking process. We have a porch café and an enormous gift shop at the end of the tour. We make sure you leave here with something with my damn name stamped on it. Wine charms you might use once at a party or t-shirts that say, "Is It Wine O'Clock Yet?" and on the back it says, "It is at Gelbert's!"

When I used to go out, I'd go to Napa, where fewer people know the name Gelbert and more tourists flock. I can't be anonymous in my Valley. Napa may get more press, but I will always think Sonoma's wines are better. When I do go out, I never give my last name. I've told women I worked in my family's tasting room before but never owned it. I only ever say I pour wine in the tasting room and stock the gift shop.

My parents have a condo in the city and stay there often, but the house remains in perfect condition waiting for one of us to move into it. My mother's highlighted hair hides the encroaching gray. She flits around the property, and people take selfies with her like she's Alice in Wonderland. She religiously keeps her ass and her under eyes taut with creams, facials, trainers, and various appointments. She always has an eye for making sure everything is in its place. We have a great relationship. She still cooks dinner for me when I stop by regularly a week to drop off my laundry or just tell her about the latest girl I don't want to see again, until Nat. The Nutcracker is important this year because I haven't spent that much time with her lately.

I've never felt the need to attach myself to anyone. I have my friends and my family to entertain me. And when I need to come, I've never had a problem finding help in that area. There's always a tourist or a wine club hottie willing to get down. And because of all the practice blending and tasting, my tongue is quite famous for what it can do.

The tasting room porch is packed with people sipping and snacking. Poppy started her cooking career here, providing small bites and plates for those who came to taste our wine. The current chef has been here for a like a year. I slept with her early on. She was meh. Damn. I really am a douche. The more distance I put between —Pre-Natalie and After Natalie—the more I see what a tool I was.

She flipped some kind of switch inside me. I can't get enough of the smell or feel of her. I can't be around her without wanting to be inside her in some capacity.

CHAPTER 18

DAVID

I BOUND up the stairs and push past the tourists. Michael Bublé's Christmas album is blaring throughout the space. Chris calls me over to the corner of the room with a head nod. It's a more private corner reserved for wine club member's tastings or pricey vertical tasting special events.

"What's up?" He points to the bar. I look over, and there's a bucket-like thing, and it's screaming. "Jesus, tell them to take that kid out of here." Chris shakes his head. "Fine. I'll do it. Is that why I'm here, to bounce a family with a screechy kid?"

He hands me an envelope. "There's no family to bounce." Chris's hand is clammy, and his face is white.

I cock an eyebrow at him.

He speaks quickly and quietly. "I don't know what to do. I don't know who this is. I've been here a long time, but I don't know this name. I'm hoping you might know it. I didn't want to freak out your mom, so I called you."

The envelope says, David Allen.

"Fuck." I look around the room, quickly scanning everyone, but no one is looking at me. They're all looking at the screeching child. Chris's eyes snap to mine. "Where's the family? Where's the mother? Or nanny? Who fucking dropped this off? Fuck."

Fuck. Fuck. Fuck. My skin is oscillating between itchy and tingly. Like a thousand small spikes poking me at once. What the hell is going on? Now my body is cold, and my hands are shaking. This cannot be happening. It's like an icy breeze keeps running up and down my fucking spine. David Allen is the fake name I give out to hook-ups. Allen is my middle name. Shit.

"That's just it. We've asked everyone. There isn't a family, and the baby won't stop crying. Everyone has tried to soothe it, but we're afraid to pick it up. We don't know what the laws of this are. I don't want my staff to be put in any kind of trouble because they picked up a strange baby. Who the hell is David Allen?"

I move toward the screaming bucket and look back at Chris. "Me. Tell no one." Chris pretends to button his lips, but his eyes are popping. He's shocked but not nearly as shocked as I am. This can't be what I'm terrified it is. I've gone bare with exactly two women. One of them would still be pregnant, and if it's the other, this kid would be heading off to college. I pick up the screamy thing, and there's a fancy leather bag on the floor. I grab it too. I head back to the empty tiny tasting bar in the corner and stare at Chris.

"Dude, open the letter." Like a Band-Aid. I have to just rip it open. I have to know all the details so I can fix this situation.

I rip it open. Then I thrust it at Chris to read. "The handwriting isn't great, but it clearly says David Allen is the father of this baby. The mother isn't coming back, and she wishes you well."

"Well and truly fucked. That's what that letter says. Does it have a name? Or say anything else? Does this thing have any information about it?"

Chris shakes his head no, and I pull the letter from him.

Chris points to the letter and says, "What is this letter? A J? An S? W?"

"It's just a fucking big ass scribble. I can't just call it Scribbles." The baby looks at me for the first time. I repeat the name, "Scribbles. Do you want to be Scribbles? You're a baby. How the fuck do you know I'm not saying tortilla?" It cries again. This can't be mine. There's no way. I'm going to the Nutcracker tonight, then fucking Natalie all weekend. I have a pick-up game with Mel in the morning. I'm blending the Meritage and have a sculpture I'm working on. This is not my kid.

I lift it up awkwardly and stare into the baby's eyes. I whisper, "Scribbles." It stops crying again. "Scribbles it is."

My body is now overheated, and my skin is flushed. It feels like the adrenaline high of heading into the fourth quarter of a game, and we're only behind by six. The thing calms for a second and stares at me with its eyes open wide. Fuck. Shit. Damn. Scribbles? What the hell? Christ, it's not like I can deny this. I'm in awe and freaked the fuck out. This thing has my eyes —those stupid green unique eyes with the aqua flecks in them. Becca has them too. As bright as the Irish freaking flag green. Is it possible Becca gave birth and gave it up, then someone pushed it off on me? Maybe Poppy? This is secretly Sal's kid, and they're punking me. Except Poppy would brag about being pregnant. She'll be the type of pregnant that talks too much about how she loves it.

I am not down for this. And like a nightmare, my mother walks in. She's a baby person. She hugs and holds strangers' babies. Can't put them down. When Ingrid Schroeder, Bax's decade-younger sister, was little, I swear she spent more time in my mother's arms than anywhere.

Mom beelines for the baby. I fold the note and shove it into my back pocket. The baby begins to wail again as I stick it back in its bucket. My mother looks at me and beelines for the screaming. She leans over the baby and coos at it. She immediately picks the thing up. My mother is the most intuitive person ever. She holds the little one and starts to gently bounce her. I don't move. I freeze as she naturally takes her into her arms. The kid miraculously stops crying again. My mom begins to walk outside. "Follow me, David." I grab the bucket thing and its luggage. Which seems to be just this leather bag. "And for the record, she's a girl."

I look at my mom and say, "A girl named Scribbles."

We're just down the porch and away from the noise of the tourists. My mom's voice is gentle and soft. Her blonde hair is impeccable, and her soft sweater welcomes this little girl to her chest. She's so tiny. I don't know months or what, but this kid is tiny. Shit. I'm going to need like a kid doctor or something. Or, what do I do with her? Where the hell is the mother? And who the hell is the mother? Does this belong to me now? Is it like a finders keepers thing?

"What's up, sweet face? No need for all the tears." She kisses Scribbles' cheek. She looks around again. I assume I look like a deer in a headlight. No one says a word. Scribbles stops crying for a second. My mother looks in her face, then begins to silently weep and hold her close. She's beaming a smile and staring at me. I don't move.

"Well..." A tear runs down my mom's face. She reaches for my hand while staring at her face. "Baby Girl Gelbert. If those aren't Gelbert eyes staring at me, I don't know whose eyes they are. They're Great Aunt Saoirse's eyes. Welcome to our world, baby girl. It seems your daddy accidentally did something right. And no matter what's happened to you so far, looking at your very terrified Daddy, we're going to make sure you know you're loved. Ok? You can call me Mhamó, it's Gaelic for Grandma. I don't know what else you've got mixed up in there, but we're Irish through and through, my darling." The tasting room noise fades into nothing as my mother bonds with my child. Holy shit. Mine.

"And now, sweetie, it's time to teach your daddy why you're so sad right now. I'd be upset too if I were you. I can smell you, sweet girl."

"Mom?" I don't know what to say.

She squeezes my hand. She's always been good about yelling at us in private, so we're not embarrassed, but I'm honestly shocked she's not scolding me. "Later. Whether you know it or not yet, my darling boy, your priorities just shifted. Grab that big bag. I'm assuming what we need is in it. Follow me."

CHAPTER 19

DAVID

I'M SITTING in our very yellow kitchen with my head in my hands. My mom has changed Scribbles and given her a bottle. She always said the pale yellow was soothing, and that's why she wanted it in the kitchen. I would sit in the living room closer to the liquor cabinet, but I hoped the yellow would calm my nerves. Nope. Still jangled and paralyzed with panic. My mom's called Dr. Johnson, the town doctor that's been around forever. He offered to come over and check her out. She's apparently in excellent condition for an abandoned baby. He also pledged to keep our secret. He said he doesn't see the benefit of uprooting the baby.

I'm a couple of glasses of bourbon into the day and can think of nothing except, who the hell is this baby's mother? And who would just leave a baby in my fucking care? Poor Scribbles. She lost the fucking parental lottery. Becca's been upstairs with Mom for the longest time. I put my head down on the unsoothing yellow table runner.

My sister smacks the back of my head. "You're a dad." Then laughs. Everyone needs to stop hitting me.

"You take that back. That was a low blow. I'm not a father."

"Science says different. Did you see her? She looks EXACTLY like you. It's freaky." My sister's long auburn locks are pulled back in her traditional severe braid down her back. She's as tall as I am but willowy. I used to think the wind could knock her over. She has this nervous demeanor that always unnerves people. Works really well in court. She seldom loses. She may appear delicate, but she's all fire, brimstone, and fucking steel. We fought a lot as kids. We had nothing in common except our parents, and I often think she simply tolerates me or lives to torture, but there's no one I want at my back more than my sister. She's secretly a warrior. But right now, the buster of balls that she is needs to shut the fuck up.

I swig my drink. "Shit. This cannot be happening."

"Kind of shocked it hasn't happened before now." I'm insanely careful. It's the one thing I didn't want to happen.

"Not helping. What the hell? There has a be something legal you can do."

"That's a strange thing. I did a bit of research while I was upstairs. Family law isn't really my wheelhouse."

"Of course you researched. I drink, and you research and maybe write a quick brief. Did you organize my sock drawer too while you were upstairs?"

"Fuck right off, little brother. She's not legally yours until we can begin to establish paternity." She gets a call and puts her finger up, then leaves the room. I sit up straight. And think. Maybe she's not mine. Do I want her not to be mine? Scribbles and I have barely spent any time together. She's not going to like me. Few do for more than a couple of days, except Natalie.

I slam my head back onto the table. Oh, Christ. Natalie. Natalie doesn't want kids and isn't sure she loves me yet. No. Scribbles can't take Natalie away from me. This is the worst thing that's ever happened to me. I can't imagine it's a banner day for Scribbles either, but at least she won't remember it. All the light in my heart just whooshed out of the room. Gone.

How do I even have that conversation? It's a foregone conclusion I'll fuck up that chat. She'll not want me. I need her to want me. I need her to be in love with me, then this news can be handled. I also need all the details and plans for that thing upstairs. Once I know she's mine forever, then I can tell Nat about Scribbles. That's the only plan that makes sense. Well, makes sense in a fucked-up sitcom, possibly teen drama kind of way. But it's the best plan I've got. For all, I know Scribbles' mom will be back tomorrow, and I'll have had that insane, horrible conversation with Natalie for nothing. This makes more sense. I can tell her about Scribbles once she's sorted.

My sister pulls my attention. "You need to find the mom."

"Duh."

"No. I mean legally. She's the only one who can sign over parental rights to you. Currently, if you try to do anything legal for that little girl, she has to go to the state first. She's considered an abandoned child and becomes a ward of California."

Christ. No. "Like an orphan?"

"You can't prove paternity except for a letter. And well, those fucking eyes of ours. But legally, you can't prove she's been placed in your care or that you are responsible for her wellbeing. You'd have to be tested and evaluated to satisfy the state. And if it's discovered she crossed state lines, then we're into a federal mess of possible kidnapping and reckless endangerment of a child."

"Christ. No. What the hell?"

"If she's discovered with you, legally, she'll be put into the foster system, and you'll be vetted so you can become her legal guardian. But once she's in the system, there's no guarantee she'd be placed in your care. You have a good shot if you can prove paternity. But while you wait for DNA tests, she'll have to live somewhere, and there's no way to know if she'll be temporarily placed with you. Considering you're a winemaking bachelor with a reputation, probably not."

"Can I get her placed with you or Elle and Josh?"

"We'd start at square one of the vetting system, same as you." My sister crosses her arms over her chest. She's pacing a bit. I know her. She's going over everything I just said to make sure she didn't say anything that wasn't true. She's never wrong.

"Shit," I say.

My sister bites into an apple and leans up against the kitchen counter. "Right now, she's a bit of a fugitive."

I pause to take in all that Becca just said.

"My daughter's a badass." I grin at the idea of her on the run.

"You called her your daughter."

"Well, I'm sure as fuck not letting her into the foster system." If I do nothing else for her, I'll do that. I flip my chair towards my sister.

"Then we have to find the mother. She's the easiest path to custody. Otherwise, there's a whole slew of legal stuff. And what if she has some kind of sickness or something? Anyway, it should be easy enough to find the mother, right? You could call her today, and we'll start to sort this out."

I leap up and circle the kitchen island and get in my sister's face. I say, "HOW?"

"You have no clue who she is! You're slime."

"How the hell am I slime? I slept with women. I didn't steal their credit card information. Until Nat, I slept with more than one woman a week. First, I'd have to figure out how old that baby is, then try and remember what I did nine months before that. Christ, Bec. This is fucking insane."

She bites the apple again and crosses her arms over her chest. She looks up at the ceiling like when she's trying to solve a case. Her face turns back towards me. "Get Mel and Tommi on this mystery." Bax's sister and her white-hat hacker girlfriend. Hell no. No one.

I say, "NO! Swear to me, Bec, don't tell a soul. I'm totally freaking serious. No one."

"No one what?" my sister says. I can't have anyone getting into this. Not yet. Let me sort out Scribbles, then people can know. It will be a footnote, not a plot point. Unless the mom really doesn't want her.

"Tell no one. Not until I figure out what's going to happen."

Poppy bounds into the room. Shit. "Tell me." Her damn curly hair bouncing with each step she takes. This is not what I need from my fucking cousin. Her mom still lives on the property, and she grew up in this house with us. Well, in the house that was our grandparents'. Shit. She's the worst with a secret. Not Sam bad, but bad.

"You're not the best with keeping things private." Becca crosses her arms and looks at me. How do I keep this from getting out? No one can know until I understand what's happening and how I tell Nat.

"I'm excellent at keeping secrets," Poppy says.

Becca shifts her weight and looks at our bubbly cousin. "You're having 'secret' sex with a Mafia Don, and everyone knows."

"No one knows *when* it started." She winks. And then, like a catastrophic event, my mother walks in holding the baby.

Poppy squeals and goes over to look. "Auntie Jana, who is this little bundle?" She pulls back the blanket. "That looks exactly like David." She gasps sharply and scowls at me. "What did you do?"

"Fine! Apparently, I knocked someone up, and now there's this." I throw my hands up.

"Who?"

"No clue."

Becca says off the cuff, "I'd start by checking out your greasy DMs from like eleven or twelve months ago."

"Fuck," I say.

My mom shushes us. "Do not swear in front of her. Let's go into the living room."

My mom reaches out and puts her hand on my shoulder.

"All seems to be well. She'll need a pediatrician, and we don't have her shot records, so that's an issue. But our best guess is that she's around five months old." I've been dating Natalie for five months.

I run to the bag and search for any paperwork we might have overlooked. I find an envelope in a side pocket I didn't find before. I glance in and can't believe what it is. I'll deal with it later. But no shot records or birth certificate.

We all follow my mom into the living room and flop onto different couches. It's a cavernous room formally decorated with rich azure blue velvet couches. It's all a bit poseur in my mind, but Dad loves the pomposity of it all. There are great big timber beams and insane curtains that puddle on the floor in front of the windows.

Poppy takes her from my mom's arms, and I sit on the couch and put my head in my hands. Poppy starts swinging her slightly and bouncing for some reason. She talks in a marzipan sticky sweet voice. "Oh, cutie. I'm so sorry David's your daddy. It's going to be a rough road, but we'll be here."

I flip her off, and she laughs at me.

I look around the room. "Until I can find her mother, Mom, can we please keep this in the family? I promise I'm not going to ditch the little thing. Just until I figure this shit out. I need to know if the mom was overwhelmed or heartless. For now, please keep it with just our family. Well, and Chris and Dr. Johnson. But keep the circle tight."

Everyone nods except my mom. She says, "What about Natalie?"

"No. Not yet. I will. Of course. But she has a whole history I can't go into. It's her story to tell. Let's just say she does NOT want kids in any way, shape, or form. Look, for all we know, the mom may show up in the next couple of days, and this will blow over."

Becca smacks my head again, and Poppy speaks in her stern rule-following tone. "David Allen Gelbert! Whether the mom comes back or not, you are her FATHER." My mom sits down next to me.

"David. She will always be in your life, and if you plan to have Natalie as well, she deserves to know all of your life."

"Fuck. I will tell her when the picture is clearer how we all move forward. When I know my responsibilities and whether she lives with me or wherever. I don't fucking know anything. I don't know what to do, but I'll figure it out. It's going to be my conversation to have."

Becca turns to me. "You have your answer to the Nat problem right here. This kid is your out. Clean. You can be single again. Get lots of DILF action. And banging hoes with protection again." My ever-pragmatic witch of a sister.

"I always wrap."

There's a silence in the room as the little thing snuffles out a yawn, and all eyes turn back to me.

I mutter softly, "And I don't want an out."

Becca turns sharply to me. "What?"

I confess, "I'm in love with Natalie." My mom sighs and covers her heart. I ignore her and continue talking, " Let me sort this all out before like sixty people enter our relationship, including a baby. Oh, God. There's a baby."

Poppy sits down next to me with the baby and takes my hand. "Ok. I won't tell anyone. But I won't keep this forever. If you really love her, Nat deserves a chance to process this too. What's her name?"

"Natalie. I thought you knew her."

Poppy smacks my arm. I'm so stunned I don't even understand what people are saying to me.

I say, "Everyone, stop hitting me. You mean the baby, right? I don't know. I could barely read the note, been calling her Scribbles. I'm racking my brain. I need a minute to sort."

Mom runs her well-manicured hands through my hair. "Sweet boy, you'll figure it out. How about I take baby girl tonight? Let me tell your dad, and we'll take care of her for a day or two while you figure out your next steps. I'll send him out for a pack and play."

"What the hell is that?"

"You'll learn. But you know your father loves a Costco trip." He has more money than he'll ever need, but he's obsessed with buying in bulk or big things on discount.

She puts her hand on my cheek, and I lean into it. Poppy scoffs a bit, but I ignore her.

"Whatever you need, I'm here," my sister says. She's so practical I'm guessing she means making out a last will and testament for the baby or registering her for a passport, or setting up her IRA.

Poppy squeezes my hand, then hands me the sleeping baby. I lay her across my lap, and my mom flips my arm over and adjusts the baby. She's cute when she sleeps. She also creeps me the fuck out because what the hell am I going to do?

My voice is broken, "I'm going to be bad at this."

Poppy stands and tosses over her shoulder as she walks out of the room. "You're going to be terrible at this. And then you'll be great. It's what you do. You fuck things up spectacularly, and then like magic, you turn the world around, and everyone loves you. Pisses me off that the world always rallies behind you, but

I'll be here if you need me. Good luck. I have to run and open the café." And then she's gone. Never one to compliment me without a dig. Always the perfect one. I do love her, but she bugs.

My mom stands up and leaves the room, and Becca is across the room scrolling her phone. It's just Scribbles and me on this end of the couch.

I'm fucked.

CHAPTER 20

DAVID

THE KID IS STRAPPED into that bucket thing. It snapped into the giant plastic thing attached to secret hooks I never knew existed in my back seat. She faces backward. It's a whole thing. Thank fucking God she's sleeping. My mom is laying the groundwork with my dad, then I'll bring the tiny thing over there. I wish there was even a moment of doubt, but she already looks exactly like my entire freaking family and me. I'm too in shock to even begin to deal with her the way I probably should. I pull out of Gelbert Family Winery. I can't go back to my house. I don't want her to think that's where she's going to stay. She has to stay with my mom. I don't even know all the things we need. Bibs. Those are a thing, right? I'm freaking out, and I want to call Natalie, but I know this is not her thing. This is not what she's looking for in a partner. Anxiety is creeping in, and I need one of my outlets, but that's not possible right now. It's not like I can pull out a blowtorch with this thing around, or shoot hoops, or fuck Nat into submission. My hands feel tight like the skin is too small for my hands. I keep stretching them. I reach in the back, palm the basketball on the floor, and put it in the front seat. I hold onto it, and it starts to help.

In addition to Nat not wanting kids, I can't trigger her with the foster care stuff. Scribbles will not go into the system. I'll hide the tiny fugitive at my mom's house until we can make her legal somehow. Becca can surely find a loophole to custody. Nat can't know. I can't do that to her. Not until I'm sure about everything. Or anything.

Baxter, who's known her the longest, doesn't even know she was bounced around in foster homes. She wants nothing to do with children. I'm fucked. My heart aches when she's not around me. I don't want to be David without Nat. I didn't plan this kid. She's like the Spanish Inquisition in that old Monty Python movie. Nobody expects the Spanish Inquisition. Nobody expects a baby left on a bar. I didn't plan any fucking thing. How the hell do I keep her and keep this thing in the backseat? I'm freaking. Breathe. Scribbles woke up and is making cute baby noises, but I don't know what they mean. Is that how she talks? When does that happen? Perhaps she could clue me in on who her mother is.

"Scribbles, what's your mom's name? Where do you hail from?"

Nothing. Not even a snuffle from her. I need to Google a timeline of when they talk and shit like that.

My mom said the baby could stay with them. Theoretically, the baby and Nat never need to meet. I could visit the baby at my parents' house. Fuck. I sound like an asshole, even to myself.

I'm driving in circles, and I decide to seek advice from another baby. And I only know one baby.

"DAVID?!" ELLE SAYS IN BETWEEN LICKS OF A PURPLE POPSICLE that's turned her tongue plum.

She hugs me with her non-sticky hand. "Come in. Josh isn't here."

"That's better." My hands are sweaty and fidgety. My pulse is racing. It feels like it's pre-game. I swallow down the rising puke and push forward.

"He's with Sam."

I ask even though I know he's not ok. "How's Sam doing? I haven't seen him in a couple of days."

"He's catatonic. He's a shell. I mean, can you blame him?".

"How are you doing?" She shrugs, and I pull her into an embrace.

She holds on tightly. "I wish I could understand. I don't think this is as simple as Sammie getting bored with Sam. There's something I don't understand, but it's not like I can go after her. I don't know where to start. I miss her."

"Me too." She wipes a tear from under her eye and straightens up. She puts her hands on her expanding belly.

"Ok. Why are you here?"

"I need your help."

"Well, Emma will be down for another hour or so, and these daemons only want to eat Popsicles. I've got time. It's like the 9th circle of food hell. I'm either puking or eating a fucking neon-colored ice pop." She rubs her stomach, which has really popped over the last couple of weeks.

"Ignore me and my Fred Flintstone feet. Did you know they didn't even return to normal before that asshole knocked me up again?" I pull a tight smile. I usually find her misery funny, but I can't think of anything else. And everyone in town is aware of her thoughts on her swollen feet. And then there's a wail from the car.

"Why aren't you laughing at me? That's one of your favorite things. And what is that?"

"That's what I need your help with. I don't know what to do."

Elle tosses the ice pop in the bush and waddles to the car. I unlock it, and she opens it. She bends in, and I hear a tone of voice I wish I knew how to imitate.

"Oh. Precious babe. What is it you want? Come here." She expertly pulls the child from the seat that took me forty minutes to figure out how to get her in to. "Who are you?" Scribbles scrunches up her face and cries again. Elle puts her on her shoulder and begins to sway a little bit, and she stops crying.

I say way too loudly, "Sorcery! You're a witch. How did you do that?"

"Practice." The baby pulls at a blonde strand of hair that's come loose from Elle's messy bun. She's in leggings and an oversized crisp white button-down and flat pointy, red shoes. Although miserable and pregnant, she looks more put together than most women I know, except my mom.

I'm still standing in her doorway, and she walks up, pops a hip, and holds the baby there. "She's a redhead."

I nod.

"She has distinctive green eyes."

I nod again.

"Where's her mom? DAD!" She squeals a bit. "Holy shit, you're a dad! Gelbert is a baby daddy."

"Please stop saying that. I don't know what to do with her." I'm numb and panicked as Elle speaks.

"First thing would stop calling her 'her.' What's her name?"

"I've been calling her Scribbles." The baby responds to the name. That's not a good thing. She thinks her name is Scribbles. Have I doomed her already with my jackassery?

"Get inside. You need wine, and she needs a new diaper."

"I def don't know how to do that."

"As luck would have it, there's a tutorial about to happen, just inside that door. Go get her car seat."

Elle pushes past me with the little girl. I go to the car, reach into the seat, find that hook thing, pull out the plastic contraption, and grab the baby's luggage.

I enter, and she's lying on a tall table in Elle's front room. She's tracing her belly with her fingers. And she seems to be making all kinds of sounds like she's laughing.

Elle looks up and busts out laughing. "Baby girl, you're in trouble. Your daddy just brought in the entire seat, base and all. Just put it down. We need to work on this first." I hand her the bag.

Elle turns the bag around to examine it. "This is gorgeous. I mean designer gorgeous. Holy shit, this is expensive, and Chanel. Did you buy this, or does baby Scribbles have really good taste?"

"It came with her."

"Like fries on the side of a burger?"

I smirk at her jab. "What do I do first?"

Elle keeps one hand on the baby and steps back so I can get closer to the table. "Always keep one hand on the baby while they're on the changing table."

"There's an entire table dedicated to changing diapers? I definitely don't have this."

Elle puts a hand on my shoulder. "Put your hand lightly on the baby." I do it and look at her. "You should see both of your eyes. You both look like you just found the monster in a horror movie. It's going to be ok." Scribbles kicks her little legs. She's got some power. I smile at her.

"She's so soft."

"Yes. Babies are. She won't break. But she could fall off the table." I look down at her as her eyes meet mine. I put my finger in her tiny hand like I've seen in movies. I'd like to say I don't have a moment where I literally feel the earth shift. I don't want to be a cliché, but I am. All the parts of me and my heart and brain begin to make room for her. I have no power over it.

My voice cracks a bit. "Now what?"

Elle puts her hand on my shoulder. She runs me through taking off the diaper and how to appropriately use a wipe. Then I get it on her, and there's no poop, so I feel good at this. She tells me about the magical stripe that lets me know she's wet.

"Good. Now dump the diaper into that thing over there."

"Do I need one of those things too?" It's like a tall skinny garbage can that sucks up diapers.

"We have an extra one. We also have an extra crib if you need it?"

"Why?"

Elle moves around the room picking up small toys and arranging pillows. "Josh bought one he liked. Silly man thought he could decorate. I was willing to put up with it, but now that we're having twins, we need matching cribs, or my OCD will have me climbing the walls. Josh doesn't remember where he got the other one, and we, thankfully, can't find it. So. Extra crib. And I'm not saving it for the next one because that's simply not happening." I smile and laugh at her. Elle's very particular about where things go and how they should look. She ducks outside for a moment and comes back with her discarded ice pop wrapper. My formerly alpha grunting man friend, Josh, found the one woman on the planet who can put him in his place. It's glorious to see.

She scoops up the baby and heads to the kitchen. Next thing I know, she has a bottle in her mouth. "Hey! What did Natalie say about this baby? How are things with you two?" Now I'm nervous. Natalie's rental cottage is on the LaChappelle/Whittier property, as is the house I'm standing in. Her cottage is up a different driveway from Josh and Elle's. Hopefully, she won't know I'm here. I didn't even think this through. She could totally see me leave. Shit.

Effortlessly, Elle continues to feed the baby and pour me a

glass of LaChappelle/Whittier Merlot. They do make a kick-ass Merlot. I take the glass from her, but before I do, she sticks her nose in the glass and takes a big sniff.

"Sigh." I sit on the couch with the bag on my lap, and she joins me. "Did you go through the bag?"

"It's all bottles, diaper junk, and a blanket." I don't mention the envelope.

"Put your wine down. Open your arms." I do as I'm told. She puts the baby in my arms, and I hold the bottle.

"See, it's fine." It's not. I'm pretty sure she's going to choke because I'm holding the damn bottle wrong.

I say, "No one knows. I don't know how to tell Natalie. It's a whole thing. She doesn't like children and doesn't want them."

"And you want her." Elle leans forward.

"I'm in love with her." Elle gets up and grabs a Smurf blue Popsicle. She gestures to me, and I shake my head. I'm not a big Popsicle fan.

"Shit! Gelbert, this is a big boy day for you. You're a dad. You're in a real relationship. You really are coming into your own."

"No. You don't get it. I'll lose Natalie if she learns about this baby. And I don't know if the mom is coming back. The note just said she's mine and she couldn't handle being a mother. That's all I could understand. The rest was scribbles."

The aha plays across her face, then she glares at me. "That's cold. You must have done her dirty." I most certainly never did anyone dirty. I was always clear with my intentions and the aftermath of each encounter.

"You're saying the mother of this baby left her because I didn't call?" I cross my legs and get more comfortable. For once, I'm not the worst person in a scenario.

Elle places her hand over her heart, and her emerald green eyes soften. "That was a horrible thing to say. Sorry. I hate this woman. I want to bury this woman. Who leaves a sweet face like that? And you don't know her?"

It's the thing that will drive me mad. I have no fucking clue who this girl's mother could be. There's a movie montage of faces and evenings playing on a loop in my brain, and I have no clue which one it is. "I don't remember any clingers. I always wrap up. I mean always."

"Somebody got through because this precious little miracle is here."

"Not so much a miracle as a complication."

She smacks me in the head. I swear if one more woman hits me today, I'm going to lose it. "Fuck you, asshole. I swear, Gelbert, if you don't start seeing the world more clearly right now, I'm going to keep smacking you. Stop whining. You're not the same douche nozzle I first met." That was bad. I was insanely drunk and high when Josh introduced us to her. I called her a bitch because she didn't want to sleep with me. I was a fucking moron.

She continues, "You're not him despite what you tell yourself. Stop it. It's time to be better. Give her a name. She's a person. She's your person. And you need to be hers. Whether you planned it or not"

"We'll see."

She raises her hand. "Asshole. Give her a name. Right now. Do not be douche, David. Be the other one." I look at her face, and it makes me smile. "And make it a really good one. She's a tough little fighter. I can tell. Look at the way she's trying to touch your hand. She knows she has to fight to make you realize you're her daddy, not an asshole."

"I don't know how to do this." If I name her, then this is real. If I name this sweet, innocent little fugitive, it's as if I'm betraying Natalie in some way.

"Not yet, but I'm here. She can't be much younger than Emma. I'd say she's four or five months."

"I've been with Natalie for five months. She was born while I was with Nat."

"Does Nat know you love her?" Elle's voice is soothing, and Scribbles' eyelids are fluttering.

I turn my gaze back to Elle. I shift on the couch, so Princess S and I are more comfortable. "Yes." Elle smiles and seems to be swooning a bit.

"Then you must tell her. I won't tell anyone, but only if you name your baby girl right now." Elle rubs her hand over my daughter's head.

"What if she has a name?"

"Give her a name from her dad. And if she has one from the woman who walked away from her, trust me, she doesn't remember it or want it. And it's not worthy of her. I hate pregnancy as much as the next gal—"

"Not all women hate pregnancy."

"They should. But I can't imagine anyone doing this." I stare at her flaming little redhead and those wild green eyes while she continues to suck the bottle down. She's a part of me. Freaking me out. She has a heritage I have to teach her about. This little abandoned outlaw has a history and a legacy. She has family and hopefully a decent wine palate.

There was a woman who lived right next door to my favorite person, my great-aunt Saoirse. They let the world believe they were neighbors. But if you paid attention, you knew one of those houses was for show. They're idyllic houses located just outside of Cork, where my family roots lie. They were built side by side with very little room in between. I used to think both Saoirse and her "neighbor" hung the moon. She was vibrant and fearless, and I was always mesmerized by her. She and my Aunt Saoirse traveled the world and always stopped by Sonoma on all of their trips. It was an annual event until Saoirse died. Her companion/neighbor was Auntie Mame, in my mind. Always adventurous and encouraging the best in people and never bothering or believing the worst. She grew up in some terrible conditions but always said she'd found Saoirse, so she must have done something right in her life. She's a fighter, too.

When I was eighteen, my parents shipped me off to Saoirse and Ireland for the summer to work on a sheep farm. Thought I'd learn some work ethic. I learned how to drink whiskey and swear in Gaelic. Best summer of my life. I lived in the empty house while they lived together. I kept their thinly veiled secret my whole life. They once described their relationship as living outside the law as people viewed it. Saoirse died about eight or so years ago. We went to the funeral, and I comforted her like the widow she was. The love of Saoirse's life, her fugitive desperado partner, still lives in the house they secretly shared.

When I ran from the NBA draft, it was their doorstep where I turned up drunk, scared, and scarred. She took me in without question, and I stayed longer than I anticipated. I worked the land again as I had several years earlier. I learned how to stand up for myself without my fists. I learned I'm funny and comfortable with who I am. I learned I'm a hell of a lot different than my father leads the world or myself to believe. She taught me there's not a whole lot of difference between brave and stupid. I learned sometimes it's ok to be the black sheep. And I learned it all from Sadie, the outlaw.

"Sadie," I whisper to her. She's staring at me while she drinks her bottle.

"Hi, Sadie." Elle kisses her forehead. "Welcome. And good luck."

CHAPTER 21

NATALIE

I DIDN'T EXPECT to see David tonight. He just crawled into my bed. I turn over and kiss him. He holds me tight. I slide my hand down his stomach, and he catches it.

"Sunshine, is it ok if I just hold you?"

I'm confused, the Parade is always up for it, but this is nice too. "Are you ok?" I ask him.

"I am. I just missed the smell of you. The feel of you. I promise to slide my cock into any and all holes you'd like in the morning, but I'm exhausted. I just needed to see you."

That's about the loveliest thing. He needed me. Not wanted me but needs me. I need him too. I lay my head down on his chest, and he pulls me into his side. He plays a little with my hair. I feel his breathing regulate quickly. No one falls asleep faster than David Gelbert. I snuggle down and close my eyes, and as I drift off to sleep, I hear him.

"I love you so damn much, Natalie Lloyd. Remember that."

It's incredibly lovely and sweet. The words are still clogged in my throat, but I tighten my grip on him. I hope he knows.

"Come on." He's up and bouncing around the room as sunlight streams through the window. It's created highlights in his hair, and he's even more stunning. He throws some clothes on the bed, and I realize he's serious as he heads out to the living room.

I dress quickly.

"Where are we going?"

"Breakfast. I'm starving, and I have a full day of bullshit. I wanted to spend some time with you this morning." I go up on my tiptoes, which isn't enough, and wait for him to lean down to me. He does and slants his minty mouth over mine. His tongue sweeps in and out, and his hands find their way to my ass. He squeezes and kneads it and moans into my mouth. This man.

"Fuck."

I pull back. "What?"

"If we fuck, I won't have time to eat before I go out and meet Luis at the property."

"Can we, maybe, I don't know, do it quickly?" I curl my hair around my finger, and he growls. He pulls out a chair.

"Hard and fast it is, my lady."

My eyes flash desire at him. He kisses me roughly, then puts my back to his front. "Yes, please and thank you very flim-flam-ming much," I say. Then he peppers little bites down my neck, and I squirm while he laughs at me.

He's in my ear, and it's hot and low. "Bend over, Nat. I'm going to fuck that pussy from behind." He reaches into my cotton I'm-not-seeing-him-tonight panties. And quickly swirls my lady liquid over his fingers. A quick swipe up and down the hot zone, and he rips my undies down. Before I know it, I'm bent over the chair, and the Parade is ready to launch. He's kissing down my back, and the anticipation is killing me. He kisses down my butt. I flinch.

"Settle girl. Not today." He growls, then nips at my bottom

while his fingers thrust up into me, and I lurch forward. "Fuck, then pancakes."

"Mmmm. Yes."

"And now I want to lick raspberry jam off you again."

"We're out."

"But I'm in." And he thrusts all the way inside of me as we both gasp. And then he gets down to work. He pulls my hips to him, and I look back at him. He quickly bends down and kisses me as I welcome the Parade.

"Totally worth being late for," he says. I smile at him, then he slams into me, and I begin to moan.

"Can I take your order?" We're at Creekside Diner, and I've never been here. When we arrived, he nodded to a familiar group of men. They all greet him warmly, except his father. Apparently, all the dads of the 5 gather here to have coffee and breakfast once a week. They do it like their fathers did before them. I greeted them earlier, Arthur gave a gruff hello, but Will Whittier hopped up to give me a hug.

Poppy strolls in, waves to the dads, and sits down. David rolls his eyes. "What do you want, Pop?"

"Just here to grab some take-out."

"And—"

"Hi, Poppy!" I do like her a lot.

"Hi, Natalie. How are you?" David leers at her. They must have had another fight. They tend to bicker.

"David, you should know that my mother is currently with yours." He grips the table. This is a nasty fight.

"And what is dear Aunt Tina doing with my mom?"

"Holding things and setting things up. Things that should be set up in other places."

I shift in my seat. I think perhaps I need to leave them alone to work things out.

David says, "Where and when things get set up is at my mother's discretion. Oh, and mine. Not your mother's or yours. But thanks so much for the input and the ever-helpful meddling. You're a lamb to care."

His tone is sarcastic, and I don't know what to do.

"I'm having pancakes," I blurt out. I'm so flim-flamming confused right now.

Poppy forces a smile at David. He says, "You should be going, right, Poppy. My cousin. My blood and family. My loyalty will always lie with you, my sister from another mister."

She stands up and shoves him a little. I smile as I think David's teasing her.

"Nat, it's lovely to see you. Come by for lunch if you want. Tuesdays are usually slow, so we can chat and catch up."

The waitress nods at Poppy. She grabs a giant bag of food and turns to leave, but of course, David can't let her just go.

"That's an awful lot of food for someone so slight, Pop. Feeding the neighborhood or just a giant 6'5" Italian?"

"F U, David. FU." Then she curtseys and leaves.

David takes a sip of his coffee and stares out at the dads. There's a strange silence as he shuffles the menu. I know he knows by heart. Something's off.

"I don't know why but I'm going to ask this again. Are you ok?"

He snaps his attention to me and takes my hand. His face returns to normal David.

He says, "I will always be ok, if I have you. Poppy and I had a fight. It's always worse when she gets her mom involved with my mom. It's an age-old trick of Poppy's. Aunt Tina is kinder and more rational than my father, but she still a hardheaded Gelbert who thinks she always knows what's best for people. She gets my mom up in arms."

I run my fingernails up and down his forearms. He grins, and I see David clearly again.

"If there's anything you need."

"I know. I have a lot of shit on my plate, and sometimes it gets to me."

"You should go shoot hoops," I say brightly. He kisses my hands and then sucks on my fingers. I laugh at him.

"Yes. That's exactly what I'll do after breakfast. Well, maybe after I do you again."

I smile and sip my own coffee, my eyes never leaving his. Those words are getting harder and harder, not to say.

CHAPTER 22

DAVID

I'M EXHAUSTED after three weeks of juggling Natalie and Sadie. Plus, I have a project I'm working on for the new Pro/Ho tasting room and winter pruning. This is an entirely new level of fucking tired.

We have blocks of vines all over the valley and even out to the coast. Eventually, we'll go all estate with the vineyard property we purchased last fall. For now, I'm driving all the hell over the place to check on things. Sam is useless. He doesn't even come to Wednesday nights at the Starling Bar. He mopes around, and his beard is repulsive. It's so long, mountain-man nasty, instead of normally trimmed. Tabi offered to trim it for him, and he kicked her out of his house.

Sadie lives at my mom's house. Today is the first day she's at my house. Nat and I are perfect, but she knows I'm tired and distracted. I always pivot and change the subject. I won't lie to her. Just dancing around my reality is enough for now.

My mom thinks it's a good idea for me to take Sadie for a couple of hours today. Elle has assured me I'm prepared for this, and she will answer her phone if I call. I don't think I'm ready for this, but it's not like I have a choice. Sadie's starting to sit up a bit on her own. She does fall over a lot, so she's not so good at it.

"Hello. I'm your father. I know that sounds very *Star Wars*. But we haven't hung out a whole lot, and I want to make sure you know who I am." Sadie makes a soft snuffling sound and then gums on the primary-colored plastic keys Elle gave her. I think they look like a dog toy, but you can't take them away from Sadie. "Hi. I don't know what else to say. I'm supposed to get you used to my voice. So, I guess I'm keeping you. Your grandfather loves you but is disappointed in me, so he's looking for your mommy."

Jesus, what am I doing? I have nothing to say to this girl. "But don't worry, I'd never give her another crack at destroying your little Sadie ego." I nod, and she slams her little hand onto the ground. We're on the floor. I have her propped up against the couch. "Natalie changed everything. Natalie is wonderful and you might meet her someday, if I can figure out how to do it. My point being, until Nat, I didn't hook up with the most upstanding of women. Good gals, all of them, but I can't vouch for the chick who ditched you." Sadie laughs. I smile back at her.

"She ditched the cutest, sweetest Sadie in the world, and left her in my care. She doesn't get another chance. I mean, when you're sixteen, you can decide, but my instinct to protect you from this skank is strong." She pulls on my hand and shrieks a happy shriek. Her smile and eyes are big and bright. She keeps looking at my chest. I read babies should be presented with black patterns and shapes to help stimulate their brains. I don't have shit like that in my house except for the tattoos on my body. I took my shirt off. She keeps slapping the grapes on my arm like she knows it's her destiny.

"Shit, girl. I'm gone for you. I want to protect you from everything. Also, you may never kiss or hook up with anyone. You know how girls date their dads? Don't do that. In fact, don't date at all, and we'll stay cool." I pick up her little hand and high-five Princess Scribbles.

I pull out the list of things I'm supposed to do in this couple of hours. I scoop her up, and she keeps trying to pick the tattoos off of me. It's charming. I wish I could think of a better word than cute, but that's just Sadie.

And as cute as she is, I am glad she's going back to my parent's house later. I told Natalie I was having dental work done for the next couple of hours. It's the only mid-day activity thing I could think of, and I wouldn't be able to talk or text. And might lay me out for the night if I'm exhausted.

I place Sadie lying on her puzzle mat with the shit hanging over her. I call it the dojo. Because she tries to kick and hit the little squeaky things hanging down.

Next on the list is feeding her. She seems fine. I'm going to let that one slide. Burp. Ok. My mom included diagrams. I pick up Sadie. She's so delicate, I'm terrified I'm going to break her somehow. I gingerly place her over my shoulder and start patting her back like the picture. She's squirming and making silly noises. She squeaks, and I cannot tell you how adorable a baby burp is. I laugh despite my intense fear. That's done. And I rocked it.

I hold her in front of me and kiss her nose. It's a cute nose. I'm assuming it belongs to her mother because not one of us has a button nose or those little lips. This girl. This girl that belongs to me is cute, and we're getting along. Then the horror of her face makes my entire body freeze. Her face gets redder than anything I've ever seen, and she squinches into the tightest ball. There's a split second of silence as her mouth opens as wide as it can, and then it begins.

This ear-piercing screaming could seriously kill a man if it continues. Prisoners could be tortured with this high-pitched squeal. I begin to bounce her gently to stop it like Josh does with Emma. Does not work. In fact, pisses her off. I hold her up and smell her butt. Nothing seems to be wrong there.

I check the list. Tummy time is next. I panic. She's angry I messed up her schedule. I mean, this screeching is terrible. I inspect her quickly to make sure there's nothing I'm missing. Then I quickly move the dojo to the side and put her on her stomach. Then I back away from the wailing machine and wait for it to end. But it doesn't. Holy shit. It's worse. It's all worse. Somehow this minuscule fucking person is louder. Cats and dogs are going to start showing up here because of her screech. Hell, lost sailors at sea can hear her siren call. She's worse. This is some serious, painful crying. My heart is out of my chest that she's this upset.

I snatch her up and put her back on my shoulder. Maybe she needs more burping. She seemed to like that. And now I've put the Miami Sound Machine of Death directly next to my ear. I panic. There's something wrong. I mean, seriously wrong. I try to take her out of her tiny pink outfit to make sure there's no splinter or a sharp knife sticking out of her somewhere. I can't explain the look of pain and the sheer volume of screeching. She seems fine. Not bleeding. But now she's angrier. I've made her even worse.

Her whole body is mottled with bright red anger. I've seen women pissed at me before, but usually, a quick drink or dinner would satisfy them. I don't think being clever and charming is going to fix this situation.

"Sadie. Sadie. Shh. Please. Please, Sadie girl. Scribbles. Shush. Hush. Shh. Shh. It's ok, baby girl. It's ok. I got you." I bounce her up and down and sway. I try to sing over her volume. I can't think of anything else but the Dixie Chicks, "I'm not ready to make nice. I'm not ready to back down." Nope. She doesn't get the irony and isn't even remotely soothed. I am reaching for my shirt—we're going somewhere with people who know what the fuck they're doing because clearly, I do not.

I grab my shirt and knock over the can of powdered formula. Shit. Shit. Shit. The bottle. Could she be this mad over the bottle? Fuck. I panic. I scoop her up in just her diaper with the pink thing hanging off her feet. I couldn't get it all the way off because she was thrashing so much.

I say to her in an authoritative but kind tone, "Sadie. Chill. Chill out. Chill out for Daddy. Daddy needs to calm down. SHHH. Fuck. Calm down. I'm sorry. Daddy's sorry. Sadie, please chill the fuck out." I hold her a little like a football while I scramble for the tin of formula. I manage to get the lid off, but I spill half the container. There's a scoop, but I don't know how many scoops to give her.

"Sadie. Quick, how many scoops of powdered space food do you get?"

She answers by screaming so loud I can't fathom how the police aren't here investigating a mass murder. I shove some of the powder into the bottle. I'm covered in it. It's starting to make me sticky as it clings to my skin. My shirt is only half on. I add water. I fill the little bottle with water while trying to bounce her on my forearm. None of this is fun. Why the fuck do people choose this? What the hell? Josh and Elle are fucking crazy. They're going to have three screeching shit machines in their house, voluntarily.

"Sadie, I'm working on it. Give it a rest. Come on, Sadie. Cut me some slack, Scribbles. Sadie, damn." I feel like she's been screeching for a couple of hours now. Even though, in reality, it's been like ten minutes. Ten minutes of time-bending hell. Baby screaming time is the most extended increment of time known to man. If this bottle doesn't work, I may lose my mind.

I put her up on my shoulder again. I'll deal with the deafness later. I scramble one-handed to put the ring thing back on, then the nipple, and shake it all up. I put her into the cradle of my arms as she continues to hate me and wail. She's all woman. Most of them hate me and wail at me when I don't do what they want. The difference is, I want to do what she wants. I just don't know what the fuck that is!

I give her the bottle, and her tiny hands instantly wrap around it. She blinks the tears from her eyes and begins to suck. "Damn, girl. You were hangry. You are totally my kid. I'm a fucking genius for figuring out what you needed. Food."

I've never felt more elation of accomplishment than figuring out how to stop Sadie from crying. I made a half-court shot at the buzzer once. This is fucking better. Five minutes ago, I never felt more like a failure in my life. This is something. Finally. I rub my thumb over her light hairline and smooth back her crimson wisps. She's staring at me while sucking it back.

I glance at the list. Shit. The burping comes after the bottle. Makes sense. Think of it like chugging beer. You chug a bottle. You're going to belch. I'm afraid to move out of the kitchen, but I want to sit on my couch. I grab the list and head over there. She doesn't seem to mind the movement and the bottle is almost all gone. The list says not to give her another one. Just the one. Her eyes are fluttering closed. I want to let her sleep, but the beer-belching thing comes to mind. I hate feeling full like that.

She finishes, and I pull the bottle from her lips with a tiny pop. She stares at me like she actually sees me and not a blob. "Sadie. Sadie Baby Girl. Daddy's going to burp you now, ok. Don't cry again. Please. Let's all just sit in this little victory for a second, ok." I place her on my shoulder and begin patting her back, and like a fucking champ, a significant Gelbert-worthy belch erupts from my kid.

"Awesome job. Top-notch. High marks for that one, kid." I kiss her tummy, and she giggles. So, I do it again. She's smacking my head with her stiff robot arms. She snuffles and coos, and I put her clothes back on. I check the stripe on the diaper, and she's still dry. Thank God. I don't think I'm ready for that, solo. I cradle her in my arms. I told her I'm her father. I called myself her daddy. I've never done that before. I'm not sure I hated it.

She squirms, getting comfortable, and I cover her with a blanket. I know I'm supposed to do that burrito wrap thing, but I'm not leaving her with the blanket alone. She'll fall asleep in my arms. After that, she can sleep on the couch. If it's good enough for me, it's good enough for Sadie. Actually, I'm going to need a better couch for her. She should have better things.

"I don't know any fairy tales. Sorry. Um. I guess we could get some. Or your grandmother most certainly has some. She can read them to you. Oooh. I do know one. Settle in. This is a good one. Once upon a time, way back in 2015, there were five men, Steph, Klay, Dray, Harrison, and Andrew, and they were mighty warriors. Golden warriors with the power to command a magical sphere."

CHAPTER 23

DAVID

MOM: David. We need to talk about Sadie.

DAVID: Ok. Soon. I have too much Pro/Ho stuff today, then hanging with Nat. Love you. Kisses to Scribbles.

MOM: Fine.

I'm standing in the Pro/Ho tasting room. My own fucking space. Well, the 5's space. But it's more mine than even my house —my mother decorated that. It's finally framed, mudded, and plumbed. They were able to salvage a lot of the original structure while expanding the footprint. We can stock, sell and pour our wine from here. The permits for everything have been filed by the ever-efficient Natalie. The electricians will finish up in a few days, but I'm installing the piece for our counter today.

I took all of those old metal signs they found on the property, mainly in the red equipment barn. I've sanded, restored, and welded them together with some of the original barn wood into a counter. I used the original sign from the property about tractor repair service to be the base of the counter. It's the first thing you'll see when you walk in. The rest of the signs are a mishmash of local wineries that no longer exist. Or better yet, some are the farms that formed the valley to begin with. The farms are gone, but now they're familiar names of streets and roads around here. Like 'Hap' Arnold, the road's namesake, where our new winery finds its home. We found a rusted-out sign you can just make out that says, "El Rancho Feliz." They named their farm the Happy Ranch.

My phone dings.

BECCA: Have you told Natalie yet?

DAVID: No. Why?

BECCA: Dear Auntie T is on a rampage of forthright high horseness.

DAVID: Fuck me.

BECCA: Just thought I'd give you a head's up.

DAVID: Poppy up in it, I'm sure.

BECCA: I'm staying at my house in Napa, where it's all family-free.

DAVID: Good call. Can I come?

BECCA: NO. And Dad's on his sister's side. Not yours.

DAVID: There's a fucking surprise.

BECCA: Not.

I scrub my hands over my face and try to shake off my anger at my aunt. She can't help but get involved. I'm sure my dad is yelling at my mom, and poor Princess Scribbles has to endure it all because I'm a fucking pussy who can't tell his girlfriend he has a kid. I turn around and try to get my happy back.

There are giant wooden double doors on this little shack. Tabi insisted there be a peephole speakeasy door, Prohibition style. So if people want to come in, they have to knock, then someone will have to slide the window open, and whatever they say will be the correct password. I give the whole thing about a week before we're super fucking sick of walking over to the door and going through Tabi's little skit. She can do it all she wants, but the rest of us will tell her to fuck off very soon.

I glance out of the back windows of the tasting room to the

old barn that will become our crush pad. The steel tanks go in after we pour the concrete next week. I'm putting in a hoop. I know we'll all use it, but I need it. We're going to be working out here, and it's far from my house. I need the ability to shoot the rock whenever I want.

The vines looked good and are starting to swell. I know when they pop, I'll get misty looking at vines that belong to us. Bax and Tabi's house will sit at the far end of the property, and it's still for shit. This dilapidated old farmhouse that they dream of renovating is still a disaster. We all banded together to try to get the winery and tasting room up and running by spring. Tabi and Bax's dreamhouse has to wait. The crush pad and lab are a priority to be functional before the next harvest. The bottling equipment and labeler will wait until after their house is done. We can still do that at our assorted family wineries.

I have too much energy. You'd think running a winery, dating someone seriously, and being a dad of a toddler would send me to sleep, but I have a twitch to be active. I swear if I were a different dude, I'd be a junkie. I need something to do with my hands always. The ADHA bullshit testing I'd been through when I was younger was endless. Once diagnosed, my father thought it was a neat little excuse to hang his hatred on. He probably still thinks it's something you can snap out of. Not sure we'll ever figure out how to be in the same room together, and I listen to all of my mother's crap as she explains how much she loves the man. He does treat her better than the rest of us. Even perfect Becca isn't above his insults. Asshole. Not sure how I've gotten to be thirty-six years old, and still can't fucking understand how he has a successful winery, a full group of loving friends, and a devoted wife. All l see is his mistrust and disgust with me.

When I was playing ball, we were good. I knew what he expected. Our goals aligned and we were in sync. Once I gave up basketball and came home to work, things went to shit again. My grandfather was a loving guy, so I can't even blame his attitude on that shit. Whatever.

I crank some Zeppelin, pull out my drill, and start attaching the metal and wood panels to the top of the barn wood base I built. To the credit of the rest, they let me run with this idea. Josh is too busy as babies number 2, and 3 get closer. Tabi and Bax are incredibly busy trying to get a baby of their own. Sam's still MIA, obsessed with finding her. He's finally started showing up on Wednesday nights, but he's kind of a shell of himself. Fucking freaky. We've all read the note, and it's cryptic. He moved into his parent's house back at the Langerford vineyard. He really only talks to Josh and Elle.

My mind drifts to Sadie. It's been a day since I've seen her. Things are amping up here. My mom has it handled, though. Sadie seems to like me now, and I like being with her as well. It's fucked up. I miss her when I'm with Nat, and I desperately miss Nat when I'm with her.

Natalie and I are still clicking, but she still hasn't told me she loves me. I know she does. I continue to tell her, but I'm biding my time. The longer the Sadie secret festers, the more anxious I get about the I love you. I need it. Once I have it, I'll feel confident enough to tell her. We still don't know who the mom is, and there's no custody loophole yet.

The temporary door on the tasting room keeps flapping and squeaking. It's windy out today and not very nice. I glance at the door just as I'm securing the last piece of the countertop. I see the wind blowing around my favorite blonde hair. My entire being lightens. Different from when Sadie's mood elevates me. Fuck I love her. She won't leave. I won't let her. We can figure it out.

Done. I'm done keeping them separate, and I'll fight for both of them. I'm going to tell Natalie this weekend. Time for me to control the narrative. I think we're in a solid place. She just needs to meet her. If Princess Scribbles can charm my dad, she can undoubtedly turn Natalie.

I turn Zep down and yell, "Get your cute ass in here. Don't fucking lurk." She steps through the door and puts her hands on her hot and haughty little hips. My heart really is hers. I can't explain it. But lately, there's an icy little bite like a papercut every time we're together. I'd feel better about telling her if she'd say the damn words.

I need my mom to hold on for a touch more. I just need to put the words together. Sadie seems happy, though. The only one who ever balks at the situation is Poppy. She and her mom chat nonstop about the situation to my mother. Aunt Tina and my dad make the perfect siblings, always knowing what someone else should do instead of looking inward.

Natalie still hasn't moved. "Come here. I need the taste of you on my lips." She grins and rolls her eyes at me. But she does walk over, and I lean over the newly finished bar and give her a quick peck to the lips.

"Wow. David, this is gorgeous. You were right. This is so much more than just a tasting room. It's a vibe."

"Babe, I won't lie. I know what I'm doing when it comes to dazzling." I leap up on the bar and swing my legs around to trap her. She's eye level with my dick, but I need to overlook that fact. She cocks her head, realizing what I've done. "I wanted to give the people something beautiful to look at. Right at eye level."

"I get it. The Parade route wasn't available all the time, so you had to do this piece of art counter."

I smile at her. "It's not art. It's just a counter." She smacks my legs until I open and release her from between my legs. I jump down off the counter, scoop her up and reverse our position. I kiss her, and her soft lips transport me again to a place I never thought I'd want to be. Utterly committed to her. She nips at my bottom lip, and I seize the open mouth opportunity to get my tongue into her. I'll take any part of her. There's nothing like the taste of my Sunshine. She tangles with me, and the kiss begins to amp up. I grab the back of her head and pull her hair a touch to put her where I want her. She moans.

"Well, Natalie, is this an invitation to christen the space?"

She smiles. "No. Kissing is all we have for a day or two if you know what I mean."

"I most certainly do not. I get to play this body anyway I want, so I'm not sure what these new restrictions are about."

"It's you know, women things are happening."

"Period. Who cares? I feel like if we put my head in your mouth, we could work around the problem together."

She laughs. And I continue, "You know I don't need that part of you to make you come. Has anyone ever sucked your tits in the most perfect manner where you lost your mind and came so hard you blacked out?"

Her face flames for a second. She's so embarrassed by certain things it's insane. But she never stops me. She secretly loves it.

I say, "I'm not going to stop teasing, biting, sucking until we both come." I kiss her hard, and she gasps into my mouth. I move her closer and squeeze her perfect ass a little too much. "And there's always this." Her eyes darken as her whole demeanor stiffens. I kiss her neck, and she relaxes into my touch.

She sputters, "Talking about my rear end like that makes me squirmy. Stop it."

I have no clue if squirmy means someday I get through the back door or if it's a no-go.

She kisses me quickly and changes the subject. "Start talking about this artwork. Is that what you've been doing with all the time away from me lately?"

Shit. I dig my tongue into her mouth again. Never gets old. It's always thrilling to kiss her. I'm a jackass. But I'm going to tell her. No matter what.

I pull back and smack her delicious ass. "It's a bunch of metal. Not art."

"Bullpoop. I saw the new thing you made leaning up against your garage when I stopped by earlier looking for you." That's scary as fuck. What if I was there with Sadie? The pop in from the love of my life shouldn't be stress inducing.

I say, "Fucking around. It's for the new nursery for the Whittier babies." And right there is my first out and out lie to her. It's a thing for Sadie's room at my parents' house I'm just fucking around with. It's some welded metal in the shape of a seahorse. Like the things, she likes to bathe with. I dash over to the cash register and find a pen. I date the top of the Post-it in my color and write down what I just said. I put it in my back pocket. I'm going to write down every lie I tell her and hand them to her after I tell her about Sadie this weekend. I hope it will show how much she means to me. Or I'm the same lying shit heel I've been most of my life.

"What was that?"

"Secrets." And that is not a lie. I smirk. Hoping charm covers up panic and guilt.

She smiles and says, "That's art." She needs to stop being kind to me.

"No. That's boredom." Art classes always bolstered my GPA and grounded me so I could stay on the team. I don't have the concentration for reading literature. Math, I can do, but long passages of reading are really hard for me. It's why I was promised no paperwork when I went to work with my friends. It takes me ten times longer than anyone else because I can't focus on it. The welding shit helped me focus in college, and I've stepped it up since I've had more responsibility at Pro/Ho.

Not being able to do all the paperwork shit and purchasing stuff are things my father and I fought about a lot when I tried to work for him. He'd yell about being efficient, and I'd tell him to fuck off. My brain doesn't focus that way, but that's not something he wants to hear.

That's who Arthur Gelbert is, efficient. When I was growing up, drawing, welding metal, and basketball made sense when words and my father didn't. But it's not art. I walk away from her, so I don't have to discuss this further. I put down the drill and take off the goggles from the top of my head. She jumps down and follows me, but I duck behind the bar and point at her.

"Sit." She drags a high-top chair from one of the little tasting tables over the counter. In the future, the chairs will only be at the scattered high-top tables in the little garden area. Tabi's having it cleared just behind here up on a small hill, so people can sip outside and look over the property. Her house will be mostly hidden, but people could actually see us working in some of the barns if they wish. We're still debating about putting in a cave or just using a warehouse for barrel aging. I'd love a cave, but it's a considerable expense to dig out and get right, and I'm not sure I have the balls to ask Josh for even more money to invest. I know he has it, but it feels strange asking your friend for money.

I grab twelve glasses and line them up in two rows of six.

"What are you doing?"

"Fixing your palate, Sunshine." That megawatt smile beams at me. She's been begging us all to teach her everything we know about wine, but the problem growing up in it is you don't know anything different. I'm not sure what she knows or what she doesn't because it's so innate to who I am. But I do know she sneered her little face up at the mention of Merlot. The movie *Sideways* really screwed over that amazing little grape. Sam was prepping a wine club family variety pack shipment, and we did a little tasting a couple of days ago. Not that he was any help, but he did go to each winery and pick up a couple of options for us to taste. We narrowed the family selections and decided on the newest Pro/Ho Merlot called: "Yes, You Are Drinking F'ing Merlot." I named it myself. Bax hates the name, but since I'm the only one consistently doing any fucking work at Pro/Ho, the name stays.

I pull out the bottles, line them up behind the glasses, then pour a splash of each into both sets of glasses. Then I grab the little buckets and hand one to her.

"You can spit if you like. It's only going to be a sip or two of each one, or you can drink the two glasses it's going to add up to."

She grins and pushes the bucket back to me.

"What are we drinking?"

"Merlot." And there's that nose crinkle. "You've got this grape all wrong. It's the velvet on your tongue, it's the lube in a good red blend, and it's the easy Sunday morning feeling."

"If you say so."

"It's my very favorite grape. It needs the right soil and temperament to flourish. It's the velvet in a blend smoothing everything out. I love it on it's own but when blended just the right way, it's magic. You have to pay attention, but it can thrive when given the right path. It can be tricky to blend sometimes, but it's so worth it. When you marry two or three distinct varietals together, and they taste better together than alone, there's no other feeling than doing it correctly." I smile at her and push an errant hair back. She leans into my touch.

"And what if you blend them incorrectly?"

"Then it all goes to shit."

I wish she knew I was currently speaking in metaphor. I need another Post-it.

CHAPTER 24

NAT

I'M RUNNING my hands through his red scruff, and he's smiling like a dog in the sun. He's said it. He's said it many, many times. I feel it from him. And I can't possibly imagine being without him. I have to tell him. I've only ever said these words to inanimate objects and a mistake of an ex. My heart is guiding this moment, and for the first time, I can believe what he keeps telling me. I'm lying on his chest, and the world of perfection is swirling around us. He kisses me sweetly, then flops back down on the pillow.

The scent around us is the mixture of us, and it hints at forever. I was complete and settled into being very good at my job and having a few friends around who would drift in and out of my life. Then Baxter Schroeder. Taking the job as his assistant in Washington DC changed my entire life. I never thought I'd have friends who stuck around. When Tabi called me and told me he needed me on his campaign bus, it was the first time someone didn't forget me after they left. I've always kept friends and lovers at arm's length because history has taught me everything is temporary.

Then Bax sat me down and invited me to help build Pro/Ho

into something. Then Tabi, Bax, Josh, Sam, and this gorgeous, thoughtful, playful man lying under me gave me a home. I've never had permanence in my life, and that's what this man promises me. I was put on this earth for this moment, and it's about to swallow me whole.

"David." He cracks his eyes open and moans. Then he runs his hands through my hair. We're still slick with sweat from the amount of sex we keep having. I vamp. I'm not sure I can say this, and I'm not sure I'll ever be able to repeat it, but if I don't let it out right now, it might choke me with emotion. It's so big I can't contain it.

"David."

He whispers, "Yes, beautiful." I move my hand to his heart. I feel it beating, and I know it's for me.

My shaky voice says, "I love you."

He says nothing but curls his arm around me tighter. I wait with bated breath to hear his reply, to hear the confirmation I'm not alone.

"It's about damn time." True to form, he says what he wants, not what I want to hear. But it's what I need. He knew we were fated. It just took me a while to get here.

"Nat." I brace myself to hear it reflected back at me. "I'm starving." I sit up and glare. He's always starving. The sun is streaming under the curtains in his bedroom. He has this bed made of big thick wooden beams. It could be out of a ski lodge or a cabin. It's the safest place in the world. I watch his incredibly toned butt walk across the room. He glances back. "Are you checking me out, Sunshine? It's making me squirmy when you look at my rear end." He wiggles it.

"Hmmm." I sigh.

"You are a super-secret little sunshiny slut, aren't you?" I bite my lip, and he leaps back onto the bed, scooping me into his arms. His tongue makes itself comfortable in my mouth once again. I'm all his.

"And I love you. A lot. Like Kevin Durant a lot. You know that. I've told you that. But there are things I need to tell you about my life. Things you need to know and be a part of. Come on." He jumps off me and flicks his head towards the door.

"What things?" This sounds ominous. He tosses on a t-shirt, then pulls me off the bed and into his arms.

He kisses the top of my head. "Be gone furrowed brow. I'm not married or a convict. No worries. But we need food. You've fucked me silly. I'm starving, and my cock needs a minute before I make you come again. Seriously, you've been so open and honest about your life. It's time for me to come clean about something. But it won't change the fact I've never been so hopelessly gone for someone in my life. You are mine. And I'm yours. That's not only a fact, but it's forever." He shrugs as if it's not a monumental statement. He pulls on his sneakers.

He hugs me to him a little too tight. He says, "We're a done fucking deal. You're my north star. You're my special edition Doritos." I try to wiggle away from him. This really is too much. I just eked out an 'I Love You,' and he's talking about marrying me.

His hands are on my shoulders, and he captures me with his eyes. "I never want you to doubt my feelings for you. When you're ready, I want to give you everything. But I know that's not something you're used to, and I know you well enough to know after we have our breakfast chat, it's going to be a minute before you want to see me. But I'll be here, waiting. Always."

He cups my face and kisses me softly. His tongue licking my lips until I open to him. As I do all the vulnerability, worry, and doubt about the things he just said flood into him and evaporate.

He pulls back, still holding my face in his. "I want NO ONE in my life more than you."

He lets go and turns away. There really is something else. All that time away from me. What the hell is he hinting at? Is he sick? Or moving away? Secret identity? I gasp. I don't know what he has to tell me, but I believe he loves me. Thoroughly and completely.

I say, "You can tell me anything. I can take it." He pulls on a pair of cargo shorts over his shoes. He probably didn't think it all through. He does that. I'm a little sad because his perfect bubble butt is covered up.

His voice cracks a bit. "I know you can. But I'm not sure I can."

I panic. "Are you sick?"

"No. But it is a permanent thing. And I just misspoke. I want no one in my life the way you're in my life."

"You're scaring me. And I'm starving. And stop talking in riddles. They're ways of saying nothing and everything, and I'm too orgasm-brained to figure it out."

He slaps me on my ass and says, "Get dressed. We're heading to L'ours Noir. I need a Joe Bear scramble." He calls the Black Bear Diner by a made-up French name, thinking it makes it fancy because we're in Wine Country, and everything has to be fancy. But it's just a delicious diner with giant plates of food.

"Wait. I thought we were supposed to go to some brunch with the 5 because Elle got new dishes she's insanely excited about."

He yells from the bathroom, "Nah. I need you to myself. We have much to discuss, my secret Sunshiny slut."

I head to the kitchen to find my bra. On the way, I hand his old Sonoma High School hoodie on my head. It drowns me, but I roll up the sleeves and pair it with leggings. He laughs at my strange get-up, but it's so I can throw on my bra once I find it.

There's an aggressive knock at his door. He comes out and smiles at me as I duck behind the kitchen island to find my underwear. He doesn't get to the door fast enough. It's kicked open. I pop up, then realize my breasts are out. I quickly zip up in front of his mother, who is carrying a baby.

I don't know what is happening. David's eyes shoot to mine.

"David Allen Gelbert. My darling. You can't take a hint. We're done. It is time for you to grow up. I'm siding with your father and the family on this. Clean up your own backyard. Do you hear me?" I can't focus on anything except the redheaded child she's holding. I like Jana a lot, and I've never seen her angry, but right now, she's furious.

"Mom. Can you come back in like an hour? I need a minute to clarify things. Please." He seems desperate for her to leave.

"Not one more second. I love this one more than I can ever tell you, but it's time for you to step up." She steps to the side to let a bunch of movers carrying a crib and other baby-like things inside David's house. He's staring at me, and his eyes are very wide, but I'm sure they don't compare the width of mine. This is a kooky and ooky feeling times like a thousand.

His face snaps to his mother. "David! Tell them where to put your daughter's things."

His face shoots to mine. My entire body is one giant wavy line. I can't keep my feet planted, my head is light and dizzy, and my stomach churns. I'm swaying back and forth. He sees me. He doesn't run to me to see if I'm ok. But turns to his mother and nods. He takes the baby, who looks so much like him it's insane. She lights up when he holds her and his expression slashes me. Slashes through all we just said and shared. He's in love with her.

Most women would swoon at the way he looks at his daughter, but it just tells me he's been lying to me. I don't have his whole heart, and I gave him mine. I don't know what to make of that. I don't know my place, and it feels very much like when a new baby would replace me. Four different foster homes made room in their lives for a baby by giving them my room. I turn and throw up. Jana runs to me.

"I didn't see you there, Natalie. Dear, are you ok?" I continue to dry heave, and I hear the baby babble behind me. Jana rubs my back and rinses the sink. Then she gets me a glass of water. I drink it greedily after rinsing out my mouth.

"Are you sick?" She turns to David and says, "I can take the baby until we know you're not contagious."

David speaks. Our eyes lock as I wipe my mouth with a paper towel. He never looks away. "She's not sick, Mom. We're all fine. She's just in shock, and I need you to leave."

I say the first thing since that baby came here. "No worries. I'm on my way out."

He shifts the baby to his hip as if it's the most natural thing in the world. When did this happen? How long has this baby been around? We've been together for almost six months. She's clearly bigger than a newborn. I don't know baby sizes. But did he know about her when we got together? Has everyone been keeping this from me? I'm so embarrassed. Who is the mom? Did he love her too? Oh. No. They're together, or they're co-parenting. I'm an accessory.

I turn to grab my bag from the couch.

His mom leans back on the counter. His voice is strong and dominating. "Nat, stay. Mom, get out. Natalie, don't you dare move." The baby girl makes a noise. He lowers his voice, but it still has the same power. But now, it has a syrupy sweet tone to it. "Sadie, you're going to the dojo. Daddy needs to talk to Natalie. And then we're all getting some goddamned breakfast."

"David. You can't kick me out." His mother crosses her arms and glares at him. He doesn't hesitate.

"Yes. I can. Thank you for everything. I have it from here. I will call you. Take Dad and go back to the city. Far from me." At least he chose me over his mom.

"I have news about Sadie's mom. Becca called with the particulars of what you'll need."

Both of our heads snap to hers. He leers at his mother and grits his teeth. "GO. I don't want to know. Get out now so I can repair this damage. You are not currently welcome here, Mom."

She fixes her hair by fluffing up the ends with her fingers. Then she walks over to David. She glares at him. The movers come out from the back bedroom, hand David a bill and leave. Jana kisses the little girl.

"Sadie. Mhamó loves you." Jana tears up a little as she kisses the little girl, who grabs a fistful of her hair and yells gibberish. "That's right, sweet girl, I love you. Your Daideó and Mhamó love you so, little one. Good luck with your daddy."

David looks frustrated. "Why do people keep fucking saying that? I've got this. Those are Aunt T and Pop's words, not yours."

"All they did was open my eyes. You've never been responsible for anything in your life except vines, and it's time to step up."

"I never expected this from you, Mom. To only see what people are telling you. Get out. Get the fuck out right now."

His face has fallen at her words. I want to go to him, but the baby is in the way. She turns to me. "Natalie, it was lovely to see you. Good luck to you too." And with that, she turns and walks out, closing the door behind her. David and his daughter turn to me.

His face shifts to that of concern and love. "Nat."

"Stop. I don't think I can handle this. You know I can't." He puts his hand up to me. I can't deal with all of this.

"Then let's go slow. This is Sadie Gelbert. My daughter. This is what I wanted to tell you about over eggs. The timeline is a little accelerated. I don't have toast and raspberry jam in front of you but let's remedy that."

"No. I can't handle this." Tears fill my eyes, and my body goes into emotional lockdown. I know how to do this. I can feel it happening. Cold frost starting at my toes, it will creep upward until I'm closed off to him. It's not happening fast enough. I need to shut this situation down, now.

His voice is clear but altered. It's not my David. "You can handle this. You're the strongest person I've ever known. And what I was going to tell you, until we were so rudely interrupted by life, is I've been falling in love with two of the most amazing people I've had the privilege to know."

I look at my purse on the couch, and it's too far away for me to escape. And he's blocking the door.

I'm numb and stunned, and I want out of here. My purse might as well be a hefty garbage bag because the history of my life seems to be repeating itself. At least I got to say I love you once in my life. I meant it. And that's what's really going to suck.

CHAPTER 25

DAVID

SADIE HAS GONE QUIET. "Nat. Come on. Everything looks better after pancakes."

"You lied to me."

"Look. I was not good with this either. I didn't think I could do it. But with practice, I'm ready to do this. You don't have to. You just need to let me love you, and you love me. And I only lied to you three times. I wrote them down. This, I just didn't tell you."

"THIS IS A HUGE THING NOT TO TELL ME." Sadie starts crying, and I bounce her on my hip, go to the drawer near Natalie, and pull out the magic neon primary-colored keys. She takes them greedily, smacks them against my chest, then puts them in her mouth.

"I'm terrible with babies. I can't do this. I can't with babies." I know that it has nothing to do with her prowess with babies. I've seen her with Emma. It's the lying thing. Or the no children thing. But those are things we can get past. I'm desperate for her to stay and talk this through. Sadie squeals and I smile at her. Nat's face falls. Shit.

"Look, I'm pretty terrible with babies. Ask her. I mean, I kind of suck at it. It's all about test and adjust. You try one thing, then pivot to the next. It's a lot like playing man to man rather than a zone defense. It took me a minute. I'm not good, and I'm terrified to be with her for more than a couple of hours."

I see her wind up a bit. "How is this possible? HOW?!" Sadie howls and I grab her bunny. She tucks it under her neck and puts her head down on my shoulder. I instinctively kiss the top of her head. Then, I bounce just a little as I talk to Nat.

I say, "I don't know much, but I do know screaming at them is not their favorite." I pull the dojo from the closet, and Sadie starts kicking. I put the mat down, then her in the middle of her favorite chaos, and she goes to work, spinning and pulling on the stupid plastic fish. I look over at the kitchen. She's still frozen in place.

Nat smiles, and a tear goes down her cheek. I rush to her, and she backs away from me. Shit. This is precisely what I thought would happen. I hoped it wouldn't. I've been waiting for her to tell me she loved me. I thought it would be weeks ago, but I can't fucking change this moment. I've kept this from her for five weeks. That's it. We can surely survive this.

I stare at Natalie's beautiful blue eyes as they slowly cloud over. I've broken everything I thought I'd fixed in her soul. She was so shattered, and I painstakingly and carefully picked up as many pieces of her lovely soul to put them back together. With each moment we spent together, she opened my heart and mind more. We were meant to heal each other, and now I see it. I've destroyed her, and I'm not sure if it's just Sadie or my dumbass plan of not telling her until she was totally in love with me the way I am with her.

"You're not safe anymore," she utters, and it's terrible. I mean, like a javelin through the fucking heart terrible.

"Stay here. In fact, give me your bag."

"What?"

I snatch it off the couch before she can and smile at her. My entire body relaxing as I look at her. She needs to know I'm the same as I was twenty minutes ago. My mother doesn't matter now. "Please don't leave. We're not done."

"I think we are. I don't live that far. I can walk," she says resolutely.

I smirk at her. "The climb up to Lookout cottage will take you and your short legs like three weeks. I don't have that kind of time to nurse you back to health after you try and scale Mt. Whittier. You're not dressed for it, and you really should reserve a Sherpa well in advance."

The corners of her mouth turn up slightly. She doesn't want to laugh. I've got her. "Stay right here." Sadie is howling, so I pick her back up and thrust the damn keys in her hands, and she starts jabbering away. I look at Natalie watching us.

Sadie throws her keys to the ground, and they land at Natalie's feet. She bends over and retrieves them. It's like she's on instinct. Then she walks to the sink, rinses them off, and hands them back.

"Here, baby." She steps back as if it were her job to retrieve them, and she didn't actually want to perform this task. I'm well and truly fucked again. But maybe I can convince her this is who we can be.

I hurry to the backroom that's now officially Sadie's, I guess, because my mother decided it's time for me to be her dad. Fuck Jana and her timing. This whole plan reeks of my Aunt Tina— she's been yammering at my mother to cut me off and let me handle my mess. Poppy. Fuck that. Everyone else in this village gets help. I needed it and took it. My cousin can be an annoying goody-two-shoes rule follower.

She has this streak of stubborn right and wrong. I'm in the room searching for Sadie's luggage. The only thing Sadie has of her mom's. I sling it over my shoulder and pull the car seat from under the extra blankets out of the closet. I reenter the living room, and Nat has her arms wrapped around herself.

"Let's go. I'm going to kill someone if there's a line for a table."

"You still want to go to breakfast."

"Yes."

"With the baby?"

"Sadie."

She stares at me. "How do we have a conversation with her with us?" Her face is all screwed up in confusion.

"You seem to know less about babies than I did. And trust me, I knew like a minuscule amount." I shrug. Charming has to work. She has to come with us. If she's still talking to me, I have a chance to dig us out from under this. I can absolutely figure out how to fix this.

"Where has that seat been?" Nat starts circling toward the front of my house. I don't know if she's trying to get away or needs to move.

I slowly follow her, keeping an eye on Scribbles. "Back closet, hidden. And I know you're going to think that's more betrayal, so stop right now. It's all part of the same betrayal. There's no reason to get more upset or angry with every little thing that gets revealed about Princess Scribbles." Nat cocks her head. "Long story. Let me shove some maple syrup down your throat. Kiss your sweet sticky lips, and we'll talk about this. I'll tell you everything. I know it's all fucked up right now—"

"You just swore in front of the baby."

"Sadie." She won't say her name. She's already detaching from us. Shit.

"You swore."

"She doesn't understand language, and really when you're a baby who is a product of a one-night stand and abandoned by your mom if fuck is your first word, you're entitled to it. Would that really be the worst thing?"

"Yes. Her first word should be dog or mom. Wait. Ships and crackers. Abandoned?"

I nod. Her eyes go to Sadie. This isn't how I wanted them to bond. I wanted them to like each other or at least do it for me. I don't want their bond to be one of abandonment and pain. Nat won't come near me, so I step to her.

Sadie's cooing and really helping my case. This is the Sadie I need to woo Natalie. Satan Sadie is not anything Nat's prepared for at this time. I take Natalie's hand and pull her with me. I hand her bag to her.

"You can go. If that's what you need. But I'll follow you. I'll be wherever you are. Hell, you work with me. You can't escape me. I have to tell you, as dark and crappy as all this seems, for the first time in five weeks, I see a pinhole of something bigger than both of us."

"You can't make me love your daughter." Her voice has an edge to it, I've never heard before. She moves her purse in front of her like a shield.

"Sadie," I whisper.

"I won't. I'm incapable. I don't want any of this or anything to do with that baby."

Say her fucking name, Nat. Please.

"Sadie. But you want me, right?" I find my footing quickly. I'm not a guy who's good with no. Competitive nature and all that.

"I don't know." I open the door, then grab the car seat. I'm an expert at getting it in and out now, and I can do with Sadie in my arms. I settle her and hand her Vino Bunny, the wonder Rabbit, and she grabs it and instantly puts an ear in her mouth. She's kicking in excitement, and I gaze at her lovingly. I kiss her nose, and she shrieks with laughter. I smile and look over to Natalie.

Tears are pouring down her face. I close the car door and open the passenger door.

She turns and goes to her own car.

"No. That's not how this works. You let me apologize and explain. And you listen. Then you take time to work this out, come back to me, and we live happily ever after. That's the fucking agenda here, Natalie."

She turns to me. "Not my agenda. This is how I work. This is actually what I'm designed for. Impermanence. Moving on. The only thing constant—"

"Is change, and it can be a good thing," I finish her sentence.

Her blue eyes are already puffy from the tears. Her words come out in bursts through her controlled hysterics, and it's the most painful thing I've ever witnessed. I'm horrified by the redness overtaking her skin. I don't know if it's anger or sorrow, but I know I'm responsible.

"I was going to say, the only thing constant is there's no room for me."

My mouth drops into a horrified expression. She puts her car in reverse and pulls out of the driveway before I can even close the door. Sadie starts yelling from inside my car, and I can't go after Natalie. I have to take care of Sadie. And the thing she just said slams into my heart and my head, and I'm terrified it's true.

CHAPTER 26

DAVID

"SADIE, Daddy fucked up. I mean fucked up. I never intended for Nat to be your mom. I think you have one of those. Although I can't even come up with an image, let alone a name to give you who she is. But you'd like Natalie. She can be like your buddy, and Daddy can go on loving her. The worlds can remain separate like they were." I slam the steering wheel. I just needed a couple of hours, and this shit wouldn't have blown up like this. Playing catch-up sucks, but I was always good at coming from behind. The underdog position is one I'm familiar with. But I should have had home-court advantage. Fucking Poppy.

I turn back to Sadie, and she's going to town on those plastic keys. "Time to meet your village. And you have my permission to hate your Auntie Poppy. Everyone will be there except Uncle Sam. Maybe we don't call him that. But he'll come around eventually, and I'll tell him about you. But everyone else finds out now." In my heart, I know nothing can ever be separated again as much as I want it to be.

I look in the rearview mirror and grin. "You and me now. Well, you and me and, when she'll talk to me again, Nat. That's the way it's supposed to be. I have to fix it. I'll fix it."

I PULL UP THE HILL DRIVEWAY TO ELLE AND JOSH'S HOUSE. ONLY my family, Elle, and Josh's makeshift grandmother, Mrs. Dotson, know about Sadie. She's been babysitting in a pinch.

Elle told me if it came up, she would tell Josh, but it's my duty to tell all of them. I pull the car up in front of their house that overlooks the vineyards of LaChappelle/Whittier. It takes my damn breath away every time. My house is down in the valley and moderate. I've been saving and saving. I want to build something on a plot of land I bought just up the valley four years ago. It's actually near Prohibition's new site. I haven't told anyone, and I didn't want to build anything alone, so I let it sit. That's how I ended up renting the bungalow downtown and waiting for the perfect moment to build. Done waiting. I'm going to build a house with Natalie. I'm so gone for that chick. Sadie starts fussing and pulls me out of my funk. I'm sitting parked, looking at the house.

"Ok, Scribbles, let's rip this Band-Aid off. And whatever your new Auntie Tabi says to me in the next ten minutes, disregard it. I love you, and I'm going to make sure you have everything you need, expose you to the best music, sports, and art, and love you." I pick her up, and she settles a bit. I hold her close and kiss the top of her baby hair head. I whisper, "It's ok, baby girl, I'm done hiding you. It's time you meet the rest of your family."

I hitch my non-manly, leather diaper bag on my shoulder. The envelope is still in it. I've never told anyone about it—it's a cashier's check for $233,610. The exact cost of raising a child to seventeen, according to Google. I was going to give it to Josh to invest for her, but now I want to give it back. My baby can't be bought.

I run my hand over the scruff on my chin. Bax is standing at the window. He waves tentatively, and I hear him call for Tab. I hustle to the door and walk inside without knocking. Elle turns, as does everyone else. Evan, Jims, Sal, Poppy, and Bax's sister, Tommi. The whole fucking gang is here.

"Oh. David. Is everything ok?" Elle waddles over to me. Sadie fusses, and she takes her. "Little stunner, come here. Daddy has some music to face. How about some Cheerios?" She's using the cute baby voice people automatically use when holding a baby. "Or whatever whole grain, natural, organic, cardboard O's your Uncle Josh will allow in the house." She bounces her a bit. I kiss the top of her head, and when I look up, I'm staring at lots of open mouths.

Tabi yells from the corner, "Who the hell gave you a baby?" I hold my hand up to her and push my way to Poppy.

"A fucking ambush. Are you god damned serious right now? You couldn't give me a heads up like a decent person? She knows. Are you fucking happy now? Little snitch. Living in your moral compass sucks. I'm going to fix this, but it was never your place to be any part of this. Stay the fuck away from my daughter and me."

Sal, her massive not-so-secret mobster boyfriend, steps in front of me with aggression I could never mirror. He's a scary muthafucker, but this is family business. Mine.

"Yo. Pop. Back your goon down." She pats Sal on the shoulder.

His deep voice fills the room. "Don't, David. Don't disrespect her. Or me, you punk piece of shit."

I don't back down. "Sal, this about her disrespecting me. And you of all people should understand me trying to handle family business on my own."

I step back and turn towards Poppy. "Should I have told Nat sooner? Absolutely, but it's not your call, Pop. Butt the hell out of my life. I didn't even get to tell her because you and your mom decided to get mine all riled up and ruin my life. You have one of your own to ruin." Sal bristles, and again she lays her hand on him like a choke chain on a dog collar.

Josh pipes up, "He's not wrong, Pop." Josh has been on the receiving end of Poppy's right and wrong lectures throughout the years. We love her, but enough already. Brother got my back.

Poppy says, "Could everyone stop? I did right by that little girl," she yells, then buries her head in Sal's chest.

Sal says in a growl, "Walk away, Gelbert. Walk away from me."

"Not your call, Poppy," Baxter chimes in, and I cross my arms over my chest. I don't need to say anything else to her. Neither of these guys has any idea what's going on but blindly defended me. I'd do the same for them.

I shake it off and walk from Sal, and he ushers Poppy to the kitchen, and I'm left facing everyone else.

Tabi steps in front of me. "I believe I asked a question. Who the hell gave you a baby?"

I exhale. "I don't know."

Evan squeals, "Congratulations! This is amazing." He hugs me.

"Thanks, man." I grin.

Jims Langerford puts his arm around me and speaks to his husband, "Evs, baby, can you go check on Elle? We have a few domestic issues to discuss." He turns to me and playfully slaps my face repeatedly.

Tabi steps forward and pushes me. "Who the fuck gave you a baby?"

Josh crosses his arms over his chest, Bax puts his hands on his hips, and they both stare at me.

Tabi presses, "Answer me, Gelbert."

"I seriously don't know. I'll answer all questions later. Nat just found out too. I have to go and see if I can fix things. Elle, can you?"

"I've got her. We're old pals." She smiles broadly. "Her best friend will be up in a minute, and the two can jabber at each other." I grin that there's another generation to weave their own story.

Josh says, "Woman! Hellcat, what are you talking about? How do YOU know this baby?"

I put my hand on Josh's shoulder. "I asked her not to tell anyone. My fault, not hers. Go broodish on *me*. Later. I have a relationship to save." She babbles while holding a little snack cup of dry cereal. She's pulling Elle's hair and almost singing. Then she laughs and throws something at Tabi and melts her heart. I see my brazen friend go all gooey inside.

I take her from Elle, and she whacks me in the face with the red and blue cup. Then it falls to the ground. I go to pick it up, and Josh clears his throat.

Elle looks at him. "It's fine. Sorry. There's no 5-second rule in this house because the germaphobe is afraid our daughter, and now yours, will eat carpet fibers and choke." Everyone laughs then turns back to me.

"This is my daughter, Sadie. We think she's a little over six months old." She screeches in delight and reaches for Elle. I hand her over, and Elle bounces her a little. "I don't know who her mom is. I've been keeping her a secret from you and Nat for about a month and a half. That's when I found out myself."

Bax says, "Why keep this from us? We could have helped."

Tabi hits her husband on the shoulder. "No. We wouldn't have helped him lie to Natalie."

Bax turns to her. "We could have helped with the baby. Eseís chorís kardiá omorfiá."

Tabi kisses him quickly. "At least you called me beautiful while you called me heartless." She shrugs.

Jims asks, "Does Sam know?"

Josh scoffs, "Because he's come out of his house in the last two months? I'm not sure he's bathed since November." We all look at each other, then Bax breaks the silence. He walks over to Elle and takes Sadie into his arms. She stares at him.

"Hi. Wow. So beautiful. And you're strong like your daddy, I can see it. Sweet, sweet girl. I'm Uncle Bax, and if you ever need anything, don't ask your Aunt Tabi. Come straight to me." He pulls her into his chest, smells her head, and smiles. Then he turns to me. "We've got her. Tell us the rest later. Go get Nat."

"And don't fuck her over," Jims adds.

"She's leaving me. She doesn't want kids."

Josh nods his chin at me, and I turn to leave. Tabi gives her parting shot, "Do not lose my friend and our only non-family employee. Also, how the hell do you look like a natural with that baby? You. Fucking Gelbert. You're a father."

Elle answers for me as she slurps a new ice pop, "And a damn good one, Tab, so fuck off." Tabi throws her arms around me.

"Then congrats, Gelbert. She's going to love being spoiled by her Theía Tabi." I squeeze her. She whispers in my ear, "I'm so thrilled for you, David. Go put your life together." The door flies open, and there's literally a yeti walking in the door.

Evan's hands fly to his throat as if he's clutching pearls. "Dear brother-in-law, this is too much hair for anyone to carry off. I beg of you to let me fix this." The yeti waves him off and surveys the room.

"What the hell?" Sam looks to Josh, who is now holding Sadie. "Did you have another fucking kid while I was buried in my sad potato-chip-crumble-filled depression grotto?" Sam steps to Bax, and the whole room waits.

"Hey there, redheaded stranger. Holy shit, you're a Gelbert. How long have I been in the fucking sadness isolation cave?" I slap him on the back.

Poppy reenters the room and says, "Too long. You get to tell

us one sad thing, then onto David's good and bad things."
Fucking suck-up trying to make it right. I glare at her and turn
to Sam.

Sam holds out his hand and embraces mine. Our eyes meet.
He says, "All the pictures of us are gone or destroyed. She erased
them all from my phone and hers. There's just the one from the
fake New Year's Eve party that Elle posted on Instagram." There
are groans and gasps.

Josh puts his hand on Sam's shoulder and says, "There will
never be a minute where any of this makes sense. Stop trying to
make sense of it. There's nothing to solve. And I need you to
come back, man. Gelbert's a father, and I don't have the strength
to mock him enough alone." He smiles and nods at us.

"Who's her mom?" Sam asks.

Bax answers, "Best guest? Anonymous skank." Everyone
laughs, including Sadie. It's the best sound in the world, and it
proves she's on my side. She thinks her mom is a skank too.

I squint and point to Bax. "Bingo."

I turn back to Sam. "Sadie, this is Sam. Sam, this is my
daughter, Sadie. I have to go fix something. And take a fucking
shower. You stink."

I kiss Sadie on the head and run out the door. I jump in my
Range Rover and head back down the hill to Nat's rental cottage.
I guess I never noticed everything about her screams temporary.
I have to change that. She cannot leave.

CHAPTER 27

NATALIE

I'M FOLDING. It's the easiest thing I can do right now. It's the thing that needs doing. Lookout Cottage, what the Whittiers call the cottage I'm living in, is immaculate and in order. I'm ready to go. I head back into the bedroom, and it hurts to look at the odd pillow on the bed. David needs a unique pillow, and I bought one to match his at his house. It's the closest to living with someone I've ever gotten. I fix the bed. Then I place the pillow into a fresh garbage bag. I toss it by the front door. I dump the hamper into another garbage bag and place it in my suitcase. I begin to leave the room but remember I forgot something. I dig out his sweatshirt and put it with the pillow at the door. Shared property sorted.

I wrap my arms around myself and stare at the door. I know him. He doesn't give up. I'm ready. I will not cry again, and I will not let him inside my home or any part of me again. The urgent screech of his wheels around the last switchback warns me it's showtime. I pull my hair up into a knot on my head and prepare for battle.

He doesn't even knock. He bellows, "Get out here, now. Not only are we not done, but you have not been dismissed. You ran away. Face me and this. And at the other end of our talk, if you're still definite about ditching the love of your life, I'll respect that."

He's such a fire-trucking nerfhead. I whip the door open. I say, "No, you won't."

He uses his panty-melting smirk I'm powerless against. I breathe in sharply. He says, "No. I won't ever stop proving to you we are written on the pages of history."

"Stop. Where did you read it?"

"Some novel Tabi had in the office. But it's true. I belong to you, and you belong to me."

I keep my distance and make sure my shoes are still on my feet so I can run to my car. "You belong to someone else."

He rubs his hands over his face and through his hair. He's trying not to yell at me. "You need food. Let's go. I really need food."

"You still think I'm going to mother-trucking breakfast with you?"

"Big guns, Nat, pulling out the mother-trucking. You need pancakes more than I thought. And you can either get into my car, or I can carry you there. Sadie's taken care of. I have nowhere to be. She's not in the car waiting for you—just us. You mean more to me than way too much syrup. Sweet Cream Pancakes aren't going to cut it. I think we're in a Stuffed Blackberry French Toast situation. With extra raspberry jam."

"That's so much sugar," I chastise, and my resolve weakens. I want him to tell me it's all a joke. I don't see a way past all of this, but I owe him a conversation. I owe myself solid closure. That's what this meal will be. "Fine. Just breakfast."

He turns back towards his car and says, "For the rest of our lives. Breakfast for the rest of our lives or no deal."

I roll my eyes. "No deal."

"Fine. We'll start with today's sugar coma. Get your sexy, cute ass into my car before I attack you. Has anyone ever told you how fucking utterly delectable you look when you're haughty and life alteringly angry at me?"

I grab my purse and the garbage bag and pull the door behind me. Infuriating. The man is infuriating.

"Bringing refuse?"

"These are your things."

"Funny." He laughs at me, and it pisses me off.

"What is?"

"You still think there's my stuff and your stuff. Aside from Sadie at the moment, everything is ours now."

"No, David. Stop saying things like that."

He slides into the driver's side after closing my door. He flashes those electric green eyes. "I can stop saying them, but it won't make it less true." He waggles his eyebrows, and in a flash, he steals a quick kiss. I let him have it. It will be our last.

I HOLD THE CUP BETWEEN MY HANDS, AND HE ADDS MORE CREAM to it. We haven't spoken since the car. He knew I needed a second to collect. I appreciate the mental space, but my body will never collect itself around him. My blood rushes, and my heart beats a touch faster every single time he looks at me. I think my hair and nails grow faster. It's what I thought love felt like, but it turns out it's not quite it. I'll ignore my physical response to him and focus on how this all won't work. I'll sob tonight at what I've lost, but I need to maintain. I started forming things to say ever since that child appeared on his hip. I'm in shock.

He's leaning back on his side of the booth with his arms stretched out open. That's who he is, an open book. Mostly. There's the whole hiding a kid thing.

I sit up a little straighter. I say, "As a foster kid, you try to be the solution, not another problem. You don't make yourself too noticeable so you can stay put. I have had my tubes tied, and I told you I don't want children. Did you think I'd look at Sadie and magically melt?" I have not had my tubes tied, but if he can lie to me about something life-altering, so can I.

His lips curl up as he leans over the table. "Why the condoms, Sunshine? If I'm clean and you can't get pregnant? Makes no sense. Make up something else. Try again." He grins, and now my blood boils that he caught me in a lie.

Then he says, "Um. Yeah, I did think you'd melt. I mean, I eventually did. Look at her. She's adorable. And she looks like me. And from all accounts, you love me and like the way I look."

I scoot back as far as I can. "She's adorable, but I remain me, and I don't want children. We're at an impasse. I won't be able to get over this anger."

"This is where your logic is getting fuzzy. Be mad at me for not telling you. Be furious about that. But I'm not asking you to have children."

He's got to be kidding.

"YOU have a child. Your daughter will always come first. You didn't tell me about a child. She should have been conversation number one."

He's usually snarky, but I see him shift to agitated as he shreds a napkin onto the table. "You're right. What I should have said to you on our first day together was, 'Oh, by the way, I've slept with a woman who will abandon our child and proceed to dump her at my family's winery in a couple of months once we're happy.' It would have made more sense than my hopes and dreams for Pro/Ho. Thanks for fucking clearing that up, Nat."

This cold sarcasm is usually reserved for his father. Other than yelling at his mother today, I've never really seen him this frustrated. We've never really fought.

I push back. "Hey. I'm the one who has to deal with all of this very suddenly. You've had time to adjust. You can't be mad. We need to deal with your lies."

"Lies. There were three." He digs some ratty Post-It notes out of his back pocket and places them before me. "There. I wrote them down so I could make sure to tell you about the three times I lied to you. I'm terribly sorry. The lie and the apology are on the notes." I don't pick them up.

"You can't be angry with me. You're the liar."

He runs his hands up his face and glares at me. "I can be angry at the way you're refusing to actually talk about this. You're just vilifying me instead of discussing it all. How do we move forward? No more how I tricked you from the beginning. You know that's absurd, right? I didn't know I had a kid until we were already dating for five months. I told you I loved you before Sadie was ditched on a tasting room bar."

I spit my words, "And then your priorities shifted, and you hid the most important thing in your life from me."

He slams his hands down on the table. His giant palms covering most of his side of the table. "What are you talking about? Did you feel slighted these past months? Did you feel me love you less?"

We both sit back, and he lets my venom settle over it. I chew my pancakes, and he pops a piece of bacon into his mouth. He sips his coffee, and his eyes peek at me over his coffee cup.

"Who said she was the most important thing in my life?"

Wind sufficiently knocked out of me.

CHAPTER 28

DAVID

WE'RE STILL SITTING, saying nothing. We're simply eating. I'm just picking at the remnants of my meal. She's not responded to me. This is not how we end. I know how her head works. She's packing. That's what the pillow nonsense was about. I shrug when she looks at me. Now Sadie's in the open, and I won't hold back my thoughts anymore. Well, maybe just the one. The one where I want to fuck her into submission right here at the table. I'll keep that one to myself.

"You can't just leave." All my cards.

"I can. It's the best plan. It's the only one I can live with."

I don't let her off the hook. "Yes, but we didn't come up with it. I fucked up. I get that. I'm sorry. I had my reasons. I'd be happy to tell you all of them. Especially if I can write them in jam across your body. I am sorry you're so upset. I was trying to figure it all out before we ended up in this discussion. You're right. We should have solved this together, and I fucked that up. But we're still in a relationship. You promised to be in this with me."

"That's a horrible thing to say to me. You made me promise something impossible. I'm still stunned, shocked, and hurt. Why the fuck didn't you tell me?" I stretch my legs and brush by hers, and she jerks them away at the moment of contact.

"This. I needed to know how you felt about me and for you to know how deeply I feel for you before all the Sadie rained down the chaos."

She looks down at her lap and says, "It's not enough. None of it. Your excuse or your reasons."

"I love you." The people around us turn to watch us.

"Not enough."

I lean forward and take her hand, and she doesn't immediately pull back. I stroke the back of her hand with my thumb, and I see her wheels turning.

She looks into my eyes, and I'm hopeful. I can't help but see hope in those eyes. "Did you really think throwing on a Santa hat and doing an Irish jig could undo a lifetime of shoddy memories and heartbreak?"

I don't hesitate. "Yes. Yes, I did. Because I didn't have a shitty childhood like you. Parts of mine sucked. But I won't let you use that as an excuse. You should at least understand I don't want Sadie to live through what you did." Bam. Elephant laid right on the table. She tries to pull away, and I don't let her. "I'm going to change it up for Sadie. But I don't know what it's like. In all of our moments together, I thought I was doing something nice and building something with you. I want to do everything for and with you. You belong with me. Sadie is a different thing, and we'll figure that out, but you're not even giving us a chance to acclimate."

"It can't." I change tactics. She's already shut down, and I'm at a loss.

"What we have is at least enough to hang a tomorrow on." I think that's my best beg.

"Is it?"

Crushed. Fuck.

My heart's tearing like when you try to rip tissue paper. It's not a straight tear that can be tapped back easily. It's delicate and jagged, and I have to stop her from ripping it in half. I just realized I have such a full and robust heart. I don't want to lose it.

She's staring out the window at Napa Street, holding her coffee cup in her hand. The sun is playing with me. It's illuminating her from behind, and she looks even more perfect, almost untouchable. She was so completely mine hours ago, and now the table seems too wide to reach her. I stare at her cream skin and delicate fingers as she shifts the coffee cup. She's too good for me. She's realizing it right now.

Clever will only hold her attention for so long. I'm going to lose her, but I think I would have lost her either way. At least by lying to her for a little bit, I got a couple more moments I can hold onto as perfect. When she leaves, and she will, I can replay them in my mind like game highlights. I'm looking at her, aching to comfort her and take away the pain I caused. The only things I know with absolute certainty are:

1. I will love and care for Sadie always and make sure she's safe
2. My knees will eventually need to be replaced because of basketball
3. I will never love someone again the way I love Natalie Lloyd.

She says without looking at me, "I didn't know there were three of us in this relationship."

I pivot again. No more gentle. "That was a bitch move, not telling you. My bad."

"That's your apology?"

"No. I've said I'm sorry, so cut me a moment. I fucked up. I get that, but I'm trying to fix this. I'm trying to tell you how much you mean to me. I'm not ready to walk through this life without you." I roll my eyes and shake my head. "I get it, I have a kid now, but that doesn't change who we are."

"No, but it changes everything about our relationship. Because we're not the only ones in it. That relationship doesn't exist anymore if it ever did."

She has a good point, and I see a tiny speck of light at the end of my loneliness tunnel.

"Then give us a first date."

She sips her tea and glares at me. I see the slightest smile from behind her teacup.

"Come on. I love you. When's the last time you went out on a date, and you already knew you were adored? And the sex would be good. Meet her. Meet me as her dad. Date us. I need you, Nat."

"I'm aware. Doesn't change the fact I'm pissed."

I grin and tease her a little. "And you love me." I start swaying and humming Al Green.

"No. Do not, David. Do not. No one wants to hear this."

I whisper, "Let's Stay Together." I bite my bottom lip. "I. I'm so in love with you." I stand up. She slinks under the table.

She bites out her words. "Check. Get the Check."

"...since we've been together."

She stands up and tries to leave. I'm going to let her. Her eyes fill with pain again, and charming isn't going to cut it. I stop singing. I blurt out anything I can think of to make her stay.

"I love you so much. Carry that wherever you're going. I will love you until the end of next week." I smirk. She's not amused. "I'll love you forever. I thought you got that. I will never stop fighting for us." The entire restaurant is looking at me. Neighbors, peers, and familiar waitresses. They're all waiting with bated breath. Her face morphs into a look I've never seen before.

She deserves to put me in my place. She deserves the anger and the scene she's about to let loose. I only hope my heart can take it.

She turns to me. "Fuck you, David." My entire body slumps as I realize I drove her to swear. This is more painful than I thought it would be. Christ. My eyes fill with tears she deserves to see but doesn't deserve to take the blame for. "Fuck you. Fuck you for making me believe a different life was possible for me. Fuck you for loving me and lying to me. Fuck you for building me up only to shatter me. But most of all fuck you for hurting me so much I'm saying the word fuck. And in public too."

Sharp and dull pains ravage my body, and I know the only thing to do is nothing. If I keep pushing her, I'll lose everything.

I'M SO NOT USED to having my day revolve around her nap schedule. I've been spoiled, I get it. But I'm also used to Natalie. I miss her so much it aches. I didn't know heartbreak cliches were true.

I sleep surrounded by pillows. It's a poor substitute for the little pixie. The other night I woke up and decided to drive up to Lookout cottage and crawl into bed with her. I got to the door before I saw the car seat.

I keep forgetting.

She's not mine.

I have a kid.

I pop a beer and settle into the couch. Sleep not coming. Sadie will be up in an hour or two. I'll watch some ESPN classics. See what games they're telling me are historic. I hope it's an epic Lakers/Celtics playoff game. My father insisted I watch hours and hours of old game tapes of the greats. Bird and Johnson were always my favorites. So graceful and skilled. Their focus and clear love of the game would amp me up to play.

It's an old Rockets game with the Twin Towers. I start to drift off. Maybe I can grab another hour. I wake up to a scream so piercing it's like someone's been shot. I leap off the couch and bolt to Sadie's room.

The smell is overwhelming, but the sight of that little girl pulling herself up to standing and the walls with shit handprints on them is the most shocking thing I've ever seen. She's sobbing and falls down onto the mattress. I look at her, and her little sleep outfit is caked to her. Her diaper not holding anything in. Everything is covered. I lift her up by her armpits and head to the kitchen sink. There's a hose in there. I peel off the outfit, but she's still sobbing. There's more than there should be, and I panic. There's something seriously wrong. This isn't normal. She isn't normal. She's in pain. There's too much poop. She doesn't usually poop this much. This is beyond me. I have to get her some help. I grab a kitchen garbage bag and swaddle it around her waist. Then wrap the rest of her in towels. I wash my hands as best I can, but I don't have time to do anymore. She's sick or something. I grab my phone and keys and bolt to the car. It's seven a.m. I don't know where else to go. My mother's out of town. But this is medical. She needs medical attention.

I'm holding her and driving. I didn't trust the car seat. I'm going as fast as I can while being insanely careful. I leave the car at the entrance to the hospital. I don't know where the emergency entrance is, but I know the people inside will. It's only when the air hits my chest do I realize I'm only in basketball shorts. No shirt, no shoes, and no wallet.

"Help. My daughter needs help."

"Insurance and ID, please."

The staff is staring at me. She smells terrible. It's in her hair. I don't know what to do, but these people should be more concerned. She's sick.

"I can run and get them. I don't have them. Help my daughter. I don't know what's wrong with her. Please."

"My hands are tied. The emergency room is down the hall but without—"

I roar, "NOW. Help her now."

The woman steps back, horrified at me. She should be. She should be grabbing a doctor immediately.

"Dude. Are you ok?" I turn sharply at Josh's voice.

"Something's not right with Sadie. There's crap everywhere. There's something wrong. It's all up her back, in her hair. She won't stop crying. There's too much. This can't be right. Something's wrong with her. Help me."

Josh bends over, laughing. How the hell can he fucking laugh at me?

"Jesus. I thought there was something really wrong."

"What the fuck are you saying to me?" Sadie still squirming in her dirty towel ensemble, and everyone can hear the white kitchen bag rustling.

"I thought there was an emergency, but no, you're just a dumbass. She's fine. Except your daughter is dressed like a homeless person in winter."

I punch his shoulder. "Explain!"

He reaches for my crap-covered daughter, and I surrender her.

He holds her at arm's length. "Hey, girl. Daddy's never experienced a blowout."

I turn to him while grabbing the anti-bacterial wipes on the counter of the hospital check-in. "What the hell is that? She's ok, for real?"

Josh says, "She is, Daddy. You put the diaper on wrong, you fucking idiot. Come with me. Elle's getting an ultrasound upstairs. Peds and OB should be able to assist us."

I exhale and shake a bit from the surge of adrenaline. I bend over and put my hands on my knees. Thank Christ it was nothing but a mess. The entire room begins laughing at me. And

I find the humor in it immediately. I laugh too. I start wiping down my chest and gesture to the crowd.

"Shit. Man. I was out of my head."

He raises his eyebrows and cocks his head. "Oh, I get it. I get it a lot. Lots of shit. Now imagine you had the kid, and Natalie was pregnant."

"Your sugar mandates makes a little more sense. Fuck. We're a mess."

"Nope, you are." He snaps a picture of me still covered in Sadie's shit, and I know it will come back to haunt me one day.

We follow Josh up to the OBGYN wing. He disappears for Elle's appointment. The nurses and staff coo over Sadie and offer to help clean her up. They find me some enormous pink scrubs and a shower to clean myself up. I'm drinking shitty coffee and trying to remember a time where I wasn't terrified all the time.

Josh joins me. He attempts to give me a dead leg, but I react too quickly.

"Elle ok?"

"Yes, they're finishing up now. She'll pee, then we'll go. The twins are on the smaller side, but that's totally normal, so I hear. But her blood pressure seems to be holding this time."

I shake my head. "How are we supposed to do this? She's so much more fragile than I thought a baby could be."

"We all are." He nods. "So your intention is to leave her alone." Natalie conversation. The 5 keep texting, but I've been ignoring them while I settle into my sad Sam reality of loneliness.

"It is." I nod.

"This is to prevent you from breaking?"

"Yes." My voice is smaller than I intend it to be.

"They're also much more resilient than you think." He slaps my shoulder and settles into his chair.

I take in what he's saying. But Josh loves to give advice. He always thinks he knows best.

"You can't sit back and let shit happen to you." He grins at his joke. "You've always been able to slide by. Do you want a different life?" This man upended his entire world to grab a chance of happiness. He built a successful business and life far away from here, then he met Elle, and she reminded him what was important in life.

"Get off your ass, Gelbert, and fix this. We're here if she still walks away, but you owe it to her and you to see if you can have all of it."

I slam my fist down on his thigh, successfully giving him a dead leg. He groans.

"Asshole."

I smirk at him as I jump up and retrieve Sadie from the nurses. I look back at Josh as Elle appears at his side. "I'll think about it."

"Yeah, you will," Elle chimes in, having no idea what we're talking about. "Can I call you the King of Shit?" She smiles.

"Not yet. But soon." I look at Josh. "Thanks, man."

As Sadie and I make it to the car, I whip out my phone and look up hazmat cleaning services. I am not scrubbing those walls.

"Sadie, girl. How about a trip to see Aunties Mel and Tommi? Daddy needs to discuss a few things with them. And Auntie Mel has the skill set we need."

She coos and puts her hand on my chin. I love when she does that.

CHAPTER 30

NATALIE

TABI: Girl, what's your damage?

NAT: Nothing.

TABI: Nobody reacts like that if there's not something lurking. Tell the newly crowned Theía Tabi.

NAT: I'm fine, thanks for asking.

TABI: Duh. You're the most put together person I know, of course you're fine.

TABI: But you're not. There's a crack in your liberty bell—do you want to tell me?

NAT: Tabi. I swear there's no damage. There's no problem. David and I had a very nice time and that time has passed.

TABI: You're talking like a yoga instructor.

NAT: Ok.

TABI: I hate fucking yoga. Cut the shit.

NAT: Please let me have a minute. Must you be so blunt all the time?

TABI: It's my gift. Call me if you need me.

Of course, there's damage, but it's none of her concern. I fell in love with way too many people who had no idea over the years. And here's a man who I can't get enough of and is falling all over himself to be with me. And yet, I'm still keeping him away. I'm so confused and lost. I should talk to someone, but my only real friends are his best friends.

Which is somewhat problematic should anything continue between us because inevitably, things move on. Then I'll be left without friends or a home again. After growing up in the foster care system, it's not a totally unfamiliar feeling. I'd show up, and if there was a girl my age, I'd become friends with her friends. I'd become invaluable to the family. But make sure I was invisible as often as possible. No swearing, no rocking the boat, and strictly following their rules. I have the ability to see the holes and just fill them without being asked. It's served me well. If I became invaluable and invisible, then maybe I didn't have to leave.

I'd do the dishes, laundry, and pick up after the other children. I'd help cook or run errands on the rare occasion I'd be trusted with money. But then something would happen, a vase would get broken, or one of the biological kids would be embarrassed by my clothing at school, or they'd want to steal from their parents. I'd get blamed. I'd lose whatever friends I'd made since they all belonged to the biological kids. I'd pack my meager belongings into a new garbage bag and be placed in another home.

When I was younger, the pattern wasn't about being blamed and shipped out but replaced. It was common for me to move along once their lives started to take the shape they wanted. Many good people thought they were so benevolent to take in a child in need, but it was always more about their ego than my welfare.

I still look up one family on social media. I used to send a Christmas card to them. They were the kindest. I was with them for about a year and a half when I was seven years old. It was the first time anyone had thrown me a birthday party. They were kind and funny. They included me in everything, and they were loving. A younger couple with no children. Then she became pregnant. It was a complicated pregnancy and birth, but I loved that little baby. Which made it especially painful when I was suddenly sent to a new home. They were careful not to ever call me a sister. The father tried to explain. He said they couldn't afford us both. It had nothing to do with who I was. He'd lost his job. He said someday if things turned around, they'd look for me. The mom never even said goodbye to me. He told me it was too painful for her. Still, I was eight years old, and therapy has told me this is the actual root of my abandonment issues, not when my addict parents ditched me.

They have four kids, who are now almost grown. They never sent a card back to me. I've made very few attachments in my life since then. It's too much when they choose something or someone else. And I can't be rational when they want to stay.

Baxter has been the most consistent person in my life. When he left Sacramento to run for Congress, I was devastated. It was such a familiar feeling of not knowing why he left me behind. I'd been indispensable. We'd been friends. I moved from DC to Sacramento with him when he moved offices. And although in my past that quality has been exploited and abused by boyfriends and foster families alike, Bax always noticed everything I did for him. Yet, I was never in love with him. Bax was always like the brother I never got to keep. Then Tabi called, and they folded me into their life here. Then there was Gelbert. He's their friend. And now I'm alone again. It's all suddenly too familiar.

I desperately want to be chosen and stay. But I can't. It's a baby, and she deserves a life I couldn't have. Sonoma feels like home for the first time in my life. I finally belong somewhere, and I don't know how to make it last. I don't know how to not be in love with David Gelbert.

I'm staring out at the valley on this makeshift patio outside Lookout Cottage on the LaChappelle Whittier winery property. I can't stop staring at that bell. Even though Sarah and Will wouldn't take money, I make sure to leave baked goods or flowers for them almost daily to show my appreciation. I've cleaned up the landscaping and even planted new flowers. I'm thinking of creating flower boxes, but I don't know if Sarah would like them. I have to feel her out.

"Nat?" I jump at a female voice. No one really comes up here unless they're coming to see me. I also didn't hear her drive up here.

I stand and turn around. It's Becca Gelbert, David's sister. "Hi. Is something wrong?"

"No. I just wanted to come and say hi. I had to drop off some legal things for Elle to sign. And then, well, you're here, so I thought I would say hello."

I motion to the chair next to me. "If you're here to advocate for him, please don't." I don't know what to think of all of this. We're not friends, and she always seems so closed off unless she's around David.

She sits on the edge of the chair with her legs together, and I slink back a bit. She's a bit intimidating.

She stands and puts her hands on her hips. She looks at me very directly. "I'm not good at girl talk."

"Good. I'm not talking. Say what you need to say, then you can tell him you were here."

"Your eyes are very red." Becca blurts out truth. It's what she does. My eyes are red. Interestingly, she points out facts, but it all drips in judgment.

"That happens when you cry. You're a bit awkward." I push back against her with all my defenses up.

She says, "I don't stand on ceremony. I didn't get the flourish gene like my asshole brother. He's always been an ass. But he's different now."

I grasp her meaning, and now I hurt even more than I did before. "I get it. The man is softened by the baby. He's a completely changed and loving human now that he has a baby. You can go now."

"No."

"No, you won't go?" I start to stand up, and she pins me to my seat with her steely gaze. Her eyes are so similar to his.

"No. I mean, he's completely changed. As if something unlocked within his soul and brain that made him the person we all hoped he'd become. But it was you. Not the baby."

I fall back into my chair. Her words stealing all my breath.

I scrape together my voice and manage to say, "You've pleaded his case. You can go now."

"I wasn't pleading his. I was pleading mine. I want to keep this version of my brother." She stands and makes an awkward gesture of squeezing my knee. I wish I knew how to grant her wish. And mine. I want to keep this version of her brother too.

PART 3

MERLOT

CHAPTER 31

DAVID

I DON'T KNOW what the fuck I'm going to do. There is no way Nat is sticking around and figuring out what all of this is between us if there's a fucking baby hanging around.

BECCA: *For what it's worth, she's miserable too. But she's not an asshole. I had a family lawyer draw up all the paperwork. You just need to find her.*

DAVID: *You're an asshole.*

BECCA: *Do you want me to drop off the papers?*

DAVID: *Drop them at Mom and Dad's house, not Pro/Ho. Heading there now. All I need is the mom's signature, right?*

BECCA: *If you can find the skank.*

DAVID: *Maybe she's not.*

BECCA: *She ditched a baby. But she ditched her in the right place.*

DAVID: *Were you just nice to me?*

BECCA: *Consider it an early birthday present.*

I'M BARELY IN THE HOUSE WHEN THE MAN ACCOSTS ME. HE KISSES my daughter, then pulls her up and rubs his nose on her belly.

"Jana, come get the girl." He passes her off to my mom, and she acknowledges me but is wholly involved with Sadie. We've talked on the phone. I apologized for swearing at her. I also know she's still upset she got talked into an ambush. She made me apologize to Poppy. Which was annoying, but I did it. But no fucking way am I talking to the barbarian that is my Aunt Tina. Thankfully she's on another cruise spending her brother's money.

My father puts his hands in his pockets. His voice is angry, and he's wearing his resting asshole face. "You let her slip off the fucking hook, son."

"What are you talking about?"

"The mother. You still haven't found her. Looks like you're stuck now."

I shake my head. How is he this way? I'm shocked he has friends, let alone friends like Will, Adrian, Costas or Jim Sr. He's an asshole. Been an asshole my whole life. I listen every time my mother tells me his good qualities, and it's my mother I choose to believe. I often think she could have done better, and she reminds me my dad saved her. Whatever that means. And that she loves him more profoundly than I could ever understand. If she loves him the way I love Natalie, then maybe I could understand.

"Dad. I'm trying really hard not to blow up at you."

"Blow boy. I'm not spending my fucking golden years raising your child."

"Wow. Sadie is your grandchild. And she's out of your house and in mine. Golden years? Really? You'll never retire. I'm raising her. I'm almost thirty-six years old. It's not like I knocked up someone in my teens and ruined all my chances."

"You did that one all by yourself."

I fucking hate him. "Your hatred of my daughter stems from me walking away from fucking basketball? My daughter, the one whose belly you just rubbed, the one I love and can't wait to be all the things you weren't.

He pours himself a drink and sits down. He crosses his legs perfectly and puts his arm across the back of the couch, then flicks his eyes to me.

"Cut me a break."

He did not say that.

"You? Shut the fuck up, Dad." I move towards him, and he pisses me off by not even moving a tick of his mouth. "You rode me every day of my life about your shit. I am an adult with a successful business, a daughter, a—"

"But you fucked up your romantic life. Like you have for the past fifteen years."

I sit down opposite him and look at him as a puzzle to solve. I can take all the insults he's about to hurl. Still, if I've learned nothing else from sweet Nat, it's to listen to what people are actually saying so you can figure out what they really mean. I've never stopped long enough to listen. My mind always buzzing. I didn't hear when Natalie told me she was scared and alone, over and over. She let me know exactly how she'd react to Sadie, and I ignored it. I glossed over it and covered it up with Christmas lights and oral sex. I didn't listen. But I'm going to listen to the asshole sitting across from me and really try to get it. And if I don't, then fuck him. I'm done.

I nod to him.

"I pushed you because you could have been something." I crack my hand so hard as I tighten my fists, but I don't say anything. "You threw away NBA fame and fortune. The way you look, the way you played, you could have had endorsements and a different life. You wouldn't be stuck in a dead-end vineyard job."

"I thought you loved it."

"I do now. But, I wasn't handed a glittering other path. You were and you shit all over it." He sips his drink. I want to leave, but Nat's voice is in my head. Just listen. What did I just hear? And then it dawns me.

"You're jealous. You're jealous I had a way out of this life, and you were stuck. You're jealous I love it here. I love everything about the terroir and grapes. I love this lifestyle despite you. You wanted to go pro." His face is red and flustered. He was a decent linebacker at Arkansas in his day. He must have failed to go pro.

I say, "You wanted fame. Is that why you tried to distribute Gelbert so widely we almost lost the winery? Jesus, Dad. Do you like anything about your life?"

His voice is the weakest I've ever heard, "Yes. You, your sister, and your mother." I look at him.

"Then stop fucking hassling me. Forgive Becca for not being bolder in life. Let Mom have more fun and be a nicer goddamned human."

He pinches the bridge of his nose. "That little girl," he sputters out.

"Sadie." I'm pissed.

"She's the best thing about me."

I'm completely undone. Confused and floundering to catch up to whatever he said. "What are you talking about, you lunatic?"

"She's hope. She's a fresh start. And somehow has given me some hope too. I don't like thinking about all this shit. It's a waste most of the time. I have no regrets in my life. Life is what it is. And I won't apologize for trying to get you to be your best. But I will apologize for blustering and trivializing that girl." Again. I'm confused.

"Sadie?"

He shakes his head. "Natalie." The man mystifies and stuns me. "You deserve someone who understands your complicated and asinine brain the way your mother understands mine."

"And Sadie?"

"Son. I will always want more for you than I have. You'll see. Now that you're a dad, I hope I make more sense to you." I pause and look around a very familiar room that seems to have taken on a brighter quality to it. I start picking at a thread on my shirt. I fidget with it while I process all he just said. He sits patiently and lets me. He's not yelling or demanding. He's not mocking or chastising me. He's waiting to hear what I have to say.

"Nat taught me to look beyond the words people are saying. Thank her. I'm out. I don't want to rip your head off as one of us leaves the room. Perhaps that's progress."

"Are you leaving Sadie here tonight?" He asks.

I tease him. "You just said you didn't want to spend your golden years looking after my kid."

"I'm an asshole, remember? There's nothing I want more than some baby cuddles right now."

"She's pretty good at those." I smile and realize nothing is ever black and white. Not even my dad. He's not just an asshole.

"She is," he says.

"I'll pick her up in the morning. Fuck off, Dad," I say in a very pleasant manner.

He smiles at me. It's an earnest moment of affection. It's strange, and I'll have to see if we have a different relationship on the other side of this mess.

He says, "What was that for?"

I shrug. "Habit."

I walk out of the room, and I hear him exhale loudly and laugh. "Fuck off right back atcha, son." I grin at our new version of I love you. It's better than the old one where we said nothing at all.

I'm going to go find my mom and kiss Sadie goodnight. I'm getting used to her. What I really need is a night's sleep and to dive into some winter pruning tomorrow. But fuck all that.

Tonight, I need her more. I need her more than I've ever needed anything. I know she won't answer, but I try again.

DAVID: I know you're ignoring me. But please tell me you're ok. I need you.

NAT: Leave me alone.

DAVID: Today was a better day than I thought it would be. I wanted to share it with you.

NAT: Leave me alone.

DAVID: Tonight I will. But tomorrow all bets are off. Night, Sunshine.

She's hurting, but someday I hope she understands how broken my heart is too. Thank fucking God it's Wednesday. I'll go get drunk with the guys. Or whoever the hell is at Starling Bar. I don't care. I only care if there's alcohol. Being a single dad doesn't allow you to get black-out drunk, but she's tucked in my mother's arms and whiskey is calling to me.

CHAPTER 32

DAVID

IT'S three days after my bender, and I'm still a touch hungover. I fucking rang my own bell. Tabi bursts into my house. Because why would she fucking care if I need privacy. Sadie is on her belly and looks towards the door. Tabi scoops her up, and I hand her a burp cloth because she drools like a mutha right now. Tabi doesn't miss a beat and puts Sadie on her shoulder, and baby girl starts playing with Tabi's necklace.

She points violently. "Fix this fucking shit right now."

I stand up and ignore her, walking towards my kitchen for a green juice. I grab one and close the fridge, and gesture to Tabi. She shakes me off. She hates juice. I sip the juice, and I can see her getting irritated. I won't react to her. She's all bluster right now. She won't yell with a baby on her shoulder. She's bouncing now, and the Sadie magic lightens her mood.

"I'm serious. Whatever you need to do to apologize to mopey Natalie, do it." She turns her head and greets Princess Scribbles. "Theía Tabi is here. No need to censor. Let it out, Sadie." Sadie throws her head back and laughs as Tabi tickles her belly. She then dips her down head and pulls her up suddenly, much to Sadie's delight.

"You do know it's not all me, right?" I toss the empty bottle from across the room into the recycling. Nothing but can. Then I grab a water and gesture to her. She nods, sits on the couch, and stares at me while I lean up against my kitchen counter.

"She's the one who is threatened by a baby. I told her I'd choose her too. I told her I'd work it all out." I don't even know if Tabi knows Nat's backstory, but I let a piece of it slip.

I say, "How the hell am I supposed to fix her lifelong abandonment issues?"

"Don't leave." Blunt as always.

I defend because I'm tired of everyone thinking this is all my fault. The lying, absolutely. But I would have lost her sooner if I told her right away. Maybe, that would have been easier.

I say, "I haven't left her. She won't listen. She thinks I'm already gone. Shouldn't you be off doing something for the fucking winery we own? It's my day off, not yours."

She's still swinging Sadie around. "I don't like anyone else you've ever dated. Or banged or forced me to have a meal or a drink with."

I roll my eyes and push off the counter towards her. "They weren't all bad. Gabrielle was great." Not really. The woman is a fleeting shadow in comparison to Nat.

"Ouch." Tabi grabs Sadie's hand and pulls her hair out of her tight fist. Sadie laughs and laughs. Tabi offers Sadie her finger, and she immediately tries to put it in her mouth. I offer Tabi her slobbery plastic keys.

"Ok, stop pulling on Theía Tabi and take your keys, demon grip." Sadie giggles and grabs the keys, and smashes them into Tabi's face. I reach out for the baby to relieve Tabi. To her credit, she pulls her onto her lap and away from her face. She bounces Sadie while she talks. "Gabee. She went by Gabee. Like babee. Uck. No. Fix this."

"How the fuck do I do that?"

"Need her. Show her every day."

"I do need her. Every moment of every day. I need more Sunshine in my life, but she thinks I left her."

Tabi throws a pillow at me. "Get out of your cock's head. Be her friend. You did leave her. You left her every day. Once this cutie came along. You scheduled yourself around her, and you are not on her doorstep right fucking now, you pussy."

"What? We are friends." Now, I'm defensive. But, I'm not the one afraid of going forward. Which is the fucking strangest thing. Nat left me. Not the other way around.

"No, you're not. Your cock wants her so badly I feel it from here, and thank God this tiny one can't understand. But you could be her friend. Have her help you with something. Let her feel connected to you in a way that doesn't involve bodily fluids or the winery."

She gets up to go and kisses Sadie on the head before depositing her back into my arms. I look at that little face and smile. She's calm and sweet right now. I'm sure as soon as Tabi walks away, Sadie will begin to roar, I'll have no fucking clue why, and I'll want to punch a wall until she falls asleep. I didn't know I'd have to teach her that when you're tired, you sleep. When you're hungry, you eat. She doesn't get these concepts yet. I throw her on my hip and walk Tab to the door.

"What do you need help with? Make it up if you have to. She loves to feel useful, and she's really good at it. She's already part of the 5. We can't lose her because you're too much of a douche nozzle to figure out how to keep her."

"I'm raising a human, running a winery, hell, we're building a winery, I might need a minute...." And then something occurs to me. "I know. I know exactly what to do."

I kiss Tabi on the cheek as she turns to go. She kisses Sadie again, who screams at an ear-piercing decibel. Not a cry but a squeal of some sort. It's a new noise, not one I'm a fan of. So loud. How are babies this freaking loud?

"Ok. That's all yours. Call me if you need me. I'm headed out to meet with Luis to see if they can pull the porch and stairs off my nightmare of a future home while they collect the burned-out pieces of that weird little shed behind the big red barn. I do not want to know what that was used for."

"Ew. It's where he kept chickens. It's a chicken coop, you idiot."

"Or a murder shack."

"Are you still freaked out by the ghost cat on the property?" Tabi's certain part of our new Prohibition Winery site, and her new homestead, is haunted.

Tabi waves her hands around. "She had to come from some-where. I gave her the evil eye the other day and nothing. She's a pure demon cat." Her watch pings. "Oh, shit. I need your help."

I put Sadie back down. She's starting to crawl all the hell over the place. I've blocked off a safe zone with pillows. I place her in the pillow palace and turn back to Tabi. "Shoot."

"Interesting choice of words. Be right back, you jackass."

"Dude. Cut with the hostility." That's enough from her already. She runs to her car and is back in a flash.

She says, "Look, bitch, I'm hormonal. Taking shit to try and amp up the baby factory, and I need an outlet." She shoves me. I used to be her favorite punching bag in high school when she had nasty fights with her dad or hormones got the best of her. I know she means none of it. I speak fluent Tabi sass talk.

I cock my head to the side. "You need to scream at me some more?"

"Yes! Muthafucking asshole, I do." Sadie shrieks in delight and rams her head into a pillow. She's either an idiot or a genius. Jury is still out. I turn back to my friend.

I say, "Let it rip, my dearest friend." There's no below-the-belt with us because other than her fucking Bax for years, we have no secrets.

She yells at full Tabi, window-shaking volume. "Thank you. Now get the fuck dressed." I have my shirt off. Scribbles likes tracing the tattoos with her finger and then hitting them. I grab a shirt, and she sets up a pharmacy.

"I need you to shoot this fucking needle into my dumbass stomach. I can't do it again." She rasps the end of that sentence and lifts her shirt. There are series of minor bruises around her belly button, like a sickening smile.

"Christ, Tab. Are you ok? What the fuck?"

"Infertility sucks is what." She cranks this big pen-looking thing two turns and hands it to me. She makes a dot with a Sharpie next to the darkest of the bruises on her stomach.

"Here." She points. "Shove it in and push. I have to do this right now, and Bax is in a meeting." I do it without hesitation, and she winces.

"If it works, you can pick out the middle name." She flops into a chair. "You've seen Bax. He's nutty for babies, and I want to give them to him. But after getting everything checked out, my body isn't cooperating. My piece of shit ovaries need help."

"Sorry."

"Not your place, Gelbert. No fucking sympathy from you. Just shoot me up when I need you. And tell no one."

"Why?" She's usually an open book. Her inability to hide emotions is legendary.

"I'm not ready to face it all, and I don't want sympathy. I want solutions and answers. I just want to be pregnant so badly. It's so fucking frustrating and disheartening every month when I'm not. I thought that's what I was designed for, and I'm broken."

"You're not broken. You're perfect." I say, and she softens her face for a moment. Then she throws off the moment.

"I'm also pissed when I think of all the unprotected sex I could have had. No chance of accidents. Unlike you."

"Ok." I smile and let her have the shot.

"You folded like a bitch there, Gelbert."

"For you, I always do."

She tries to make it to the door, but I yank her wrist and pull her into my arms. I can always get her to open up. Sam makes everyone feel better, but I can make anyone tell me what's wrong. I can't always fix it, but at least I can be there. We stand in an embrace for a minute or two. I feel her whole body relax, then I hear her sniffle.

"I got you. You'll be the next one to get knocked up. Well, if Elle and Josh slow down a touch. How about this? You can have my next illegitimate skank baby." She laughs, and I kiss the top of her head.

I shove Tabi out of my house and close the door. I can't imagine what they're going through. I scoop up Sadie. I can smell she's also just taken a dump.

"Ok. Let's clean that ass. And your loud Theía Tabi just gave me an idea."

CHAPTER 33

DAVID

FUCK I'M TIRED. I'm bouncing her on my hip. She won't leave my fucking side without squealing. She slept in my bed. I surrounded her with pillows, but she kept wiggling until she was right at my side. We were up like three or four times last night. I don't know. It all blends together. This is the first time I've noticed her growing. She's out of all of her teeny clothing into the next size. I have a shit-ton of clothes she's never even worn before. She's too big for them. It's wild.

Today she's wearing a Warriors' onesie. It's the first thing I bought her on my own. She looks so freaking cute. I keep taking pictures of her. I can't believe how different she looks, and she's only been in my house for about a month. We think she's seven months old.

I need to know for sure. There are no medical records because we don't know her name, and if we start some, they have to be on the DL because she's not legally mine. They went ahead and gave her the shots that were due at six months. "Ok, Princess Scribbles. We can do this. Shh. Daddy needs you to shh. So here." I've been withholding the bottle to use it to make this call. She takes it greedily and shuts up. My girl can drank. Tip it up with the best of them.

"Prohibition Winery, this is Natalie. How can I help you?"

"I need your help," I blurt out.

"No. Will there be anything else, sir?"

"Well, I wouldn't call me sir if you don't want me to come down there and start disrespecting your wish to not have sex with me." I wink at Sadie. Then I realize just how creepy that is.

I wait for the laugh that's not going to happen, then she sighs. "David."

"Sunshine. I am well aware of what you want. There will be no Parade today. I get it." She hisses a touch. "Stop it, girl. It was a joke. I really do need your help. Like a friend. Not some down and dirty innuendo like I need you to help the semen out of my cock."

She giggles. And now I really do need her to help me out with that last thought. You know what else a baby does in your home? She limits your libido. And limits where and when you can masturbate. I schedule it around either naps and head to the shower or the brief moments I can pawn her off on people. Last week, I couldn't get it to go down, so I dropped her off at Elle's for like half an hour. It's the least sexy thing ever. It's biological, but now thinking about Nat's lip curl, my entire body is vibrating with want. I need to cancel the Parade before it takes on a decidedly Mardi Gras place in my very Disney household.

"Hold on. I have another call."

I put Sadie in her swing and strap her in. I've learned she can't just balance, and I'm grateful for quick reflexes. Caught her just before trouble. But I can't hold her and have a cock-stirring moment. Ew. Just ew. And my cock is super mad at me right now. I believe it's his longest time-out since sophomore year in college when I thought sex would jinx our chances of winning the NCAA Tournament. Five weeks I went. We got knocked out by a first-round bracket-busting dark horse, freaking Lafayette College. I fouled out on purpose when the writing was on the wall and was balls deep in a couple of cheerleaders before the final buzzer.

She's back, and my soul zings at her voice. "This plan won't work."

"What?" I'm honestly confused as to where her head is at. I know Bax and Josh asked her to stay through Pro/Ho's opening. I figure I have seven weeks to fix this shit.

Her voice is a bit strained. "Trying to be Tabi and Bax."

"Oh, hell no. I don't have time for that shit. Those idiots waited for twenty-some years to actually be together. No. Not looking to woo you when I'm fifty-five. We work together and you stay friends with my friends. I miss bouncing ideas off of you and having a conversations. Can we do that? I'll pawn Sadie off on someone, and let's eat food and look at each other in a purely platonic way. Not angry. Not naked. Just talking. I'll wear actual clothing and not my basketball gear. And you can take the angry stick out of your ass for a second."

She laughs, thankfully. She says, "Lunch. Lunch only."

"Yes. Duh. It's not like I can whip it out and have it charm you like a snake from a basket. A salad and some grilled meats of some sort laid across the top. That's it."

"Swiss Hotel at one." I get the irony of Switzerland, and I know she wants to meet on the neutral Plaza ground. But nope.

"The Swiss is mad at me right now. I left a dirty Sadie bomb in the bathroom and forgot to wrap it up. Poppy's."

"That's hardly neutral ground."

"I didn't know we were on opposite sides, friend. Poppy's still pissed at me. I may have screamed at her a bit. She likes you better, so really, it's in your favor, not mine. You can even keep her in our fake break-up if you like."

"There's nothing fake about it."

"You keep thinking that." There's a pause, and I bite my lip.

"Fine. Poppy's. But if anyone else we know is there, we leave."

"If that's the rule, then we best just drive out to a field and eat sandwiches made at home in the car. It's Sonoma. You can't walk a block without running into someone you know. And I do mean you. I know you've only been here like eight months, but that's plenty of time for the entire town to know you."

"Fair enough. You have thirty minutes." She's cute when she's curt.

"Thanks, Sunshine."

"Natalie," she corrects me. "You called here because you knew I had to pick up."

"Yes. That's exactly why I did that." I hang up and bust out the group text.

DAVID: BABYSITTER ASSISTANCE, PLEASE. 1 TO 31SH.

SAM: Why am I on this chain? I'd only regale your child with tales of heartbreak and woe. And a very strange Etsy store I'm opening to unload all the things I've built to screw Sammy.

JOSH: Sam, we had a meeting. You're done being maudlin. Grab your running shoes and meet me at my house in an hour.

TABI: Can't. I'm covering the phones for your lady. Well the lady you lost and are desperately trying to get back. Her. I have to cover the phones for Nat.

JOSH: Jesus, just shut up Tab.

BAX: Meetings. But kiss her cute feet for me. And Christ, you do talk too much, my love.

SAM: Gross, man. Did you guys see that octopus documentary with the guy who lives in the house that's like on a tide pool? I think I have that relationship with my microwave.

JOSH: Not fucking around, Sam. Get over here. Elle's in the city.

BAX: Are we all going to that fundraiser thing for the museum? Is it a Pro/Ho, or is this an individual thing?

TABI: You have to go because of City Council. But I think Jims is going.

JIMS: I am. Evs will be away, so it will just be me. Tab—be my plus one?

BAX: Isn't she my plus one?

TABI: Nope, Jims doesn't have to shake as many hands. I'm going with him.

DAVID: ASSHOLES! BACK TO ME. I NEED A SITTER.

EVAN: Give me that little bundle. You can drop her off at our house. I'm working from home today.

JIMS: So am I, and I don't want the baby here.

EVAN: Tough. You need to get used to it. Next month is coming on quickly. (heart emoji baby emoji baby bottle emoji heart emoji)

JOSH: Another freaking baby?

BAX: Yeah! I love this.

TABI: WHAT? Blessings! Who is this stranger baby?

JIMS: A little girl we're adopting from Africa.

DAVID: That's incredible. I'll drop your practice baby off around 12:30, thanks.

JOSH: Congrats. That's amazing.

SAM: For the record, I knew and kept the secret. Suck it, bitches.

DAVID: You haven't been out of the house in a week. Who were you going to fucking tell? Your Taco Bell dust bunnies? Go run with Josh. I'm out. Thanks Ev.

CHAPTER 34

NAT

I KEEP REARRANGING the bread in the basket. Surely it looks better with the lavash crackers angled towards the sun like tulips. Then I change seats to see it from his perspective. He's been out at Pro/Ho's future permanent home most of the last two weeks. I've only seen glimpses of him and done most of my work remotely. Usually, the office phones are rerouted to my cell. I only go in when I know one of the other guys will be there. Since we only do tastings by appointment, there really isn't any reason for anyone to stop by. The moment he spoke, my entire body began to get shimmery and rattle. His voice was low and sexy. I wanted to claw my way through the phone and attack him. I want to lick him all over. But I maintained for my heart and my sanity.

It's been working out just fine for now. As long as I make myself indispensable, they won't think of firing me from Pro/Ho until after the opening. I did agree to stay.

The tasting room was one of the last good times I had with David. I haven't been back out to the property since, even though I should. I should be helping to merchandise the place and paint the inside, but I don't want to run into him. And now, I'm sitting in his seat at this table just to make sure he has a good view of the flim-flamming bread. This is hard.

It's sunny today, and because it's winter, it's that crisp kind of sunny day. No humidity, fog, or haze to muck it up. I look through the giant front window. His ginger hair looks sun-kissed and perfect. His features are sharp and defined, and now my conviction gets hazy because he's in ideal light. My heart hurts, and my kitty cat weeps. My brain is fuzzy just at the sight of him. Floopy belly central over here. It's a bit chilly today, and he's wearing a navy pea coat and dark jeans. They hug his athletic thighs, and the collar of a crisp white button-down peeks over the top. Such simple clothing, but on this man, it makes everything complicated. He looks so blanketing sexy in the most basic of clothing. He's all sharp angles and sexy lines.

Even though I have to separate from him because there's no future, it doesn't mean I'm not still in love with him. He looks around the restaurant, which isn't that large, but it does give me one more moment to drink in the sight of him. Phantoms! This was a bad idea. He does all the things to me, and I don't know how to make them stop. I want to tear my clothes off and gently move the artfully orchestrated breadbasket to the side and be his lunchtime special. Finally, he sees me, and his face bursts into a smile so immense the world could never mistake how he feels about me.

I stand and smooth down my heather gray sweater dress. There's a zipper down the back I once wore at the front. It was his favorite toy for the evening. He kept zipping it up and down throughout the evening when no one was looking. He'd growl each time. The zipper's in the back today.

He kisses my cheek, and I hear him inhale.

"Honeysuckle. Always sweet. That's how you smell to me."

And he smells like smokey citrus and cedar. And it's not fair he looks the way he does and smells like that.

"Stop. Please. Let's do this friend thing correctly." I hold out my hand, and he shakes it and holds on too much.

He says, "I'd tell Tabi she smells like a spice rack if she were here. Same diff." He takes his coat off. Then he unbuttons his sleeves and rolls them up. His vine tattoo snaking its way to his wrists. The tattoo I've licked and nipped at. The one I consider to be mine, but it's not. He speaks again through his smirk.

"Your dress is on backward. Need help with that zipper?" He raises a darkened paprika eyebrow, and I attempt to not squirm in arousal. "Then again, maybe it's not on backward, if that's how you play it. I'm game."

I roll my eyes at him and look at his hands as they splay out in front of him grabbing his napkin. "Why is your phone on the table? You never leave it out." He's one of those guys who can't carry it around. He doesn't usually care.

He's clear in his intention and hides nothing from me. He says, "In case Evan needs me." Then he cocks his head. Reality smacks me in the face. He had to get a babysitter to come see me. His focus will never be me. It will always be her.

I find my voice and say, "What is it you need?"

"Do you really want me to answer that? I have a list of places I need to put my tongue. You mean like that list of needs?" He smirks, and I want to lick him again. I want to climb him and have him hold me and tell me this will all pass. This will all be alright. I want him to know my heart better than I do. He's staring at me, and I need to move this along to survive.

I say, "Why the lunch meeting?"

He sits back and motions the waitstaff. A large burly man lopes over to us. "She's not here, but she left instructions about what you should eat."

Just like a Gelbert, to rob me a choice.

David says, "That's cool with me, Nat?"

"No, it's not ok." I don't always order the same thing here, and how could Poppy possibly know what I'd like. "May I please have the chicken salad sandwich on a soft sour roll, not the croissant, without the pickled onions and fries instead of chips? An Arnold Palmer, light on the lemonade. Oh, and no walnuts, please." A familiar waitress walks up, and smiles at the two of us placing food on the table.

Burly man says, "So, you want this?" He places a plate in front of me, and it's my exact order. Damn her. David is served a burger and fries with a side of minestrone soup. I want soup. But I don't want minestrone.

"Yes, but—" And the woman is back with a cup of Dungeness crab bisque and an Arnold Palmer. A pilsner is put down in front of David.

He sips. "Pop thinks of everything. She always knows what people should eat. It's why she's so good at this." David tosses a fry into his mouth and nods at the staff.

He says, "Mel found some potential Sadie moms." And thud. It's like he dropped a poop in the middle of the table. He takes a bite of his burger.

"And how is this my problem?" I act like I don't care about the outcome of this situation.

He chews and sits back. "Damn. Drop the attitude. I didn't do this to you. I did this before we met. Before you went ahead and changed my DNA and life. Give it a rest."

I don't know what to say when he's being angry but saying considerable things.

I say, "I'm sorry." I soften and take a giant bite of my sandwich.

"Thank you." He nods.

I talk through my bite even though I thought it might just keep me quiet. "You don't want to apologize?"

"Again with this? I already have for not telling you sooner about Princess Scribbles." He shrugs at me, and I want to smack his smug face. But I'm confused about who he's talking about.

"Who? Is that a cartoon character or something?"

"It's Sadie, and it's a funny story."

"Tell me." I smile, relieved that the burden of conversation flips to him.

"No. You can't hear how she became Princess Scribbles and insist on pretending you're not part of my life. So, friend, I say again. Cut the shit."

I cross and recross my feet under the table and ensure my napkin is secure in my lap. His lips wraps around his burger, and I watch as he bites and chews. I can't look away from his mouth. He licks the ketchup from the corner of his mouth. Not fair.

He says, "This is not how friendships work, buttercup. It should look like this—I harass you, you give it back to me, all in good fun. Then we talk sports."

"I don't want to talk sports."

"Then I guess we'll have to go back to being in love." He shrugs.

"DAVID!"

He laughs, and I realize he's trying to wind me up. He takes a bigger bite of his burger. I shift in my chair, and he watches every tiny move I make. Every part of me aches. It hurts to be this close and distant at the same time. I have to find the building blocks of protection inside me.

He says, "Plus. For once, I have nothing to apologize about." This knocks the wind out of me. I sit back in my chair. He doesn't want to apologize to me for having a secret baby? I look at him sideways and open my mouth, but he cuts me off before I can speak.

"I've already apologized for lying to you about Sadie, but as for Sadie herself, nope. Not even a little bit. I love you both."

I don't want to delve into my jealousy over a baby. I'm going to let it go. I'm actually going to need to probably grow up a bit too. Am I really jealous of a baby or pissed off he lied? Either way, I think it's possible I need to talk to someone. He needs me, and at the base of all the flim-flamming stuff floating around us, I do care for him.

I say, "Tell me what you need." I can do that. I can be here for him. I can figure that out. Make it about the business of friendship. Because the idea of apologizing for knocking someone up before he met me really is batcrapcrazy.

"Mel found three moms, and I need to know how I should proceed."

"Three?"

He nods. He's unapologetic about that too. He's said that his past made him happy in his present. I wish I could get there with him.

He continues, "I got her all of my texts from Verizon, and she went through them in the timeframe of Sadie's conception. We narrowed it down from sixteen." I wince as he says this. He seems fine with it. I knew he slept around. That's not the wincey part for me. A couple of weeks ago, he called that night 'an accident.' Now it's a conception. His heart has shifted even more.

I ask, "Her conception?"

"You know, the night the lights went out in Georgia."

He smiles, and I say, "Ok. But how—"

He holds up a finger, shoves some fries in his mouth, washes them down with beer, and continues. "Mel and Tommi trolled the DMs of my David Allen account. Yes, I'm that slimy. I have a fake social account for my fake name in order to hook up. Mel used some facial recognition software and matched the prime candidates up against their social media profiles."

"Ew."

"That's exactly what Melissa and Tommi said. They couldn't believe how slimy my DMs were. I did not want to read them. There were many women in there I didn't hook up with because they were seriously sketchy. Then they narrowed it to seven. Five were in my texts, but only three had texts two days in a row. Which means I slept with them."

"You only text women you sleep with for two days?"

"Yes. Once for the hook-up and, my mom raised me right, once in the morning to either check on them, say goodbye or thank them."

"You know you're a douche, right? A kind of man whore."

"Oh, I'm aware." He raises his glass to me.

"And when did you stop this douche behavior?"

"The first day, you sat at Tabi's desk at Prohibition."

Wind. Knocked again. I smile at him. I can't help it. The red scruff on his chin and his ruddy complexion are my own personal fantasy. He probably always will be. I'll remember this always as my forever, almost. His shirt is bucking open a little like he's been lifting even more. His chest is bigger and more defined.

He puts his beer back on the table. "Sorry, but it's true. Come on, let me turn that sweater dress around for you." He smiles again.

"You're still a little douchey." He holds up his fingers and pinches them shut, leaving just a smidge open. I giggle at his joke.

"One is a teacher in Reno. One is an insurance person in San Jose. I'm really hoping it's either one of them so this can all be easy and done."

"You think this is going to be easy?" He leans back in his seat, and I lean forward. I really want to know how he thinks this is going to go down.

"Well, if Sadie wants to see her mother, it won't be hard to get to San Jose."

I'm mid-swallow but just actually hearing what he's saying.

"You're keeping Sadie?" I'd held out a secret hope we'd work it out if Sadie went back to her mother.

"Of course."

My heart both drops and soars. He's the kindest man, and he's no longer just mine.

David says, "I need to find her mom so she can sign an agreement. I need her to waive her parental rights. I don't even know Sadie's birthday or her medical history. I need her birth certificate. Currently, if anyone complains or contests my custody, she can be taken away from me. I have a DNA test, but that proves paternity, not custody. She'd have to go into the state system until I petition for legal rights. Or her punk-ass mom who abandoned her can just sign some papers."

My body responds to the triggers of the state system, and suddenly I see a way through this for me. I'll help him find the mom and put closure on all of this. So she has a permanent home. If it can be done before Pro/Ho's opening day, then all the better. Button it all up neat as a pin and move on.

I'm stunned. All this time, I thought he was racing to find her mother to return her to her life. Then I thought we might have a chance. Wow. I'm such a selfish, myopic person. How did that happen? How did I miss that Sadie was permanent? That he wants to give her the one thing no one's been able to give me. A home.

I'm quickly becoming the villain in a children's novel. Oh, crackerpots, I'm Count Olaf. I'm a baby hater. I'm an unsupportive person. I am horrible. I have to fix this. I have to be there for him. I can't be a baby hater. I don't have to have them, but I don't have to hate them. I can't be with him, but I can be there for him.

"Nat. You ok?" My face must have gone white since I'm clammy. I wipe my hands on the napkin. I turn my focus back to the green eyes that will always comfort me despite all that's ending.

"Yes. I'm going to be ok. I had the wrong impression, that's all. What about the third woman?"

"Momtestant number three is an executive VP of some kind of complicated media job thing in New York. Works in television. If memory serves, she was here for her sister's wedding. And I'd slept with her a couple of months before when she was in town for the bachelorette. There are four sets of texts to her."

"You slept with that woman twice? I thought you didn't do that." My heart seizes a bit. Did he lie about that too?

He puts a hand up to me and says, "Calm it down. I told you this already. I told you there was only one woman I slept with twice in the last decade besides you." He did say it. I remember, but I thought she'd remain anonymous.

"You liked her," I say quietly.

"Not enough to pursue her, obviously. Whoa. Are you seriously jealous of a woman I barely remember from long before I met you? Who may turn out to be a soap opera evil baby ditcher?" He grins at my flash of emotions.

I shift in my seat again and pull a lavash cracker from the basket. I instantly put it back. I don't want that. I swirl my straw and don't look at him.

"Nat. Answer me, jelly, jelly, jelly jealous, Nat." His voice is adorably singsongy.

I collect myself enough to say, "Yes." It comes out as a croak.

"Because you think bathroom banging Momtestant #3 makes what I feel about you less?"

I nod. It does. And now he's tied to her forever. I don't have that.

His entire voice gets softer, "Sunshine, I can only tell you so many times how I feel about you. It's up to you to believe."

I bite my lip and shove my knuckle into the divot of my chin. It's a pressure point that instantly stops me from crying. I collect, and look back at him.

He says, "Can we put our problems to the side for a moment?" And squeezes my hand. He lingers too long as his thumb sweeps over my knuckles. There's love in every touch, look, and word he says, but it's not forever. I know it. And it's not enough.

I sit up straighter in my chair. "Do you remember these women?"

"I do. I'm not that much of an asshole. I do. I remembered two of their first and last names. The woman from Reno, I don't think I ever knew her last name. That's what I'm going to tell Sadie when she asks about her sleazy dad's hook-ups in the future."

"You can't tell her that!"

"I can. It's part of my scared straight program. Let her be afraid of hooking up. Then I don't have to buy a gun when boys come snooping around." I laugh at him.

I take out a notebook and start to make a list of things we need to do. I look at him. "You show up and talk to these women. This isn't a phone or email situation. You owe it to these women to talk to them and ask them to sign those papers."

"I owe them nothing." David's voice takes on an edge. His anger comes to the surface so quickly. He bubbles over, and it dissipates quickly, but he can go there instantly. He needs to go shoot some hoops or weld something. My shiny inner soul smiles, knowing he's not using his favorite anxiety outlet, sex.

I say, "You have to visit them." He nods at me. "And take Sadie."

"What?! She dumped her. Why the fuck would I allow her to shit on her again?"

I take his forearm then let go quickly because our skin blisters when we touch. I downshift to friendzone. I can do this.

I say, "Calm. If you truly want her to be yours." This is the hardest thing I've ever said in my entire life. I breathe in, then exhale quickly, trying to calm myself as I give away the only person who has ever truly loved me. His eyes bore into my skull and heart and the further down regions, but I say what he needs. "You have to know she doesn't really want anything to do with her. You need to see their connection, or lack of it, to feel secure that no one is going to take Sadie away from you." My heart drops into my stomach as I say her name for the first time.

"But what—"

"Then you'll know. You'll know she has two parents to care about her. And if not, then all that love you have has a perfect landing spot. Plus, it's not like the rest of your tribe is going to let her go without a fight."

Me not so much, but Sadie, they'll bloody a knife, a fellowship of the rings, mother of dragons fight for that little girl. Even his dad would carry an ax into battle for that baby.

"David, you need to know she's yours forever."

He crosses his arms over his chest, and his shirt pulls tight on those biceps. I can see the shadow of the rest of his tattoo sleeve. How the hell am I supposed to walk away from that? Oh yeah, there's no room for me. I almost forgot. A stolen lunch or maybe a couple of hours, but that little girl really does need to come first.

"How do you know me this well?" He's slashing at my heart. Of course, I know him this well.

"That's what friends are for. Now, let's set updates for us to visit." I pull out my phone, and he takes my hand.

He shakes his head in disbelief. "You'll go with me?"

"Yes." I can't help but say yes to him.

"This might be the best friend-lunch I've ever had. Conversation, great. Resolutions, great. Food, great. Only hitch is that I'm not currently eating at my favorite buffet."

I look down. When I look up, his eyes are darkened.

"We're friends, David. That buffet is closed."

"For now."

Damn his ego.

CHAPTER 35

DAVID

NAT: You have this. She's got this. The two of you make the best team.

DAVID: The three of us.

NAT: Stop. You know I'm not staying past Pro/Ho's opening. We're not a team. We're an alliance working towards a common goal. Then we'll go our separate ways. And I'll send a Christmas card every year.

DAVID: Cool. Cool. Tell me where to get the mail forwarded. If you leave, then Sadie and I will simply go your way. I hate packing, but I guess we could hire some movers to do it.

NAT: Stop

DAVID: OOOH! I just overheard a couple people talking about a Parade coming to town.

NAT: Shame I'm going to miss it. Too busy with work. I'll have to be a bystander watching the Parade pass me by.

DAVID: As your boss, I decree you should work less and maybe look into settling down into a good spot to at least watch the Parade.

NAT: You're not my boss.

DAVID: A little bit I am.

NAT: Yes. A little bit you are.

DAVID: BRB. Just got here. Thanks, Nat. I don't like to do anything without you, but I certainly didn't want to do this.

NAT: You're welcome.

For the past week, we've been inseparable. Clothed, but inseparable. Almost becoming friends. I have a secret that's going to come busting out of me soon. I love her even more on such a deeper level now. The more time I spend with her, the more I realize I won't be without her. I don't know how to get her past Sadie.

Sadie has quickly become, in tandem with Nat, essential to my life. And probably the most important thing I'll ever do. I need all this to be behind us, so I can focus on getting Nat back. Wouldn't it be nice if this first one was the mom?

Natalie stayed back at the hotel. I didn't think we needed one. We could have driven back tonight. Nat thought if Marjorie is the mother, she might want to spend time with Sadie. It's a nice thought, but she ditched the little girl.

We found Marjorie on social, and I do remember her. It was a drunken evening, and she was pleasant enough. She has a quirk where her voice gets really squeaky when she's excited and sneezes like a freight train when she climaxes. I stopped it all from going down a second time after three sneezes. Nearly suffocated me when her legs clamped together mid-sneeze.

She's got bright eyes that, if I look at Sadie, could be shaped like hers. And her nose is a little button nose like Sadie's. I'm glad Sadie didn't get my ramrod straight Irish nose. She has enough from me already. The ginger is strong with this one. Her hair gets brighter every day. I'm driving to get coffee with this woman. I have the paperwork tucked into the diaper bag along with the check. I'm drumming my fingers on the steering wheel. I fidget with the radio, but there's shit on. I keep looking for something to listen to, and nothing feels right.

"Sadie, there's nothing to listen to. Do you want to sing to keep Daddy calm?" At a red light, I glance back at her, and she shrieks and throws Gibby, the giraffe, at me. She misses, but I appreciate the effort. She begins to slam her little hands onto her snack cup. Then she grabs the handles and flings them all around.

"Shake it, Sadie. Come on, shake those Goldfish. Shake a shake shake." She takes the handle and begins to jerk her arm around while they make a solid rhythm.

But after a few shakes, I realize I didn't put the lid on correctly, and Goldfish crackers fly everywhere. Some hitting her in the face. She's stunned for a split second. I glance back as I pull back into traffic, and she's winding herself up.

"It's ok, Sadie. It's fine, baby girl. Just Goldfish." But I said the word, and now she reaches into her cup, and it's empty, and I'm stuck driving, and there's a fucking nightmare unfolding. I can't stop it, and there's nothing I can do about it until the next red light. Shit. It's like a slow-motion accident of horror and cuteness. Satan Sadie is coming out to play, and I'm not sure I can stop her.

"Sadie. Sadie. Sadie." I snap my fingers, hoping it distracts her. I find the shiny object theory works well for us. If she's upset or persistent about something, I just replace it with something else. Or distract her long enough with something else until she forgets the thing she was upset about. But I have no tricks up my sleeve. The radio is going in and out. Shit. Snapping not working. Her face is squinched up and red.

I sing, "Sadie! Sadie Married Lady." I was in *Funny Girl* in high school. I did it for the girl playing the lead, who delightfully took my virginity during play practice one random Wednesday. But I ended up having to play Nicky Arnstein. I was blinded by teenage pussy and my desire to explore it for the first time. But I got to seduce her and then blow her off each night in character. Our fated love ran the course of the show and junior prom. We parted ways in the summer, just in time for my first taste of tourists. All those bored girls dragged into the tasting room by their parents, ripe for the taking. Josh and I got good at picking them up. If they came into my winery, I'd suggest they go to his and vice versa. One of us could usually close the deal on a set of sisters or cousins. As we got older and legally able to drink, we were in frequent play in the tasting room. Sam and Bax totally dogged with us. Sometimes we'd need Tabi to get into the mix and pretend we were protective and safe older brothers. Tabi always got more ass than all of us, though. It was an excellent sexual scam until they all went off to adult.

But somehow, I still know this song from the play. The screeching is out of control as I get lost in pussy nostalgia. I shake my head to get it clear, and begin singing.

I adapt the words.

"Sadie, Sadie, baby lady. How that baby license works on Daddy's nerves and hotel clerks. Sit you in the softest seat. Sadie Sadie, baby lady, that's you."

It works, she calms down until we get there as I continue to belt out my made-up Sadie song, and she sings along with gibberish. I forget the window is down, and everyone looks at me while I park, but I can't stop, or she'll start crying until I can cram a Goldfish down her gullet. I pop out of the car, singing louder as she watches me come around to get her. I lean down to grab her, and I scoop some of the Goldfish from the seat and plop them into the cup. She sticks out her tiny tongue. She does this when she's hungry. I hand her the cup, and she instantly shoves her hand inside. She doesn't want anyone to hand it to her. She wants to work for the fish. I admire that. She didn't get that from me. I stand up, hoist her on my arm, and grab the bag.

I look over at the patio where Marjorie is sitting. Her dress is too revealing for coffee, but I get it. I said I had to speak to her about something important. I'm a douche. I should have rephrased it. She looks surprised as she stands and puts a hand up slowly to kind of wave to me.

"Ok, Scribbles. We're on. Let's go see if the sex sneezer is your mama." She babbles the letter D. I like to think it's for dad. She can't get to her fish, so she babbles and hits my chest with the cup over and over. I make my way over to Marjorie without stopping at the counter to get anything for me. She looks stunned. She never thought she'd be confronted with the baby she abandoned. Shit. I thought I could play this cool, but this woman let this little lady go. Without a note or a goodbye, just a cashier's check. How the fuck did a teacher get that kind of money to try and buy me off? Without an explanation. She dumped her in the world and thought I could handle it. Well, I'm stepping up now. I don't care if you're a freaking teacher. You suck and don't deserve this baby.

I don't break eye contact as I continue dragging a highchair behind me as I make my way to her. She grins quickly because Sadie is offering her Gibby. It's all the girl really has to offer, and she's giving it to the one person on the planet who deserves nothing from her. I should have brought Natalie to calm me down. I place Sadie in the chair, and she's still babbling like a moron. Marjorie looks down at her, and she's speechless. That's right, you demon, look in your daughter's face. My hands are balled in fists, and I can't sit down. I keep rocking the chair that's in front of me back and forth.

Marjorie has the nerve to bend down into my daughter's face. Sadie seems fine with it. Not pissed or indignant. But fine. She reaches out her hand, and Marjorie puts her finger in it. She wraps her fingers around in a little fist, and my heart hurts. Sadie will always choose her mom.

"And who is this little surprise? So sweet." She stands back up, and I am disarmed by her. Ok, maybe a slight overreaction. Perhaps Sadie's just friendly to her sweet teacher voice.

"Hi. Um."

"David? Are you ok?" I wipe the sweat from my upper lip.

She's not her mom. Marjorie sits back down, and Sadie reaches for something random on the table. I hand her a napkin, but don't look away from Marjorie. I sit down.

"I think I'm fine. You don't know her, do you?"

"The baby?"

"Yes. Her name is Sadie. She's my daughter."

"Wow."

"Yeah. Wow. And she's not yours." Marjorie sits back as if I've offended her. "I mean, not rude like that. Sorry. But, you didn't perhaps abandon her at my family winery?" I should be smoother than this.

"Your family has a winery? I thought you were an architect?"

"Do they serve booze here? Never mind, I'm driving. Um. Can I have that glass of water?"

She slides it to me, and I finish it in one gulp. I'd prepared a million things to say to Sadie's mother, but I never prepared what to say to the ones who aren't her mother.

"I'm going to say a lot of things. Let me preface them with I'm sorry. I used to be a douche nozzle. You're about to find out just how big."

"Oh, I remember how big you are." I grin. It's nice the Parade is remembered fondly. As all Parades should be.

"I'm not an architect. But if it's any consolation, you're the only one I ever told I was an architect. It wasn't my go-to. And my name is David Gelbert. Not David Allen."

"Of Gelbert Family Winery?" I nod. "Why did you lie to me, and why?"

"Shh." I reach into the diaper bag and pull out Cheerios. My secret Sadie weapon when I need her to be occupied. Her best friend Emma loves them, and even though she's younger, she keeps up with her like a champ. Sadie's like some kind of math OCD genius. She arranges them for like ten minutes before she eats. I can get a full thirty minutes of conversation with thirty

Cheerios. Then, like a cat to a can opener, she perks up and starts babbling again, reaching for the bag like a junkie. She babbles the D again. I grin, knowing it has to be me. I'm the D. I put five down on the highchair tray, and she goes right to work arranging and stacking them.

"That's adorable."

"What?"

"You with her. And her intent look. Now I understand you lied to get me into..." she whispers, "bed."

"Let me stop you. I lied to almost every woman to get them in bed. I get that wasn't the ideal way to meet someone, but there it is. I've recently been informed I was a career douche nozzle. And for the record, you can say bed in front of Sadie. I don't think she's catching on yet."

"Wait, shit. You thought I was her mother? You thought I could do that to a baby?"

"No. No." She stands up and throws her napkin down on the table. I stand up and put my hand on her forearm. "Please. Let me take my head out of my ass and try to explain myself. I'm sorry for all of this. I just didn't know what else to do." Sadie begins to ramp up because the Cheerios are gone, and I hear her say, "Ch Ch."

My head swivels. "Hey, sweet girl, are you looking for Ch Ch Cheerios?"

"Ch Ch," she responds.

I look at Marjorie in total shock. "Holy shit, did you see that? She's a fucking genius." I say to Sadie, "You got this, girl. Cheerios. That's right, Ch Ch."

I put down more Cheerios, and she goes back to work. "Marjorie. Please let me buy you more coffee or a tea or a gallon of milk. Do you need lunch? I'll have a honey-baked ham delivered. Anything. Just sit."

"I don't want a ham." She should be indignant. I didn't think this through. Of course, they would be offended. Yikes.

"You and I had a great night. I do remember lots about that night. I lied to you because I'd already lied to your friend about who I was. She was from the area, and I don't like to give out my last name because it becomes about my family winery and not me. I know that's vain and stupid, but I kept up the lie because of your friend. You were wearing a blue dress with pink flowers. You have a dog named Ruffles after the potato chip. I promise you, whoever I was that night, it was a version of who I really am. If I'd met you without anyone from the area, I wouldn't have made up those things."

"Really?"

"Yes. And I want to be completely transparent. I'm involved with someone for real now."

"Really? I've been on a bunch of dates with someone as well." She's haughty and ridiculous. But I hope I didn't do more damage by showing up here.

"That's great. But I need to explain I had sex with you in the window in which Sadie was conceived."

"Oh."

"It wasn't personal. I have to find her mother to get her to sign over her parental rights. I want to release her from Sadie's life, but I have to find her first. You were my first stop, and I can tell I'm going to need to hone my pitch a bit."

"To say the least. So why bring her along?"

"Because no one can lie to that face. A genuine reaction would be hard to fake. I saw the truth when you greeted her. Your warmth and openness. You wouldn't be able to leave her behind."

"Were you worried I might change my mind if I saw her? I mean, if I was her."

"Yes, but I'm also worried about someone changing their

mind down the way, so I wanted to be able to confront them with this sweet face and have them choose for real."

"You are a douche nozzle."

"Oh, most definitely. A big one."

"Who is she?"

"No clue, that's why the coffee."

"No, the woman who held your attention?"

I smile. "Oh, Natalie. She's amazing, and I'm in love with her. And she's in love with me, and we're not together because she's not sure about all of this."

"She needs closure too, then. She needs to know the mother isn't going to come and take Sadie away. Or you."

"Come again."

She leans forward, and I'm listening intently. I reach behind me and put five more Cheerios down.

"You were a jock, right?" I nod. "Stop acting like a cliché. Stop pushing forward on instinct and think about the impact to the team. She doesn't want to invest in this little girl, or you, if either of you is going to be with the other woman."

"I don't want anyone but her."

"If her mother wants her back, you'll still get to see her. Your girlfriend would be cut out of the picture. You'll always be connected to the mom."

Shit. Natalie is afraid of losing. I thought she was afraid of winning. Of getting things, she's always dreamed about, not the losing part of it all. I'm unable to prove to her she won't lose. If that's the case, then what the hell am I even doing.

Without looking away from Marjorie, I put another five Cheerios down in front of Sadie, and she squeals, "CH. CH! D! Ch."

"I won't lose Sadie. I can't. I'm in it now. I'm in it with Nat and Sadie, and I have to figure out how to mesh all this together in some kind of family stew."

"I wouldn't present it to her with the stew reference. Sounds like a pot of misfit ingredients." How is the sex sneezer this wise?

"But if you cook it long enough." Marjorie is shaking her head no at me, and I hear it. Stew isn't sexy, despite what Sam says.

"Thank you, Marjorie. I hope this guy is the one for you. And I'm sorry for all of this."

"Be well. And take care of this tiny, fantastic joy. Bye-bye, Sadie. Bye-bye." She does that whole hand open and shut thing with both hands as Marjorie coos bye bye to her. Then she kisses me on the cheek and leaves.

DAVID: *It's not her.*

NAT: *I'm sorry. I know you want this over with.*

DAVID: *You know you're not losing me, right?*

NAT: *I do know that. You're a good friend.*

DAVID: *Drop the act. We could never be friends. Not while I still want to lick you. And I'm madly in love with you.*

NAT: *Stop saying things like that.*

DAVID: *Cuz you'll get the wrong idea?*

NAT: *It complicates everything.*

DAVID: *Then be with me, and then it's all easy.*

NAT: *Now I'm getting the wrong idea.*

DAVID: *Is it that I want to dump cold water on you or the idea where I move you into my house and never let you out of our life? Which one is the wrong idea?*

NAT: *Let's start with you feeding me dinner as we drive home to Sonoma.*

DAVID: *Deal. But let's stay the night.*

NAT: *Separate beds!*

DAVID: *Keep telling yourself that.*

CHAPTER 36

NAT

SADIE LOOKS EXHAUSTED. I even held her for a moment today. But she's getting cranky and crying. David makes her a bottle and gently puts her into a sleeping outfit. He narrates everything he does, and it's like crack to my kitty. Even my ovaries are responding as her eyes look adoringly at him, and her hand tries to peel up his tattoos. The moment where he has to make a choice is long past, and I see the choice. It doesn't make me want him any less. That's the haunting right there.

I have my feet curled up underneath me on one of the couches. The front desk was so charmed by Sadie they upgraded us. We have a suite with a dining room, living room, and several bathrooms. The walk-in closet is larger than my first studio apartment in DC. There are two queen beds. I insisted, and they brought up an actual portable crib, so we didn't have to set up the pack n play. I'm told she won't sleep in it anyway. She prefers the bed surrounded by pillows or a crib.

He lifts the glass and brass coffee table over his head like it's nothing and puts it in the front hall closet. Then he takes the extra cushions off the two side chairs and creates a barrier. He plops her down with brightly colored plastic rings, and she quickly goes to work on stacking them. He sits across from me on the other couch. He's wearing those dimdarn sexy gray sweats, and a soft baby-blue t-shirt fitted tightly across that rippled chest. I can almost see his abs—my mouth waters. I'm wearing a cream t-shirt I know he likes and polka-dot jammie shorts. We stare at each other for a moment. I clutch the coffee mug full of Merlot between my hands.

"If I don't come over there and kiss you, I'm going to die."

Sadie squeals, but he doesn't look. He keeps staring at me. And my resolve is gone.

I sit up a bit and he licks his lips. "Well, I don't want you to die." I smile a little, and he leaps past Sadie and her pillow fort and I'm in his arms in an instant. His lips are warm and inviting and perfect. I surrender to the fireflies low in my belly. And sigh. He takes the mug from my hand and puts it on the ground, his lips never leaving mine. He nips at my lower lip and lowers me onto the couch. He's on top of me, and all the gloom is pushed from my mind and heart. I nestle beneath him and open my mouth slightly. His tongue licks the inside of my mouth slowly and softly. He's teasing me, and I love every second of it. Then he claims my mouth like I've so desperately wanted him to do for so long. I denied it, but his tongue is aggressively tangling with mine. Our hands are groping and pulling at the odds and ends of each other. I feel myself buck my pelvis forward, seeking relief.

"There's my Sunshine." His Parade comes to life, and he grinds down on me while his hand pinches my nipple under my shirt. We're gasping and desperate for each other.

Then the pillow fort comes down, and she's pulling up on the couch. Or trying to.

He groans, and we both look at the little face. She smashes her tiny fists into the side of the couch, laughing. I wiggle from underneath him. The heat between us remains, but my senses return. I smile from the corner and wrap my arms around my middle. David flops face-first onto the couch with a giant moan and I laugh. Then he sits up and scoops her off the floor.

"Ok, you little cockblocker, time for bed."

She babbles, "DaDaDaDaDa," and his face lights up.

"Sadie, Nat is not impressed with the fact that you're babbling Daddy now. She should be. She will be, but for now, cool it. I'm trying to get laid, and you are not helping." He foists her over his head, and she's giggling. He settles her into his side and heads to the bedroom.

I stand there, unsure of what to do.

"NAT! Come on. Help is required. It's why you came along, right? Jesus, you're lazy." I laugh at him and step into the bedroom. He's got Sadie in one arm, pulling the crib with the other.

"Take her." I put her in my arms, and she puts her hand on my face. For a brief second, I wonder if there's something wrong with me that I don't feel a pull towards her. Then she yanks my hair.

"Careful, she's got a fierce grip." I get my hair out of her hands, and she's looking around to see where David is. He's pulled the crib out of the room. I follow into the hallway, and he's arranging it in the walk-in closet. It's like her own personal sleeping chambers. He grabs the baby monitor camera from his bag and sets it up. Checks his phone. He turns to see the two of us. He looks beyond the baby and leers at me. Then pulls off his t-shirt. I lick my lips in response.

"Yeah. There it is, Sunshine. That bubble gum-pink tongue that I'm going to need on my cock soon."

I blush a bit, and Sadie whines and reaches for David. He scoops her up and grabs Gibby and Vino Bunny. He plops all of them into the crib. Then puts a giant puffy book of animals in there. His phone plays Nick Drake's "Pink Moon." She settles into the crib. He crouches down and puts his hand through, and holds her fingers for a second.

"Night night, Sadie. You bubble butt beautiful baby." She giggles slightly, then rolls towards him, pulling Vino Bunny's ear in her mouth. He leaves and pulls the door almost shut.

I don't even get to say a word before I'm bent over the bed on my back. He's on top of me. Heat pulsing between us. Our eyes are dark and wild as we slip into our sexy roles. My hands claw at his back. My mouth and legs are completely open to the man. His hand snakes up my shirt, and he squeezes. He pulls back from our tongue war and says, "You know I'm going to need these. Why didn't you remove your bra?"

I giggle. It's my David. Mine, on top of me, joking with me. "I wanted to give you a challenge."

"Fuck that, Sunshine, you're already too much. Do you mind if I rip this from your body? I need your nipples now."

He scoots off the bed and jerks me to standing. His hand is up my back. He snaps the band quickly, and it releases. I gasp. His hands are on my nipples, and he pushes the cups out of the way. His large, commanding hands that can palm a basketball and manipulate metal. They're rough and soft at the same time. He's kneading and pinching, and I might just go over the edge with this. He takes my mouth aggressively and I'm thrilled we're not going to make this some gentle lovemaking session. Not that our relations have ever been super gentle, but I want the Parade, not him, in the long run. It has to be that way. But right now, he's all mine. My shirt is lifted, and his mouth is on my nipple, his hand on my ass squeezing me closer to him. He bites, and I inhale sharply. I moan. I reach down and stroke him through his sweats. He moans back. I reach my hand to his waistband and into his sweats. When I touch him, I feel the pre-ejaculate and push it down over his shaft. He amps up his kissing, and it's assertive and all encompassing. I'm lost in a thrashing of tongue, lips, and teeth.

"I've missed your mouth." I gasp. He looks up at me.

"In that case." He throws me on the bed, and my polka-dot shorts are gone in an instant. I'm spread wide for him as he looks at me. His gray sweats hiding nothing. I see his complete outline, and my mouth waters.

"Eyes up here, missy." He grins. "I need to watch you come on my face. I need to be coated in you." He licks me without warning. Strong, flat tongue from the bottom to the top. My lady button buzzes on contact. I love when he does that. "You're so fucking gorgeous."

"That's because I'm almost naked, and you're horny."

He lets go of my legs and planks over top of me. "No. Don't ever think that. Your pussy is perfect, don't get me wrong, but your face, your heart, your soul are such perfection. You're so gorgeous, everywhere. I've missed you so much."

"Stop. Please just—"

And reality interrupts us. He leaps off me, and as he's out the door to fetch a screaming Sadie, he says, "Don't move."

I scramble for my shorts and put my shirt back in place. I jam my forefinger knuckle into my chin, but it doesn't work this time. I cry, just a little. I'm not sure if it's because I really do want what he wants. Or if we're both delusional.

I curl up in the other bed and pull the covers over me. I stay like that for half an hour. He comes back, and I feel his lips on my ear. I pull my eyes shut.

"You can fake pout sleep all you want. But we're both coming tonight. You want to play out some sleep or corpse kink, go ahead, but the Parade float is all inflated."

I crack open my eyes, and he's facing me, kneeling on the floor.

"I'm sorry, but the Parade is canceled tonight, David. Please.

Please let me sleep. You sleep in the other bed in case she needs you in the night. That way, I might not wake up."

His face falls. "I see what you're doing. You can't hide from us forever. It will be the worst wedding ever when you are at the altar still pretending we're not together."

"Please." My voice cracks. He kisses me softly on the head as he stands up.

"Night, Natalie. I'm now going to say two things you don't want to hear. You're welcome to come to my bed and just sleep. I miss holding you as much as everything else. And I love you."

I say nothing as he climbs into the other bed. Every piece of me cracking as I reject happiness again.

———

I WAKE TO HIS ARM PULLING ME CLOSER AND HIS SMELL comforting me. I snuggle deeper into him. I don't know when I crawled into his bed. It was a dream I had. But, apparently, it was a dream I made come true.

"Shh. Put your head to sleep and let me just love you." I kiss his forearm and let him.

CHAPTER 37

NAT

IT WAS a close call in Reno. It's been a couple of days avoiding him after the strange drive back to Sonoma. We barely spoke, and both just took care of Sadie to avoid talking about us. I miss him. It was the best sleep I've had since I found out.

We can't be in the same room like that again. He left me in the middle to take care of her, and he should. But I'm the one who lay there feeling as if the baby had won. Am I genuinely jealous of a baby? I'm horrible. There's only so much David to go around, and my piece of him keeps getting smaller. I don't want to spend another night crying. I snuggle down into the blanket on this couch. It's not the most comfortable, but it is beautiful. If I lived here for real, I'd replace it with something cozier but not as chic. But I'll be gone soon enough, so it's fine. I hear a car come up to the cottage, and I know it's Will Whittier. He always brings me a wrapped dinner on Sundays. Like I'm an orphan. Oh, right.

I slump on the couch and wait for his signature knock and his quick rendition of "Dancing Queen." Not ideal, but it always makes me laugh. All my work is done for tomorrow, and I need to check back in with Bax. He has several consulting gigs now, and I'm hoping to jump from Pro/Ho to his gig. He'd let me live wherever I want. I'm so used to missing David that I'm used to the pain like people get used to a bunion. It's all I have left of him. I'm not ready to give up the pain. Eventually, I'll have to take care of it, but the pain is manageable for now. Most nights.

Not tonight, though. Tonight, it's a dark and twisty pit of *what could have beens* and *why can't I justs*. I can't cry again. My hair's in a random headband, and I have on my sloppy PJs. The ones no one ever gets to see but bring me great joy. I'm in floral leggings and a gray Washington Wizards shirt that goes down to my knees and is in that wonderful t-shirt phase where it's almost see-through. It's so thin. It's about to be too late for this shirt, so I wear it sparingly. There's a single banging knock. That's not Will. I open the door, and my breath is gone. White V-neck contrasting with the delicious ink on his biceps, tight jeans, ginger hair askew, and a sly smirk on his lips. He looks me up and down and licks his luscious lips. He looks way too good.

He puts his hand up to stop me from saying anything. "Shh. No fucking talking about anything. I need you. Do you need me? Just for tonight. I know the rules. I know you can't with me or us —just tonight. Just be with me. Let's be us for one night. It's fucking unbearable how much I miss you. I know I just said we're not going to talk. But I'm going to kiss you now unless you slam this door in my face. And if you don't slam it in my face, I'm going to slam your body on that far wall and fuck you until you can't walk tomorrow."

I nod, and before I'm done, his lips are on mine. I'm a full pour of whiskey as heat floods my system, and I feel like I've just been served. I gasp into his mouth, and his tongue is instantly inside mine. His hands mold me to his body, and I clutch at his biceps. The kiss is uncontrolled and unselfconscious. We go for every inch of each other's mouths.

He picks me up, and I hitch up against him and grind like an alley cat in heat. He growls and nibbles my neck.

"Here's your only choice tonight." My whole body lights up. He needs to be in control, and I'm happy to relinquish all say tonight. It means that tomorrow I don't have to take responsibility for all the things he did to me.

"What's my only choice?" I throw my shirt to the side, and I'm topless. He looks to the ceiling.

"Choice revoked. I'm going to do all the things. I was going to ask how you wanted to come first, but I've just decided for you."

He whips off his clothes as he bounces on the bed and pulls me to him. He buries his face between my boobs, and his hand moves down towards my waistband.

"By the way, these are fucking hideous. They look like grandma curtains." He puts his hand down the front of them, and I'm so ready. "So perfectly wet for me, aren't you, my Sunshiny slut?" I gasp as his fingers swirl around my lady button. His lips are on my nipple as he slips a finger inside me. He pulls it in and out, and I squirm to get more of him.

"Answer me. Are you wet just for me?"

I gasp. "Only you."

"Fuck, Nat." He puts another finger inside and pumps harder and I can't take his tongue on my nipple. I call out. It's a sneak attack. I didn't even feel it build when my body begins to convulse.

"Jesus. You're going to snap my fingers off with that powerful pussy pulse you got going. Fucking come again. Come on, let me feel it." He kisses me quickly and deeply. He doesn't stop the motion of his fingers. He puts me on the bed, and now his mouth is on me. He sucks my enter key into his mouth. I can't take it. I scream. I'm so sensitive and ready. My entire body lifts off the mattress, and he pushes me back down. I can't take it.

"David. Stop. You have to stop."

He lifts his face. "Oh, Sunshine, I'm just getting fucking

started. You're going to be rung out when I'm done. Then you get to be on top. If I only get one night, it's going to be epic." He pulls his fingers out of me and crawls up my body, kissing as he goes. He arrives at my face, and I look into his eyes.

"Let me make sure both of us are spent tomorrow, my love."

"No love talk."

He notches himself, and the Parade is on in one thrust. I arch into him. He kisses me. "Impossible. No matter what happens, there will always be love between us."

Then he smirks, thrusts enough to push me into the mattress, and I surrender to his magical member and the night.

"David," I say breathlessly as we settle into a grinding thrusting pattern, and I know I'm going to come again. I'm going to keep coming. Oh. My. I'm saying coming. I want to release everything and fall into the abyss of tingles with him.

I KISS HIM SWEETLY, LEANING OVER THE BED WHEN I RETURN FROM the bathroom. His hands behind his head looking comfortable. Our situation crashes down on my shoulders, and I feel worse than before. He kisses me, then gets out of the bed. I don't stop him, but I want to.

He pulls his pants on and grabs his t-shirt. This all feels wrong. Even though I got what I wanted, I didn't. He's looking at his feet, then finally looks into my eyes.

He says, "It will be more difficult to leave you in the morning." He grins, trying, and I see my David slip away behind a veil. I've had about a hundred orgasms, and I'm trying to swim in the serotonin, but it's all too painful.

He snaps to snark mode. "Ok. Um. So, I love you. I will always love you. How about when Sadie goes to college, we continue this? That cool with you? Wait for me."

I smile and try to laugh. He's pacing the room. He glances up at me, and now I know he's flipped to irritated.

"Come to me, Nat. It's on you. Whether you believe me or not, every moment of my day is dimmer because of your absence in my arms. I don't say shit like that. That's how you know it's real. You make me speak like I'm a Netflix boyfriend."

"David." My voice is so small.

"You may think that little girl fills my soul. She does, but not all the way. Not like you. Not like when you smile at me and see who I am, despite all the jackassery I've pulled, the women I've slept with, and the shit I've screwed up. You look at me, and my life is in focus. It's clear what happiness looks like reflected in your beautiful blue eyes." He holds my face for a moment, then pulls back physically. I pull back mentally.

I'm standing in front of him, completely naked. This won't do. I turn from him, and he follows me into the living room. I grab my Wizard's shirt from the floor. I put as much distance between us as I can in this tiny cottage, but he stalks right after me.

He takes my arm and spins me towards him. His face is pained and stern. "Nat, if you see your life somewhere else, then please go. If you think you'll find what we have again, I wish you well. Because you won't. This is the thing I thought I'd never get. The thing I thought was a freaking myth. How the hell does everyone I was brought up with get to find their soulmate? Bax and Sam always believed it's just what you do because that's all we were exposed to. Josh begrudgingly came around to Elle being his one perfect thing. Forever wasn't for me. I was resigned to keep banging twenty-year-olds for another couple of years, then settling down with the one who annoyed me the least. We'd have a life full of sex, and I'd have my conversations with my friends because we'd have nothing to say to each other. But each time I'm with you, there's not enough time to tell you all the things crowding my head. We could seriously get to the end of our days, and I would have like six more things I needed to tell you. But none of that fucking matters. This is now on you. Choose me or leave. I can't take it. It's just fucking cruel to have to see you every day. If I could leave, I would. I know you can't take it either."

I pull on my jammie shorts. I refuse to be pantless while I stand up for my feelings.

I say, "I get it. This isn't my home. I'm cast out again."

"Jesus, Nat. I don't know what you want from me any longer. I was your fucking home, but you're the one choosing to cast out yourself."

"But—"

He interrupts, "I will never get over you, but at least I can try and not be Sam. He's so devastated he can barely move around during the day. I just want to be the sad single dad who once had everything on the horizon. But just like the NBA or Pratt or my dumbass sculptures, I let it all slip away. I can't leave here, but if I could, I'd give you this town. Fucking keep it. But you being around is too fucking painful. I love you, but stop dicking me around."

"I'm not. And all those things you let go of because of your dad."

"No. You told me to listen, why aren't you? Look, my dad and I talked. See—more shit to tell you. Fuck. Stop dicking me around."

"I'm not." I stamp my foot and move to straighten already perfectly piled books on the shelf.

"You are. You won't tell me why, and then there's this let's be friends bullshit. I only did that so you'd talk to me. I don't want to be your friend. But apparently, I am so fucking whipped, I'll create an imaginary friendship. I'll fake caring about your paperwork. I'll make sure you have orgasms, and I'll pretend you still love me while we have sex. Super cool deal for me." He punches the couch, and the frame shakes. He stalks around the room. I've never seen him this way. He's shaking his hands like he needs to fidget.

"Stop it. Don't do this." Don't cheapen what we feel for each other.

His voice is beyond angry. "Why the fuck not, Nat?" I don't answer him. He nods. I see the pain in his eyes, and it matches my heart.

He throws his hands in the air. "Got it. You get to walk away with your closure and your dignity. You're not begging me to be with you. Fabulous. Then leave. Get out. Get out of my town. It will be painful to be here without you, but it's excruciating to be here with you and not be with you."

"No." I made a promise to Bax to stay. I promised to see the opening through. I'll go eventually.

"Is it your damn work ethic? You feel the need to finish things. And you blame me?"

"Yes, I still do."

"Bullshit. You've shut down Natalie, who has compassion and kindness. The one who loved me for me. I'm done being your punching bag to rectify your past. I will take a lot, clearly. But we finally found the line where I'm just a fucking clown in your parade of selfishness. I'm sorry I had a better childhood, but I'm not sorry I tried to give you a better adulthood. When you're old and look back, you'll have only yourself to blame. I won't fucking take that role." His hands are flailing, and I need him to stop. The volume and anger are so much. I wish I were different. I wish I could give him a better ending. I don't know how to move past my pain.

I place my hand on his chest. I want to calm the beast. "Stop. Don't talk to me like this."

His words are biting, and his chest is hard and unyielding.

"Fuck off."

"You don't understand," I plead as I follow him around the small cottage. He walks outside and paces in a bigger circle around the makeshift patio.

There's a big bell in a tree just off the patio. The LaChappelle bell. It used to be rung to signal that police were coming to raid the winery during the Prohibition era. They're the only winery to never get busted. That's why they call this cottage the Look-out. I stare at the bell, so tough and rigid. It's still intact and beautiful, but it doesn't ring. It's stuck in the tree that's grown around it. That bell is annoying the heck out of me. I don't want to be the stuck bell, but I am. I don't know how to get unstuck.

He's planted so far from me. "As you walk away, remember this, I chose you. I continued to choose you. You didn't pick me. Fucking hurts more than I ever thought possible. But this time, you're the one choosing to pack and leave. Sadie didn't ask for this any more than you asked for the childhood you ended up with. Fate put her in a better place to grow up. Is that it? Do you resent her for falling into a better life than you did? Tell me you're not that person."

"No," I say, immediately trying to convince myself as well.

"I desperately wanted to change the past for you, to make it right, and now I have that chance with Sadie. But lately, I've realized if any of your past were different, you wouldn't be the perfect human I'm completely in love with. I don't want to change your past. I wanted to build our future."

"David, it's not that simple. We have to deal with the lies."

He rolls his eyes. "Broken fucking record, Nat. You seem to be stuck hiding behind some righteous indignation there. Doesn't look good on you. I'd ditch it. Maybe the next man you choose to ruin by walking away will buy your shit. You abandoned me. You shut me out. You wrote me off. You told me there's no room for me in your closed life. Enjoy the silence."

"I don't know what you want me to say." I put my hands on my hips, trying to look as if I know what I'm doing. No room in my life. That's funny.

He holds his hands out in a praying motion. "Please leave Prohibition. Leave me something. Don't make me fire you."

"You can't. You waived that right in the HR document."

He smiles slightly. Then it turns.

He's in my face in a flash. "Fucking hell, Nat. It's too painful to see you. Don't you get that? It's maddening to know you love me, and you're choosing to be an asshole. You're choosing for us to be alone in our misery. I'm starting to remember quotes from coaches I used to have. If you have to force it, it's not right. I'm done trying to convince you to love me. To be with me. It's awful."

"You think it's any less painful for me?" I yell right back at him.

"Yes. I do." He crosses his arms over his chest.

"Why?"

"You seem fine. I'm barely holding it together. I'm consumed by thoughts of you."

I yell, "I'm a mess, OK! Happy now?" I throw my hands in the air and walk away from him. I pick up the chairs and rearrange them on the little patio. I make sure none of the chairs face the stupid flim-flamming bell.

He smirks, and I want to hit him. He's got his hands in his pockets, and he's staring at me.

I continue, "I'm destroyed by every moment and every thought. I build myself back up and compartmentalize. I have a lifetime of moving on, and for the first time, I'm not sure how. This place, these people, I thought I'd found my place. And you. Oh God, you. David. It's too painful—every night, I sit here and let my stomach eat away at itself, knowing you're giggling and playing daddy without a thought for me."

"First of all, you insane woman, I'm not playing. I am daddy. I am Sadie's daddy and love all of it. Even the colossal blowout shits where I run to the hospital. I do. When whoever signs over parental rights, it will be elation and relief like I've never felt. She's pride and hope and joy. She's all of that and more. But it's a different love."

"I can't be happy with what's leftover."

His shoulders fall. "And finally, there's my why. It's everything I hoped you weren't. Great. Thanks. I'm out. Think about a new job. Or let's think of a way to completely avoid each other for a moment. Until my winery opens its doors. Then if you have to be there because apparently, you can find it in your heart to be there for Bax, I'll nod, and you can take the fuck off from there." His face is cold, and his eyes are clouded over. I finally did it. I pushed him away successfully.

"David." I move towards him, and he moves away. He's rejecting me altogether. I knew he would if I told the truth. That's always how this goes down.

"Nope. No David. No. All in or all out. That's the terms of our relationship, and since you have all the power, I'm guessing it's all out."

I try to touch him, and again he yanks his arm out of my grasp. "Please understand."

His voice is sarcastic and low. "Seems it's time for me to leave. Enjoy your fortress of solitude. Remind me to write you a good letter of reference when you eventually get the fuck out of my winery and life."

He slams the door of his car. I run into the house and crumple onto the floor. I stare at the door, knowing he's never coming back. I always succeed when I set my mind to a task.

It's a long time until I finally hear the gravel crunch under his tires. The engine flares. I hear it get fainter, the sound of everything shattering around me.

CHAPTER 38

DAVID

I'M STILL FUCKING PISSED she won't even try to figure this out. There's nothing else I can do. I have to get over her. Pro/Ho's opening will be a dividing line. Hopefully, I'll have this custody shit worked out, and Nat will be gone. As long as she's in my sphere, there's no way I'll ever get over her.

I won't return to full douche nozzle behavior, but I will be bringing back a bit of that. I'll take Sam. The two of us can drown our sorrows in a sea of stranger-danger pussy. But I swear, I'm thinking of getting a vasectomy.

"Sadie, girl. Your daddy is a complete tool. He was just thinking of getting snipped so he could go back to a life of casual and freaky sex. Yes, he was. Your daddy's a horrible person, but he loves you. He loves you so much." I really do. There'll never be a day where I don't love both Nat and Sadie. I'll have to figure out how to live with the pain of losing one of them and not blaming the other for the loss. It's not Princess Scribbles' fault. It's the damn leaky condom's fucking fault.

I look back at her—she's fighting a nap—and I realize that damn leaky condom gave me the whole world. I reach back and squeeze her tiny feet.

I turn my mind back to the drive. I'll redirect my anger. Maybe it will help dissipate the fear that I'll lose both my girls in two days.

Headed to San Jose to meet up with Momtestant #2. This one I'm a little scared of. If memory serves, she's a bobcat in a burlap sack wild. There was some biting, and not on my part. My back had scratches, as well as my kitchen cabinet. I sanded it down, but she took a fork at one point and made her mark, as she called it. I'm surprised she didn't pee on everything to mark her conquest. If this is Sadie's mom, it might explain her stubborn streak.

She's been whimpering and crying for the past half hour. I'm trying to ignore it. She doesn't want to be in her car seat. She kicked and arched and pushed on anything her little eight-month-old body could to not go into it. I took her away from Emma and Elle because this woman could meet with me now. She's way attached to them. She likes to drum on Elle's enormous stomach. Since Natalie is barely speaking to me, trying to put distance, which is a load of bullshit, I didn't tell her I was about to meet Momtestant #2.

Sadie's livid I took her away from a play-date. But it's not like the babies were doing anything together. Emma is a little over two months older and pulls up on every fucking thing she can. And Sadie sits and laughs at her. Then she falls over in order to make Emma laugh. The two of them howl together. I was in such a rush to get to Heather, I agreed to watch Emma next week so Sadie could have another opportunity to play the clown. I groan, realizing it's two butts to wipe.

Sadie's cried herself out a bit and is doing the eye flutter thing. I reach down into the diaper bag on the front seat and pull out Gibby. She takes it lazily, tosses her thumb in her mouth, and finally loses the battle with consciousness.

It's not that long of a drive, and since we've decided it's nap time, I'm hoping she'll stay asleep. She's bad with the transfer. The moment you move her from one location to the other, the nap is over. I have a policy that she stays where she lands. She's napped all over the house. I've even sat in the car for an extra hour to keep her napping.

I have an hour-and-a-half drive ahead of me. An hour with just my head to keep me company, and that's not a good thing. Heading down to San Jose and that stupid old song keeps running in a loop in my head. I don't know any words except "Do You Know the Way to San Jose?"

I know what not to do this time. I think. This woman, Heather, is completely different from the school teacher in Reno. She's a tech warrior who wears battle gear for fun. I picked her up at a bar in Napa as she was escaping from a corporate retreat. I was utterly enthralled with the number of buckles I'd have to release to get to her. She was wearing a soft chest plate. Like an umpire almost, but fitted and not bulky. She also had neoprene that hid not a curve. She's a voluptuous and incredibly sexy woman. There was something about her I couldn't turn down. The following day she was up and gone before I could even formulate a plan. I was never sure if I wanted to see her again because I liked her or if it was so I could be the one to leave. The sex was plentiful and kinky, and I hope to God my sweet Sadie wasn't conceived while I was spanking that woman's ample and delicious ass and riding her into the headboard. She does have a hall of fame ass.

I HAVE THE PAPERWORK IN FRONT OF ME, AND SADIE'S SUCKING down a bottle. She's changed and happier with me again but has a death grip on Gibby. I know she's still tired. It's fucking weird how well I know her. I'm exhausted because I screwed up her nap schedule again this week, so we were up watching Sports Center highlights late last night. At least she got a little sack time in, on the way down here.

I have the Cheerios waiting in a bag under the table so she can't see them. I'm ready to battle with this imaginary army of people who want to take my daughter away. I'm sitting outside at Roy's Station. It's a coffee and tea place with killer quiche. I hand Sadie one of the pouch things that have like a whole meal smashed up in it. She greedily takes it. When the aliens come and tell us all we have to eat pureed things from pouches, this generation is the only one who will be ready. Sure we had Go-Gurt, but this entire chicken dinner in a tube thing is a genius and a scary development.

I see a shock of platinum blonde hair in dreadlocks emerge from what looks like a vintage Camero. All heads turn as she begins to walk towards me, the undulation of her hips calling out to everyone in the universe, 'Not only do I like myself, but you fucking love me and can't have me.' Every head is turned towards her powerful energy.

I want Sadie to be that confident in life. Imagine if this were her mother. Maybe she'd get that indefinable ability to tell me to fuck off if I told her what was best for her in life. If Sadie got to go to art school instead of taking the basketball scholarship because it's what would make her happy. If she had this woman's gumption and determination, that would be a good thing, just like it would have been lovely for her to have the sweet warmth and openness of Marjorie.

I wave to Heather as I smooth Sadie's flyaway hair. Heather stops dead in her tracks. Her voice is loud and commanding. It carries across state lines.

"Fuck No. Fuck to the HELL NO. I'm into daddy kink, but I am not into daddies. I do not fuck fathers as a rule. No matter how hot."

I stare at her, and she nods at me. I salute her. She laughs. "You're still a hot piece of ass there, David Allen."

I yell, "Gelbert. It's David Gelbert."

"Fuck yeah, it is."

"I'm sorry I lied to you."

"You might be a DILF, but I don't do that shit."

"Kids? Or men with kids?"

"Both. I had my tubes tied five years ago. No, thank you. Take care." And like that, she's gone.

She's still in the parking lot yelling to the patio. Sadie begins chattering, and I hand her some Cheerios and smile. At least I know who her mother is now. Momtestant # 3. The only woman besides Natalie I've ever slept with twice in the last decade.

"Sadie. Looks like we're going to New York."

CHAPTER 39

NATALIE

I'M SWEEPING because that's something I do often lately. I'm doing it before they paint tomorrow.

I sweep the tasting room or clean the offices. I Pledged the desks last week at the Plaza space, and Sam complained that everything smelled like a hospital with everyone sucking on lemon drops. He's better, but still a little slovenly. I'm going to sneak into Sam's house tomorrow and clean it. Without Pledge. He hasn't been taking care of himself, and it's all I could think of to help. Josh slipped me his keys and is going to make sure he's out of there. He told me to hire someone, but it makes me feel helpful and needed. It's comforting to me, like an old routine.

I will also do anything I can to keep from thinking about how David's going to New York to be with Sadie's mom. Bax told me he found her. He couldn't be bothered. They'll probably decide to become a family. She'll get the last little space of his heart that was reserved for me. That should help me move on more quickly. There's not even a sliver of space for me.

"Nat?

"In here."

Elle appears in the doorway. She's wearing a flowy, yellow,

and black floral dress that makes her look almost ethereal. She always floats into a room. Her blonde hair is pulled into a severe ponytail down her back, and her emerald eyes are sparkling and mischievous most days. Today is no different. But she is enormous. Her face is puffy, and her belly enters the room about a foot before she does.

"This is starting to look amazing. I was just coming to check on the paint color. Where are the dry swatches?"

I point to the wall with four stripes of color that all look the same to me, but she begins to inspect each one.

"How do you feel?"

"You don't want to know. I've been banned from discussing it. I'm supposed to focus on the joy."

I laugh. "Who banned you?"

"Everyone. Including sweet, accepting Sarah! I don't think there is a moment in the day where I don't feel like I'm the size of an Adirondack chair and as puffy as the Michelin Man. I can't eat without acid reflux; I can't sleep without hip pain and it's not like I'm getting laid. My only joys are ordering people around, decorating, and freezer pops. Oh, and counting down the days until the succubi are expelled! Ten days and fucking counting, or I'm ripping them out of there myself."

I smile at her misery. She's the most amazing mother. It's the pregnancy part she's not good with. And I put away my triggers about her pregnancy. There's bigger stuff for me to worry about.

She waddles to the nearby wall. "Which one do you like, Nat?" I'm kind of stunned she's asking my opinion.

"The one on the left," I lie. I don't see a rooting difference between any of them.

"Liar. Come here." She places a hand on her ever-growing belly.

She points to the one on the left. "See, this one has an undertone of blue." She holds up a white piece of paper. Looks like an index card in front of the color.

"And this one has a rosy undertone."

And suddenly, I see it. I take the index card and move it to the next one. "What do you see?"

"Yellow," I say.

"Exactly. And the last one is just a flat gray. But which do you like?"

"My opinion doesn't matter here." Elle turns to me, pushes me down in a seat, and takes one opposite me. She's licking her lips. This usually means she wants a Popsicle lately.

"We have green or purple," I say.

Her eyes light up. "You stocked this place with ices?"

I nod at her. "Just a couple. Just in case."

"You really are a wonder, Natalie. Green, please. And of course, your opinion matters." I wince. She's the only person I've ever known who volunteers to eat the green ones.

I scurry across the slate floor tiles to get it. There's a small freezer in the backroom where there will eventually be merchandise. Elle picked out these frozen silicone ice cubes to chill wine quickly without watering it down. She wanted them frozen here if anyone wants to buy a bottle and find a spot to sit and have a sip. She always thinks everything through to the end. I do that. It's how I know how everything will end.

"You didn't answer me," she calls after me, and I yell back as I snip off the top of the tube of electric green ice.

"Rosy one."

"Good eye. See, when you pause to look, you can see all kinds of things. That's the one we're going to go with." I hand it to her. "Thank you so much. These ladies are overheated today and driving me insane." I grab another chair and place it in front of her.

"For your cankles." Elle bursts out laughing as she lifts her feet to the chair. "Because they ain't ankles, and they ain't calves." She arranges the gauzy blue skirt over her legs as she leans back. I pick a piece of lint off my red brick shorts. I've paired them with a Pro/Ho t-shirt that says, "There's just not enough to go around."

"You're not here for the paint color. You already knew which paint you were using. You must be up in the rotation—the never-ending group tirade to get me to reconsider being with David." I cross my arms and stare at her as her tongue becomes toxic green.

"You're too good. Did you know I'm an orphan?" I'm a bit stunned, and I lean forward just a bit. "My parents were killed when I was in college. I know it's not the same, but in this situation, I think I might be able to give you a little insight."

"What situation?" No. I lean back and look at the bar over my shoulder. Then snap my head to the other side to look away from David's masterpiece. I exhale.

She says, "The situation with the 5."

"No, thank you, Elle," I say politely.

She flexes the toes of her perfectly pointy woven azure flats. She says, "You don't know me well, but I'm not good with the word 'no.'"

"Meaning?" I know she's close to David and Sadie. I don't want to hear it. I'll shine her on. Today I secured a job with a lobbying firm in DC. I'm leaving on the day of the opening. I'm only going to tell Bax before he hears from somewhere else.

"When I came here and accidentally found family and fell on Joshua's dick."

"What?"

"History. Look, it took a while to feel a part of the whole. I rejected all of it. I was good on my own. I knew how to do that. It seemed easier. It's not."

"We have very different situations." I grab the broom and begin working again.

"Forces were working against Josh and me at the time. Keeping us apart for a moment or two. But in the end, our biggest hurdle was us. I worked very hard at keeping love out of my life to protect me. And that's exactly what you're doing."

"I'm not." She can't know what I'm feeling.

"I knew what it was like to have someone make my favorite dinner on my birthday, and I'm so sorry you didn't. But now you do."

I whip around to her. "Why does everyone think they know how I feel, or think they know exactly why I don't want to be with David? We're not friends. We're not family. Thank you for your visit, but I have to go."

Elle stands up, well struggles to stand up, and groans a lot. "Please don't run. I can't fucking catch you carrying two cranky as hell cantaloupes in my stomach."

At the door, I turn back to her. "Elle. I like you. But I don't need another person, who barely knows me, lobbying for David to tell me how I should feel in this situation." I never raise my voice, and right now, it's loud as anything.

"Why do you think we don't know you? I'm thrilled to have met you and shared meals, parties, coffee and holidays with you over the past nine months. I'm not lobbying for David. I'm lobbying for love." Her voice cracks. "Fucking hormones. Wait." She puts her hands out as if she's trying to steady her emotions and her balance. I make sure she's not going to fall, but that's it.

"You don't get to do that sitting on the perch of your perfect life. I'm sorry about your parents and for what you went through when you first got together with Josh, but your life is flipping perfect, and mine is a mess."

I walk out but hear her calling after me, "Mine was a mess. A huge fucking mess and I fought hard to be with Josh."

I stand just outside of the tasting room, listening to her.

"The ladies are kicking up a storm on this. You'd better listen to them. They're like tiny annoying oracles. I fought to be a part of this wide and massive family. I don't understand why you won't."

Tears are streaming down my face, and I walk away quickly before she can respond to what I yell over my shoulder, "Because there's no room for me, and it's better to find out now than later."

She yells from the door, and I don't turn around, "Then why are you still here? If there's no room for you in his life, or ours, then why are you still here? I cry bullshit, young Natalie."

I storm away, wishing I could summon a tiny bit of Tabi and tell her to leave me alone in the rudest way possible. I turn and yell back, "I read that KT athletic tape in thin strips in a cross-hatch pattern can help with ankle swelling."

Elle waddles out to me. "I'm going to text you a number. Use it or not. But I can't be stopped. I'm a force of nature. You're lucky these double basketball hell beasties have me at a disadvantage. Dammit, Nat, stop. I can't run." She stops and stands there as I keep walking. "Are there extra ices?" she yells.

I pause and look back at her. "In the mini-fridge."

She yells, "Thank you. For everything you do. You don't have to be my friend because I'm already yours."

I'm at my car, but I don't get in. I slide down to the ground and sit there. I pull my knees up and bury my head. The sun feels warm and lovely on the top of my head. I don't know how long I sit there or if I wanted her to catch up to me. I look up when I hear the slurp of a freezer pop.

I'm looking at my phone. I say, "Thank you, Elle." It's the number of a therapist.

"You're welcome. Come here. There's no way in hell I can go down there. Trust me, the 5 have your back. At least I do. And I can make Josh do almost anything." I stand and walk into her outstretched arms, and she keeps talking, "Except I can't stop him from knocking me up. We got you, girl. Sammy would say the same things I am if she were here. Damn hormones." Her voice cracks again. "Now, let's talk about a place where your man makes sense again."

"He's not mine."

"You should tell the universe that."

My breath catches.

I lean back against my car. She grabs at her stomach and then pees. Just pees. She looks up at the sky as if she can't stop herself.

"Fuck me. Call Josh." She looks at me, and I must look to be in total confusion. She laughs hysterically. "I'm in labor, not incontinent. Drive me to the hospital." Shit, her water broke.

I open the passenger door and get her inside. Then I fly around to the driver's side.

Before I get in, she looks at me. "Can you just grab one more green ice?" I smile at her as she rubs her belly.

CHAPTER 40

DAVID

SHE TEXTED. I don't know what to do with this information.

NAT: I have to tell you something.

I was driving and trying to get through security and missed her text. It's from hours ago. I respond and hope she'll tell me why she's contacting. I was pretty clear that we're done.

DAVID: Will you answer if I call?

I walk around with Sadie on my hip. She's been extra clingy lately. I swear she's an entirely different Sadie every two weeks. Every time I think I have something solved, there's a whole new girl I have to contend with. Every trick has stopped working. She even hates Ch Ch now. I'm pacing. It's been a forty-five-minute delay at the gate. Why the hell did she contact me?

NAT: What do you want, David?

DAVID: You and courtside seats to the Warriors. But I'll settle for another truce. I'm answering your text from before.

NAT: Your friends are all pissed at me because I won't be with you.

DAVID: Why don't you tell me why you texted and I promise not to mention when I'm thinking of bending you over my couch to hate fuck you from behind.

NAT: I'll pretend that too.

DAVID: Don't be cute. You don't want me, fucking fine, but don't take away my hate fuck fantasies. That's all I have left. I have a thing. What do you need?

NAT: Oh! You're at the airport. Elle is in labor.

DAVID: Fantastic for them. I'll call Josh. You don't have to be their messenger any longer. I know you want nothing to fucking do with me.

NAT: I'm sorry.

DAVID: No, you're not. You're starting to reflect someone I don't know and that might be the hardest part of this. I was in love with someone who would never be this cold.

NAT: Please stop. Good luck in New York.

DAVID: Fine. Take care. Lose my number.

I'm zoning out on takeoff thinking about our text exchange. I was too mean. I don't have time to fix it now. I refocus on Sadie. I lost the love of my life, but I won't lose the other.

My sister and everyone else refused to come with us. I'm the idiot with the screeching child on a plane. Some bitch had the audacity to ask me if I could pass Sadie to her mother because she might have better luck. I snapped so hard my jaw cracked and freaked everyone around us. "I am her mother," I roared at the woman, and Sadie got even more upset.

Holy shit, don't fly with a kid. It's terrible. The kind of terrible I could never imagine. I think Sadie is vibing off my constant bad mood lately. Someone suggested I give her Benadryl to put her to sleep, and I thought it was barbaric. But now, if I had a fucking pot gummy, I'd give it to her. Shut up, Sadie. It's just an airplane. Fuck. I pick her up again. At least I was smart enough to buy a second seat. I walk up and down the plane bouncing and shushing, hoping it will work this time. The flight attendant puts her hand on my back, and it's so comforting I might marry this woman.

This is a shit day, and it's only going to be shittier. The only flight we could get gives us enough time to get to Sadie's mom's office. Sadie finally snuggles into my chest, and I beginning to hum. The flight attendants sigh. I'm like DILF clickbait, and I could care less. I whisper as we go back to our seats. Doesn't matter how frustrated or upset I am with Sadie when she puts her tiny hand on my face, it all disappears.

"Sweet Satan, Sadie. I swear parenting is a manic-depressive ride. How can I love you so much in one second and want to leave you with the pilot the next?" She coos quietly and sticks her fist in her mouth. I kiss the top of her red whisps. "Behave, ok? Cut Daddy a little slack. He's kind of terrified of your corporate giant mommy."

Her name is Josephine Delgado, and Mel, Tommi's girlfriend, hacked into her schedule. I put myself on it, and I know she has nothing after my meeting but lunch until her haircut at two. Mel is a scary good hacker who uses her powers primarily for good. She's a down chick. Killer basketball player. Only one in town who can consistently almost beat me in one-on-one.

Josie, as I knew her, is insanely successful. She does something in media and television, and we're on our way to the Viacom CBS offices. I'm not sure if she's responsible for all the crime shows with initials or not, but I would like them to stop coming up with new ones. I'm not really prepared to go toe to toe with her. I'm grappling with what to say this time. Now that I know she's the one who abandoned Princess Scribbles.

She wasn't a corporate anything on our nights together. She was soft and warm. And funny. She kept up with me and made me laugh. There are hook-ups, and there are hook-ups that make you feel a little less alone in the world. She was the latter. Josie was hammered at her sister's bachelorette party in San Francisco. I met her at a bar, and we went to a hotel room. She stayed in the morning and told me she lived far away from her family and didn't have the best relationship. We talked about fathers and mothers and expectations and being doomed. She said she had found a way past all of it but felt guilty about doing what she knew she was put on this earth to do. That conversation came back to me as I stared at her corporate profile picture. I feel guilty, and I'm not doing everything I was put on this earth to do.

I think I secretly knew she was Sadie's mom all along. It was slightly more than a hook-up, but neither of us wanted anything beyond the fantasy of breakfast together in bed. She was interested in what I had to say and gave my words weight. No one really does that. Well, Natalie did. I will never let Sadie think she's less than in any way.

Her mom and I had drunk sex the first time. She told me where to meet her the second time. After the wedding. I went to the bar with very low expectations. That night was lots of drunken sex but also again sober in the morning. I want to believe Sadie was conceived in the morning when we chose each other in the light of day. When we came together, vulnerable for just a moment.

This assistant woman has no idea who I am. I told her I represented a winery interested in getting into sponsorship. Pro/Ho got me in the door, and I'll arrive as David Gelbert. Not David Allen. I'm not trying to surprise her or trap her. It's just the only way she had an opening to see me.

I have a suit. I thought for a moment I'd change out of my jeans and white oxford, out of respect, but then fuck it, she didn't have respect enough to keep her daughter. Or to even bother telling me who she was. Or to tell me she was pregnant in the first place. Scribbles, and I don't owe her shit.

Sadie's calmer now that we're in a cab. I'm worried about the lack of a car seat. I didn't think of that when I jumped on the plane. I do have the annoying umbrella stroller, but it's a huge fucking hassle.

When we arrive, I look up. It's what you do in a city. Manhattan is more condensed than San Fran, and that city is jam-packed. At least this part in midtown is all glass and steel and people. Sadie keeps blinking, trying to take it all in. It's adorable. I sit on the edge of a planter. It's sunny and pleasant out. I have her face me. The more I think about the connection with Josie, the more I realize maybe I've been a tad unfair to Natalie.

My own sack of shit ego weighing me down. I should have let her off the hook. Let her relax before I pounced on her. I can't and won't get over her. I have to try one more time. Or maybe I flat out tell Nat I'm going to fight for her. Even though Josie and I shared a moment, Natalie validates and loves me in a way no one else on earth could dare to. Shit. I need her. I have to get her to get over her shit too.

We need to come together in this, not blame the past. I've let every decision and choice happen to me. The only significant choice I've made in my life was to ditch the NBA draft. UNLV, sports in school, my friends, were handed to me on a silver platter, and even this thing I'm holding in the sunlight. Sadie happened to me. Natalie was there in my winery office. The winery our parents created, and we took over. Happened to me. I'm letting Natalie leave me. I'm letting it happen to me. Bullshit. From today on, I'm the one that chooses what happens. I didn't realize I was a passenger in my own life.

"Sadie. We're going to meet your mommy. I don't know what's going to happen. But it's time to choose things. And despite our beginning, Princess Scribbles, I choose you. Whoever is upstairs doesn't get to have you. Ok. Remember. You're mine." I kiss her cheek. Then she leans forward and opens her mouth around my nose. "The kiss needs work, Sadie. Don't quit your baby job."

She yells. She's so loud. She starts babbling DaDaDaDa and pulls my lip with her fingers. I kiss her hand and pull it away.

"I will never leave you. I will never let you go. Ok. Also, Natalie is mine. Time to let her know. You'll like her. She's going to be your mom, too, whether she wants to or not. I've told her, but she's not getting the message. We're a conclusion, not a question. Stop asking, you freaking pixie."

Sadie babbles again, and I cuddle her close. I'm not sure when my heart opened this much, but I don't want it to close again. I strap on the Baby Björn. I'd use the stroller, but I forgot to pick it up as we deplaned. Doesn't matter. I'm a God of the Baby Björn. I'm an expert now, and Sadie happily plays with the straps. Now hands-free, I text. I'm ready.

DAVID: *Be prepared.*

NAT: *For what?*

DAVID: *For everything.*

NAT: *Tornado, Bear Attack, The Warriors trading Steph Curry?*

DAVID: *You better stop it because it makes me love you more when you're this fucking cute and sassy.*

NAT: *Why are you nice to me?*

I push call. She sends me to voicemail. I call again. She picks up.

"David." Her voice is breathy, and I have to look at Sadie's face and remember to rain on my Parade.

"I love you. I love you. I love you. And you're a fucking moron if you think I'm going to let you go. All that shit we said needs to be talked about, but I love you."

"It's not about a lack of love, David. It's about my place." I pace in front of the building. I need this sorted or at least started before I confront Josie.

"It's next to me."

"What is?"

"Your place in the world. Next to me. You hurt me by not choosing to stay with me, but I realized I don't have to be hurt. I reject your choice."

"You are in New York. The two-timer?"

"Yes. And I'm terrified to go in the building." There's a pause, and I know her. She's thinking about how to be my friend.

"Do it for Sadie. Just keep thinking about that. One foot in front of the other, all for her. I have to go."

I slip this in before she can hang up on me. "All for us. My entire world is all for us."

She hangs up and lets me have the last word for now. After this is settled, one way or another, I'm going home to explain to my girl how she's a fucking idiot. Then I'm going to screw her into next week. It's time to show her, not tell her, I love her.

I make one more call. "Elle." I drum my fingers on the top of Sadie's head. She giggles.

"What's up? Is Sadie ok?"

"Seriously, you think I'd be calm if something were wrong. Do you still have a construction crew hook up?"

"Yes, but Pro/Ho has a contractor."

"I don't want to pull him from the tasting room job or Tabi and Bax's house. Tabi will kill me. I need a favor. I have an idea."

"Don't go hurting yourself."

Natalie doesn't trust anything good. She never expects people not to disappoint her. She loves to be efficient and work because she knows what to expect. I want to give her something she can always depend on, no matter what her fucked-up brain says to her.

Elle says, "I'm listening. But you know I just gave fucking birth, you asshole." I did absolutely forget. "Sorry. I'm exhausted, and my nipples are the size of dinner plates."

"Hey. We're not nipple talking friends. Sorry."

"I know. I miss Sammy. But what can I do for you?"

"Speak to me of babies."

"They're perfect. Healthy, happy and completely nestled in their daddy's arms. I'm going to need a date night soon. Well, once I sleep for like a week."

I catch her drift. "I'll take Emma if Will and Sarah can take..."

She fills in my sentence, "Samantha and Maxine."

I gasp. "First off, you named your kids Sam and Max. What are they? Old canasta players? Who's Maxine?"

"My mom. And we're calling them Mini and Maxi."

"That's either the cutest or the dumbest thing I've ever heard."

"Whatever. What mountain can I move for you, Gelbert?"

SADIE IS SACKED OUT FOR THE MOMENT. THE MOTION OF THE elevator to the billionth floor has her eyes fluttering. I'm sure she'll wake with a start to announce us for our fake meeting. I check-in at the front desk.

"Sir, um. Can I take your bag?" The woman is snide, and I'm disappointed she's a cliché.

"No, that's fine." I nod.

"Or your baby?" she says in a tone dripping with the East Coast, Manhattan disdain for anything that makes too much noise. Of course, West Coasters have the same thing when we're asked to dress up.

"Nope. We're all set. Can you just point me towards Josie Delgado's office? I have an appointment. I'm David Gelbert."

"You mean Ms. Josephine Delgado. Please follow me."

Two women are sitting at the reception desk. One is quickly cleaning up the knocked-over business cards and the container of mints Sadie made quick work of. The woman ahead of me, the sweeter of the two, smiles at me. I'm trying not to think about the puke rising in my throat. I could lose my daughter in a matter of minutes. The door opens. The office is everything you think an exec's office should be. It's all windows, ego, and high-powered lacquered wood. She sees me, and her face drops for a second, then a steely gaze settles quickly as she turns her eyes back to the assistant. I stand there frozen.

The Sherpa woman who guided me to the office says, "Can I get you anything? Coffee or water? Um, a bottle?" Sadie squeals at the b-word.

She says, "Nothing. Thank you, that is all. Leave us." The door closes, and she sits. I unleash Sadie and place her on the floor with some blocks and Gibby. She sets to building them up and tearing them down.

I cross the room. We stare at each other while I reposition the chair to keep an eye on Sadie and look at her mother.

"How much?" She raises an eyebrow. The frost coming off this woman is palpable. She's gonna Elsa me in a minute.

I'm confused by her phrasing. I cross my legs. "She's almost a year old. But you of all people should know that?"

"I knew you'd come for more money someday." She reaches into her desk and shuffles something around. I reach into Sadie's luggage and place the envelope with the battered offensive cashier's check on her desk.

I say, "You mean to add to this amount. Sure. Let's say I'm here for money, you lunatic, let's say all of it."

"You want all my money?" She pulls something up on a computer.

I blow out a scoff. "No. I'm not here for your fucking money. I'm here for her and a signature."

Josie is nonplussed. She sits back in her high-powered exec chair. I'm not intimidated. I've been inside this woman. I've been inside enough that my super-sperm busted the condom. She says, "How did you get in here? I have a meeting any moment."

I pull out my wallet and a Pro/Ho business card. I throw my license and the card across her massive black marble desk. She seems like a detail gal, so I'll give them all to her.

"You lied to me."

I shake my head at this woman.

"M'kay. I can see how my different last name might be the real issue with our relationship. You have a meeting with me and your daughter. Who you abandoned. And didn't tell me about it. Want to revisit my lie? My last name. Boop. That's the whole lie. You. Damn, you got a trunk full of explaining to do, sister."

She glances down at the identification. "She's not my daughter."

All the air in the world fills my deflated and defensive body. I'm able to exhale again. I lean back, put my hands behind my head, and relax because she's not going to fight me on this. But I do need her story. I need to tell Sadie why she left her, why she doesn't want her.

"Hate to break it to you, but DNA says differently."

"I can't have a daughter. I tried." She runs her well-manicured hand over her already silky-smooth immovable hair. It's in a perfect long, low ponytail. The rich walnut waves I remembered have clearly been tamed for her life here. Her eyes are a light brown that complements her slightly olive complexion. I'll be interested to hear if Delgado is Spanish or Portuguese in origin.

I gesture with a come here hand. "Spill it, woman. Give me the whole story. And when you're done there's some paperwork for you to sign. Then we're gone."

"Custody." I'm no longer afraid of getting what I deserve and what I want. I can still be the black sheep, but now I get what I want.

"Parental rights. Paternity. Full iron-clad custody. You get none, and I get all. Custody implies temporary. I want no money, no claim to your future money, only Sadie."

Her breath catches, and she looks at her for the first time. Then, she whispers, "Sadie." Then she turns back to me. "Would you like a drink?"

"That's the best idea you've had since dumping Sadie at my winery." I wipe my sweaty hands on my jeans. She goes to some secret executive bar and pours two glasses of something brown. She hands me a glass, then sits on the couch across the office. I join her, scooping up Sadie to bring her closer to the couch area. Josie finishes her drink and pours another from a decanter that sits on an incredibly sharp and dangerous coffee table. I instinctively put my hand on the corner closest to Sadie.

Josie begins speaking in a compromised voice. "I thought I was missing something by working all the time. I love what I do. I love my life, but I was worried I'd get to the end of it and have regrets."

"Regret leaving her?" And now the puke rises again. I sip most of my drink.

She looks down at her feet and sits on the edge of a very expensive leather couch. She says, "Regret not having a child."

"And now?" I ask.

"I know there's a lot of judgment. And I'm the villain in her life story."

"We'll see about that. Can't say I'll understand, but I'll listen. What do you know now?" I turn my chair, so I can see both women. My fucked-up family.

"Now I know how awful it was to be pregnant. I know what it's like to give birth." She swallows her drink down, then wrings her hands as she places the glass on the table. "I know what it's like to stare at her desperately wanting that thing to kick in. That gene of overwhelming love. It never did. In five months, I never felt anything but resentment and anger."

"At her?" Really. I mean, I was mad she fucked up my relationship, but never anger. I stand and reposition Sadie back where I can see her. She's crawling everywhere.

"A little at you. A lot at me. I got into a real 'why me' spiral. I don't have that thing, and I've learned it's ok."

That completely knocks the wind out of me. "Are you sure it wasn't postpartum depression?"

"I'm sure."

"Tell me now. Tell me, you never want to be her mother?"

There's a pause. She crosses her legs and looks at Sadie, who is shrieking up a storm. "Maybe like an aunt? Or nothing. I gave up that choice. I'm a good aunt."

"Wait, Sadie has cousins?"

"She does." Her voice is quiet. I don't know what to think of all of this.

"When's her birthday? I feel that it's soon."

Josie nods. "July 14th." The anniversary of my first kiss with Natalie is July 21st. Sadie was already in the world. July was a pretty momentous month for me last year.

"Hey, Scribbles. Your birthday is in July. Holy shit. We thought it was in August." She looks at me and pulls up on the coffee table, then flops back onto her butt. She gets up again. That's my girl. Don't ever give up. But then she starts grabbing at art things strewn across to make the hard edges of this office softer. I pull up a wicker ball and hand it to her. She happily throws it and contemplates walking to get it but crawls instead.

"That. I don't have that."

"Basic human decency?" I say.

She smiles at me, and I stand around Sadie, gently guiding her away from corners and sharp objects. Using the shiny object method of replacing the danger with something dumb to occupy her for a moment.

"Your instinct to protect her. It's like you're guarding the President. Keeping everything in her periphery safe. Always scanning the horizon to make sure she doesn't run into danger or snipers."

I laugh. "I forgot you're funny, Josie."

She smiles a sad little smile. "Only my family calls me Josie. I'm Jo or Josephine to the rest of the world."

I scoop up Sadie and look at her. "You might not have the instinct, or even like me as a person, but the moment the condom broke, we became family, Josie." Tears fill her eyes. I finally see the humanity I knew she was burying. I sit down with Sadie, and she reaches for Josie. Josie takes her hand, and Sadie pulls it towards her face. Then she scrambles over to Josie and puts her head down on her lap. I've seen her do that to Elle. Josie runs her nails through her hair and begins full-on crying.

"Are you ok?"

"I don't know how she could remember this," she sputters.

"What?" She wipes her eyes and collects herself.

"I used to lay her on my lap like this and run my fingers through her hair." She blubbers a bit. "And I haven't cried in five years." It spills down her face, and I scoot closer to her on the couch. Sadie stays put, and I pull Josie to my shoulder. She sobs and sobs. Sadie and I wait for her to get done. I pray this flood of emotion doesn't alter my world again. I can't handle losing them. I'll crumble back into the man I don't want to be.

"Shh. It's alright. Josie, tell me what you want."

She straightens up, and Sadie lifts her head. I pull her into my lap and face her forward. Josie crosses the room, finds tissues in a drawer and pours another finger of whiskey. She turns and leans back against the bar area of her deep dark wooden cabinets that line the wall. She crosses her arms and stares at me.

Then she slowly walks to the front of her desk and drags the legal papers to her. She takes out a pen. I'm elated and incredibly dejected at the same time. I'm actively watching a woman give away her child. Sadie. This obnoxious, loud, screechy, stubborn, determined bundle of perfect girl is being discarded by her mother. But when we leave this room, she's legally mine, and that's everything.

Josie stops herself from writing and turns to us. Sadie is still reaching for her as if she knows. She must, on some cellular, spiritual level, know this is her mother. I hate they'll permanently be bonded in a way I never could be to her. Is that fucking selfish? Hell yeah, but I'm the only one in the room who loves her.

Her voice is more shattered than I thought, "I know I don't want to be a mother to any child. It doesn't work. I don't work that way. This career, my social life, my charities, my houses-"

"Houses? I should have cashed that check."

Josie chuckles. "Those are the things that make me happy. I've struggled a lot with thinking there was something wrong with me or that I'm a puppy killer like that two-toned Disney villain."

"Cruella de Vil?"

"How the hell would I know? I wasn't any good at being a child. I never liked any of that. I've always been thirty-eight at heart. And I like it that way. Poor sweet girl was born because I thought there was something wrong with me she could fix. But it turns out there's nothing wrong with me. That's not my path. I'm just so sorry she got caught in the middle of it."

I rush to the woman and plant us in front of her. "You may have gone about it in a fucked-up way, and perhaps you should have got a pet before you decided to give birth...."

"I don't half-ass anything."

I laugh. "But without knowing it, you saved my life by

creating one. I love my winery. I love my family's winery. And I've found the woman I want for all time if she'll ever call me back. But I am as sure as you are in your path that Sadie is mine."

Sadie flips backward and laughs. "Way to ruin the moment, Scribbles. She's currently peeing. When she flips back like that, I know I have to change her."

Josie looks at me and places a hand on my bicep. "I'm so sorry. Will you tell her I'm so sorry?"

"No. You will." I give her some side-eye, and she knows I won't let her off the hook. I don't want her money, but I do want to guarantee at least one conversation with Sadie. I back up and grab the diaper bag. "Is there somewhere I can change her?"

Josie smiles and clears her desk off. "You can use this." I hand her to Josie, and she awkwardly holds her as Sadie bounces in her arms and squeals that high-pitched nightmare squeal. I set up the changing pad, wipes, and disposal bag.

"It's fascinating how quickly you can become an expert at something when you have to." I pull open the diaper and reach for Sadie. "Or want to." I go about unsnapping and cleaning while Josie paces.

I say, "However you define it, you're going to be her mother. I would like it if you could plan on meeting her at least once to explain all of this. Or more if you want. But as of today, you are a footnote, not main plot."

She nods and paces. "I'd like to know her. I think I'll be better when she's older. Is that ok?" She comes into my view and stands there. Sadie is reaching for her, and I hand her the plastic keys to keep her occupied. She slams them onto the desk.

"Sure. But you're either in or out."

"You are a good dad. Did you always want this?" She truly wants to know, and it's not anything I've ever really thought about. Maybe the couple of weeks leading up to my mother dumping her at my place, but it just happened.

"There's no want. There's only what is. I'm her dad, and I'm going to raise her, hopefully with Natalie at my side, but if not, then by myself."

"Why by yourself?" Josie crosses her arms over her very beautiful blush pink blouse. She's got a pointedness to her, but she is beautiful. Sadie has her nose and her mouth.

I open up to the mother of my child, "I can't imagine anyone else at my side but Nat, so there's just her."

"We'll circle back to the idiot who won't be with a hot, kind, wonderful, skilled single dad like you, but I do want to know her."

I pick a clean Sadie up and grab a pre-made bottle. The smartest thing someone ever told me was to never warm up a bottle. That way, they're used to drinking it at room temperature, and you're always good to go.

She takes it greedily.

"I won't lie to her. She will ask about you, and I won't lie. I won't vilify or embellish, but I will tell her how Sadie and I met."

Josie smiles. "Fair enough. And I'll be available for questions. My family lives in Petaluma, and I have a sister with kids. They're older from her first marriage, but they are her cousins. I kept this from her. It wasn't easy, but I did it. I'm going to fly home this weekend to tell them. After all of this, I see that they deserve to know."

"Want us to tag along? Sadie could always use more family." Her face falls, and she drops her head into her hands. When she looks up at me, I see Josie, not Josephine.

"You would do that for me?" There are tears in her eyes. I don't know what the family rift is about, and it's not for me to know.

"I'm a much nicer person than you. And I'm not doing it for you." She laughs and glances at her daughter.

"I'd very much like to meet your sister. I have a village helping raise Sadie, but it would be nice if there were more babysitters in the mix. Can she meet her grandparents too?" Josie's eyes fill again. "I'm sorry. I didn't mean to upset you."

"No. No. You didn't. They've passed. I think that's part of the reason I kept her. My mother's nickname was Grace. That's what I called her when she was born."

I squeeze Josie's hand. My daughter has a mom name and a dad name now. She can be both. Mostly mine. Like 99.6% mine and 0.4% her mother.

"Sadie Grace Gelbert it is then. But I have to warn you, I won't stop her from contacting you or reaching out to you. I won't stand in the way of any relationship you want to have with her, but I will cut it all off if you give her false expectations. The very first time you promise her something and don't deliver, whether it's a phone call or a trip to the Maldives, I will cut you off without a second chance. You only get one chance. Use it wisely."

"No one talks to me like that. You got some balls on you, Gelbert." I lean into her and narrow my eyes.

"And not only have you sucked them, but they also made this one of the loves of my life." I kiss the top of her head as Josie signs over all parental rights to me, laughing.

She hands me the papers. "Can I take you two to lunch? I'd like to hear about her future stepmom and how you're going to get her back."

"I could use a consult. We accept."

Her voice takes on a more serious tone, "Thank you."

"For what?"

"Confronting me like this. Making me accountable and showing me that I'm not the villain."

"We shall see, Cruella. I plan to make you the ultimate scapegoat for everything that goes wrong in her life." She laughs very hard.

And just like that, Sadie Grace is mine. And she got a part-time sugar mama. We all exit the office together. Josie has the diaper bag.

She shifts her weight. "Keep the check. For her."

"I'll keep it for now, but I'm not sure what to do with it."

"Fair enough," Josie says.

I ask, "Why didn't you tell me?"

"I CALLED THE WINERY AT LEAST SEVEN TIMES. DAVID ALLEN WAS never working."

Oh, snap. I wish I could be angry at her, but if she'd found me, I'd never have found Natalie. I laugh at her. "I guess he wasn't. Sorry about the wrong name."

She nods sharply at me. It's easy to talk about in hindsight, but I can't imagine what she went through. "Someday, if you want to talk about the struggle of being pregnant and birthing all by yourself, I'll listen."

"You really are dreamy, David Allen." She squeezes my shoulder and looks again at our daughter, who's babbling the D-word again. I look to Josie. "That's right. The first word, Daddy. Or Cheerio. We're still debating." She smiles a sad little smile at me. I can't change that for her. I got what I came for. And she has to live with her guilt for always. I won't take that from her or try to make it better.

"Hey, why do you call her Scribbles? Does she like coloring?"

"She can barely hold her food. Your handwriting is for shit." She laughs heartily. "All I got from the note was that it was for David Allen. And the baby was mine. What else did you say?"

"Her name and her birthday. Sonoma Grace Delgado."

I can't stop laughing. "Dumbest name ever. Sonoma is a stripper name." Josie laughs. "You think that note said Sonoma Grace Delgado?" I nuzzle into my daughter, "Your mommy is fucking crazy, girl."

She laughs and puts her hand on my shoulder. "You have no idea. Sadie, girl, let's see if we can get Daddy to talk about this, Natalie." Sadie bounces at the mention of Nat's name. Or she's just bouncing, and I'm imagining it. I grin and push the elevator button. As we step inside, I realize although her birth family is all here together, it's not Sadie's home or her real family. The buzzer hasn't rung yet. Some people used to call me the 4th quarter demon. I thrived on being down towards the end of the game and coming back winning. There's still time for a fourth-quarter rally.

CHAPTER 41

DAVID

SHE WON'T RETURN my calls. I haven't slept since New York. I'm a fucking zombie. No, I'm worse. I'm a retired power forward who returns to the game for one more season to cash a check—a shell of my vibrant self. My pep talk was for shit. There's no rally to be had. There's no sleep and no hope.

Sadie won't stop crying. I don't know what to do. She's hysterical. I'll sacrifice a toe for her to stop crying. Is there an ancient baby God I can pray to?

I don't even know how she still has a voice. I don't know what the crying is about. I mean, there's a ton of disgusting drool. Is she hungry? If she's thirsty, she most certainly should drink, which she's not doing. I can't possibly change her again. Her ass is raw from all the over-changing. And then it's been over-butt pasted. She's not having any of my tricks. Or me. We keep napping on the couch for approximately twenty minutes. I'd be better off if the baby would just waterboard me.

I wake with a start because she's screeching again. Screeching, screeching everywhere I go. People give us a wide berth as we walk around. It's the wailing of a foreign ambulance all day and night long. Why hasn't the biological need to sleep and eat overtaken her?

Brave, who cares. Fuck it. I need reinforcements. I tried to fix this on my own. About to throw everything we own against a wall.

I PULL UP TO MY PARENTS' HOUSE, AND LITERALLY, THE BEACON, the little siren that is Sadie, is wailing. Really shaking the lungs now. Siren Sadie is Satan. She hates me so much. She's kicking and slobbering on my shoulder. I've totally failed her, and she's only been officially mine for a little bit.

I walk up to the front door. My mom whips open the door, looking perfect. I have bags upon bags under my eyes. I'm not even sure this shirt is mine; I don't know where it came from. It's covered with spit-up, drool and food. Maybe it's mine. I do know I've been in the same boxers and shorts for close to seventy-two hours. But now that I'm in public, it's all out there. I'm entirely underwater.

"Mom, Mom, I don't know what I'm doing. This is awful. Awful, and I can't do it. So tired. She hates me and the world," I plead."

My mom unstraps Sadie and takes her in her arms. I feel the physical weight of her leave my body, and relax just a smidge.

Then, I watch as my mother puts her up on her shoulder and instantly puts her fingers into her mouth.

And Sadie stops.

I rasp, "What kind of black magic do you possess?" Why do women intuitively know what to do?

"Hey, New York City lady. How are you, baby girl?"

She's going to town on my mom's knuckles. She places an open hand on my cheek, and I lean into it. She says, "Are you ready to be a big girl now? Is that what you want to do, be a big girl with teeth?" She raises an eyebrow, looks at me, and winks. "Honey, she's teething."

I place a hand on Sadie's head.

"But why? Why is she screaming like this for days? Why has she been this miserable? And what are you doing with your finger?"

She turns into the house, and I follow the two of them. Sadie can't stop smashing her little mouth around my mom's knuckle. "Massaging her gums. They're all inflamed and red. She's about to cut a tooth which means something super sharp is pushing through her little baby gums. And she's never known pain like this, my love. We all become a bit immune to pain. But this is new."

"Shit."

"Exactly, and she doesn't know what to do with the pain because it won't go away. Think of your worst toothache. Now imagine you don't know why it's happening."

I turn in a circle on the royal blue intricate hall carpet. "Why, why don't they tell you that? According to lists, this shouldn't happen for like a month."

She sits down in the living room, and I flop onto an adjacent couch. She says, "You should tell Sadie her timeline is off. Babies totally respect set milestones." I roll my eyes at my mother.

She says, "I'm going give her a little Advil and put her down. Go put some damp washcloths into the freezer for later."

"Thanks, Mom." I put my head down on the couch. I'll do the washcloth thing in a minute. I just need to get my head straight for a second.

I wake up as my sister hits me with a pillow. "What the hell, Bex?" I glance at my watch as if I've been asleep for a decade. It's been fourteen minutes. But it was a solid fourteen. I stumble over my words because, literally, my head will not form sentences.

"My niece is tucked in. You look like shit. Mom will be down in a minute."

I sit up and rub my face a little too vigorously. Becca sits on the couch opposite me.

I say, "Ever the tactful one."

"You also smell really rank. I filed all the papers, and she will be yours without hassle."

"Thank you. I should shower. A guilt-free shower would be awesome."

Becca pulls her feet under her and adjusts her watch. "Isn't showering always guilt-free?"

"Not when you have a baby. When they're napping, you have so much to get done showering gets shoved down the list. And when she was still in that bucket thing, I'd strap her in and sit her just outside of the shower. Now I have to haul the pack n play into the bathroom and shower."

"Just stick her in the thing. No need to drag it to the bathroom. She shouldn't have to see you shower."

"I end up showering at night a lot. But, Bex, don't have children. You can't just leave them alone for a second. I may have fucked up the teething thing, but I know that."

She shrugs, and I want her to head off to wherever stuck-up, clueless women congregate. She puts her hands on the back of the couch. She says, "Are you ok?"

I pause. We've always sniped at each other. We're so freaking different. She's uptight and proper and always has been. Someday I hope she lets loose just once. But we do care about each other.

I say, "No. I'm not ok. Maybe after a full night's sleep when Sadie's like twenty-five, I might be ok. But now, not."

"I went to see her."

I lie back down and prop one of the very many blue throw pillows under my head. "Sadie. I know."

"Nat."

My heart thrums and then aches. It's a dark and bleak path of fucking nothingness.

"She looks like shit too. How badly did you fuck all this up?"

"Cool. I was worried I might forget for the briefest of moments how shitty everything is. Can always count on you, sis."

"It's what I do best. Go shower." She leaves and yells back through the house, "Love you."

I mutter, "But Mom loves me best." My head hits the decorative pillow, and my eyes are closing as I hear her give me one last jab.

"I heard that, and it's all the horseshit."

I wake to my hair being stroked. My head is in my mother's lap. As an adult, I shouldn't like it that much. But then again, I've only really been an adult for like seven months. "It's been a couple of hours, honey. You have to get up and clean yourself up. We have some chicken leftover. Your father did take-out last night while I was in the city, and he way overbought."

I grin. My dad is not good at emotional stuff, but he's always doing or buying things hoping everyone understands. My mom loves the take-out from Pete's Henny Penny in Petaluma. He made sure there was some for her when he got home.

She says, "And there's extra coleslaw and those wedge potatoes." Those are my favorites. I'm the only one who eats that.

"Did he get the mac and cheese too and fried pickle spears?" Those are Becca's favorite.

"And the elote for Poppy. I guess in his mind, he really wanted an old-fashioned family dinner."

"You know those always resulted in fights."

"It's funny what your mind chooses to remember. I only remember all of us being together laughing."

I grin and sit up as she pats my hip. I smooth my hair down and run my hand over my chin. It will be a full-on Sam beard by tomorrow.

I swing my legs up onto the couch, and my mom puts them in her lap and smacks them. "Silly boy thought he could do this by himself. Nobody can. I don't care if you're a woman, married, partnered couple, young, or old. It really does take a village, honey. Why didn't you reach out?"

I pull my feet from her and grab Sadie's bag. I grab the bottle and formula powder. I'm going to make her a bottle.

She puts her hand on my forearm. "It's all taken care of. Go. Eat, sleep, and shower while Sadie's asleep and I'll be here when she wakes up."

"How did you get her to calm down so quickly?"

"The tiny bit of bourbon on her gums. Then I sent your father out for all the stuff we need to help her through teething. This we know."

"I don't know what to do. I didn't know what to do. I haven't slept. I'm terrified I was doing something wrong. I don't know what the fuck I'm doing."

"Coming here was a good step." She squeezes my ankles. My entire being is becoming unmoored. I felt adrift with no fucking purpose and weighed down by all the fucking purpose all at once. I'm coming apart.

"Two full days, Mom. Two days of nothing but fucking it all up. How do I do this?" I pull at my out-of-control filthy hair.

"You're already doing it."

"I'm not doing anything. I'm just desperately trying to make her feel ok."

"That's what parenting is."

"Parenting is being like this freaking tired and this useless."

Ridiculous, I'm ridiculous. "My whole life is a scratch, Mom. I'm barely holding myself together." She scoots down the couch, and I lean into her. If I were a crying sort, this would be my moment. If I were a drunk, this is my rock bottom. And if I were a genius, it would be when I'd figure it all out. But I'm not. I wipe my eyes by squeezing them shut and pinching the bridge of my nose.

"I can't fix things with Nat. I can't raise her alone. I can't even figure out when my daughter is in pain. She was in pain, and I didn't know it. I'm not fit for this. I'm terrible. I told Sadie to fuck off. I called her an asshole. Not to her face, but I said it. And I sure as fuck thought it. My ego was hurt, and I told Nat to fuck off too. I told her I didn't need her. But I do. And not just for Sadie. I need her because she's the missing piece of me. I screwed it all up. Epically. I'm going to die alone, and they'll take my daughter away from me."

My mom begins laughing hysterically. And then I do. My sister walks back in.

"Come on." She motions for us to follow her. I get up and pull my mom towards me.

"David, honey. That's what being in love feels like with both of them." She puts her hand on my back and urges me forward.

My mom and I walk into the dining room, and Dad has made a massive spread of the leftovers. We all take our regular places, and my dad puts the baby monitor down next to my plate. I nod to him as he sits at the head of the table.

My father places his napkin on his lap. He says, "It's getting cold. Everyone eat for Christ's sake. It's just teething."

I smile at him, and he looks down at his plate. Then I bite into a giant piece of fried chicken. God, it's perfect.

CHAPTER 42

DAVID

I WAKE in my childhood bed. I take a piss, then head down the hall. I don't know what time I passed out. I know it was after a shit-ton of laughs and chicken at my impromptu OG family dinner. No Poppy or Aunt Tina. Just the four of us. I tiptoe down the hall in the dusk and peek inside what used to be a guest room. It's now a full-on fucking Sadie circus, complete with an oversized big top canopy. She's snuggled up with Vino Bunny and Gibby, the giraffe. Her arms are splayed over her head. She's open and tired. I kiss her gently on the forehead and head back to my room. I'm still in my nasty teething nightmare clothes. I find an old Lakers jersey and some sweats. I pass out again instantly.

"IT'S TIME, DAVID." I ROLL OVER AND SEE MY MOM SITTING ON THE edge of my bed. It's bright daylight, and she's opened all the drapes. I sit up and prop pillows behind me and proceed to rub the sleep out of my face, grateful for my lack of morning wood. Even the Parade is exhausted.

"Sadie, okay?"

"She's napping."

I shake my head quickly. "What freaking time is it?"

"It's two."

"Did I miss a day?"

My mom laughs. "No, but it is time for you to wake up and get your daughter and go. Your dad put together a teething survival kit with instructions. He was really good with teething."

I blink rapidly to wake up more. I don't remember my dad being good at any kid stuff except sports.

"How will I know I'm not doing anything wrong again?" The panic is back. I feel as if I'm in a well and can't climb out. I'm no good to Sadie, and I've ruined everything with Natalie.

My mom stands and starts picking up my nasty clothes. "Just give them what they need and keep giving it to them. You're going to be wrong, and you're going to be right."

"Them?" She pops her hip and gives me the mom side-eye. I still don't know if she means more children or Natalie.

"Trust me, when you're right, it will outweigh all the times you're wrong. Loving her means you're doing the right thing, sweetheart."

I blurt out, "I can't get Nat to love me again. I can't get her back." I look to the ceiling and exhale all my breath in a second.

"That certainly doesn't sound like the man I raised. Remember when you set up an art walk in our house behind the couch? Then you made us buy tickets to come to see your three paintings? You sold dollar tickets to all of our family and friends. You made thirty dollars that day, and when I asked what you were going to do with the money, you said, buy more art supplies."

"And Dad put me in basketball the next day," I huff.

"Yes, but to his credit, he never told you to stop painting." I've been so busy looking for ways to twist the past in my brain, I forgot to get a second opinion.

My mother takes a tone with me. "My darling. Despite what I've tried to teach you, you've never really had to work for a thing in your life. You had natural gifts and parents with deep pockets."

I nod. It's the same revelation I came to in New York. I let things happen to me and never really worked at anything.

"Josh worked his little tush off practicing basketball, football, and distance running to be as good as you. He never was. Your palate for blending is something you loved and have developed, but you have a scary natural gift for it. When you got a full ride to UNLV and got into Pratt, I was so proud of you."

I stand up and begin to pace and look at my mom. "But I didn't go to Pratt, did I?"

"Own this, right now. Your artwork was good enough. Your grades were good enough. You were amazing. Who knows what you could have done? You didn't have to work for it. It's just there. It's an innate talent. Just like basketball or wine. You worked for all of those, but in the end, you started way ahead of everyone else."

I walk into the bathroom and splash water on my face. My mother follows me in and my entire teen years come crashing back to me. Leave me alone. I want to wallow in my ineptitude, and she wants to relive my glory years. I've been a go-with-the-flow guy for a long time and never really noticed I was drifting, not floating above the fray, but drifting to the most straightforward scenario. The only place I've probably never taken for granted is in the wine lab. I feel lucky to be there every day.

She says, "When you went to UNLV, it broke my heart a little bit. I wanted you to follow your artistic journey. But your heart was with sports, and I'll always want what's best for you, so it's fine. That's what parents do."

I look up in the mirror and see her in the reflection. She's looking at her nails. There's nothing left to hide from anyone—time to be raw.

My voice is softer than I intend. "I didn't want to go to UNLV. I did it for Dad. It was the easiest thing for everyone." I turn slowly, and she's staring at me with an open mouth. I quickly try to fix it. "Disregard that shit. I just let that slip, but I'm so fucking tired." I have no self-control or filter.

"Why didn't you ever tell me that you wanted to go to Pratt? Do you still sculpt?"

"Just at night or when I can't sleep, or you know when the anxiety comes. I said I wanted him to be proud of me."

"Why not tell me you wanted to be an artist?"

I put my hands on her shoulders. I want my words to have weight. I say, "Because I was more than okay being a vintner. It's who I am. It's what I do. I truly do love blending."

"You always have. And you have a gift. Again, something that you were born with."

"All due respect, bullshit. I worked my ass off to be as good as I am at it. But it never seemed like work because I love it. Maybe that's why I didn't see how I should value it. My favorite thing is to take two separate and unique things and combine them. Pulling the very best of one and bringing out the very best in the other, but maintaining their separate unique characteristics. To create something that never existed in the world. That no one thought possible. Meritage is the challenge I adore. It's not always perfect, but it's always worth the effort. Always worth the journey."

My mother smirks at me.

I see it. I'm an idiot. I know how to fix this. I say, "It was her. She's the reason I became a complete person. She pulled out the very best of me." We stand in my idiot revelation for a moment, and Sadie's cry bursts through the monitor clipped to her belt.

"Darling boy." She turns from the door. "You're going to have to work for something for the first time in your life. It's going to be hard, and it's going to be ugly and messy. But don't let this moment go."

"Mom, she knows how I feel. And she can't get past Sadie."

"Give her what she needs. She's an incredibly independent woman."

I pull the comforter up on my bed, and my mom helps from her side. We move the pillows into the perfect position in tandem.

"She needs space. But she's been independent her whole life. I want her to know she doesn't have to be alone. I'll be there. But Sadie is a part of me know, and that's a lot to ask."

My mom puts her hands on her hips and tuts. "No one can resist that little girl. And she might know how you feel about her, but have you shown her?

"You're sculpting more because of her. Does she know that? Show her you love her. Let there be no doubt." I take my slender mom into my arms and hold her. She comes up to my shoulders. It's cute when she hugs me around the waist. We stay like that until Sadie wails again. I unclip the monitor from her belt and look at my mom.

I say, "I've got this."

She smiles at me. "Yes, you do."

CHAPTER 43

NAT

THE CLOSER THE DAY GETS, the tighter my chest and resolve get. It's time to put this chapter behind me. But all of my hurt, love, and excitement are just below the surface. I thought things might be a little different after our conversation about New York. But he's been silent.

I'm like a placid lake. Smooth as glass on the outside, but turmoil and life swirling underneath. The slightest raindrop will cause a disturbance, and the whole thing will blow up. Pro/Ho opens soon, and the flurry of activity is remarkable. The steel tanks aren't operational yet, but they are in the big red barn. Tabi and Bax's house is still a disaster, but the tasting room is incredible.

I'm going to finish all my duties early and take off. I'll stop by Elle's and say goodbye. I want to see the twins now they're not so squishy and new. They came home yesterday.

I couldn't sleep and have a secret project that has to be done under cover of darkness. I broke into David's place while he was sleeping. Lucky for me, though, his car wasn't at his house last night. I'm sure he's out. He's found a way to have a life. It was Wednesday, and the guys always get together at Starling Bar. He probably hooked up with a tourist and dumped Sadie off on his mom. I get really sick to my stomach every time I think of him with someone. I gave him up, but that doesn't mean he still doesn't feel like he's mine.

Besides my other fundamental issues, I cannot leave a job half done. So here I am with a series of flashlights set up to finish all the polishing touches on Pro/Ho's tasting room. The electricity was all messed up. The electrician is coming out to fix it tomorrow. They're having a soft opening in a couple of days. I'm not going to go. I'll slip out after my job is done. I wanted to hang some of David's pieces that his mom helped me find. In addition to the ones I stole from his workshop, he has others tucked into the barn here and at his mom's studio.

I reached out to some sculptors to get a price range he should sell his work. I know he's a brilliant winemaker and vintner, but he can have this too. I want him to have this. I've been so selfish through so much of the past five months, worrying about how everything affected me or how to protect my heart, but the truth is it's crushed, and I have to work through it. But I still care.

Some sculptures are animals in funny hats or glasses, all created from metal. But the six and twelve-bottle racks he made with recycled metal and license plates are freaking stunning. I've added them to the cash register inventory already. Those are what I'm setting up when I hear the door creak. I crouch low and crawl into the center of the darkroom underneath the beams of flashlights. There's a large figure in the door-frame brandishing what looks like a large piece of wood. He reaches for the light switch and feels around a bit. There's a cold chill down my back, and I can barely breathe. I'm here alone. Literally in the middle of nowhere by myself. But when am I not by myself? Fine. Come kill me, homicidal wood-brandishing maniac. What does it matter?

Then the wood slips from the man's hands, and I hear, "Son of a bitch. Shit. Fucking splinter."

"Bax?"

"What the fuck, Nat?"

I stand, and he flips on the light. I didn't know the lights had been fixed. Bax is dressed in pajamas.

I put a hand up to say hello. He stares at me, then at his hand. I walk behind the register and open a drawer. I grab duct tape and tear off a piece. I take his hand, and he lets me. I examine which way the splinter has gone into his finger. Then I secure the tape and pull it in the opposite direction with one quick motion.

"Ouch. Shit." Then he looks down, and I flip the tape over, showing him the splinter. "Wow. Thank you. And why are you here? You totally freaked me out."

"You. You're kidding, right. A woman alone in the wilderness."

"This isn't quite the wilderness. Tabi and I are camping on the property for the night."

"You are only here because she has a magical hold on you. You hate the outdoors." I look at him sideways.

"I don't hate it, but yes, I prefer a hotel. She wanted to sleep among the vines, and she has a rather stronghold on my libido. I'm a bit addicted, so I relented." I laugh.

The stools are in the storage shed, and there's nowhere to sit in the room. I head over to the bar and slide down on the floor, leaning up against David's handiwork that's the tasting bar.

Bax grabs an open bottle and slides down next to me.

"Write this off, will ya?" He sips from the bottle and passes it back to me. It's fitting I'm leaving in a day, and the last person I get to spend time with is the one person who changed my life. Despite my broken heart and my broken life, I wouldn't change a thing. Not even the broken condom. He's a better David with Sadie. And that kills me too.

"You want to tell me why you're spending your nights here? You used to do this back in DC. You'd go to the office in the middle of the night to avoid something. What are you avoiding?"

I sip and hand the bottle back to him. I pull my t-shirt down. It's bunched up in the back and is bugging me. "Nothing. I wanted to put these art pieces in the merchandise area."

"I thought Elle already merchandised everything before the babies?" I pop up and grab one of the six-bottle wine racks. I hand it to Baxter. He turns it around in his hands, and his eyes glaze over. "This is freaking cool. Where did you find these, and why the 4 a.m. placement?"

My voice breaks as I say his name out loud, "David. He did these, and I thought the world should see them."

Bax puts the wine and wine rack down and pulls me into his side. It's the raindrop that breaks the surface of my placid lake. I curl into my friend/boss, and despite every professional bone in my body, I sob. I crumple into a puddle on his chest. He doesn't move or say anything except, "Let it out. Let it all go."

He's the most stable man I've ever known. Kind and considerate, and always intuitive. He has trouble sometimes seeing things clearly in his own life, but the clarity with which he sees others is astounding. We stay like that until I have snot running down his pajamas. He pulls my chin up to him.

"I'm going to get you a tissue, and then you get to tell me all the things. All the things. I know you. You're getting ready to run. You're buttoning up everything and neatly trimming all your loose ends. But before you go anywhere, you're going to need to tell me why. I don't want to hear that it's Sadie, David, or even my often inappropriate but well-meaning wife."

I am breathing in and out so violently I might hyperventilate. I lean forward, and Bax rubs my back. "Just breathe, Nat. There is nothing we can't solve together." My heart seizes for a moment. This man literally has my back, and I didn't even realize I'd opened myself up so much that he is my family. I get myself under control, sit across from him, crisscross apple sauce, and regulate my breathing. Trying to not let it catch in my throat. I take my hair down, then pull it back up into the elastic. I wipe under my eyes. I breathe.

Bax reaches for a clean bar rag and hands it to me. I blow my nose, and he hands me the Pinot Noir, named, "It's Peen NO, not Peen Yes." It's the dumbest name for a wine, but they were all drunk and couldn't stop laughing. It's not going to be distributed. It's a limited release, so they went ahead and put that on the label.

"Do you want all of my messed up?"

"Well, if you've decided to give it to me instead of David, clearly it needs to come out because you're doing a shitty job of burying it."

"He knows lots of this. I grew up in the foster system after my mother overdosed and my father went to prison for drug trafficking and voluntary manslaughter."

He covers his heart with his hand.

I scold him. "Be Bax. Don't be sympathetic. Take this in as facts. Don't sympathize or editorialize. Please just listen. I bounced between lots of homes and never really found a forever place. Still haven't."

"Bullshit." His words erupt from his mouth. I glare, and he covers his mouth and nods at me, his blond bangs flopping over his ice-blue eyes.

"There were lots of nice people, but I learned not to unpack. I kept my things in a garbage bag the state provided for me. When it was time to move, they provided me with a new one. I've never owned furniture because I'm always ready to move." I put my finger up to stop him from talking. I gut-check myself to tell him the next part.

"I've been through a lot of therapy, and even though I know the issues, I haven't really been able to change them. Do not feel sorry for me!" I've been through even more therapy lately.

"Wouldn't dream of it." He takes the bottle and swigs.

"At each home, I thought if I was indispensable and perfect, they'd choose me. That I'd get to stay if I was the best dishwasher, sweeper, organizer of toys—I'd get to have a family."

"Shit." He can't help himself. There's a warm glow building inside of me as I share all of this with Baxter.

"It turns out I do like being indispensable, but I no longer think I have to be that to be accepted."

"Did you get close to adoption?" He shifts and crosses his legs to face me. They're long and off to the side. He leans back on his elbows. I grin. When Bax first hired me, when he was a lobbyist in DC, he would lay down in his office like this. I'd sit across from him late at night, and we'd work through who he could go after on the Hill to get a bill on the floor. He made me feel important for the first time in my life. My voice was heard. He's doing that again right now. And I went and fell in love with his spiritual brother from another mother. This is a man who gave me a glimpse of what a happy life could look like.

I move the wine towards the middle of us. "Once."

"What happened?"

I don't hesitate. My voice is cold and flat. "They got pregnant and needed my room for the baby." And just like that, I've laid out my buffet of nuttiness for Baxter to absorb. He exhales, and instead of saying something, he sweetly takes my hand.

"With all due respect, you're one of my closest friends, my trusted confidant, you know me better in some ways than my wife, but you're a fucking moron."

I yank my hand away. I stand up and turn in a circle looking for my things. I just told my friend my most intimate secret and why I have to leave, and he called me a moron.

He's up in a flash, blocking the door. "Moron. A baby creates more love, not less. I've never seen him this hurt and joyous at the same time. That's the torture of love. The high and low. You can't possibly think what you're feeling is unique."

I put my hands on my hips and stare at him. "And how would I know?" That stops him, and his face falls a bit. I grab my stuff and sling my bag over my shoulder. I square my shoulders and prepare to walk away from this mess. His mouth drops open a bit as he looks at me.

"Holy shit, Nat. Has anyone ever told you they love you?"

"Only one person."

Bax pulls me to him. He whispers, and the sound of his name fills the room and my heart. "David." I nod. He doesn't hesitate, "I love you, Natalie."

A voice startles both of us, "I love you, Natalie." Tears are streaming down Tabi's face as she steps into the tasting room. "And you are damaged! I fucking knew it. You thought we'd pick him over you."

I nod.

"We pick you both. Bax is right. You're a fucking idiot. You're goddamn stuck with us whether you can get past this dumbass —" Baxter hisses at her. She glares at him. "Whether you figure this out or not with David. No matter where you go, we're still going to love you, and you always have a place in our lives. And I know Elle, Josh, and the whole of the 5 feel that way. Well, maybe not Sam. He's numb and is still like a fucking cranky ass bear who can't find any salmon."

Bax stares at her. "Your point, my love?"

"Oh. Well, even being an asshole, Sam loves you too."

I step back from Bax and stare at the two of them. I suck in a breath.

Bax says, "Cry if you need to, but you're not leaving. You're too important here."

Tabi pulls me to her. "Honestly, you know more about Pro/Ho than all of us. We don't even know where you keep the fucking Post-its."

I answer automatically, "Well, you were each assigned your own color, so if you scribble a note and leave it on my desk, I know who it's from. Yours are the green ones."

"Why green?" Tabi asks.

Bax clears his throat. "Point. Missing it." His wife grins at him. He says, "Nat, eventually we're going to have children, and they're going to need you too. They need an aunt like you. The rest of them are disastrous in their own way, and you'll be the calm one. The one who always knows what they need."

Tears run down my face. Tabi pulls me to her and squeezes too tightly. "I'm buying you a dresser tomorrow, and I'm going to help you unpack personally. No more living out of your suitcase or your—" she throws up some air quotes "—bullshit garbage bags. Enough. You need furniture. And we're getting you a place you can decorate. Elle's good, but you can't tell me the way the guest house is decorated is how you would do things."

"I don't know how I'd do things. I've never let myself think of any place like home."

Tabi says, "You are home. I see you, dumb bitch. Gelbert's your home too." My body floods with warmth at the thought of him. Is that what home feels like?

I say, "Do you have any idea what's it's like to dodge the question, 'Hey, where you from?' I'm from nowhere, and I was conditioned to take up as little space as possible. I trusted that little sliver of space David made, and it was taken away."

"First of all, melodrama, that was a wide muthafucking berth, not a sliver of space. And you took it away. You chose not to be from somewhere. Because we all see it, even if you don't, you're from here."

I crumple again at the words I've never heard before.

Bax adds, "But we can't fix you and Gelbert. That's between the three of you."

I nod. And say words I've only ever dreamed of saying to friends or family. They come out in a rush, "I love you too. Thank you." My breath catches on the last word.

Bax picks up the bottle of Pinot and hands it to Tabi, who takes a sip. He says, "Have you ever said that to anyone before?"

"Once." I never got to say it to him again. I want to. I'm aching to say it, like a kid who wants to eat all of their Halloween candy at once. I want to tear into all the KitKats and tell him I love him. I'm just not sure how to move forward.

Bax kisses the top of my head. "Feels good, huh? Maybe you should repeat it."

Tabi smacks him. "You just said we weren't going to help fix things." Tabi teases her husband and best friend.

I say, "No worries. I have an idea."

They light up as I use a phrase they evoke to each other. But I really do have an idea. I've never fought for anything. I've never thought I deserved anything good. And now, as I pause for a moment to look around at what I've created and become a part of, I realize I've been fighting all along, but it's been for the wrong thing.

CHAPTER 44

NAT

I'M STILL PICKING myself up from my late-night talk with Bax and Tabi. I have things to pick up around the Plaza. I called the woman Elle recommended and talked through some things. I'm going to start seeing her.

I don't even know how to start the conversation with David, but I did get him this dumb little thing. It's a custom little shirt dress for Sadie that says *Meritage, an unexpected blend*. It was the only thing I could think of to prove I'm willing to try. I think I'm willing to try. I still have a lifetime of triggers but it would be nice to know Sadie. The alternative seems like a bad idea since I've never felt so empty in my entire life.

The thought of him is where my sunshine comes from. Any sunshine I have inside me is because of the way he makes me feel. I'm willing to test Bax's theory that the baby makes room for more love, not less.

I don't want to be Sadie's mother. And I do need to know what's going on with that. I need to know if he slept with the mother again when he went to New York. I know he spent time with her and her family in Petaluma. I don't know how all of that went. But I want to start the conversation. I ache. I miss him so much. Everything is in shadow when that colorful man is absent. Being with him is like the part in *WandaVision* when they moved from their black and white existence to the color. He does that to me every time.

I'm checking on the florist for the arrangements being created for Pro/Ho's soft opening. They're going to be gorgeous. I'm nervous, thinking about seeing David at work tomorrow, and decide to grab an ice cream. Ice cream always helps—especially Sweet Scoops. I scan my texts, and I have a ton from Bax asking me if I'm ok. And true to her word, when I left my little guest cottage today, there was a dresser sitting outside the cottage. It had a note on a green Post-it that said, "UNPACK NOW!"

I stop in my tracks and see him scanning the Plaza looking for someone. She's strapped to his chest, flinging her arms and legs all around. She is cute. She's wearing a Gelbert Family Winery hat. Jana probably had it made for her. Or probably Arthur, the secret softie. He sent me a note two days ago that simply said,

You're way too good for my son, but I'm asking you to talk to him. He's a miserable bastard without you. And I sure do like you better than him.
—Arthur Gelbert.

I think that's officially the last person in his extended family of the 5 to try and mend our relationship.

I back up, trying to get around the corner, even though that would have me squarely in view of Poppy's Café, which I've also avoided. He sees me looking at him. We stare for a moment, then I put my hand up and turn away. I'm not ready for him.

His voice booms down the block, almost shaking the

windows of the stores. He's in front of the alley that leads to Murphy's Pub.

"THAT'S ENOUGH. Stop moving. Stop moving, right now."

I put my hand up, and he stops in his tracks. I pull out my phone and text. I am in no way prepared for this. My notes for this conversation are still on my computer. I haven't printed them up yet. This can't possibly happen now. I typed them up after my run-in with the happy Schroeder/Aganos duo. Also, I don't want my business displayed to their entire town.

NATALIE: I don't have time right now. I agree. Lots to discuss, but we can set up a time to talk in the next day or two.

He pulls out his phone and stares down. His face is all heated up and gorgeous right now. He has a bit of auburn scruff on his chiseled chin, and I want to scrape my fingers through it. Or feel it in other parts of me.

"No fucking way, Lloyd. We talk now. Right"—he covers Sadie's ears—"fucking now."

I back away a bit like a deer caught in his headlight. More like a sexy tractor beam. I quickly type.

NATALIE: Sorry, David. I'm not prepared for this. How about tomorrow morning at say nine?

He starts moving towards me slowly like he's trying not to scare away a squirrel. "You keep texting as if I care about anything you've sent. Tell me. Tell me what it said." He's still yelling, and we're attracting a small crowd. He looks around. "Disperse, gawkers." Then Sadie lets loose with a high pitch squeal for emphasis. "GO AWAY, everyone. I'm trying to get my life straight. We'll take out an ad in the Sonoma Index-Tribune and tell you all how it went, so watch for it. We'll even get Robbie to take our picture to please you looky-loos. But go the fuck away."

One woman gasps. "That's a baby."

He rounds on her, and this could be my opportunity to escape, but I'm compelled to see how this goes down.

"Mam. Kindly move along, and unless you're willing to raise my daughter, I'd"—He covers her ears again, and she starts babbling loudly—"go the fuck away. You're messing with destiny."

CHAPTER 45

DAVID

I COVER Sadie's ears and scream at the exasperating woman running away from me. "STOP, YOU GORGEOUS INFURI-ATING WOMAN. STOP RUNNING RIGHT NOW. AND I PROMISE YOU I'LL STOP BEING AN OBTUSE DOUCHE NOZZLE."

I look around as people laugh around me. I growl at them, but it stopped my girl in her tracks. And she is that. She is, without a doubt, mine, and it's time to prove it to her. I start strolling to her so as not to spook her. I tiptoe, and she grins. I hunch over and put Sadie's finger to her mouth, and the two of us say, "SHHHH." I then say the rest of the line for Sadie, "Be very, very quiet. We're hunting rabbits."

I continue to tiptoe to Natalie at the block. Her hair is slightly longer than it was, and I'm sad I didn't watch it grow. The blonde is matching the sunlight all around her. Her blue eyes are wide and softened. Her peachy skin is luminescent. She's wearing tight cargo shorts and a blousy blue top that matches her eyes and her checkered Vans. The most beautiful she's ever looked is either mid-orgasm or the night of New Year's Eve when I first told her I loved her. Until now. She's wearing my new favorite outfit. The one that will forever say, this was the moment.

I didn't see our issues because I can hear about her past, but I don't know the emotional part. I don't know what it's like to be alone. I have no more tremendous privilege than that. I've always had money. I'm athletic. I'm white. I'm a man, but never knowing a single moment where I wasn't loved or surrounded by almost too many people is unimaginable. I don't know what it's like to have no one to talk to or about. I cursed everyone's involvement in every aspect of my life. I hated my overbearing, disapproving father, but I always had someone, and I always will. The difference is I'd trade all of my giant ass extended family, except for this leech hanging off the front of me.

I'd trade them all for her. I want to be her person forever, and I want her to be mine. I want us to be hers. All my insecurities, flaws, and issues are validated in her smile. Her heart hard-won but completely worth it because I'm complete in her eyes. I'm not the black sheep with anger issues. I'm not the man whore who can't focus on one woman or one thing long enough to succeed. In her eyes, I'm David, the artist, and vintner. I'm hers to laugh with or sit in silence and grope each other. Because I can *not* keep my hands off that little pixie.

I didn't see that all of this was our problem. Not hers to snap out of, but mine to reassure her she doesn't have to be alone another second of her life. That Sadie made more room, not less. I want all her moments, all her kisses, and feisty, nervous speeches. I will listen forever. We need and want everything she can give us.

I plant myself in front of her, and she looks at her feet. They shuffle back and forth, and they're so fucking cute. Sadie reaches for her, and she smiles warmly at her. She puts out a finger, and Sadie tries to put it in her mouth.

I put my hand on the top of Sadie's head. "She's my purpose, but you're my reason."

She stares at me. "You are NOT that poetic. Did that just come to you? Did Bax write it?"

"Stop it, Sunshine. Let it go. Let them come down. Drop your bullshit walls. Being on this side of your chilly ass fortress fucking sucks."

"You swore in front of Sadie."

"Turns out I can't stop, so I'm just going to teach her not to use it until she's older. You're avoiding again, Sunshine."

"Stop calling me that? Why do you do that?"

I move towards her, and she doesn't flinch again. Sadie is cooing and kicking, but I overlook it. She's reaching for Nat again. This time she's doing her best to ignore her, but Scribbles is pretty fucking animated right now. I put my hand on her head, and she laughs.

"I'll never stop calling you Sunshine. And if you don't get it, you're as dumb as I think you are."

"I'm not dumb."

"Yes, you are. You don't see. Everyone and everything is brighter with you around. We all grow like plants and flowers and vines in your gaze. I mean all the families. You make Will Whittier seem dull and bland, and that's fucking hard to do. You're the light to everything around you. I thrive in your well-lit stare, and I refuse to let you take it away. I need you. And whether you want to admit it or not, you need me. You need Sadie too."

She screams at the mention of her name, and that baby shriek is ear piercing and distracting to everyone around us. She starts kicking and making her happy little jumps. The drool is flying as she whips her fist out of her mouth. It flings onto Natalie. She stares at her chest with the big blob of drool. I smile sheepishly as Sadie seems to be laughing at her.

"Shh. Sadie. Don't ever make that noise again when I'm trying to woo the woman. Ok. Girl." She shrieks again. I look back up at Natalie. I say, "Women. You can ask them, tell them, yell at them, and until they decide on their own, it's like I'm speaking in a foreign language." I shrug, and Natalie smiles. Yes. It's like she's cracking open, and all of her light is starting to spill into all the dark and abandoned places in my soul.

Her mouth drops open. "I don't know if I can do this." I take her hand, and Sadie is jabbering away. Natalie leans forward, takes a scrap of the blanket, and wipes her drool.

"She's teething," Natalie remarks.

"Nah, she's drunk." Natalie laughs. I say very clearly, "I want you. I choose you. Actually, that's a lie."

"You don't choose me?" Her face falls.

"No. I had no fucking choice in the universe's decision. And neither do you, so the sooner you get out of your own way, the sooner I can be kissing you."

She steps towards me full-on, smiling now, and I lean forward. Sadie kicks her in the stomach.

"Hold on." I unsnap the Baby Björn, and Sadie shrieks again and starts wiggling to get down. I look around and see Mrs. Dotson, Josh's kind of grandma. The woman has to be like a hundred, but she's spicy as hell. She's coming out of the ice cream shop.

She waves, and I quickly stride over to her, yelling behind me, "Don't move, Natalie. I mean it, don't freaking move."

She wiggles her hips back and forth. I want to bury myself in her. I grin at her and waggle my finger.

"Not a muscle, Lloyd!" I see her start to tear up, but she doesn't move. Good girl.

I thrust Sadie and her diaper bag into Mrs. Dotson's arms and say, "Hold this a sec."

She takes Sadie into her arms and smacks the back of my

head. "Go get that girl. Fix it. She's the only thing I like about you. Well, her and this one." Mrs. Dotson kisses the top of Sadie's head, and I grin at that saucy senior and bolt back down the block to Natalie. She's still angry at me from when I used to run through her flowerbeds as a kid. I almost get to Natalie, and then I remember how I wanted to show her.

She looks confused as I bolt back to Mrs. Dotson and fish out an envelope.

I run back and hand it to her. She opens it and sees a battered cashier's check and another folded official document.

"What's this for? David. This is a random amount."

"It's the cost of raising a child to the age of eighteen."

"It's too much. You can't give this to me."

"I'm not. Josie is. She won't miss it. Put it towards something you want to do. I know it won't erase your upbringing, but you said you wanted to help other kids to have a better childhood. Consider this a payment you should have had all along." Her eyes fill, and I wipe under her one eye.

Her voice cracks, "And this?"

"This is a deed to some property. It's in your name. I thought you might want to build something of your own that possibly we share with you, for like forever or whatnot. But it's yours. You do with it what you want. But no matter what you'll always have a home here."

She opens her mouth, but I don't let her say a word and sweep her into my arms. Tears streaming down her face, she looks at me. I don't kiss her. I need her to choose me. She looks at me. Her eyes tell me everything, as they always have. Long before she could identify the words aloud, she said them to me this way.

"I love you so very, very much."

"This is what I've been saying. You seem to be the only one who didn't know that. God, woman. Now can we be a family?"

"But what about me not wanting kids."

I push hair back from her face. So perfect. I rub my thumb over her cheekbone, and I see her melt into my touch.

I say, "Well, that's not gonna work because I'm gonna marry you. I wanna spend the rest of my life with you, and whether you like it or not, Sadie's gonna be hanging around for a while. But you don't have to be a stepmom. You just have to live with us until the end of our days. You get to raise her and take her love as well as mine. Forever and ever. It really doesn't seem as tricky as you're making it."

"What about her mother? You were with her? Were you with her again? Are the two of you together?"

"You'll meet her. She's great—beautiful, smart, selfish, scared, and confused. But she's a part of Sadie, so that makes her wonderful."

She cocks an eyebrow at me and looks crestfallen. Could that be jealousy? Whatever help she needs to get past her block to happiness, I'll do. Gurus, acupuncture, ashrams, doctors, supplements, meds, whatever. We just do it together. This separate life is nothing. It's a terrible limbo, a waystation to happiness. It's so close, and yet we can't get to it.

"I'm confused."

I grin. "I forgive Josie."

"How?" I guess that's beyond her comprehension too. She's never really been forgiven or had to forgive because she wasn't invested in or invested enough for it to matter. Jesus, I've been selfish, looking at my situation and expecting it all to magically be ok without listening to what she was actually saying. It has nothing to do with Sadie and everything to do with being scared of loss.

"I've never been one to hold on to all that shit. Except with my dad, but we're fighting it out. Being a dad now helped me see him a little more clearly. There's still a lot to our relationship I don't get, but at least now we're communicating. Grudges and pity are a waste of time."

"Pity, I'm familiar with."

"Do you think I love you because I pity you? Or I did the holiday thing because I felt bad for you."

"Yes."

"I did it because I wanted us to have memories, good fucking memories, as fast as possible. I wanted to be your foundation, your past, present, and future immediately, and I couldn't figure out a better way than to replace your bad memories with good ones."

"You want to be my past—"

"Present and future. We've been over this. I've been stumbling through my life, never veering towards any particular path except wine. I've never fought for anything except with my dad. I gave up on dreams or ideas, and in return, I was angry. I fought all the time. I picked fights or was an asshole to people because deep down, I was fucking mad I never bothered to fight for anything. It seemed easier to live with this angry flame in my stomach I thought was part of me. And then you kissed me. And the flames disappeared, and in its place was hope, confidence, belief, and love. You saw all that turmoil and didn't bat an eye. You dismissed it for the nonsense that it is. Without telling me to. I began sculpting again. I went to the 5 and told them I didn't want any admin part, and I didn't want to hire a winemaker. That Sam and I could do it for real. No more dicking around and pretending."

"Oh, David." She sighs.

"If you get to be an adult, I get to be one too." I wink at her. I say, "I told them that I love blending two to three things, that shouldn't be together, to make the very best version of what something could be. You, Sadie, and I, we are my ultimate challenge. And I will fight with everything I have to make sure I spend the rest of my life perfecting that perfect Meritage blend to be the best that it can be.

"Now, that, I did write. On the plane home from meeting Josie, and it's been running through my brain ever since. You wouldn't see me, so I got really good at it. Did I rush it?"

"No. I'd say the last thing we've done is rush."

"You done?"

"Done with what?"

I say, "Are you done wallowing and feeling sorry for yourself?"

"I uh, I."

"You love thinking the world owes you something because you and my dad could really get along. "

"I'm seeing someone."

My heart drops.

"A therapist. That Elle recommended. I am ready to fight for something for the first time in my life, too."

I grin at her. "You are?"

Her voice is strong and clear, "Fuck yeah, I am."

I scoop her into my arms. "Well, that was easy. We're fighting for the same thing."

"Fuck yeah, we are."

"That word from your mouth is killing me." My knees are weak. And that word is making my dick hard.

Her sassy little mouth opens again, "What are you going to flim-flam fucking do about it?"

"This." I wrap her legs around me and begin to carry her towards my car. I know she can feel the Parade at total inflation. I keep walking.

She asks, "Where are we going?"

I turn the corner. "Home."

"What about Sadie?" I look over towards Poppy's, and she's

pouring iced tea on her patio. I hitch Natalie up a little higher and keep walking.

"POP!" Her head turns, and she sees me walking towards her. Nat buries her face in my neck and begins to kiss it quietly. "Hey, Sunshine. Ease up on your tongue work, or I'll fuck you against the wall of Casa Mia's entrance. It's been way too long." She giggles into my jaw.

"What, David?" Poppy smiles when she sees Natalie in my arms.

"Can you grab Sadie? She's with Mrs. Dotson around the corner."

"Can't leave. Short-staffed. I'll text Josh. He's at the Pro/Ho offices. He can grab her."

"Cool. Thanks, Pop."

Natalie breathes in, and I pull her back just a little and look at her. I kiss her as gently as I can, given the fact I'm not sure I'll make it back to my car before pulling out my cock. "See, having a big family pays off." She smiles.

Poppy yells after us, "Josh wants to know how long he's keeping her?"

I yell back, "Until tomorrow."

And then my Sunshine yells, "Better make it the day after that."

I look at her, and we put our foreheads together. All the jokes are made. And our angst and anger are done for the moment. "You know, now is our forever. Got it? You stubborn, closed-off witch of a woman."

"Witch?"

I say, "If you're not, then how do you explain the spell you put on me?"

She rolls her eyes and says, "Did it hurt?"

I grin, and we play our game. "Hurt what?"

"When you fell from Heaven?"

I say as I lower her into my passenger seat, "Life without you is like a broken pencil...pointless." She laughs. I cock my left eyebrow and say, "Be with me."

"I don't know that one."

"It's new. I've never said it before. Surrender all your armor, all your doubts, and embrace the family that's in front of you and all around you. We choose you. I will forever choose you. I love you so very much, Natalie. In fact"—I gesture behind me—"I'll choose you over that shit machine if you want." She laughs.

"Despite my best efforts to sabotage my life, I choose the two of you too. I want to know her. I am going to stink at it. And I don't want to step on toes."

"Her toes are really tiny. It's easy to avoid them." I smile.

"You're the reason I was ready for her. Without you showing me what it's like to truly love someone, I never could love her the way I do. She has you to thank for a home. Let us give you one back. You can't take that away from us. You're the Sunshine in all of our days." I take her hands as I kneel beside my car.

"Well, how the hell am I supposed to say no to that?"

I kiss her like forever's not long enough. I slide my tongue into her mouth, and I'm shocked birds don't break out in song.

I ask, "You'll stay with me always?"

"Where would I go? I'm finally home. You're my home."

The end.

EPILOGUE

"YOU CAN'T GO. Not allowed. Because then it's only my children and Samia at this fake one-year-old's birthday party," Elle yells at Natalie. She continues to shuffle Sadie towards the door. Natalie shrugs. She hugs Bax and Tabi and heads out. Elle continues to demand we stay. It's hard to ignore Elle, but they keep on moving. Proud of my girls.

It's the official Pro/Ho opening after a months of delays and last minute problems. Natalie moved out of the LC/W cottage two months ago, and is getting used to having a third party around.

Today is perfect, and the five of us were all here to cut the ribbon together. Natalie provided very large scissors in our signature Post-it colors.

Emma got the shaft. In the lead up to the opening in all the chaos, they forgot her first birthday. They blame the construction delays, I blame the two tiny shit machines that keep them up all night.

We've all been sworn to secrecy that we'll never tell Emma they forgot. I make my way towards the car. Sadie is squawking because she doesn't want to leave her best friend. Her first birthday is this week and I have a very special celebration planned. We'll celebrate with everyone later. My mom hugs me, and we accept all the congratulations from our families. But we have places to be and adventures to be had.

"Son. This is quite a thing you've done." My father slaps me on the back and I feel the weight of it. I know he's talking about all of it. We'll never be buddies but for now, we're good. We find ourselves in an epic Gelbert détente, lately.

I glance at Nat, and she's so incredibly beautiful. She's the sunshine in all our days and is reaching her rays even further.

Natalie has decided to dedicate part of the property I gave her towards building a nonprofit for the foster kid experience. She's already filling my house with suitcases. She and Sadie are off to a rocky start, but they seem to adore each other. She also asked if I wouldn't mind if I helped her build a house for us.

"Sorry, Elle, but Sadie has exotic places to be that aren't fake birthday parties."

Elle has taken way too many pictures of the kids together so she can prove to Emma one day that she did get a party. Sadie crawls, very quickly now, back to the group. She pulls up to standing next to her newest friend. Evan and Jims' new daughter, Samia, is in the group now. She's just a touch younger than Emma and older than Sadie. She fits right in the middle. The three of them are scary together, and the thought of their future fills me with dread. Sam approaches me and throws an arm around me.

"Dude, we have a shit-ton of work to do. You're just taking off?"

"Funny, from the guy who only just remembered we own a winery. Fuck you, man." I hug him. It's good to see him back to a version of himself. He's been running with Josh daily, and he's starting to look a little more like my friend. He bulked up a lot on his already large frame, and I'm glad the sadness seems to be subsiding.

I raise an eyebrow and lay down a challenge. "When I get back, I'll play you for who gets the first crack at the Zin we found at the back of the property." We both want to harvest it and make it something special, but we do not see eye to eye on what it should be.

"You're on. Have a good trip."

"That's it, no crack about anything."

He grins and starts to walk away. Then turns back to me, "Your hair looks fucking dumb all gelled up at a kid's birthday party, but I thought you already knew that."

I flip him off and scoop up Sadie Grace. The other love of my life is already waiting at the car, having collected all the Sadie paraphernalia from around the tasting room. Bax, Tabi, Will Whittier and my dad are inside pouring for the first of our real in-person customers. I hope we sell out. I've always dreamed of being a sellout.

SADIE'S SECOND FLIGHT WAS MUCH DIFFERENT. ESPECIALLY WITH A second set of hands and a dash of Benadryl. Nat squeezes my hand as we exit the plane. Sadie's strapped in, and we search for our rental car. I know the roads, and Nat can't help but stare at the insane beauty of the rolling green hills. I breathe easier here somehow. Must be in my DNA. We're exhausted but expected. I want to get to our destination as fast as possible. Sadie is sacked out in the back. Nat keeps snapping pictures of her, and the views outside of her window. Then she gently falls asleep with her hand on my thigh.

I turn down the familiar lane on the outskirts of the tiny town. I jump out and open the gates. Once I drive through, I close them again to keep the sheep contained. I assume there's still sheep. The little road winds a bit to the middle of the property, then splits evenly between the two houses. The cliffs are on the backside of the cottages, but you can hear the waves crashing on the rocks. One house is dark, and the other has smoke coming from the chimney. It's all lit up, and there are bright red flowers in the flower boxes that adorn the windows. It's as vivid as my favorite memories. And as stereotypically cliché as anyone would imagine.

I wake up both my girls with gentle kisses. The head for Sadie and those perfect pink lips for Nat. The moss is bright between the flagstone walk I laid for them so long ago. I knock, and the cheerful but aged face of Sadie appears. She claps her hands in front of her and shrieks with delight.

She pulls me into a tight embrace, then reaches for Natalie. Nat shifts Scribbles to my hip and hugs a woman she's only ever heard about.

"My dear troublemaker. You look good."

"You look old. But good."

"Cheeky bastard."

I grin, and Natalie laughs. "That he is," she says.

I take Nat's hand and turn back towards Sadie in the doorway. "You once told me when everything made sense, I'd know my life's purpose. And then I'd know it was time to raise a glass. Sadie, this is the love of my life Natalie Lloyd, and this is my daughter, Sadie." Her eyes fill instantly as she takes Scribbles out of my arms. Her whole being fills with joy. That's what my girl does. Fills everyone with the same joy. Both of them, actually.

"Goodness, little girl. Well, if it isn't the love of my life staring back at me. Those are my love's eyes you're sporting, little darling. You have Saoirse's eyes just like your daddy." I nod.

I wink at her and say, "Sadie, I'm here to raise a glass."

"Then we should get cracking. There's a lot of joy to be celebrating. And I have a yarn or two to spin about your daddy." She says to Sadie.

Nat squeezes my hand. "I'd like to hear those as well." The two enter the house, and I pull Nat back to me. Without a word, I kiss her so completely we can barely breathe. She instantly floods me with sunshine. But she always does. I can't wait to find a moment to fill her up as well. I pull back and shake my head at my filthy mind.

"What?" She asks.

"Nothing. I'm still a bit of a douchenozzle."

She puts her hand on my cheek. "It's ok. You're my douchenozzle." I kiss her hand and pull her into the neat little cottage that means the world to me. And has my whole world inside of it.

The End.

Thank you so much for reading!! I hope you loved David and Nat as much I loved writing them.

If you want to hear how **Elle tamed Josh** before their gaggle of girls you can find their story here. An enemies to lovers forced proximity tale. They started out hating each other, but with enough wine anyone can fall in love.

LaChappelle/Whittier Vineyard Trilogy
Crushing,
Rootstock
&
Uncorked

HEY KELLY, WHAT ELSE CAN I READ?

If you're so inclined to leave a review on Goodreads, BookBub or Amazon, I'll be your best friend. It really is the lifeblood of the indie publishing world. Thanks.

Now here's some other books I've written.

Rockstar Romance Duet
Shock Mount & Crossfade
A reverse age gap love triangle AND a second chance romance that all begins with a spilled glass of wine and a broken watch. Only overlap is a kiss. And everyone gets an HEA! Meghan Hannah's a mess of herself and if she's not falling in love she's falling down. She'll have to learn to stand on her own two feet and finally trust her heart or wind up ass over elbows again.

Present Tense
OUT JANUARY 13, 2022
A Chi Town Story Spinoff- It took 20 years for the to get their first chance at a second chance romance.

Side Piece.

Tess and Alex are completely swept away in an epic once-in-a-lifetime romance right up until they catch planes in opposite directions.

The workaholic standalone story of Tess & Alex, where they cheat on their jobs not each other.

She's a romance writer and he's a political podcaster. Sex is the easy part. But can they actually stop working long enough to find love?

Perhaps there could be more if only their schedules overlapped long enough to fall in love.

Other Five Families Vineyard Books

Josh & Elle
LaChappelle/Whittier Vineyard Trilogy
Crushing, Rootstock & Uncorked
Tabi & Bax
Stafýlia Cellars Duet
Over A Barrel & Under The Bus

All of this release information and random fun stuff will be in my newsletter. I'll do the work for you. You don't have to remember all of this. I'm here for you. Sign up at
www.kellykayromance.com

ACKNOWLEDGMENTS

It seems redundant to thank a reader while they're reading. So I'll just tuck this here, and when you need to be appreciated, come on back and read it. Thank you. You're the magic. You're the fulfiller of dreams. Thank you so much for finding me and supporting me. And you're pretty. And special. And strong. And funny. And interesting. And smart. - Thank you.

For such a solo activity, you'd be surprised at the size of the village needed to create a book. And as my village expands, so does my gratitude.

The ever-growing text chains with my friends are my lifeline. Thank you to all of you who text back. I love you.

And Evie, it kills me you add seltzer to Barolo, but I'm grateful you drink it with me on the other end of the video chat. Someday we'll revel in the same room.

Drunk Book Club- that's right, I said Drunk Book Club. You're a constant source of laughter, fun, and support. And my TBR brims over like my wine each time we gather. Thank you.

Tim Hogan- Jesus, I'm happy you're in my life. I love this cover as much as the others. You're Double Gold.

Aimee Walker- Editor of my dreams. I need you in my

corner always. Coming up with that 11th-hour clutch catch of Nat and David at a birthday party one book back- Damn. Thank you for your joy and expertise.

Emily Helmke- Thank you for your support, love, and mad grammar skills.

Thank you so much to Becky Burrier for Beta reading, doing all the work of a PA without all the glory, and for being on the other end of my rambling video chats making lists that keep me organized and happy.

Chuckie Smallz, Charlie Bear, Pumpkin Pie, Baby Boy, Little Man, and all the names you won't let me call you anymore, my big man of 10 years old- thanks for putting up with all of Mommy's book madness.

Eric- the ultimate partner in all things. Love you. You're the reason.

In my research to give Natalie some light and shade, I discovered the amazing work Tiffany Haddish was doing with Foster Kids. And I read her story about the trash bags, and it stayed with me. Hence why it appears in the book.

I'm going to be donating a portion of my sales to Tiffany Haddish's She Ready Foundation. If you have an extra buck or two, it's a pretty good way to spend it. If not, no problem. I'll donate for you! She's made it her goal to empower, support, and encourage foster children.

A LITTLE ABOUT ME

I used to create "dreams" with my best friend growing up. We'd each pick a boy we liked, then we'd write down a meet-cute that always ended with a happily ever after.

Now I get to dream every day, although now it's a little steamier.

I'm a writer, married to a writer, mother of a creative dynamo of a nine-year-old boy and currently a little sleepy. I'm a klutz and goofball and love lipstick as much as my Chuck Taylors.

Good things in the world: pepperoni pizza, Flair pens*, wine, coffee, laughing with my friends until my stomach hurts, a musician at the top of their game, getting lost somewhere I've never been, matinee movies on a weekday, the Chicago Cubs, a fresh new notebook full of possibilities, bourbon on a cold night, Fantasy Football, witty men, walking through the local zoo in the rain and that moment when a character clicks in and begins to write their own adventure. I'm just the pen.

*purple is my favorite Flair pen

Made in the USA
Las Vegas, NV
12 December 2021

37376141R00188